Invisible
(The Story of the USS Manta Ray)

By M. E. Nyberg

~.~

For Dad

~.~

~.~

).(

Book design by Don Mangione

~.~

ISBN 13: 978-0-9970986-6-2
eISBN 13: 978-0-9970986-7-9

Registered with U.S. Library of Congress
Copyright # TXu 2-147-103
Writers Guild of America West Reg# 2035484

~.~

Other books by M E Nyberg

...

The Profound Art of Omens
The Man Who Would Be Coyote
The Wicker Woman
Invisible

~.~

www.menyberg.com

~.~

~.~

Table of Contents

—

Chapter 1: Queen of Battle

*B*lack gives the impression of emptiness. Void.

It lends itself to timelessness. There is no *time* in black for it lacks form, definition, no distinct features or qualities except a feeling of vastness; or the opposite.

I'm accelerating, a steady rhythmic pulsation, concentric circles expanding in rapid succession. The feeling the *pulsing* creates is a mix of rapture and disquietude both; the rapture in the form of a soft velvety massage inundating my senses. The nervous tension comes from the sensation I'm losing form, losing touch with my physical body, becoming lighter, more electrified with each wave. As the vibrations increase, the patterns thin then disappear until nothing remains but a blinding white light, then a sudden and shocking advent into black.

The *void* possesses a chilling density, like plunging into a vast primordial ocean, the weight of water pressing in from all sides. I feel that I'm drowning, afraid to breathe, to let go and drown; fear the horror of it, water filling the lungs, the moment of death. I smell of the sea in my nose, the taste of salt in my mouth; drowning within a sea of darkness.

"Commander Murphy? Are you okay sir?" The young man's voice pulls me from the darkness into twilight.

The wide expanse of ocean is like a cold slap in the face; the horizon stretching for mile upon mile. Thoughts not entirely my own, pour through my mind like opening a sluice. I'm on the bridge of the Manta Ray, a U.S. Gato-class attack submarine, returning from patrol; two grueling months at sea. It's July 1943, the entire world at war. Ensign Duncan, in his beige officer's uniform–blonde hair, cap and black tie– is staring at me. Sailors in white hats and blue fatigues, their sleeves rolled-up over their biceps, are on watch, scanning the azure Pacific with binoculars.

"Are you all right Lieutenant Murphy?" Duncan's voice locks me into the moment, the thoughts coursing my mind dissipating like smoke and *the war* forces itself back into my consciousness. I shake the *dreams* from my head, focus on the ocean surrounding us, the threat of an enemy submarine lurking the waters always present.

"What is it Ensign?"

"Sorry Mr. Murphy but it seemed like you were in trance. You sure you're okay sir?"

"I'm all right Eban. Just a…*feeling*…for a moment." The eastern waters unfold before us; storm clouds hugging a dark horizon. "Looks like a squall is moving in."

"Speaking freely sir but you've been going at this job for two solid years. Maybe it's time to take a break. Word back at *Pearl* is Admiral Hess wants you commanding a new boat, a new submarine. That would give you five, maybe six months back stateside wouldn't it? Time with your wife?" I gaze at the gold band on my ring finger, pull her photograph from my breast pocket–a picture of a fair-haired woman in a flower-print dress, the words: *'Mike, come home soon, all my love, Hildy'* written across the bottom in cursive.

"How's your family back in Iowa Eban?" I ask to divert his questioning stare.

"Watching the corn grow." Our discussion attracts the attention of the sailors standing watch in the shears above; a smattering of jokes about farming and pigs. "Look alive you guys," he barks. "We ain't home yet. Look sharp, we're still in combatant waters." The men in *the sail* return to their vigil, scanning the horizon to the north and south, the sub vulnerable on the surface during light. Seaman Wyatt is abaft us on the cigarette deck, watching our rear. The sun looks like an amber jewel setting in the west. The men are joking; we're heading home.

The Manta Ray pierces the waves. Her long slender deck awash with the spray of the sea and the boat herself seems as if dreaming, lulled into a narcotic half-sleep by the slow rocking of the ocean. The sound she makes cutting the waves is like the gentle sighing of a woman. *She* too is heading home after a tough aggressive patrol, her battle armor dented and bruised.

Twilight paints the sea around the boat in mystical brushstrokes, the Trade Winds cutting a warm breeze across our bow. We're moving through a living wonder, a gigantic body of living, moving life. Strange ideas, notions about future things, future technologies, continue to reverberate through my mind. Vague notions of a distant time, free of the fetters–and horrors–of constant war.

"How many patrols has it been Lieutenant Murphy?" Duncan enquires from behind his binoculars. "Seven, right?"

"Six, fifth under Canfield. Our first patrol I was his ensign, second a lieutenant JG, the last three…his first officer. I thought you knew this already."

"Who did you start with, *Mac*? Commander MacGuffin?"

"My *NCO cruise* was with Commander Kornbluth. His last successful patrol before his boat went down in 1942."

"God rest his soul," the young man says, genuflects and returns to his binoculars.

The gold band on my left hand catches the last rays of the setting sun. I study the photograph of Hildy in the flower-print dress. It was her gift to me, prior my first voyage. A very potent good-luck charm to date. The moment I place the photo back into its pocket, all hell breaks loose, the *Bells of St. Mary*—the attack warning siren—cutting through the tranquil twilight like a knife.

Without thought, I'm heading below, down the ladder through the cramped confines of the conning tower into the subjacent control room where Quartermaster Bill Taylor, a lean raven-haired sailor, is talking to Peter Bremer, chief of the boat. Bremer always looked raggedy and gray. He was only forty-six years of age. Men are scrambling to battle stations, their shouts filling the compartment.

"What's happening Bill?"

"S-J contact Murph," Bremer interjects through his beard. "Another goddamn convoy. We barely got enough *fish* left to fight with," he says referring to our few remaining torpedoes.

"What's the difference Chief?" Quentin Sorel says from the bow-plane controls. "Canfield would go in with clubs and knives if Pearl Harbor let him."

Captain Canfield, a gangly chisel-faced man, enters through the oval watertight door and looks everyone over with steel-gray eyes, having heard the remark. He cuts a swath through the group, heading up the ladder into the conning tower. I follow him like a shadow. Inside the conning tower, he hovers behind radar technician Roosevelt Herndon sweating over his screen.

"What's the skinny Rosie?"

"Radar contact Skipper. Closing. Four, maybe five blips, behind us. Could be a pod of whales."

"Or a southbound convoy. Bearing?"

"Three-double-zero, relative. Couple miles back Skipper. It might not be anything." The look on Canfield's face says other. He shouts down the hatch into the control room.

"Chief, all-stop."

The boat shudders to a halt, the men's voices instantly quieting. He climbs the ladder through the top hatch to the bridge. I'm right on his heels. Duncan has his binoculars trained to our rear. Ominous gray storm clouds are closing-in from the east.

"See anything Ensign?"

"Think I see smoke on the horizon Captain," he says extending his arm. Canfield addresses the northwest with his binoculars. "Pretty far east for a Japanese convoy sir. Could it be one of ours?"

"Negative Mr. Duncan."

Our second officer squeezes through the hatch and joins us. "Boat at general quarters Skipper. Engine room standing-by." Ellis Stewart was 6'3" and weighed 220 lbs.

"Very well," Canfield grunts, not removing his attention from a thin wisp of smoke hugging the narrow band of gold along a lonely western horizon.

"What's cooking Dunc?" Stewart asks, reaching for seaman Wyatt's field glasses.

"Smoke at two-double-niner Lieutenant," he says, pointing with the length of his arm. Stewart focuses on the same spot Canfield is hawking. The wind whips salt in my mouth, the taste as familiar as the moment.

Duncan realizes the lookouts in *the sail* are also gazing west. "Hey, you guys look sharp up there, this could be a set-up." The men return to their assigned areas of observation, scanning the ocean around the boat.

"What do you make out Stewart?"

"Not sure Skipper. Hard to tell in the dim light." He hands me the binoculars. "Let *eagle eyes* here have a look." He shoves the apparatus into my chest. "You're the hero with the night vision. Have at it, son."

Dark-gray clouds reach for us from the northeast, bringing a pattering of raindrops. Keeping my eyes sharp on the smoke trail, I bring the lenses up to my eyes and *dial* the focus wheel in on the target. I can just make out the masthead of a Japanese merchantman coming over the horizon, the setting sun framing the ship's rigging in silhouette. We sway with the pitch and roll of the boat, the sea becoming dark and turgid. I can see Canfield watching from the periphery of my vision.

"Well?"

"I see masts. They're coming over the horizon now, maybe four ships…freighters. Lead ship, definitely a Japanese *maru,* I can tell by her forecastle." I lower the glasses, rain settling on my eyelashes. "Enemy convoy Captain."

Canfield grabs the battle phone. "Helm bring her about, right full rudder. Come to course two-eight-zero. Tell Lloyd to put all four engines on-line. Get us over there, flank speed." The boat instantly responds. I feel a rumble pulse through her superstructure as the Manta Ray carves a perfect white arc amid the dark turbulent water. The speaker under the stanchion comes to life.

"All ahead full Captain, course laid two-eighty west. Eighteen knots."

"Very well," Canfield responds, returning to his vigil, fixated on the targets now before us. "Make out any escorts Murph?" By *escorts,* he means *men-of-war,* destroyers or sub-chasers.

"Too dark to tell, but the convoy looks big. They're not freighters Captain. I think they're tankers, or troop transports. Heavy in the water." We gather tightly, like a pack of wolves staking out a herd as night tightens its velvet hand across the ocean's horizon.

"Right in the crosshairs," Stewart whispers. "Are we going straight in Skip?" Canfield remains silent, locked on the target. "You think they've spotted us?" For some reason everyone looks at me. I gaze over my shoulder at the dark rain-laden eastern horizon rolling in like a runaway freight train, the sun having already taken her golden beams deep into the west.

"Not a chance. They couldn't possibly spot our smoke against this canopy." This causes another protracted *stalking* of the slim silhouettes rapidly emerging to the northwest.

"Stewart, ready the boat for attack. *Approach* personnel to their stations."

"Aye Skipper." He instantly disappears through the hatch into the belly of the submarine. Canfield toggles the *squawk box* beneath his elbow.

"Bill, what's our range?"

The box squelches. "Four thousand yards Skipper."

"Standby to dive. We'll commence underwater approach at one thousand. Ready forward torpedo room."

"Aye-aye," the box responds and goes silent.

After another thorough scanning of the sea, he looks at me, a familiar grin turning up the corners of his mouth.

"What's your gut saying Murph? A set-up, or a bunch of poor dumb sons-of-bitches about to meet their maker?" I stare into the man's eyes. We're going to kill these men, sink the ships beneath them. He sees the look form on my face. "What is it? What's wrong?"

The gravity of the situation coats me like a heavy rain. We're at war, *kill or be killed*, the endless spilling of blood upon the planet. Except these men won't bleed, just drown; slowly sink into a lonesome sea, a vast primordial ocean, men with families, stories to tell their children, hopes and dreams, cast adrift into a vast and unforgiving water-world.

"Mister Murphy, I've asked you a question. Are you all right?" The harshness in his voice snaps me back into the present; a strange feeling overwhelms me, the senseless futility of war. Today, we could save these men, let them pass. Return them to their families, allow them the dignity of living. "Mr. Duncan, escort Mr. Murphy below. I don't think he's feeling right."

"I'm all right Captain. Yes…a sure thing." He fixes on my gaze, as if seeing into me, reading the thoughts passing through my mind. The box squawks beneath Canfield's elbow, breaking his vise-like grip on my attention.

"Two thousand yards Captain, closing rapidly."

"Mr. Duncan, get the lookouts below." Duncan relays the captain's order. The men in the shears join seaman Wyatt on the bridge counting off as they disappear down the hatch. Duncan double-checks the cigarette deck.

"All lookouts and crew below Captain."

"Very well," he says returning to his solitary vigil, a soft patina of raindrops coating the sub. After scanning the sea around the boat, he lowers his binoculars and gives us *that look*. "You boys know what?" We wait for him to continue, the rain speckling his beige uniform with dark brown spots. "War is exactly like gambling. Despite the risks, how much you've lost, or got sitting on the table, always one more…one more roll of the dice." The wind cuts into us from the east and the sea begins to rage as the front hits us. His eyes burn into mine. "Clear the bridge."

"Aye sir," Duncan responds, leading the way below.

Canfield grabs the battle phone. "Prepare to dive." I follow him into the tight confines of the conning tower, pulling on the hatch lanyard and Duncan twists the steel wheel taut.

"Top-hatch secure Captain."

"Diving Officer…take her down."

A-OOGAH-A-OOGAH blasts through the diesel-laden air, shaking the webs loose and every sailor dons the same mask, a submariner's war-face.

Canfield is instantly at his station at the periscope. "Close main induction, rig out bow-planes."

"Aye." Bremer shouts from his station in the control room below us. "Induction closed. Green board."

"Very well. Open all vents."

The boat commences a rapid downward pitch, the sound of the wind and waves changing to a soft embryonic quietude as the boat glides into the deep. The pressure tightens about the sub like a cottony embrace. Canfield nudges Stewart and points at me. He hands me *the Com*, the command set that talks to the rest of the boat. I feel its familiar contours and key the button.

"Come to sixty feet. Level off at periscope depth."

"Leveling off," Bremer shouts up the hole.

"Blow negative to the mark."

"Negative to the mark, aye Mr. Murphy," Szotsman shouts from the diving manifold. The boat hisses and levels. I can feel the mounting pressure exerted from the sea.

"Chief, put air in the boat." Bremer releases some of the *condensed air* to compensate for the new pressure from the sea and confirming that the boat is, in fact, airtight.

"We're at *pressure*," he informs me. "Good trim," he adds, confirming the Manta Ray is balanced and level.

"Silent running. All ahead standard," Canfield orders. I repeat his words into the handset and the Manta Ray kicks in her electric motors, silently stalking her prey from below the waves. I feel it more than hear it, the boat growl, then *purr*.

"She's got the scent," Canfield whispers to the men. "The hunt is on."

"We're at periscope depth," I inform the skipper. "Ahead eight knots. Silent running. All stations manned and ready."

"Very well." Canfield motions with his thumb. "Okay Ensign, let's take a look." The boat's attack periscope is elevated to eye-level. Canfield turns it three hundred and sixty degrees around the boat in low-power magnification before flipping the handle to high-power and locking on the targets. After several minutes of this silent waiting he whispers, "Slow to one-third." I repeat his order to the boat. "We're getting close. Don't want to chance them seeing our *feather*," he says from the eyepiece, referring to the wake the periscope makes cutting the water. He slams the scope down. "Lt. Stewart, how many *fish* do we got left?" he inquires asking for our torpedo count.

"Four in the bow Skip, two aft," he responds, indicating a very productive patrol. All eyes and ears are glued on the captain, waiting for his next command, quick in coming.

"Tell forward torpedo room to ready tubes three through six." I punch the Com, repeating his words. Ned Binkershon, the forward-torpedo chief, confirms the order.

"Forward-torpedo room responds Captain."

The conning tower grows as silent as a cemetery, the crew waiting on the next order. Canfield gives the thumbs-up and the periscope is again raised to eyelevel and the entire process repeated carefully, methodically; Canfield scanning the sea three hundred and sixty degrees about the sub before locking on the targets ahead.

He works the scope left then right before locking on the first target, the boat pulsing under the thrust of her electric motors now driving the vessel. The men in the conning tower wait, the entire boat becoming eerily silent.

Duncan is focused on the stadimeter opposite the captain on the periscope shaft. Perspiration beads on the foreheads of the men crowded in the tower, a nervous tension escalating in the compartment. We were running roughshod into the belly of the enemy. It was Canfield's MO. He had made a name for himself and the boat for these very daring tactics and *his boys* were along for the ride, *All the Way,* the motto of our boat.

"What's his range now Goldman?" Canfield asks our sonar operator.

"Approaching six thousand feet Skipper."

"Bearing. Mark."

"Now bearing two-eighty," Duncan says from the stadimeter column.

"Helm, come to two-seven-seven."

"Aye, coming to two-seventy-seven degrees," *Easy* Lesky echoes and there's a slight pitch and roll as the rudder fights the sea to align the vessel with these new coordinates.

Canfield checks his watch. "Flood tubes."

I key the button. "Open outer doors on tubes three through six."

He drops the scope and sides up to Bill Taylor near his station at the TDC, the torpedo data calculator. "What's your *Indian* intuition saying?" Bill was half Native-American, from Pittsburgh via Santa Fe.

"A sure bet." Normally under the operation of a more senior officer, Canfield decided to give Taylor a shot at operating the TDC during a pre-patrol exercise outside Pearl Harbor. Bill scored all direct hits.

Mocked as beginner's luck by an admiring crew, Canfield never removed him as operator. *'The kid's half Navaho, it's in his blood.'* Skipper's voice repeats in my head returning to that moment in time. Taylor was only an ensign.

"Bill, set torpedo depth at twelve feet," Canfield says. "Speed, thirty-six knots. Sixty-degree angle on the bow." He glances at Stewart. "Tell Binkershon to activate the contact exploders. I don't give a hoot-in-hell for Navy regulations. I don't trust those goddamn magnetic exploders as far as I could throw one. Up scope."

Taylor twists the dials of the TDC. State-of-the-art and top-secret in 1943, for whatever unknown reason, the machine looks mockingly antiquated to me in that moment; wheels and dials. I find myself strangely drifting, as if in a dream that might dissipate, or crack and shatter like a reflection in a mirror.

"Torpedo room responds Skipper. Contact exploders already locked and loaded."

"Four-degree spread on the *fish* Bill. Stewart, take the plot. I've two fat tankers and what looks like a transport, two columns overlapping. There's a couple of merchants in the mix. With a little luck we might nick all three of the heavies." The boat becomes nearly still, the only movement or sound, the soft clicking of the periscope in action as it floats from one target to the next. "Lesky, two degrees to port." He lowers the scope again. "Men, we'll commence firing all tubes at ten second intervals when the first ship crosses the wire at two-seven-five degrees true."

All hands respond in unison, the crew becoming tense as we ready to fire upon the enemy. We are now close enough to hear the *swish-swish* of their props.

"Two-seven-eight Skipper."

He gives Duncan *the thumb*. "Up scope Ensign." He's at the eyepiece before it reaches level. With a couple quick jerks, he locks on the first target. "Perfect…made to order," he whispers as if to some invisible person.

He scans the sea around the sub, panning the scope. Canfield was one of the finest attack skippers in the fleet; careful and methodical. "Not a damn escort in sight…this is almost too good to be real." *Real?* Is this real? Are we about to tear apart and drown several thousand human beings? It feels like I'm suddenly in a dream, perhaps a nightmare. I look at my hands, squeeze them since pinching myself would be too obvious. This is real. Real enough. Canfield is now fixed entirely on the target ships. "Constant bearing."

"Two-seven-six."

"Standby to fire." The attack crew acknowledges. We wait, all eyes and ears on the captain.

"He's at twenty-five hundred Captain," Goldman says from the sonar station.

There's a short pause then Canfield shouts, "Bearing, mark!" and our nervous young ensign nearly screams.

"Two-seven-five, on the nose."

Taylor is right on his heels. "Tracking…set."

Canfield slams the scope down and looks directly at me. "Commence firing."

Can an instant be an eternity? Can something so unfathomably broad become contained within something so infinitesimally small? I've no clear idea how long or how short this singular moment really is. It seems both, yet neither. I see all the faces staring at me, read their eyes, yes perhaps even their minds…or are *their* thoughts somehow my own? I'm suddenly the invisible person inside the man on the bridge, a mere handful of minutes ago; wondering.

"Mr. Murphy, commence firing!"

I stare at the bright red firing knob, the color of blood and fire. I see them clearly in my memory, men on fire. How can I become the instrument of these sailor's deaths? It's almost with a sense of relief when Stewart slams the plunger with his fist, shouting into the chicken-wire mouthpiece.

"Fire *one!*"

The nearly imperceptible *swish-ping* of the torpedo exiting the hull brings home a stark reality. We are the attack submarine Manta Ray, the *Queen of Battle*, stalker of the depths, one of the most effective attack submarines in the Pacific theater of war. Time stops, except for the ticking of Taylor's stopwatch that he has engaged the moment the torpedo left the boat. The men are motionless, like mannequins.

"Ten seconds," Taylor says, like reading the time of day.

"Fire *two*," Stewart shouts into the mouthpiece. The boat hisses and shudders, releasing its deadly ordnance. All ears are on the ticking of the stopwatch. This time Taylor only nods, Stewart engaging the plunger. "*Three* away." Ten seconds later, "Fire *four*," and now it's just a matter of waiting.

"All fish away Skipper." Zigmund Elder, the hydrophone operator announces. "All fish running hot, straight, and normal sir," indicating the successful launch of all four torpedoes. His curly taupe-colored hair makes him look barely sixteen years of age.

"Up scope." The process repeats, Canfield methodically scanning the sea. "Chief, you're over-compensating ballast, we're dipping the scope," he shouts from the eyepiece.

"Sorel, one degree up bubble," Chief says below my feet. "Forward trim, blow a thousand pounds."

"Flooding to the sea one thousand pounds aye," Szotsman responds from the trim manifold.

"Time on that first fish Bill?"

"Forty seconds Skipper." We all wait, counting off silently until Taylor voices the inevitable countdown. "Twenty seconds…ten…five seconds…"

Suddenly, a muffled but distinct explosion–like distant thunder reverberating off stone–penetrates the boat as the first torpedo slams into the first ship followed ten seconds later by a second explosion. The crew is jubilant.

"Two hits in the first column," Canfield says from the eyepiece. "Nice work boys."

These concussions are followed by a pause and without the slightest thought I say, "Third is a miss." Everyone looks to Taylor hovering over his watch.

"The Exec is right. Third fish has timed-out. The fourth should be saying hello…right about…now." As if rehearsed, another muffled concussion cuts the water, followed by a massive explosion that violently shakes the boat. Men reach out to steady themselves.

"Holy mackerel," Wyatt says, and Canfield looks directly at me.

"There goes the tanker." After a quick perusal he gestures for me to take the eyepiece. "Mike, take a look." I reluctantly do so, knowing what awaits my sight.

What greets my eyes is harrowing. A massive conflagration has ensued, flames swelling to several hundred feet, the water boiling. Explosions torment the flaming ship as her deck ordnance heats and blows sending shrapnel and enormous balls of flame into the night. The ship moans as if crying for help.

In the brief moment I have the eyepiece, I see them, a recurring nightmare, men on fire, like demons racing from the bowels of Hell, diving into a flaming abyss, the sea black with burning oil.

I view all this as if it's just another day at the office, returning the scope to the skipper. He offers the sight to Stewart. Our junior lieutenant takes in the sight with a profound sense of awe, perhaps a masked dread.

He whistles, returning the scope to his captain. "Damn Skipper, three hits out of four."

Canfield peruses the scene then directs Duncan to the scope. "Ensign, confirm my sightings." The young officer gains the eyepiece scanning the horizon. We all silently wait on his words, coming like an oration at a funeral, perhaps an autopsy.

"Two enemy ships dead in the water, definitely a transport the deck is filling with men. She's listing hard astern, taking on water. The tanker is on fire, fire everywhere." He pans the scope to his left. "The merchants are making a run for it, steaming south. The sea is on fire." Suddenly a massive concussion rocks the boat. "*Holy mother of god,*" the young man whispers from the eyepiece.

"What is it Dunc?" Stewart asks as Duncan shuns the eyepiece. Is it awe, terror, or some other unfathomable emotion etched upon his young face?

"The tanker…gone."

Canfield grabs the scope and scans the scene. "He's right. She's been blown to pieces. There's nothing but fire on the water. The transport is sinking. Bill, take a look." Taylor takes the scope.

"What could have done that? The whole ship…gone," Duncan says in a near-catatonic state.

"Probably carrying aviation fuel, or a munitions ferry," Taylor says from the eyepiece. "It's red hot. The water is covered with flame." Then in a mere whisper, for my ears only, "those poor guys."

Canfield's eyes cut into ours. What he says shocks me. "What do you think boys? I'd say that right there is about eight thousand tons of enemy shipping headed for the floor. That puts this patrol tally close to 17,000 tons sunk."

No one contends the claim. In the brief moment of silence, each man is left with his own thoughts. I see it clearly in their faces, thoughts about the work we've been tasked with, thoughts about drowning, the immensity of the great ocean.

Elder suddenly breaks the quietude. "Skipper, I'm picking up screws to the northwest…getting louder, intersecting course." Taylor immediately returns the scope to the captain.

"Bearing?"

"Bearing…two-nine-four degrees. Definitely closing."

Canfield trains the scope on the coordinates. "Sonofabitch. Left full rudder! Hard about!" Lesky spins the helm and the boat veers sharply, the men in the compartment reaching out to steady themselves. Everyone stares at the captain. "Helm come to one-eighty. Chief, all-ahead full." I don't like the look on his face. "It's an Akikaze. The convoy masked him to the northwest. He's got a bone in his teeth boys. He looks madder than hell." Canfield slams the scope down and glares at the men sweating it out in the conning tower. "Stewart, how many fish we got left aft?"

"Only two. The other day's attack-"

"Prepare stern tubes one and two."

Stewart stares at the man, shock indelibly on his face. "You're taking on an Akikaze destroyer?"

"Mr. Stewart, I've given you an order!"

Stewart keys the handset. "You're back in the war Collins. Load everything you got." I can hear after-torpedo chief Tukey Collins acknowledge the order in the earpiece.

Every man is now sweating. I touch my forehead, bone-dry, wonder to myself why I'm not sharing the fear I see on the crew's faces. Canfield seems amazingly calm.

"Sonar, what's his range?"

"About three thousand feet Skipper," Goldman says. "He's coming on hard, must be doing thirty knots."

"We'll never outrun him on the surface," Canfield mutters. "Men…when he's at a thousand feet, I'm going to give him both fish down the throat, then take us deep."

"Down the throat," Wyatt whispers from *the pickle,* like stating a death sentence.

Canfield scrutinizes each face. "Men, I don't intend going through another trouncing like the other night without getting in the first lick. In these seas, I'm counting on him not seeing our fish until it's too late. Clear?" The attack crew responds in unison. "Get to it." Everyone begins prepping for the attack, a renewed flurry of activity in the conning tower and control room below.

"Boat on course one-eight-zero Skipper. We're at sixty feet, full ahead."

"What's his range Goldy?" Goldman tweaks his sonar, watching, listening.

"Approaching fifteen hundred feet."

"Slow to two thirds. Up scope." The *engine order telegraph* jangles in the control room beneath our feet while Duncan helps set the periscope. Canfield locks on the target and we wait for his next command, right on cue. "Flood *after*-tubes one and two."

"Open outer doors on stern tubes one and two," Stewart repeats into the Com. After a brief moment he reports, "Stern torpedo room ready to fire."

"Bill, how're we looking?"

"It's tight but I think I have the plot Skipper. If we're going to fire it better be soon."

"Steady. He's fast Billy-boy, we don't want to give him too much of a look or he'll duck our fish. Talk to me Goldman."

"He's at twelve hundred Skipper, closing fast." There's a sudden explosion in proximity of the boat. Duncan looks at the face of every man in the conning tower, settling on mine.

"What the hell was that?"

"He's shooting at our periscope," I say as if listening to another person.

"Commander Murphy is correct," Canfield says from the eyepiece. "Even in this dim light, the bastard sees our scope. Dammit! We have to bring him in closer boys, much closer." The words roll through the men like a cold wind. The Japanese destroyer is close enough to hear her propeller blades slicing the water. "Bill, reset. I want a two-degree spread left and right. He'll see our torpedoes even at several hundred feet. I'm gambling he doesn't have the guts to *thread the needle.*" The men freeze by these words, every eye glued on the captain. "We just might get lucky boys." Another series of explosions nearer the boat has the men exchanging looks.

"Shit. That was close," Stewart whispers. All eyes and ears are on Canfield at the scope. When two more explosions rock the outer hull, Canfield calls for the range.

"Eight-double-zero." Canfield waits. More sweat pours from the men.

"Captain," Taylor interjects, "we're running out of real estate. We need to fire, or the fish won't arm themselves."

"Steady Bill, steady." More explosions nearby slam into the boat, the sound of shell fragments caressing the outer hull. The men look ready to vomit.

"Six hundred," Goldman barks without being asked.

Canfield gives us *that look*. There's another round of eye contact, the fear of our situation–now *the hunted*–upon the faces of the men in the conning tower.

"He's baiting him in," Wyatt whispers.

"Yeah, and we're the goddamn bait," Herndon hisses.

"Closing Captain."

Another salvo from the destroyer severely shakes the boat, the hull rippling. Cork insulation is knocked off the walls from the concussion outside the hull. I marvel the machine holds. Tough old boat, *'She who protects us whilst at sea,'* our boat's unofficial motto; when the sea closes in. A valve ruptures in the control room below. I hear water spraying through the expletives.

"Four hundred feet Skipper," Goldman says, a tone escalating in his voice. All eyes are glued on Canfield. *Incredible*, I think to myself. Is he purposely gambling with our lives?

After a few seconds–that feel like an eternity–Canfield says from the eyepiece, "Well men, as my old Kentucky grandmother used to say: *'Life is a game of poker, if you don't have a handful of aces you better be a damn good bullshitter.'* Mark!"

Duncan shouts out the bearing coordinates and Taylor is right on his heels. "Set!"

"Fire both tubes."

Stewart slams the plunger. "Let 'em rip Tuke! Fire one and two."

There's the immediate *swish-ping*, the pressure in the boat changing as the submarine expels its last remaining torpedoes. "Dive Skipper?" Stewart shouts, his hand on the klaxon. Canfield remains absolutely calm, casually looks at Stewart as if having tea.

"Diving Officer, emergency dive."

Stewart slams the klaxon and screams into the battle phone, "Dive! Dive! Emergency dive, three hundred feet! Rig for depth charge!"

Without thought, I hit the collision alarm and shout into the Com. "All hands, standby for collision."

"Emergency down bubble. Bury the goddamn thing!" Chief Bremer shouts. Through the hatch I see Sorel spin the bow-plane wheel like a dealer spinning a roulette wheel. Chief grabs the Aft-plane operator's collar. "Finesse her Pendleton, keep her ass in the water. Don't let her breach the surface or they'll shoot us full of holes."

The boat takes on an alarming downward angle, the collision bell clanging wildly, escalating the chaos as men scramble. Plates, cups, and equipment rattle across the deck below, the sea doors slamming shut as the boat readies for the impending attack. Everyone holds their breath as the boat pierces the depths, seeking the sanctuary of the lower temperature stratum.

"Both fish are away Captain. Both running hot, straight, and normal," Elder says from the hydrophone station.

"Lesky, hard left," Canfield shouts. "Come to zero-ninety. Left full rudder." Men reach out to steady themselves from falling. The boat screams, as if it might break apart from the pressure being placed on it. "Talk to me Goldy."

"He's coming on Skipper, no change."

Canfield shoots a look at Taylor. "When's judgment Bill?"

"I don't know for sure Captain. Best I can figure, fifteen seconds."

"Has his course changed Goldman?"

"Negative."

"Ten seconds to impact."

Canfield rails at the ceiling above like Ahab gone mad. "C'mon you sonofabitch, veer-off!"

"Five seconds, three, one…"

Nothing. No impact, only the sound of the destroyer's props cutting water. Men stare at the gray arc of the ceiling as if they could actually see the *hunter-killer* on the surface above. Ensign Duncan genuflects, silent whispers to an invisible god.

Goldman suddenly stutters. "H-He's veering. Skipper he's changing course." There's a round of eye contact before we hear it, a loud heavy thud that I feel more than hear. The men go crazy, an instantaneous release of emotion. "Hail Mary, he's hit!"

Duncan grabs my sleeve. "We got him? We got him!" The captain quiets the men in the conning tower, but we hear the sounds of jubilation echo through the boat.

"Quiet men!" Canfield shouts, listening. "Talk to me Elder. What's he doing up there?" Silence returns, like a blanket of freshly fallen snow.

"Sounds like her engines have stopped."

Canfield shoots a look at Stewart. "All stop." Stewart keys the handset, repeating his words. The boat quiets to nil, listening. An all-encompassing silence enwraps us as we ascend into the depths. "Level off."

The boat responds, leveling.

Chief pokes his bearded head up the hatch. "Boat trim. We're at two hundred and fifty feet."

A profound silence grips the crew. I swear I hear the heartbeat of the boat. Men–transfixed like boys around a campfire–listen to the vast quietude of the great ocean outside. Then we hear it, the horrid shrieking and moaning of twisting metal, bending and breaking into the deep; the slow agonizing death of a dying ship.

———

Elder turns and puts to words what we already know. "They're breaking up Captain. We got him." No one dares speak as we silently witness the destruction of two thousand tons of ship and the *death-by-drowning* of approximately one hundred and ninety men.

The sound is horrible, the ship crying out its death and slow descent into oblivion; each man left naked with his own thoughts, his own mortality, until there's no longer any thinking at all, just a deep encompassing *listening.* All eyes are locked on Elder as if he were some old sage, a fortuneteller, his crystal ball the scope glowing before him. He stares through it, one hand cupping the headset tightly to his ear.

"Anything?" He looks at Canfield and gives his head a shake, a silent acknowledgement of death. "Anyone else?"

"No Captain, quiet as a graveyard." The comment registers with every man in the coffin-like space of the conning tower. After a silent trance, Elder slides the headset onto his neck and scans the eyes of every man in the conning tower. "Nothing. I don't hear a sound above, only the other ships fading to the south."

Everyone stares at the captain awaiting his next order. Will he chance taking us above? Could there possibly be another sub-killer waiting, stalking the waters, waiting for us to surface? Canfield extends the moment like an actor on a stage.

"Silent running, ahead one-third."

Stewart echoes the captain's order into the handset. The *engine order telegraph* jangles below my feet as they relay the command to the men in the Maneuvering room. The boat shudders softly, as if shaking off a bad dream, the near imperceptible sound of her electric motors vibrating through the steel hull as sweet as humming a lullaby.

Canfield pushes his cap back off his forehead. "We did it boys. Scratch one sub-killer." Accolades are exchanged, followed by a deep encompassing quietude broken only by the shriek of the dying ship from somewhere deep within *the lonely fathoms*. No one says a word, each man quietly reflecting within his own mind *the day's work* until Canfield shatters the moment. "Lieutenant Stewart, take us to sixty feet. Let's take a look."

Stewart freezes. "Sixty feet Skipper? You don't want to stay down and listen?"

"Junior Lieutenant Stewart. Did you not hear my order?"

"Yessir."

"I want to take a look. Stay on course zero-ninety, silent running." Canfield smiles to his men. "We're fresh out of fish boys. We'll head for the barn. Keep your ears on Elder. Mister Stewart, if the coast is clear, you have the Com. First Officer Murphy, I'd like a word with you, alone, in my cabin." As he studies me–his eyes like a wolf's eyes–Elder turns, a haunted look on his face.

"Skipper…I'm picking up another set of screws." Canfield is instantly beside his station.

"Bearing?"

"Bearing…zero-ten degrees…north by northeast. Getting louder, coming on…intersecting course." All is eerily quiet, then: *PING-ping…PING-ping…PING-ping…*

"ASDIC. Damn it to hell. God damn it to hell!"

"Sir, enemy destroyer closing."

"Sonofabitch. Goddamn sonofabitch!" the captain rails at no one. "Where did he come from? Emergency dive. Chief, get us deep." Stewart hits the Klaxon twice and shouts into the com.

"Emergency dive, three hundred feet!"

"Face-dive Sorel!" Bremer shouts and Sorel spins the bow-plane control. "Flood bow buoyancy tank." The boat hisses and takes on a severe downward angle, supplies and equipment clattering across the deck floor. Sailors pull ballast levers, and the boat exhales its air.

"Screws closing rapidly. Range, six hundred feet…four hundred feet…two…they're right on top of us Captain. Splashes, depth charges on their way down!"

The first concussion is so horrendous it robs all sound and air from the compartment, a massive explosion rocking the boat; glass dials shatter, water and oil spew from ruptured pipes and valves. A column of water slams into the side of my neck and seaman Wyatt reaches over me to shut the valve feeding the ventilation system.

"Close every valve you can," I shout to the men in the control room and sailors comply, slamming watertight doors shut in preparation of flooding. The lights flicker then go out, the darkness absolute until the emergency back-ups kick in moments later, flickering precariously.

"Helm, right full rudder!" Canfield shouts. Lesky veers the boat, water gushing from an air-supply blower above his head covering him in a shower of green-water. The battle phone jangles. Canfield grabs it, listens, then slams it back into its cradle. "Sonofabitch. We busted a main in the engine room. I'm heading below Stewart." I belay him.

"I'll go Captain." He glares at me, then nods, seawater dripping from his forehead.

The engine room is flooding. Sailors are staring at the tangled mess of air and exhaust induction pipes. Sea water filling the after-hold at an alarming rate. I grab Bremer's arm, water dripping from his salt-and-pepper beard. I don't like the look in his eyes.

"How bad Chief?"

"Bad Murph, a break in the main induction manifold. We threw the starboard shaft. The brackets have been sheared off down there."

"What can we do about it?"

"Drydock her!" We stare at the pit. An alarming amount of water is entering the compartment.

"At this rate of intake, we're in serious trouble. Can *she* be repaired or not?"

"Down here? At three-hundred goddamn feet?!" He spits into the water licking our boots.

"How Chief?" He runs a hand through his greasy hair, pulling water from his beard.

"Someone has to get down in there and close-off those valves, the relief valves too…and pray like holy hell those beams don't fail while he's down there; it would take Mare Island to get the poor sonofabitch out of there." His expression turns grave. "We couldn't run the diesels."

"Who? Who'll do it?"

He grimaces. "No one wants to do it. Hell, he'd have to be half insane."

Geysers of water start spewing from the maze of pipes and electrical conduit, black and dirty as coal. Lights in the compartment flicker and spit. The clearance between the pipes and motor shaft is barely large enough to squeeze a man through. I steel myself, start under with the wrench when someone grabs my neck; Conrad Howard, our motor machinist's mate from New Jersey. He yanks the wrench from my grip.

"You California guys never quit do ya? Always gotta be the big hero, like *Tarzan the ape-man*. Get lost *Hollywood*, scram. This is Machinist's turf."

He disappears–cussing and spitting–into the water filling the hold beneath the engine-deck. Sorel is suddenly at my shoulder. "We lost com Mr. Murphy. Captain is asking for a damage report." I start for the control room when a massive explosion rocks the submarine and I'm thrown back against the engines.

Everything is swirling. I teeter between the ether and consciousness, shaking the fog from my vision when a commotion erupts. One of the new recruits, a machinist named Carley, is screaming at the top of his lungs, his voice going through me like an icepick.

When the men attempt to restrain him, he goes berserk, breaking from their grasp and punching Machinist's Mate Strejcek in the mouth, knocking Len out. He yanks a pipe-wrench from Vic Rawlston's hand, swinging it wildly at the crew. They shout, trying to bring the errant seaman to his senses but I can see plainly he's lost control, insanely demanding we immediately *surface* or he'll kill somebody.

I'd seen it before, men reaching the breaking point from the constant hammering of the depth charges slamming into the skin of the submarine, the relentless concussions nerve-wracking, rattling a man's skull; always present in one's mind, the billions of gallons of sea pressing to enter the compartment and drown everyone, a mere quarter-inch of steel between you and an agonizing death.

When Carley nearly caves-in the head of Earl Lloyd, my chief machinist, I step forward and order the man to surrender the tool or risk court-martial. His response is to slam the thing against the side of my head. I see stars exploding, the infinity of space, then a slow but steady advent into black.

Chapter 2: I'm Not Murphy

*B*lack gives the impression of emptiness.

It also lends itself to timelessness. There is no *time* in black for it lacks form, definition, no distinct features or qualities except a feeling of vastness, or the opposite. Time fails, becomes empty and meaningless; there is nothing upon which to base a calculation however diaphanous.

Without light there is no form, without form there is no perceivable place. For instance, here, now; the sensation of space, and yes…time, *the veneer of time*…the coming and going of things, of people, their whispers like prayers, obsequies.

Music is playing, over a *tinny* speaker. The soft tones make me feel as if I were floating on an ocean, a slow gentle rolling. What is this song; its quiet reflective mood oddly familiar? The answer is immediate: *A Garden in the Rain,* by Gene Austin. How would I know that? I don't know anything about *old-timey* music.

Like a swimmer from the depths I break surface, my eyes stinging from sweat. Incredibly, I'm surrounded by metal, the iron plates and rivets painted over in gray, a cylindrical room made of steel; a prison cell? There's nothing but a curtain for a door. The light seeping in under the muslin smells like coffee; and diesel fumes. Diesel fuel? When I try to sit up, a searing pain wracks my skull forcing me to lie back and stare at the bolts and rivets of my steel cage, the metal sweating like Vulcan before the flames.

Men are conversing from behind the curtain, their conversation dated, old names, old topics concerning old wars. The dark-green muslin curtain hanging from teakwood hooks is strangely familiar.

An odd feeling of nostalgia demands the moment. Déjà vu? No. The feeling is lasting, getting stronger. As if waking from a dream, I realize I'm on *a submarine.* Not a new one either, the clean sterile confines of a nuclear vessel, but an old gray antiquated submarine, the smell of diesel fuel in the air. A *fleet-boat.* I'm on a United States *Gato*-class submarine. How would I know that?

More incredible, how did I get here? I look at my hands, strong tanned hands beneath light-brown sleeves, a single gold band on the left ring-finger. The swish of the curtain portends the arrival of a bearded crewman standing over me with his mouth open.

"Hey, Mr. Murphy, you're awake. Jiggs, beat it in here, Commander Murphy's coming-around." *Murphy.* Murphy? Why does the name sound so familiar, here in this place, this *submarine*–if this is, in fact, where I am? The music changes, playing softly over the heavily painted speaker cone. For some reason the next tune is known to me also, *Sophisticated Lady,* by Duke Ellington. I gaze at the faces hovering over me–their sweaty countenances–immediately knowing their names and rank.

"Burlsley…your name is Burlsley. You're the Boatswain's Mate."

"Last time I checked." He cracks a broad grin, an upper front tooth missing from a barfight. "Boy Mr. Murphy, it sure is good to see you awake again. Coop was sweating bullets. You were really konked out, like gonesville."

"Why are you calling me that?"

"Sir?"

"*Murphy*. My name isn't Murphy, it's…" I go blank.

"Come again sir?"

"My name isn't Murphy. My name is…" No matter how I try to work my brain, I cannot remember my name.

Their expressions change radically. Burlsley turns to the other sailor. I know his name too, Jaeger. These men are sailors, dressed in blue fatigues.

"Jiggs, go get the *sawbones*, hurry."

"But Mr. Cooper is asleep in his bunk."

"Well wake him up."

When the young blonde-haired pharmacist enters, I instantly know his name. "How are you feeling Lieutenant? The guys said you were awake again."

"Your name is Cooper, Montgomery Cooper. You're from Savannah, Georgia."

"Yes sir, I sure am."

"How could I possibly know that?" His smiling demeanor inverts.

"Just take it easy Mr. Murphy. You're still suffering from the trauma."

"Trauma?"

"You don't remember?" The three sailors exchange wondering looks. "What *do* you remember?"

"Well, I remember…driving to New Jersey, from New York. There was a television in the van, one of those flip down jobs playing an old black-and-white movie, *Treasure of the Sierra Madre*, but no one was watching the movie. Some sort of disaster had occurred…in Hawaii I think…or possibly it was Japan. We were all watching the news on our smartphones, three, four of us in the van, then…I woke up here. That's all I seem to remember."

"Hey Coop, what the heck is he talking about?"

"I don't know. I'm not sure."

"What's a *smartphone*?" Jaeger interjects. "That Navy code for something? A new weapon?"

"A dream probably, nothing to worry about." His expression says the opposite. He studies my eyes with a flashlight before checking my pulse.

"Cripes Mr. Murphy, you went head-to-head with that punk Carley," Burlsley says. "I knew he was a loose cannon from day one. What did I tell everybody? Another whack-job. I can sniff those guys out a mile away."

"I saw the whole thing, ringside Commander," Jaeger adds. "It was like the second Joe Louis, Max Schmeling bout…you were Max Schmeling."

"I'm sorry but I know what I'm talking about and who I am. I don't know what your game is, but my name isn't Murphy and I want to know why you've got me in this…this submarine." I go to rise but Cooper holds me down.

"Easy does it, sir. You better just lie still until you come to your senses. I think you've sustained a concussion."

"Heck Lieutenant Murphy, you took a *wollup*," Burlsley adds. "That nut-job laid that pipe-wrench right across your head. A real cheap shot too, hitting a guy in the head with a wrench? What lousy mug does that?"

Cooper quiets him with a gesture of his hand. "Let him lie still. He's suffering amnesia from the impact. He'll come around."

"What's *amnesia*?" Jaeger asks Burlsley while Cooper studies my pupils again.

"When a guy gets knocked in the head so hard, he forgets who he was."

The curtain parts and Burlsley and Jaeger cram to one side at attention. The pharmacist stands and salutes.

"Captain."

"What's the skinny Cooper? I heard Murphy's come-to." He shoves me aside enough to sit on the edge of the bunk, crossing his gangly legs; his eyes the color of the submarine.

"Welcome back goldbrick. If you're finished with your beauty nap, Uncle Sam could use you on the bridge." He directs his attention to the other men. "I'm bypassing Midway, boys. At our current rate of advance, we'll make *Pearl* in three, maybe four days." He shifts his attention to me, smiling. "Get back and see the little woman."

I stare at the man. "Do we know each other? You look familiar."

His expression flips. "What the hell?" He glares at Cooper. "What's that?"

"Captain, Commander Murphy is suffering from the impact to his head, what's referred to in medical terminology as a *concussion*."

"I'm perfectly aware of what's happened Corpsman." His eyes cut into mine. "What do you need Murph? Name it."

"I do know you. Canfield...Oliver Canfield. You're the captain of this...*boat*...and we're at war. World War Two. My god, how could I possibly have gone...? Is this some kind of joke? What's going on here?"

"Cooper what the hell!"

"Give him time Captain, he'll come around. He's just disoriented."

"Aw heck Skipper, he says his name ain't *Murphy*, he thinks he's some other guy," Burlsley interjects; the look on Canfield's face is noteworthy.

"Thank-you for your prognosis Bosun," he states pointedly. "Now if you're through practicing medicine I'd appreciate you two jokers reporting to the Chief. Sometime today!" The sailors immediately vacate the room.

Canfield removes his cap, wiping sweat from his forehead with a dirty handkerchief before gesturing for Cooper to join him outside. Despite their whispering, I can hear their words through the curtain.

"He's suffering from amnesia sir. He seems to have forgotten who he is."

"How long will this go on?"

"Not long I think, but it's crucial he gets medical attention as soon as we get to Pearl Harbor. This could be serious Captain. A head injury isn't to be trifled with."

"Keep a close eye on him Cooper. Let me know if he gets any worse."

"Yes sir." There's a pause. "What is it sir?"

"Has Burlsley been sipping *torpedo juice* again?"

"I…I don't think so."

"What was he rambling about? Murphy thinks he's a different person?"

"He's disoriented. It must be amnesia. He seems to think he's someone else, from the future. Temporarily I hope."

"Report to me on his condition in one hour. Let me know if you need anything."

When Cooper returns, I'm sitting on the edge of the bunk.

"Whoa, hold on Mr. Murphy, you better lay back down."

"I'm all right. I'm starting to feel better." He scans my eyes with his light again and examines the bandage on the side of my head. "What happened to me Cooper?"

"Don't you remember? We finished our assigned patrol, radioed our return to *Pearl* when radar picked up a convoy. Canfield being Canfield, all four diesels went *on-line,* and we caught them last night. Jesus, Canfield goes in like Flynn, takes out two of their ships before they knew what hit them. Remember Lieutenant?"

"Yes, I know the things you're talking about. But how?"

"This is my first patrol under Canfield, as you know. I've never seen anything like it. Then it was our turn. The Japanese were on us like starving dogs on a bone. Captain wiggled his way out of it, but they must have dropped all they had. Carley went nuts, started attacking the crew. You tried to take the wrench away and took the worst of it." His expression hardens. "The guys beat the hell out of Carley Mr. Murphy. A shattered jaw, fractured ribs. He's in serious condition. All this starting to sound familiar sir?"

"It does, but how? It's too fantastic. How can I be in both places?"

"Both places?"

"Here, instead of where I'm from. Where I live and work. The laboratory…and…?"

"Sir?"

"Why are we on this old boat?"

He's incredulous. "Uh…how's that again sir?"

"Okay, I'll play along. Why are we running around the ocean, I assume, in an old antiquated submarine?" The man's blank expression concerns me. Also, what concerns me is the clothes the men wear, their old hairstyles, the old music playing…even the Waterbury watch on my wrist. It's like waking up on a 40's movie set.

There's a stack of correspondence on the desk, the Navy letterhead is an old-fashioned font, the paper crisp and new, the printing on the clipboards too. A 'near-mint' *Life* magazine sits on the tiny desk dated April 1943. I rub my forehead, stare into the man.

"What year is it Cooper?"

"Are you kidding with me sir?" I shake my head and wait for an answer. "July, July twenty-fourth," he says, purposely avoiding my actual question.

"You heard me. What *year*?"

"1943." He sees the shock form on my face. "Mr. Murphy, you better just lie real quiet. Take it easy until we get back to Pearl, get you checked out."

"*Pearl?* Pearl Harbor?"

He shakes his head. "Boy, you really took a shot. Just rest awhile Mr. Murphy. I'll check on you in a few minutes." *Murphy.* I'm not Murphy. I decide to get to the bottom of this farce. Obviously, some joke is in play and I'm soon to find myself the butt of it.

"Cooper, I'm going to walk around for a bit. Have a look around the…the sub."

"Gee, I don't know sir. I think it'd be better if-"

"C'mon Cooper loosen up. A little exercise would do me good right?" For some reason, I don't expect his suddenly accommodating me.

"Okay, you outrank me. You're the *X-0*."

"*X-0?*"

"Executive officer." His brow knits.

"Right, *X-0*…I'm the executive officer…of the S.S. Manta Ray. This *is* the Manta Ray isn't it? How would I know that?" The look on his face makes me think he's having second thoughts. When I stand my head swirls and I steady myself against the bulkhead.

"Mr. Murphy, you sure you're okay? If you have a fall you could do even more damage. This is way over my head."

"I'm all right Cooper, I'll be fine." I stand upright. "See, good as new."

He helps straighten out my uniform and follows me into a long narrow passageway made of gray steel. Pipes and conduit lace its course lined with a series of doors and curtains that lead to the officer's quarters.

Sailors emerge from the watertight door that opens into the forward torpedo room. I can see the brass-lined firing tubes, a half dozen men smoking cigarettes and laughing through the oval watertight door.

To my left is the officer's wardroom. I recognize the two young officers, Stewart and Taylor, seated at the stainless-steel table drinking coffee from bone-china cups. They're instantly on their feet, joining us in the hallway.

"Hey, look Taylor, look who decided to rejoin the war effort, mighty Mike Murphy the fleet's best first officer since Moon Mulligan." He gives my shoulder a hearty punch.

"Easy Lieutenant, he's not quite himself just yet."

"Know something Coop? You're going to make somebody a great wife someday."

"He's a little disoriented." They *gently* shove him aside.

"We'll take it from here *Doctor*."

"Yeah beat it boy surgeon, go cure the common cold," Stewart says, ruffling the medic's hair. "How you feeling Murph? Better than you look I hope." They laugh, their smiling expressions contrasting with the drab-gray environ of the gangway.

"Stewie, Bill…you're both here." My comment registers oddly with them, both sailors adopting more serious expressions.

"Get a load of this guy Taylor, like he's been on vacation or something."

"I hear the South Pacific is nice this time of year."

The curtain behind us is yanked open and Canfield emerges from his quarters opposite the wardroom.

"Lieutenant Stewart, last I checked you were the scheduled *Diving Officer*. Did Tojo call in a truce while I was in my digs?"

"I got twenty minutes yet Skip." The captain's steely gaze remains unflinching. Stewart sets his cup down and disappears through the oval port that I know leads to the control room of the submarine.

"Pharmacist Cooper, why is this man out of his bunk?" Cooper gives me a pensive look.

"Captain, requesting permission to return to my duties. I'm feeling much-"

"Denied. Get back in your bunk Mike, I want you taking it easy until we make Pearl. That's an order."

Mike, my name is Michael J. Murphy, the middle initial nothing more than a letter filling an empty box on my birth certificate, my parents unable to decide between two grandfathers, Jason or Jacob. Canfield is scrutinizing me.

"Cooper. Back in his bunk, now."

"Captain let me move about the boat. Get my bearings," I say, straightening my collar.

Canfield glares at the bewildered corpsman. "Well?"

"It might actually be good for him."

"Okay, but he as much as sneezes, I want him in his bunk. I'm not about to lose my second-in-command to a damn bump on the head. You get me Corpsman?"

"Yes sir." Cooper nudges me toward the control room.

When I duck through the sea-door leading to the submarine's control room I'm assailed by the smiling faces of the men I've been serving with. The balding George Szotsman is at the manifold bay, a veteran of six patrols. Seaman 2nd class *Easy* Lesky is singing to himself at the helm. Quentin Sorel and Ron Pendleton, manning the bow and stern planes, are swapping lies with seaman Wyatt on the busy end of a screwdriver.

—

Repairs are underway, a myriad of brass dials, crystal gauges and stainless-steel levers saturate the compartment occupying every conceivable spot. Peter Bremer, fresh from the engine room steps in wiping grease from his hands with an oily rag. He stops and shakes his head at me.

"Christ-sakes, you look like holy hell. How you feeling Murph?"

"Okay. How's the boat Chief?" I inquire, my concern for the vessel suddenly dominating my consciousness.

"Ready for the barn. They roughed us up pretty damn good that time."

"What are the damages? Anything serious?"

"You might as well hear it straight. We got our guts stomped. We fried a shitload of circuits. Connie fixed the induction leak that almost killed us, but we threw a bearing on the number-two engine and they bent our starboard shaft…its shot. Lloyd fixed the number-three diesel and stopped-up most of the leaks but we're seeping oil from somewhere. We're leaving an oil slick up there on the surface thick enough to drydock a cruiser. Let's hope we get back to Pearl before we're spotted and trailed by a Japanese sub."

"What's our injury report?"

"Three men down. Cushman, Jones and…and Carley," he says shaking his head and grimacing. "Carley's a mess."

"Yeah I heard what happened."

"Anyway, we're still in the war. Thank your Mother Superior we're out of torpedoes," he says returning his attention to the *Christmas Tree*–the primary control panel–with its plethora of red and green lights indicating the open or closed status of the various orifices moving water, air, or exhaust in and out of the boat.

The pitch and roll of the submarine–coupled with the smell of diesel fuel–inundates me with vertigo, followed by nausea and the sudden urge to vomit. I harden myself and work my way aft, through the control room toward *the head*.

I pass the radio room, realize Roscoe Jukes our radio operator is the source of the music. He's playing 78rpm records on a turntable and piping the music softly through the boat over the PA system. We often gave him permission to do so on *the return*. He smiles and nods, patented cigarette dangling from his mouth. *Jukesy* was a drifter before the war, an ex-millwright from Scranton, Pennsylvania.

I duck through the watertight door to the crew's mess bumping into Dickie Dover, the boat's baker. "Mr. Murphy, back on your feet?" He winks, continuing his chores. Dick had been a short-order cook in Kansas City before the outbreak of hostilities. The man had a near magical ability with flour, eggs, and sugar.

Within the stainless-steel eatery I find *the California Crew*, Victor Rawlston, William Toles–one of the gunners– and Anson Parmalee our chief electrician, engaged in a spirited game of rummy. Parmalee's white toothy grin and wavy brown hair remind me that he's from Berkeley and studied electronics at Caltech. Willy was from Los Angeles.

"How you feeling Lieutenant Murphy? Everything okay?" Rawlston inquires, dropping his cards, an odd expression on his normally placid face.

"I'm fine Vic. Thanks for asking."

"Sorry Lieutenant. I should'a never let that guy take that wrench from my hand. He got his payback, in spades."

"Don't worry about it." Vic was from Bakersfield. He was a good sailor, and a good mechanic; raced the dirt-track circuit back in southern California.

———

Chapter 3: The Double Man

I make my way through *the Ritz*.

The crew's sleeping quarters are filled with bunks, three tiers, floor to ceiling. No one seems to be sleeping, the sailors smoking cigarettes and drinking coffee; some reading, a few playing cards. Connie Howard is combing his moustache while perusing a comic book. Conrad always sported a large black moustache that he kept meticulously groomed.

"Well lookey what the dog dragged over the fence boys. First Officer Murphy arisen from the dead." *Arisen from the dead*; possibly truer than he knows? Is it possible that I've died, and this is some kind of purgatory, some strange reenactment of past events? Conrad frowns, concern coursing his face. "You okay Mr. Murphy? You look a little funny."

"What's new about that Connie? He always looks *a little funny*," Babineaux our chief gunner says. The gunnery crew has a good chuckle at my expense.

"Nah, Connie's right Babs. He's looking *funnier* than his usual dopey self," Dave Cisco adds, and the jokes continue unabated. When the laughter runs dry, I give Howard's shoulder a squeeze.

"How's the wife and kids back in New Jersey Mr. Howard?"

"Like I tell everybody Mr. Murphy, don't worry about the economy. Judy's out there running rampant; spending every single dollar I can ship back stateside. The economy is in great shape."

The head is just aft of the bunkroom. When I gaze into the polished stainless-steel that serves as a mirror, I see my reflection for the first time since awakening. I'm shocked. For some unexplainable reason, the man in the mirror is not the face I expect. However, the young dark-haired man in the mirror *is me*; Lieutenant Commander Michael Murphy, first officer of the S.S. Manta Ray, a United States fleet-boat at war and we're returning from patrol.

"What's happening?" I ask my reflection. It's obvious the *man in the mirror* doesn't know the answer to the question. I feel my face, its familiar contours and remember my youth, growing up in Vallejo, California. Skipping school and sneaking through the fences of Mare Island Naval Yard.

Mare Island, the great Pacific naval base, nestled quietly up the estuary from the Golden Gate. A magical world of ships, guns, and machines; lathes and drill-presses. A world of sailors, boats and tugs, but best of all the submarines, three hundred and twenty feet of sleek lean metal that could disappear under the waves, explore the depths of the ocean, like the *Nautilus* in the Jules Verne novel.

"Who are you?" I ask the young man in the mirror. He looks at me from the other side of the steel, wondering. "*Why* are you?" Again, his youthful blank stare. I have to break off our silent exchange because his eyes are my eyes and he's staring through me; an invisible man in another person's body. "This is insane. This can't be happening," he says from the mirror, voicing my thoughts aloud.

I exit the head, feeling flush. The chief steward stops and asks if I'm *feeling okay*. Charles 'Coffee' Porteru was a Cajun from Lafayette, Louisiana and earned his nickname not so much due his ethnicity than his knack for making a seriously good cup of coffee. It was his dream to become a premiere New Orleans chef.

"You look like you seen a ghost," he says, looking me over. Coffee was full of ghost stories and tales of witchcraft and voodoo, some true, some *embellished*. He reveled in holding the attention of an entire crew of battle-hardened men for minutes, hours sometimes, with stories from the Louisiana delta. "You don't look so good Mr. Murphy," he informs me. "Ya'll look half dead."

"Thanks Coffee, I appreciate that."

"You need some red-hots Mr. Murphy, cayenne, shake it up. Get the blood pumping again."

Looking at our senior steward, I'm reminded we would sneak him into the Officer's Club at the Royal Hawaiian Hotel and watch him do the *Lindy Hop* with a barmaid from St. Louis. *The Lindy* was really something to watch, especially performed by someone like Coffee who had the quickest feet of any man I've ever met. "Come on back to the mess," he says waking me from my meditation. "I'll setcha up. Get a little color in ya," he gibes.

"Consider it a date."

I wander the boat like a kid at a carnival; continue aft through the two engine rooms. Earl Lloyd, the boat's chief motor machinist, is shouting at the top of his lungs at Pat McClatchy, one of the motor machinist's mates. No one ever took offense. Earl was almost deaf from serving on the subs as a topnotch diesel mechanic. None of the men liked going out drinking with him because he always talked at the top of his lungs and he never quit talking. The more liquor you poured into Earl the louder he got until no one could stand being in the same room with him.

He shakes my hand, welcoming me *back to the war*. I pull a handkerchief from my back pocket and wipe away the grease he's left.

Lloyd commences to shout details about *the bad driveshaft* into my ear, over the roar of the Fairbanks-Morse diesel engines. When something McClatchy does diverts his attention, I slip away aft, into the stainless-steel environment of the *Maneuvering room* where the electricians answer the orders from the bridge, engaging the Elliott electric motors that propel the sub during *silent running,* when the submarine dives underwater; the diesels useless under the waves. Chief Petty Officer John Smith is conversing with Electrician's Mate Sam Torsch, standing at the ready should the *Bells of St. Mary* suddenly ring out their dire warning of an impending attack.

"Ahoy Mr. Murphy," Torsch says through his rust-colored beard.

"Feeling better sir?" Smith inquires. The two sailors were visual opposites, Torsch heavy and hairy, Smith lean and clean-shaven.

"Yes John, thank-you for asking." Smith was from Charleston, South Carolina, Torsch from Erie, Pennsylvania. "How's everything?"

"Ready for a break," Sam exhales and Smith nods.

"He's right Commander. This boat, *and* crew, needs an overhaul."

My sojourn ends in the stern torpedo compartment where a baseball game is in progress. Wally Nichols, a relief pitcher with the Cincinnati Reds, is throwing curveballs to Tommy Belcher who *caught* for Ball State before being drafted. Wallace was happily married to an heiress. Tommy was the son of a boilermaker from Muncie, Indiana.

"Hey, Lieutenant Murphy, grab a bat," Jack Georgio shouts, the torpedo crew lining the length of the compartment.

Tukey Collins and Ned Binkershon are engaged in an animated conversation about the Dodgers' current season. For reasons I hardly understand, I refer to the team as the *Los Angeles Dodgers;* they collectively howl, suggesting I '*see the pharmacist about a head-check.*' Tukey was from Brooklyn, Ned, Long Island.

"Our Exec's losing his marbles. *Los Angeles*? Sheesh," Binkershon says indignantly, shaking his head. Nothing, and I mean nothing, except the Manta Ray–or possibly their wives–were as important to them as baseball, in particular the Brooklyn Dodgers.

"You're out of your mind Murph," Collins says. "The Dodgers won't never leave Brooklyn. What ape would permit it?" he declares and Danny Dyer, Teddy Ritchie and the rest of *Tukey's crew* all voice their collective agreement, loudly.

"Alright already. Give him a break," Binkershon interjects into the melee. "Our hallowed Exec took a shot to the noodle. He's still a little numb."

"He's always *a little numb.*"

"He'll come around, right Murph?" he says shaking me like a ragdoll. When the conversation–thankfully–turns to movie stars Ned informs me it's movie night in the forward torpedo compartment and that I'm invited. "Belcher pilfered that copy of *The Thin Man.* Our coming-home present. Myrna Loy…" he says clicking his tongue and winking. "C'mon, I'll get you a cozy front row seat." Binkershon drapes a bicep around my neck and *drags* me back through the port. As we pass the radio room, Jukes flags me down.

"No movie for you Lieutenant. Captain wants to see you, in his cabin."

At his cabin I pause briefly before tapping on the bulkhead next to the curtain. "Come in."

He's at his desk, updating his logbook. "Close the curtain. Have a seat." I sit on the edge of the bunk and wait while he withdraws a nearly empty fifth of bourbon from the locker near his desk. He pours two shot glasses downing his straight before pouring another. "Bottoms up." The alcohol burns my throat. He takes time to finish writing in his patrol log, apparently more than happy to make me sit and wait for what I know is coming next. He then lights a *Camel*, offering me his pack although he knows I don't smoke. I wait, sipping the liquor, its taste like gasoline, or is it diesel fuel?

"How many patrols does this make, you and me?" he asks, knowing the answer.

"The fifth."

"That's right, five. First as a green NCO, then as a *Jag*, three as my *Exec*. Five very good, extremely successful patrols." He looks at me with his vise-like stare. "In all those patrols I don't think I've ever seen you choke, until yesterday. What happened up there Murph? You hesitated during the attack. That's a first."

"I know."

"So, you *know*. I'm asking why?"

"It's complicated."

"Try me." I rise to stroll the tiny confines of the small compartment, but can only manage a few half-turns, like an animal in a cage. "We're more than just captain and first officer you know that. Level with me. You've lost your nerve?"

"Something very strange is going on."

He stares at me through the smoke wafting toward the vent. "Like what?"

"Skipper, I don't know how to say this."

"To hell with formalities. Just say it."

"I'm not Mike Murphy."

His expression is unreadable. "Mind running that by me again?"

"I'm not Michael Murphy, the person everyone thinks I am. At least...not part of me, the guy who hesitated up there in the conning tower."

He leans back in his chair, a sublime expression on his grizzled face. "Okay, I'm always good for a joke. Who are you then, Delano Roosevelt?"

"I don't know. But I'm becoming aware of things."

"What things?"

"The future. I've been seeing it, in my mind Skipper. Feeling it...the future...the end of the war. A future world free of all this oppression, free of constant war. I know things that will happen. I'm not making this up. I'm certain of it."

He's staring a hole through me. "How?"

"I don't know."

"Why?"

"I don't know. Perhaps for some reason I can't explain right now." His expression turns grave. "Don't get me wrong Captain, I'm Michael Murphy, I know that. But I also remember other things, other thoughts...like I'm another person."

"Like what?"

"Thoughts, feelings, as if I'm somehow, for some reason, someone else. An invisible person. It's like being two people." Canfield pours another shot, downs it straight, studying me intently, scratching at his two-day stubble.

"Okay, let's say for the moment you're this other guy. What reason?"

"Like I said Skipper, I don't know, but that's why I hesitated. Killing all those men..."

"You're calling me a murderer? *Killing those men*, as you put it?"

"I realize there's a war on."

"But you hesitated because punching that plunger is murder?"

"I don't know what to think. I only know what I'm telling you is the truth. How can I be two people?"

He pours himself another shot offering to top mine off; downs his neat, putting the glass away.

"Murph, I'm going to level with you. You're the best goddamn first officer in the fleet, hands down. You're the best *approach* officer I've ever worked with. There's no one better at your job or you wouldn't be here."

"But Skipper-"

"That's a huge asset to me mister, *and* your Uncle Sam." He stares into me. "It's not common knowledge but the Manta Ray has a priority rating inside *the brass*. I get the men I want because, at the moment, I'm sinking ships. You understand what I'm telling you?"

"Yes, but-"

"You know why this boat operates at full efficiency day in and out?" He doesn't need me to answer. "Because you run it that way. It's not just the rank Murph. It's the man. Every sailor on this boat respects you because you're smart. You don't make mistakes…because the guys that do that sink their boat and drown their crews. You're the best, a natural born leader, in fact, I'm recommending you for your own command."

"My own boat?"

"There's no way we'll be sailing together after this patrol Mike. It would take a miracle. They're putting out a whole new line of boats. The new Balao boats will make the Manta Ray seem like yesterday. The cost is in the millions. Experienced skippers are in high demand."

"My own boat…"

"We'll need new skippers who are rock solid under pressure. Men who can take the fight to the enemy, punch *him* in the mouth, but get out alive. What good are we on the bottom of the ocean? I'm preaching to the choir. You know the days of the *South Pacific cruise* are over. Pearl wants results. You're all set for your own command except..." His eyes burn into mine. "Except if you go around thinking you're some other guy, you're finished in submarines, for good. They'll never give you command if, mind you *if*, they keep you in the Navy at all. You'll be shipped back stateside to a nice quiet desk job." He leans back in his chair. "Or is that what this is all about?"

"I don't understand?"

He steals a quick look outside the curtain to make sure we're not being overheard.

"Have you had it with this stinking war? Living in a steel coffin? Waiting to drown alive, in a metal cylinder, eighty screaming men trying to claw through a quarter-inch of steel plating? This isn't a romp through France, or Belgium. This is underwater warfare." He suddenly grows distant, trance-like. "One mistake, one lousy mistake and you drown eighty men alive. Eighty human beings." He stares into the bulkhead, through it, before *coming back.* "You're a smart guy Murph. Hell, you're smarter than anyone I've ever met, including the admirals." I don't know what to say, so say nothing. "Level with me boy. Is this what you're doing? Because if it is...I won't get in the way."

"You're suggesting I'm making this up to get out of the submarine service?" His stare is unrelenting. "Why? Why would I do such a thing?"

"*Why?* C'mon Mike, any man worth his rating knows you've just married Hildy."

"*Hildy?*"

"Hildy Murphy is the prettiest woman in the whole Honolulu social set…well…next to Rue Canfield. It's no secret she wants you out of submarines, and for good reason, considering how many boats we're losing on a month-to-month basis." I'm stunned by the mention of her name.

"*Hildy? Hildy Murphy*…my wife."

He studies my reaction. "Are you trying to say you've forgotten her?" I look at the gold band on my finger, her face flooding my psyche. "Every man on this boat knows you keep that little billet-doux in your breast pocket for a reason."

I instantly reach for my breast pocket and withdraw the photograph; the picture of her in the flower-print dress, her words written in flowing cursive across the bottom. Canfield sees the shock on my face.

"What is it?" I stare at him. "Speak up man. What the hell is it?!"

"This woman…is my wife." Canfield takes the photo from my hand and studies it, gazing between the photograph and myself before putting the picture back into my pocket and buttoning it shut.

"So, you forgot about Hildy. Good luck explaining that when you see her in a few days," he says and exits the compartment.

Chapter 4: Pearl

*T*he Manta Ray docks at *submarine row*, Pearl Harbor.

A contingent of officers, sailors, and technicians–but none of the crew's families–are lined along the quay to assist with her mooring. It's a solemn rather lonely greeting. A war is on, blood attrition; the submarine service is called *the silent service* for a reason.

Burlsley accepts the line forward. Sorel secures the line aft. Binkershon's torpedo crew has tied an old straw broom to our boat's mast, a *clean sweep*. The invisible man inside me is shocked, as if the small insular world inside the submarine was somehow an easy fake. It's Pearl Harbor, and it sure as hell is 1943, the aftermath of the 1941 attack still evident; the forecastle of the *Arizona* solemnly jutting from the water like a marker over a gravesite. The capital ships along *battleship row* are under various stages of repair and the dry-docks are angry, spitting sparks, hammering steel.

The teeth of war.

The ships and vehicles, the clothing people wear, hits me like a thunderbolt, confirming deeply within my mind the reality of my situation; that I'm a man from-out-of-time, a double man, awash within the twin oceans of the past and a vague misty future.

Cooper is standing beside me on the bridge, scrutinizing my expression. He squints, shading his eyes from the brilliant morning sun. "How you feeling Lieutenant?"

"Fine Cooper, fine." He knows the answer masks an inner turmoil.

"Commander Murphy, I'm with the rest of the crew at the Royal. Don't hesitate to stop in, if you need to talk."

"*The Royal?*" I echo.

"The Royal Hawaiian Hotel…where the crew stays when in port." He shakes his head while my mind drifts back to lighter, happier times, drinking and laughing; the very beginning of what has become an inexorable advent into the unknown, the war dragging into a second, probably third year. The wind snaps our battle flag, drawing me back. Despite the war, the breeze blowing offshore feels clean and pure. Perhaps the air itself is somehow different.

"I'm fine Coop. But thanks. I appreciate the invitation."

The Manta Ray, her *sail* severely damaged, is berthed next to the quay; shore-power and air-hoses laced between the dock and submarine like umbilical cords. Medics carry stretchers with the wounded sailors across the gangplank and into drab-green lorries with large red crosses painted on their sides. I watch them take Carley out, his face swollen and bruised, his ribs wrapped in bandage.

The sun coating my face with warmth suddenly takes me someplace far away…trees, a modern city, the vague features of a woman; her laughter infused within the sunshine.

Angry shouting returns me dockside; angry men shouting angry things. I'm topside with Canfield and Stewart inspecting the damage. Chief is howling. The Manta Ray's battle armor is sheared and dented. Her conning tower blackened by the enemy depth charge attack.

"Goddamn heathens!" Chief spits heading aft.

Looking at the damage, I marvel that she wasn't sunk. *Tough old boat, she who protects us whilst at sea.*

Holes are ripped into the metal cowling of her fairweather and sections of her teakwood deck are shattered and broken. The Oerlikon 20mm anti-aircraft gun is missing, completely blown from the boat.

Canfield lights *a Camel*, smiling, wearing the moment like a medal on his chest. "Stewart get that buddy of yours with the Graphflex down here. I want a picture of this before they drydock her. Take a good look boys," Canfield says waving his arm across the port. "That's the end of the reign of the *battleship admirals,* bossing the rest of the Navy around like they own us. The future is right here," he says slapping the Manta Ray's cannon. "Submarines are the future of the Navy. Submarines will own the seas." Stewart nudges him. "What is it Lieutenant?" he asks indignantly.

"Uh, Skip, am I seeing things or is that Rear-Admiral Hess headed our way in a hurry?"

Canfield's smile flips. "What in hell? What's he doing here? Bosun, pipe the admiral aboard!"

All hands stop work and stand at attention as Burlsley pipes a lean, white-haired officer onboard; the men saluting. Canfield and Hess formally salute each other, then shake hands, smiling.

"What brings you to the war Admiral? Do I still owe you from our last poker game?" Hess and Canfield did a lot of gambling together during the month-long breaks between patrols.

"Hello Ollie. No, I think you're solvent. How was the patrol?"

"We took a few lumps," he says gesturing to the bent and darkened steel.

"I see that. Everyone all right?" he asks, staring at the bandage under my cap.

"A few bumps and bruises but I figure we sent about 17,000 tons of enemy shipping to the floor on this little spree Admiral. A new record for my team."

"We'll see what the board credits you with," Hess mutters looking the boat over stem to stern, every man within eyeshot at *attention*.

"Aw hell Carl, those desk clerks undercut my numbers every single-"

"Any coffee on board?"

"Sure, the best in the fleet. As we like to say Admiral-"

"When you're done with your cigarette, I'll see you and Commander Murphy below." The crew remains at attention as our flotilla's commanding officer, is piped below.

"What gives Skip?" Stewart asks from Canfield's elbow. "Admiral Hess got a bug in his craw?"

"I don't know. Something tells me I'm not going to like it. Stewart, takeover up here," he says tossing his cigarette overboard. "Murph, let's check-in with the boss."

Below deck, Jukes is playing *It's a Precious Little Thing Called Love* by Jimmy Sauter's Night Owls, over the boat's PA. We assist Hess in acquiring a cup of coffee while men from the deck-force begin the changeover of the boat.

Carl Hess was a career naval officer, and a good one, oft-times severe, yet fair; methodically working his way up the ladder from NCO in World War One to one of the finest admirals in the Pacific fleet. He sips from the bone-china cup, cocks his head and nods.

"That's a damn good cup of coffee. What's the secret?"

"Porteru. He sneaks chicory onboard. I've watched him do it."

"I could use a man like him in my office," the admiral mutters withdrawing a pack of matches from his pocket.

Canfield flashes me a pensive look. "Give it to me straight Carl. What did I do?" Hess knows Canfield is starting to sweat. He quietly withdraws a cigar from a leather humidor, playing the moment out like a pro.

"You're injured Lt. Murphy?" he inquires, pointing the cigar at the bandage intentionally hidden under my cap.

"I'm fine Admiral. Just a bump sir." I say and he stares me down before readdressing Canfield.

"The Navy taking care of you men?"

"Yes Admiral, absolutely."

"Good. What are you a coat-hanger? Take a seat Ollie."

"Carl, if this has anything to do with our last little poker game, hell, let it slide."

"You'll get your money, you know that. Sport is one thing, this is business."

"Am I in hot water with the Ordnance Bureau again?"

"Amazingly not," Hess says biting the tip off the end of the stogie and lighting up. I see the concern on Canfield's face lift considerably. "There's a briefing in my office, both you and Lieutenant Commander Murphy."

"Oh? When?"

"In one hour."

"*One hour?*" Canfield asks and Hess scowls.

"You've something more important on your calendar Captain?"

"But we just docked. I haven't finished my patrol log."

"It'll wait."

We exchange a wondering look. "Sounds serious. What's the skinny?"

"You'll know in an hour Canfield," the admiral says succinctly, relighting his cigar, before getting up to leave. At the door he turns. "How many patrols Ollie, you and the Manta Ray?"

"This'll make six."

Hess nods, patting her bulkhead. "Oh, and Ollie, don't be late." There's no mistaking the tone in his voice–or the look on his face. He exits the compartment, talking loudly with the enlisted men. Canfield shoves his cap back off his forehead.

"Get cleaned up and into your dress-whites. Spit-shine your shoes. Something tells me this won't be a poker game."

That Old Black Magic by Glenn Miller is playing over the boat's PA, Jukes turning music like a radio program. I take a five-minute shower in the officer's head and shave at the tiny pop-up lavatory in my cabin. Taylor enters to clear out his bunk.

"So, what are you doing for the next month Bill? Sunbathing?"

"You kidding? Sleeping," he says, and we share a laugh. "Bev is flying in Mike."

"Really? How'd you manage that?"

"I made the flight arrangements through our air wing. It won't even cost me anything, at least I don't think so." He returns to packing his duffel. I can tell something is on his mind. Bill Taylor rarely came right to the point regarding personal matters. I believe he considered it impolite. "So, Mike, there's a USO dance coming up. The *shore boys* are saying the Benny Goodman band might be playing. I saw them perform at the Stanley Theater once, back in Pittsburgh. Dad took me. One of the few things he did with me before he went back…back to Santa Fe." Bill's father was full-blooded Navaho; the son of a medicine-man.

I towel the water from my chin while he shoves a book and a couple old magazines into his briefcase.

"Benny Goodman huh? I didn't know we rated that sort of thing way out here."

"Um…I was wondering if you and Hildy might want to double date? No pressure Mike…no big deal if-"

"Sure Bill. Absolutely. I'll tell Hildy when I see her. She'll be pleased."

"Bev is bringing her red dress."

"Oh? Good luck with *that* buddy."

One hour later we're standing in the reception area at Naval HQ in *full dress*; our chalk-white uniforms pressed, the black and gold shoulder-boards, sharp. Military attaches hustle back-and-forth, the urgency of war steeping the stale air. A secretary, with fake nylon seams *painted* along the back of her legs, leads us down a narrow corridor to the admiralty's private offices.

We enter a smoke-filled room dominated by a large oval table littered with papers, maps, and binders. Adjutants scurry about the men seated at the table, all high-ranking naval officers. Two civilians are also present, an elderly man with rather *wild* hair, dressed in an old brown suit and a young auburn-haired woman, *hiding* behind a pair of ugly glasses, sitting beside Rear-Admiral Bennett. We stand at attention. Admiral Hess waves us over.

"Gentlemen, this is Oliver Canfield, commanding officer of the Manta Ray and his first officer Mike Murphy. Men, this is Admiral Lance." We salute the older gray-haired officer next to Hess. "This is Vice-Admiral Greene…and you both know Rear-Admiral Bennett."

"Yes sir. Admiral," Canfield says, saluting him.

"How was the patrol Canfield?" Bennett queries us, chewing on a huge cigar. "Did you sink us an aircraft carrier?" A smatter of laughter circles the group.

"Nothing that big Admiral," Canfield says tugging at his collar.

Hess gestures toward the two civilians. "Men, this is Dr. Hoffmann and Dr. Charlesworth from the OSS, the Office of Strategic Services." Hoffmann is older, well into his seventies; Charlesworth, much younger, in her early twenties.

As I gaze at her, a strange feeling overcomes me. I cannot take my eyes from her, my attention constantly returning. Is it the deep empathic eyes hiding behind the pair of ridiculous glasses? A British woman with an elegant accent, we learn her father was a commodore second-class with the Royal Navy. Hoffmann sports a wild unkempt head of hair; his suit and tie, a *slept-in* look. Charlesworth is groomed, with no jewelry of any kind upon her person.

Admiral Lance gestures toward two empty chairs. "Be seated gentlemen. Thank-you for coming promptly." An uncomfortably sustained pause ensues as Admiral Lance lights a cigarette, looking over a dossier on the table before him. I glance at Canfield, sweat beading on his forehead. "Captain Canfield, word back in Washington says the Manta Ray is one of the finest boats in the fleet. That her crew, particularly her skipper, has nerves of steel." The admirals stare at us; Canfield tugging at his collar like a kid on a prom date. Lance looks at me. "Would you agree with this summation Lieutenant Commander Murphy?" I scan the table, all eyes on us.

"Why yes sir. I would. Definitely sir."

All eyes shift to Canfield. "I appreciate that Admiral, our boat's been lucky." Lance consults the dossier again, taking his time.

"Four battle stars, a Presidential unit citation…sixty thousand tons of confirmed enemy shipping sunk since you took command, not including this recent patrol. You call that *luck* Captain?" Canfield fidgets, the sweat on his brow forming a tiny rivulet down his temple.

"You also have a high rate of return on crew," Bennett interjects. "We have a hard time moving your men on to new construction. They're constantly requesting permission to remain onboard."

"Those guys don't know what's good for 'em Admiral," Canfield says, a trace of laughter breaking the tension. Admiral Lance gives Hess the nod.

"Men, time is of the essence, so we'll get right to brass tacks. The Manta Ray has been selected for a special mission to commence immediately upon the termination of this briefing. Doctors Hoffmann and Charlesworth will be aboard." I exchange a glance with Canfield.

Admiral Lance coughs. "Captain, what we're about to disclose to you and your first officer is classified, top-secret of the highest order. Every person in this room is sworn to secrecy. In fact, gentlemen this mission, this very meeting, doesn't exist nor will it ever exist."

"Sir?" Canfield inquires and Hess breaks the ensuing silence.

"Manta Ray is the top pick Ollie. The Chief of Staff is in full agreement."

"Yes sir, what can we do for you Admiral?"

Lance looks to Hoffmann. "Time is short so pay close attention. Dr. Hoffmann."

The elder scientist sits up, tugging at his tie. He whispers something to Charlesworth before clearing his throat.

"Captain Canfield, are you aware of the concept of invisibility?"

Canfield stares at the man. "Invisibility?"

"Yes, specifically the realignment or bending of light waves." Canfield scans the table, all eyes awaiting his reaction.

"Sure Dr. Hoffmann. I read about it in the pulps when I was a kid." There are a few chuckles from some of the men. Hoffmann isn't laughing. He looks to Lance who looks at Hess.

"Canfield cut the crap and answer him," Hess says succinctly. He looks at me and I take the opportunity to study the large paddle fan spinning slowly above our heads.

"What do you want me to say Dr. Hoffmann? Sure, I've heard of it. One moment something's sitting there, the next it isn't."

"That's not far from accurate Captain." He leans forward, folding his hands together as if in prayer. "We believe we have solved the primary mathematics behind the process of large platform wave negation."

"The what?"

"Large scale wave interference. The ability to *cloak* a large body, make it invisible. A submarine for example." Canfield shoots me a look.

"Heck Doc, why a sub? Why not a battle cruiser, or an aircraft carrier?" The admirals fail to appreciate the inquiry but Hoffmann smiles.

"An excellent question Captain, with a very simple answer, *displacement*." Canfield just stares. "Captain, what is the displacement of your ship, on the surface?"

"I don't have *a ship* Doc." Hoffmann is visibly taken aback. He looks to Admiral Lance who exhales a stream of smoke across the table before deferring to Hess.

"The *boat*, Dr. Hoffmann, is exactly three hundred and twelve feet fore to stern, twenty-seven and a half feet at her beam, her surface displacement unladed…exactly one thousand five hundred and seventy-five US tons," Hess says glaring at Canfield.

"An aircraft carrier's displacement Mr. Canfield is thousands of tons larger than that," Hoffmann says. "Please recall Archimedes' principle."

"Archie who?" A smatter of laughter breaks the ensuing silence. I realize my captain is on the spot.

"Archimedes Captain," I interject, "the Greek physicist." Canfield gives me a *look* while Dr. Charlesworth studies me from behind her glasses.

"Why don't you fill me in *First Officer,*" Canfield says coolly.

"His principle stated that the buoyant force upon an object in a fluid is equal to the weight of the fluid displaced by the object." Canfield squints.

"Precisely Mr. Murphy, very good. Therefore, a submarine is a far more desirable platform considering that a submarine is capable of sinking an aircraft carrier, given the proper conditions." There's a strained pause. "Or would you argue the last point Captain?"

"I wouldn't argue it."

"At risk of sounding overly melodramatic, a submarine is a natural predator, its low profile while at sea, its narrow wake. Deadly firepower."

"Sure."

"The displacement is a fraction to that of larger surface vessels and once underwater possesses a kind of invisibility already. Imagine if a particle field were to supplement these already impressive qualities."

"*Particle field?*"

"A particle field that could render it invisible to the naked eye while on the surface during daylight." Canfield shoots Hess a doubting look.

"I'm supposed to know what all that means?"

Hess glares at Canfield. I can hear his teeth grinding. "Canfield…pay attention. Go on Doctor Hoffmann."

"The United States fleet submarine is an electric diesel craft with massive electrical capability already in tow. We've designed a system that will tie into your ship's…excuse me…your *boat's* primary generators and batteries. This electric capability will drive the transformers that will create a field around the outer hull, a field capable of rendering the boat invisible while on the surface." There's a lengthy pause as we collectively take this in. Canfield, rather impertinently, drops his cap on the table and crosses his legs as if watching a ball game.

"So how does it work Doc?"

The question ignites a series of angry looks amongst the leadership culminating with a discreet nod from Admiral Lance, the senior ranking member present. Hoffmann defers to Dr. Charlesworth sitting beside him.

She seems stunned, completely caught off-guard and it occurs to me no one anticipated being asked this question in such a direct manner.

"I wasn't prepared to address the group Doctor Hoffmann. I mean, I've not prepared a dissertation…that's been briefed…for clearance purposes."

"Just answer the Captain's question Charlesworth. Would that be suitable Admiral Lance?"

Lance pounds his cigarette out in the ashtray. "*Damn the torpedoes, full steam ahead* Dr. Charlesworth. Captain Canfield is *onboard*. He might as well get his feet wet."

Hoffmann nudges her. "Go ahead Charlesworth."

"Um…yes…of course…right." For whatever reasons, she looks directly into my eyes for an uncomfortably long time. Where? Where have I seen those eyes before? How could I know her, have met her?

Silence hovers in the room, thicker than the cigar smoke, as she collects her thoughts. For the briefest moment I think she's actually about to faint. When she *returns,* her eyes lock firmly on Canfield and her fingertips find each other.

"Captain…we'll be applying apparatus to the Manta Ray's superstructure that will interact with an electromagnetic field generated by twin supercoils placed inside the forward and rear torpedo compartments." Canfield stares deadpan. She looks at me and our eyes lock. "These coils will be charged by your ship's five-hundred-kilowatt electrical system and stepped-up by transformers to boost the current to operative levels. The exterior antennae array, which will create a counter-field, will be tied into the ship's auxiliary batteries, effectively isolating the countercurrent necessary to excite the interference within the primary field generated by the coils."

Canfield's blank reaction is priceless. "What happens then?" he asks. I wonder if he's being serious. The admirals are grinding their teeth. Dr. Charlesworth remains unfazed, gallantly pressing on.

"The interaction of the two fields creates a transverse wave effect that, if properly attenuated, will create the desired interference pattern. This interference pattern, what is referred in parlance as *destructive interference*, is both the bending and total annihilation of reflected light off the vessel's hull." Canfield's expression speaks volumes, his lack of appreciation of the subject, especially coming from a woman.

She looks directly into my eyes again. I've the strongest sensation that I do, in fact, know her; familiarity with the things she's saying. Is it possible we've met at some point in time? How? How could we possibly have met? The thought seems ludicrous, our being literally oceans apart as it were.

Canfield addresses Hoffmann. "Has this *stuff* been tested?" Hoffmann redirects his attention to Charlesworth.

"We've had varied degrees of success, but the problem of displacement has certainly proven a thorn. Additionally, surface vessels ordnance systems are unsuitable. The attack submarine holds more promising prospects for its intended use."

"And what is its intended use Doc?"

She looks to the admirals. There's a pause in the conversation, more quiet exchanges. Eventually Admiral Hess gets the nod, clearing his throat.

"Men, we've intercepted and decoded intelligence that Japan's two super battleships the *Yamato* and the *Musashi* will rendezvous in Tokyo harbor on a specific, currently classified, date. As you already know, these ships are two of the largest capital warships in the world."

"Yeah. We've heard about Yamamoto's big tubs," Canfield adds.

"At seventy thousand tons each, the *tubs* outweigh our largest battleships by well over half. There's intelligence to indicate that one, possibly two of their aircraft carriers could dock in the same area near the target date. One, code-named *Shinano,* is rumored to be the largest aircraft carrier in the world."

"Sounds like a real tea party," Canfield gibes and Hess stares at us.

"We plan to infiltrate by submarine, attack and sink the designated targets and get out. This technology is vital, instrumental in achieving this tactical and strategic advantage." The ensuing silence is deafening. Canfield leans forward, addressing the admirals directly.

"Permission to speak freely?" They all look to Lance.

"Granted."

"Have we lost our minds?"

"Watch it Canfield," Hess barks but Admiral Lance raises his hand and Hess steps down.

"Go ahead Captain, speak your piece."

"Sir, Sagami Nada is bad enough, but Tokyo Bay? It's too shallow for submarine warfare. Infiltrating that harbor would be like sticking a finger up your ass…sir. The strait is plastered with submarine nets and underwater mines. We'll never get through. It's a suicide mission." Lance looks to Hoffmann.

"But that's exactly our point Captain, you won't be infiltrating underwater, you'll be on the surface."

"On the surface? Doc excuse me for speaking out loud but are you nuts?"

"Canfield!" Hess bellows pounding his fist into the table.

"They'll blast us out of the water before we make the breakers Carl." Hess is turning red. Dr. Hoffmann raises his fingers.

"Captain, we're taking our lead directly from the German U-boat command."

"The Krauts? This gets better by the minute."

"When our ASDIC measures became proficient at detecting their ships underwater, they simply changed their tactics and began surface raiding at night. Our warships couldn't detect them on the surface in the dark because our focus was underwater detection."

"Yeah, so what?"

"A similar tactic is being deployed here. Infiltrating Tokyo Harbor underwater is untenable, you're absolutely correct. Agreeably, it is also impossible for a surface ship to go in without being shot and sunk. Therefore, we intend to approach underwater, but enter on the surface, undetected, since their guard will be down."

"Their guard won't be down Doc. They've spotters on every sampan and behind every rock up and down the strait."

"Captain, you're failing miserably to grasp the crux of my discourse."

"Your what?"

"The Manta Ray will be unseen by the Japanese shore patrols at the strait because it will be invisible."

The reality sets in.

"You're serious. You're completely serious about this."

"Quite." Canfield looks at the admirals then back at Hoffmann. He's speechless.

Admiral Lance takes the initiative. "Gentlemen, this mission, this very discussion doesn't exist, will never exist. Should you for any reason whatsoever disclose the contents of this briefing, in any minute detail, to another living soul you will be held accountable by the highest courts of this land for treason against the nation. Are we perfectly clear on this point?" We're in a stupor, both responding in unison.

"Aye sir."

"You'll be briefed in further detail after you've departed landfall at a pre-arranged designation and time. Meanwhile, you are to proceed with stepped-up, preparations for your next war patrol to commence immediately. Any questions?"

"No sir."

"Dismissed. Captain Canfield…I want a word with you. In private."

The entire group rises in unison and begins exiting the room. Canfield whispers to me out of the side of his mouth.

"See you at the Royal, later tonight." He glances back in the direction of the admirals. "I hope."

As I exit the office, I'm *belayed* in the hallway by Admiral Bennett, steaming his way over, his cigar puffing smoke like a coal burner. "Murphy, one moment."

"Yes Admiral?" He pushes me firmly to one side, speaking uncomfortably close.

"Was it my imagination sailor or were you *checking-out* Dr. Charlesworth?"

"No sir."

"Dammit man, I've eyes in my head."

"I'm sorry Admiral, but she looks familiar to me."

He chews on his cigar, staring down my neck. "You know Lucy Charlesworth? You've met?"

"I'm certain I was mistaken sir." He stares a hole through me. I'm left to sweat it out.

"Listen Murphy. I want you to deliver a personal message from me to each and every member of your crew, one man at a time."

"Yes sir?"

"*Hands off* the lady doctor," he growls, inches from my ear. I swallow, my throat suddenly dry.

"Of course, sir."

"You tell that *seasoned* crew of yours Murphy, if they even as much as drool on that woman's shoes, some poor mother's son will be getting an ass load of me!" he shouts, drawing the attention of the people around us. "Understood sailor?"

"Implicitly sir."

He chews on his cigar again. I marvel the thing has the pith to endure it. "Hell, I just had a brainstorm. I'm making her safety and wellbeing your personal responsibility Murphy."

"Mine sir?" He glares at me to drive home his point. "Yes sir."

He drapes an arm across my shoulders, and we stroll a few paces together as if we were old friends.

"Hell, I know she's an attractive woman. Any man with one good eye can see that. But that...*broad*...Mr. Murphy, is indispensable to this mission and the war effort *and* the only child of a very close friend of mine from across the pond. We clear on that point Commander?"

"Perfectly clear sir."

"I'm delighted." He gives me one more hard look. "Her father pulled my soggy can from *the drink* when I was a virgin NCO. A German U-boat torpedoed my ship out from under me during the last one of these godforsaken '*war to end all wars*.' That kid's like a daughter to me. I hope I'm making my point clear enough?"

"Understood Admiral."

He slaps my back rather heartily. "Good man. Let me know if there's anything she needs. You're going to be like that big older brother she never had."

"Yes sir. Admiral." I salute and he *steams* his way back inside.

Exiting the smoky confines of the offices into the sunlight of the HQ reception area, I spy Hildy waiting in the wing. Her honey-colored hair is fashionably done, and she wears a paisley-print dress that shows her figure. I rush to embrace her, nearly crushing her in my arms; kiss her scarlet-painted lips oblivious of the officers and secretaries watching.

"My goodness. Someone has been at sea too long." I kiss her again, passionately. "Mike, people are watching." When I look around, I see doctors Hoffmann and Charlesworth exiting the building followed closely by two men in dark suits. I take her hand and we begin to stroll.

"How did you know I was here?"

"Rue told me. There are perks being the sister of the wife of the captain."

"I was about to call you."

"Apparently, he pulls more weight than his first officer. Is there a reason you couldn't let me know you docked over three hours ago?"

"Yes, there is."

"Why?"

"Well, it's…well…top-secret."

"Not from me."

"I'm sorry honey, but yes, this time it is."

We're interrupted by the untimely appearance of Captain Simms our immediate medical authority. "Commander Murphy, I wasn't expecting you here."

"Captain," I say saluting him.

"Hello Mrs. Murphy, a pleasure to see you again," he says, kissing her hand. "Commander Murphy, I just met your new pharmacist, Corben, I believe his name?"

"Cooper sir."

"Cooper, that's right. Bright lad. How would you rate his performance on the patrol?"

"Excellent. He's a fine young pharmacist."

"Good, I'm glad to hear you say that. He said you sustained a concussion while on the patrol?" I shoot Hildy a glance. Simms sees the shock forming on her face. "I'm sorry Mike. You probably haven't had the opportunity to, to…"

"It's all right sir. We were just getting to it."

"I want you checked out, properly. See that it's done. Mrs. Murphy, a pleasure," he says kissing her hand again.

After a few dozen steps, she takes my arm to her bosom and whispers in my ear. "Any more *secrets* I should know about? You're racking up quite a tally."

"I was going to tell you."

"That's not *top-secret* too? You've a concussion?"

"Cooper thinks that. He's only a corpsman."

"Well then, *doctor* Murphy, you're the expert. Shall we go home?"

"Yes. Please."

We escape the stifling environs of Naval HQ into the splendor of the tranquil tropical afternoon. A soft breeze lifts the finer tendrils of her lemony hair as we walk into the sun. I ask her to drive our old Plymouth around Honolulu so I can take in the sights.

"Don't you want to go home, take your bath first?" she asks, her eyes caressing me playfully.

"My bath?"

"You always go straight home, open a beer and take your bath."

"I want to see the city. It feels like I've been away for years…another lifetime." She cocks her head, starting the engine.

"Alright."

Our sojourn takes us past the grand and glorious Royal Hawaiian Hotel hovering over Waikiki Beach like a mother watching a playground full of children.

"Is that the Royal? The Royal Hawaiian Hotel?"

She stares at me strangely. "Of course."

"This is where Canfield said to meet him tonight."

"Of course, where else?" she laughs, her gaze wondering.

"Of course," I mutter suddenly remembering that the hotel had been given over to the submarine fleet, the entire hotel. It berthed the crews of the various submarines that came and went from port; a gift of thanks to the American Navy from the people of Honolulu.

It *is* 1943, the city young and active, the obvious signs of wartime tensions and propaganda in the air. The AM radio plays a Hawaiian tune by King Oliver and his Orchestra; the moment both airy and bright.

—

"Thank heavens you're finally back. There's so much I want to do for the next couple weeks. I've made a list of things that need attending to, and we've several standing invitations for dinner." She sees the expression on my face. "What? What is it Mike?"

"We won't be getting our usual allotment of *R&R*. We're being ordered back out. We start the changeover on the sub tomorrow."

"Tomorrow? For goodness sake why?"

"Well...it's a special mission."

"What mission?"

"I can't say Hildy. We've been sworn to secrecy."

"What mission Mike? Tell me. I've a right to know."

"I can't. I can't talk about it. We're under strict orders."

"I'm your wife now Michael, not your girlfriend. Wives have the privilege of knowing these things."

"I'm sorry honey, not this time. This is serious."

"So am I, very."

"Hildy...I can't talk about it. Not right now." Her expression hardens. "Honey, it's a top-secret mission." I decide to let the conversation drop, taking in the sunshine.

Honolulu, 1943, incredible. There's no doubt a war is on, the bus stops and stores littered with banners of anti-Japanese propaganda. I can't help chuckling.

"What?" she inquires. I'm instantly caught by the question, take her hand and smile.

"These poster boards, they're humorous."

"Why? What's so *humorous* about them?"

"Well...because."

"*Because* why?" she presses and there's no hiding my state of mind.

"*Because* in the future these *'dirty Japs'* as they're being labeled, will become one of our staunchest allies."

"I don't think that's funny Mike, not at all."

"I'm not trying to be funny." Her demeanor grows severe. "What is it? Hildy, what's the matter?" She suddenly stops the car in the middle of the street, putting it in park, staring out the windshield. "Hildy, you can't stop here, we're in the middle of the street."

"Why? Why not? It's *funny,* don't you think? Don't you think it's funny Mike? Ha-ha."

"Honey…I'm sorry. I was just telling you what I somehow know is fact…or will be fact." The car behind us honks, the man's arm seeking the heavens through the driver's window. "We can talk about this at home." She just stares out the windshield. "Hildy?"

"Lorna Hudgins called the other day. You remember Lorna, don't you? Commander Hudgins wife?"

"Yes, of course, but what does that-"

"He's dead Mike. His submarine is no longer classified overdue. It's official, your…*friends* killed him." She breaks, an intense sorrow welling within her; a deep, empty chasm opens up within my chest.

I take her head in my arms, tears coursing the length of my wrist. We sit in the middle of the street while the rest of humanity slowly passes by.

Chapter 5: Losing

A U.S. submariner is allowed one five-minute shower.

Unfortunately, only once a week; rigidly timed. The reason is because it takes hours, days, weeks sometimes, for the condensers to create enough fresh water to fill the boat's potable water tanks. The water is essential for cooking, bathing and drinking but as importantly, *topping off* the water reserves in the submarine's massive battery array. Ample fresh water on a submarine was more precious than gold.

The minute I'm home I'm soaking in the tub until the water becomes tepid and chases me out. I spend an hour loitering about the bathroom primping, another *rarity* on a fleet-boat. Once in my robe and slippers, clothing only a commander of the highest order would dare wear on a submarine, I wander my modest home taking in its various objects. I thumb through a dog-eared copy of Jules Verne's *Twenty Thousand Leagues Under the Sea* and recall how I've read it over and over, perhaps a dozen times, the book having been given to me by my father when I was eleven years of age, the words contained on each page creating within my young mind a vast aquatic underworld undreamed of. Beside this well-loved volume sits another classic of the sea, *Moby Dick*. I open to the first page. *Call me Ishmael…*

The house I rent from the Navy is tiny to say it politely. However, the lanai looks out over the high ground to the north, a stunning view.

A stand of old papaya trees, remnants of an old plantation, linger about the periphery of the backyard skirting a red dirt alleyway stretching into a pastel pink sunset. The house has a carport with a tiny front yard adjacent a boulevard open to the sea–all the neighboring houses lined neatly along one side facing the ocean.

Our immediate neighbors, Carpenter by name, have two boys and a large lovable old mutt named Butch. The white picket fence that separates the yard is bowed and dented from their collective assaults and Mother Nature has seen fit to cloak the wounds with jasmine vine.

Through the window I see the twins at play in their yard, Jason and Alex Carpenter, my two biggest fans, the boys sworn to a submariner's life when they're *finally past the seventh grade*. There's a treehouse, a large wooden box nailed into an indigenous tree. This ramshackle structure serves as *our boat* whenever I'm back from patrol. It isn't long before they're tapping on the backdoor. They stand in proper rank and file, Jason the eldest by 12 minutes.

"Ready to dive the boat," he informs me saluting.

"At ease," I say saluting back and Jason kicks his brother.

"Salute dummy." I get the two-finger salute from Alex, squinting in the sunlight, his schooling as a cub scout, self-evident. "Like this," Jason insists, showing him the proper positioning of the fingers. When he's happy with his brother's deportment he readdresses me officially. "First Officer reporting for duty."

"It's my turn to be the first officer," the brother contends.

"No. I'm the first officer. You can be the ensign."

"I don't want to be the stupid ensign again. I'll be the captain this time."

"No Alex, Mr. Murphy's the captain. You can be the gunner." This seems to placate the *younger* brother's concerns. "Can you come play Mr. Murphy, the sub's ready to sail," he says pointing at the collection of slapped-up lumber I remember dragging back from the motor pool.

"I just made port fellas." The disappointment on their young faces is hard to ignore. "Men, I haven't filled out my patrol log from this last patrol. When that's finished, we'll take a spin in the sub. Okay?"

"When?" they ask simultaneously.

"How about tomorrow afternoon?" We exchange salutes. "Now go stow fresh torpedoes and clean out the bilge. I want that submarine in tip-top shape for tomorrow's shakedown cruise. Dismissed." They race for the boat, a sturdy old craft, minus the gaps between her boards and the pine knots that have fallen out.

Stepping back inside our quaint little home, I'm suddenly *the stranger* again, an odd feeling clawing at my gut when I see Hildy don her apron and set to making dinner. How beautiful she looks in her paisley-print dress and *real* nylons, like a model or an aspiring movie starlet. She spies me watching, a coquettish grin forming at the edges of her beautiful mouth.

"What are you thinking?" she asks playfully. "Don't get any big ideas Commander. I'm making dinner."

The kitchen is tiny, an old chrome-laced refrigerator the size–and look–of a Buick easily dominating a third of the space. She's quite proud of this machine; having it. She complains about our friends still *struggling along with old technology*. "Millie still uses an ice-box," she informs me. "Imagine, an ice-box. Someone needs to tell Mil it's the twentieth century."

The La-Z-Boy in the corner of the living room fits me perfectly. I can feel how this chair becomes the repository of my bag of bones when I return from the arduous enterprise of submarine warfare. A wooden model of an old A-class submarine sits on the desk. I remember building it in eighth grade. On the end-table near the chair a worn and beaten toy sub is amongst the odds-and-ends. I turn it in my fingers remembering it from childhood. Carved by my grandfather for my fifth birthday; its smooth gray surface is polished into a sheer patina only a child's fingers could render.

On the walls hang nautical maps of the South Pacific, more are scattered about on the bookcases and upon a small table near the window facing the sea. Most of these maps are actual war maps, with pencil and ink marks upon their faces indicating areas of patrol, or certain *actions* or deployments. The red and gray graphite marks are indelible indicators of the horrors of warfare. I see clearly within my mind's eye the death and drowning of hundreds of men contained within these marks; the floundering of their ships, slowly disappearing beneath the waves, men cast adrift into an indifferent all-encompassing sea. I shake these disturbing thoughts from my brow like shedding rain and return to the quiet life within the seclusion of my home; Hildy singing to herself in the kitchen: *Spring Is Here Again*.

The pinewood bookcase inset into the west wall contains all my favorite volumes, *The Encyclopedia of Ships*, the Sherlock Holmes mysteries, *Treasure Island* and a well-read copy of *Ivanhoe*. I almost laugh out loud by the novice collection of editions; *Robin of Sherwood Forest, King Arthur and the Knights of the Round Table, The Time Machine*; a simpler life, where boyhood meets manhood without the repercussions of war.

There's a pipe and tobacco on the desk–although I rarely smoke–and she has bourbon and gin in crystal decanters despite my dislike of hard liquor. A desk in the corner holds blueprints of a house splayed atop it. I ask her about them. She stares blankly, her beautiful smile changing to a disconcerting frown.

"Mike…are you trying to confuse me?" My mute response upsets her. "Those are the plans for the house we're building. The house in Vallejo." It instantly floods my consciousness.

"Yes. Of course, the house we're building…in Vallejo California…near Mare Island."

"They sent those over last month for our *okay*. Seriously Mike, I don't want to be burdened with decisions about the house, the pipes, where electrical cables are supposed to go. Can you please phone Mr. Drexler as soon as possible, please? I know it's long-distance, but we'll just have to pay it. They had to stop work until decisions are made. I don't understand a thing the man talks about…*this* thing or *that* permit. What is he talking about? He gets upset because I don't understand. He gets more upset because he can't talk to you…because you're away in that…submarine. It's too much. And Rue's no help, she doesn't know. She thinks she knows everything. She doesn't know a thing about building a house. Her and Ollie have always rented. By the way, I hope you've given up the crazy notion of staying-on in Hawaii. I can't do it Mike. I can't live anywhere else than California. People are so different here. Oh, did Oliver tell you? They're going to buy the house in Vallejo, the one on Lafayette Street. Rue says if we build on Latimer Street, she's insisting Oliver move nearby. Oh, I do hope on the same street, or maybe even next door. Wouldn't that be nice, the four of us living close-by? Mike?"

"Yes honey."

Inside the desk drawer is a pistol, a US Navy-issue Colt .45 automatic. I extract it, feel its familiar weight in my hand. Without thought, I check the chamber and handle the thing as if I'd grown up using it.

"For goodness sake put that away," she says placing a pot of potatoes on the dining room table. "You're like a kid with a toy." I return the weapon to its holster and close the drawer.

Upon the small teakwood dining table–a wedding present from Admiral Hess–she places two colorful plate settings.

"There Mr. Murphy, an authentic Irish meal. Corned beef, cabbage and potatoes," she beams, proud of her handiwork, an amazing accomplishment during wartime. Something takes hold and I embrace her, kiss her scarlet lips, the taste of strawberries. "My, my…please control yourself," she says returning to setting the table. Hildy kept a great kitchen. I recall it as if these memories were not my own, but his. Again, I feel the stranger, intruding into another's life.

"Mike, what's wrong?" she asks, snapping me from these strange thoughts. "Why are you suddenly being so morose?"

"*Morose?* That's an awfully tall word Mrs. Murphy." I'm pulled to her like a magnet, put my hands about her waist, caress her shoulders, kiss her neck. Something within her releases, an inner tension she harbors, and our bodies tighten, a heat coursing the space between us like fire and nothing can stop what happens; dinner left sitting on the table untouched, the candlelight flickering, as if being shared by invisible people.

Later that evening I'm at the luxurious Royal Hawaiian Hotel in Waikiki with the rest of the Manta Ray's crew, a ritual shared by the crewmen of the boat upon returning to port. Every man is present, in one state of intoxication or another.

Ned Binkershon dusts off a stool in the middle of the bar and is already ordering me a drink. "Daisy, get our hallowed Exec a brewski, keep the glass. Okay girls gather around, no shoving. Stop squabbling about reporting for changeover tomorrow morning. Here it is, right from the puss of the bigshot himself," he says pulling me into the seat. "Go ahead, spill it Murph." Before I can respond, he interrupts. "It'll be exactly what I've been telling you girls all along. Skipper's being dragged in front of the brass for having us deactivate those lousy magnetic exploders," he says, referring to torpedo technology.

Canfield had the Ordnance Bureau in stitches by allowing our torpedo chiefs to deactivate the magnetic exploders on our Mark 14 torpedoes in lieu of the older impact exploders, despite strict orders to the contrary. Basically, the *magnetic* technology was flawed and skippers following orders were reporting more misses and failures than those that didn't.

"It's just like the last patrol ladies," Binkershon presses, "he gets hauled in by his ear, then they pin a Navy Cross on the guy. Go ahead Murph, spill."

"Oh-six-hundred. That's all I can say at this time."

"You trying to be funny?"

"Oh-six-hundred Binkershon. I suggest everybody turn in early tonight."

"Chief, the Exec trying to ruin our party?" Jack Georgio slurs completely inebriated.

"Shut-up. Well, *First Officer?* At least confirm my view to the crew gathered about your holiness. It's about *the fish*…right?"

"No."

"You trying to say this isn't about torpedoes this time?"

"I'm not *trying* Ned I *am* saying it. It's not about torpedoes."

Every man becomes introspective. The torpedo gang instantly huddles at the bar, except Collins. He looks at me, shaking his head; pulls a beaten pack of Chesterfields from his breast pocket and lights up. I take-in the entirety of my crew as wont my nature, making a mental note of every man in attendance. All the enlisted men are present except Burlsley and McClatchy.

"Where's our Bosun and McClatchy?"

Collins gives me a dour look. "Those two knuckleheads are running tandem again," he says over his whiskey. "I pity the poor stiffs that run into those two guys in a couple hours Murph. You might as well inform the shore patrol now."

"Straight to the Moka Lounge Commander, whoosh," Duncan says gesturing the length of his arm, upsetting Stewart's martini.

"What of it Duncan?" Stewart says staring at the mess. "They got a thing for those Filipino waitresses. Get over it."

"They're supposed to be here, with their buddies."

"Eban, have you even been with a woman yet?" Collins inquires.

"You need to ask?" Toles says, ordering another Martini for the lieutenant.

"More than you guys could even…so many I lost count."

"Yeah because zero ain't a number."

"Hey, lay off the little guy Tuke," Bremer interrupts, draping an arm around Duncan's neck. "He's right. They broke tradition. Those two clowns just earned yet another round of extra duty. I ain't decided *what* yet, but it'll be juicy this time around, real juicy. It all comes out in the wash gentlemen. Daisy, another round of drinks for our coveted war-heroes. To another successful patrol boys," he says toasting them. The group converges on the barkeep and the beer and drinks slosh across the old mahogany bar.

I decide to stroll the room littered with the crews of the various boats currently in port. The Manta Ray's crew is cutting loose after a long grueling patrol. Some of the men are shooting pool, some dancing with girls or each other. Everyone is drinking. Parmalee is dancing the hula in a grass skirt while balancing a bowl of fruit on his head. The gunners are engaged in a spirited game of darts with the gun battery from another boat while the sonar, radar and radio teams are enjoying the band playing Jimmy and Tommy Dorsey covers. Elder rises from his chair inadvertently bumping into me, the band playing: *Keepin' Out of Mischief Now.*

"Oh, sorry Commander Murphy. I didn't see you there."

"Where are you off to in such a hurry Zig? Hot date?"

"I'm phoning Europe in ten minutes."

"Europe? What for?" He seems oddly pensive.

"My aunts, my mother's sisters, have been out of contact for a couple months. Not a word. She's asked if I can get through on military channels."

"What town or city do they live in? Perhaps the phone lines are knocked-out."

"Anke lives in Germany, Dusseldorf. Aunt Lenka is in Poland, outside of Warsaw, and there's one in Czechoslovakia near Plzen, Aunt Vlasta. I've met them, they're all so lovely and intelligent. Vlasta plays violin with the symphony and Anke teaches art at the college in Dusseldorf." I stare into the young man's eyes as if frozen.

"You say three different aunts in three different countries are all out of contact?"

"Yeah. That's strange, don't you think? Mom is really worried. There's been a lot of anti-Semitism over there lately. That guy Hitler spouts nothing but hate. Hate and divisiveness."

"You're Jewish, right Zig? Both your parents emigrated to New York from Poland?"

"Yeah. I'm the first American-born of the family." He sees the concern on my face. I pray he can't read the thoughts passing through my mind, dark, ominous memories coming from a place I can barely comprehend. "I'll talk to you later sir," he says in response to my stare and hurries off.

"Murphy."

I turn at the sound of my name, surprised to find Lieutenant Commander Clayton Blissfeld sitting alone at one of the small tables lining the wall. I'm shocked. I barely recognize him with his growth of beard. His normally dark hair is noticeably lighter, I would even say white.

"Clay…I didn't know you were in port."

He gestures toward the chair opposite his. "We've been in a couple weeks."

"How was your last patrol?" My question goes unanswered. He seems almost catatonic. The waitress arrives with his bourbon. After she's left, Blissfeld bows low over his drink, sipping at it from the table. When he does raise the glass, his hand shakes so violently he nearly spills the contents. "You all right?" I ask. He glances about the bar, closing the space between us, his voice lowering to a near whisper.

"We got our asses kicked this last patrol Mike. Pretty damn thoroughly."

"What happened?" He attempts once more to sip the drink. He's shaking so violently he resets the glass on the table and stares at his hand. "What's wrong Clay? What's happened?" The look in his eyes is disturbing.

"We got our ass kicked Mike. Depth-charged, strafed, bombed. We couldn't stick our nose up without getting shot at."

He forces his hand beneath the table. I wait for him to shift his eyes back to mine.

"What area were you assigned to Clay?" The question doesn't even register.

"They're getting better Mike, their detection and counter-measures. They're not making mistakes anymore." His thoughts seem to wander a moment before he readdresses me, a look I've never seen etched into his normally placid face. "We're supposed to leave in two days, same area, same goddamn assignment." He stares through the table actually clenching his fists. "Is there ever going to be an end to this fucking war? Look at the shit we're in man." He studies my face. "Your next time out…be real goddamn careful," he mutters then leaves without touching his drink. I stare into the room long after he's left until I shake the moment from my mind and step back into the cacophony.

The machinists are engaged in a heated game of poker. Earl Lloyd, a bent can of beer in his grease-stained fingers, talks loudly over their shoulders while the rest of the men try to concentrate on the game.

"The sub hit a mine. I was on the bridge. Six other men were on that bridge. The sub, her whole crew, went down like a brick. Straight to the bottom, all hands. God rest their souls." He crosses himself, taking a moment to gulp his beer. "She went down so fast she nearly pulled me under. Everyone on the bridge was killed except the lieutenant and a machinist's mate named Suggs, badly wounded." The passing waitress hands him another beer. He squeezes the one he's been drinking flat then cracks open the next.

"*Anty-in* boys," Rawlston says during the pause and the machinists collectively prepare for another round of Lloyd's rambling oration.

"Our new skipper was a young cocky bastard, always in a hurry. Hurry over here, hurry over there. The crew started calling our boat *the Headless Chicken,* the wardroom *the Nursery*. We were leaving our assigned patrol sector in the South China Sea. We'd been briefed that area of the Balabac Strait was reportedly mined. Nah, not us, not our boat, right? God was on our side, right? Full steam ahead, the stupid sonofabitch…boom, the whole front of the goddam boat. Chunks of steel went up over a hundred feet. A forward capstan took the head clean off our ensign standing beside me…good-looking kid from Nebraska named Clover. His body just stood there for ten seconds without a head."

"Hey Earl, let's talk about something else for a change," Vic says taking up the cards he's been dealt, but Earl doesn't even hear him. It was gossip Earl lost his hearing working the engine rooms, but I always suspected the explosion that caused the sinking of his first boat probably had something to do with his deafness.

"The ocean is a big place. I tried to help the greaser swim, but it wasn't long before he was dead. We kept swimming but the lieutenant wasn't good at it. He couldn't swim on his stomach, always on his back, sure way to swim in circles. He tired quickly too so we weren't getting anywhere fast." He takes a slug of beer; the machinists exchanging cards and the money hits the table.

"Why weren't you wearing your life vests?"

"Who the hell stands watch wearing a life vest?"

"Eban Duncan."

"Besides him?"

"It sorta thins out after that," Vic mutters and the entire group folds their hands, Culpepper dropping three aces and raking-in the cache of bent bills and coins.

"I tried to keep the lieutenant going, keep his spirits up, sometimes pushing his feet with my shoulders, sometimes pulling him, but he knew he was drowning, probably taking me with him. Eventually he just…pushed away," he says to me, "…went off and drowned alone." He stares through the floor. "Everyone does…dies alone."

Back at the bar, Stewart is sauced. "So, *First Officer*, you get the news?" he asks ordering yet another martini.

"What news?"

"We're being ordered back to the boat, oh-six."

"Stewie, you're plastered. You better let me take-"

"What the hell's the deal Murph?" he asks becoming belligerent. Stewart could never really hold his liquor.

"We'll all be getting a belly full of it tomorrow Ellis. Let's enjoy one night of freedom," I say, and he grabs my shoulder, saluting me.

"Aye-aye Commander," he slurs, then nudges me. "Well I'll be. The old man finally made it."

Canfield enters the hotel like a hurricane making landfall, hanging his cap on the rack and heading straight for the bar. His face belies the apparent drubbing he's been through with the admirals. The crew opens a wide berth for him. Daisy, the Samoan barkeep, wipes the countertop clean already knowing his order by heart.

"Daisy, bourbon and water. Hold the water." The men crowd him like Santa at Macy's, all speaking at the same time, Stewart leading the cacophony.

"You need to knock some heads together Skip. Some joker is ordering us back to the boat, oh-six-hundred."

Chief Bremer cuts Stewart off. "The Ordnance Bureau was poking around the boat, taking measurements, asking a lot of questions."

"So what?"

"They're talking about cutting through the deck, fore and aft. Some screwball at the OB lost his mind?"

Ensign Duncan, more than *a shade-to-the-wind*, is literally on his elbow. "Skipper, they're saying we're going right straight back out there, whoosh…somebody's off their rocker." Binkershon slides up the bar knocking over Stewart's barstool.

"We've orders to report tomorrow for provisioning boss, say it ain't so."

"Hey, spread out!" Canfield barks, glaring at the entire group surrounding him. "You bunch of yahoos. There's a war on. You forget about that?"

"Yeah but Skip…"

"You heard 'em Stewart, oh-six-hundred. Sharp. And you better be standing on two legs Lieutenant because you're in charge of the detail. I and the Exec have the day off. Now get lost, all of you, hit the road!" Everyone stands with open mouths. His drink arrives and he downs it straight, slamming the empty glass on the bar. "Daisy give me another one. Make it a double." The men slowly disperse, looks of confusion on their salty faces. Only Bremer and I have the nerve to remain.

"So, how'd it go with the admirals?" He gives me *the evil eye*. His drink arrives and he downs this one straight as well. "Easy Captain."

"What are you now Murphy, my wet nurse?" He orders another.

Bremer exchanges a look, lighting a cigarette. "I don't like it. Not one goddamn bit."

"What don't you like Chief?"

"Them nabobs cutting into my boat."

"Last time I checked Chief *your* boat had *property of the US Navy* stamped into her hull-plate."

"She's my boat Ollie. She belongs to me. I know her. I run her."

Canfield laughs, a strangely disquieting laugh. "She runs you Chief."

"What's it all about Oliver? What the hell's going on?"

"You'll learn soon enough Chief, soon enough." This last remark, and Canfield's subsequent disengagement, has cryptic overtones and Bremer decides to join the other men at the end of the bar. I take his seat.

"You want to talk?"

"Nope." I stew over this succinct response turning just in time to see Dr. Charlesworth–looking very out of place–step inside the front door. I tap the skipper's shoulder and point with my chin. Canfield turns and scowls.

"Kriminy, what's she doing here? Didn't they tell her this is submariner's territory?"

"Apparently not." Two enlisted men from another boat are on her like rain on Seattle. I see the concern forming on her face as they try to coax her directly onto the dance floor. *Her face*, where have I seen it before? I take her arm, the enlisted men receding back to their table.

"Hello Dr. Charlesworth. What brings you out on a night like this?"

"Hello Commander Murphy. Thanks for the rescue."

"You're welcome but call me Mike. Out taking a stroll?"

"I thought a nightcap might help me sleep. What a day." She rolls her eyes. I gesture toward the bar and we join Canfield; the sailors staring like they'd seen a ghost step in the door.

"Hiya Doc. How's things in *funtown*?" Canfield asks. She blinks at his statement, canvassing the bar. Nearly every eye glued on her.

"I think I'm a bit out of place."

"You're outnumbered, that's for sure." Canfield yanks on the stool beside him. "Relax kid, belly-up to the bar. What gives, run out of things to talk about with that long-hair Hoffmann?"

"I thought I could use a good stiff drink," she says sitting between us.

"Atta girl, whaddya have?"

"Do they possibly have a Bordeaux?"

"A bordello? Heck Doc, I didn't think you were that kind of a girl."

She laughs, taking his arm. "Captain Canfield, you *are* a scoundrel. You're exactly as Admiral Bennett says."

"Oh yeah? What does he say?"

"That you're a scoundrel." This puts a smile on his grizzled face.

Canfield shouts down the length of the bar. "Daisy, how about a beer for the lady?" Daisy procures a can and pulls the tab, placing it on the bar before her. She doesn't appear overjoyed by his choice of drinks, taking a sip and cringing.

"Oh dear…" She peruses the bar. "What a lovely place. Is it true the entire hotel belongs exclusively to the submarine service?" I gaze into those tranquil eyes. Green.

"This is sort of our *home away from home* you might say." She notices the men of our crew dancing on the floor. I see what's caught her eye, Parmalee dancing the Hula in a grass skirt. She smiles, amused.

"Mr. Murphy, do you know that man, the one with the fruit on his head?"

"*That*, Dr. Charlesworth, is our boat's electrician, Anson Parmalee. He'll be working closely with you on the retrofit." The news doesn't impress her.

"You're not being serious?" she asks. Her smile dissipates as she studies my expression. "Are you?"

"Oh, he's serious Doc." Canfield points down the length of the bar. "And that there is your head machinist, Connie Howard." We all look at Conrad passed-out face down on the bar but still holding a can of beer upright. She looks completely alarmed. We watch as she takes up her beer and downs the entire can.

"Bleck…"

Canfield pats her on the back. "Don't worry Doc, you're in good hands. These guys are the best. They're just knocking the webs loose after our last patrol." She orders another beer, staring into space as if falling into a sudden catatonic state. Canfield and I share *a look* behind her back. "Hey, what do they call you Charlesworth…*Charlesworth?"*

"Lucy."

"No kidding? That's my dear old grandmother's name. Where's home kid?"

"At the moment? Princeton." Her beer arrives and she takes another rather lengthy draught. We share a look behind her back.

"Princeton huh? That in England?" he asks. The question makes her laugh, a laugh I've known from somewhere.

"Captain Canfield, you *are* a rip," she says pleasantly and sips her beer again. "Bleck. This is awful, truly awful."

"Glad you like it," Canfield says. She takes his arm.

"I surmise you boys are a lot more fun than the admirals, or *the men in white.*"

"Wait until you get to know us," he says, and she laughs anew. "What about Hoffmann? He a regular Joe?"

"Regular Joe?" she asks and Canfield shrugs.

"Is he okay, as most guys go?"

"Captain Canfield, Dr. Hoffmann is brilliant, absolutely brilliant. I'm fortunate to be tutored by someone so…so…"

"Pushy?"

"Believe it or not Captain, he thinks you and he will get along famously. He's very much *for* you on the project." Oddly, the remark quiets Canfield. He stares into space before pulling a pack of *Lucky Strikes* from his pocket.

"Mike, I'm going to have a smoke on the lanai," he says absently and leaves us sitting together at the bar. We both become alarmingly mute, our collective silence deafening despite the buffoonery within the bar; the men deciding to create a drunken human pyramid.

Watching the sailors tumble and fall, breaking a table in the process, I ask, "So…you like it in America?" I regret the question, thinking it ridiculous. She leans closer, our arms touching.

"Yes and no."

"Oh?"

"Four walls in a laboratory in America, isn't that much different than four walls in a laboratory in Britain." Her eyes wander to mine, deeply fathoming something.

"Have you been to America before? San Francisco perhaps?"

"This trip across the Atlantic was my first. I live something of a sheltered life Commander Murphy. They rarely let me out of my cage."

"Your cage?"

She takes another sip of beer, cringing. "That's unfit for man nor beast," pushes it away and studies me. "I'm curious, have you ever been to the United Kingdom?"

"No. Why do you ask?"

"You seem so familiar to me. Are you sure you've never…?" She stops mid-sentence, her eyes searching mine. "I'm daft. You would certainly know if you had been to Britain I should think."

We're interrupted when one of the lieutenants from another boat asks her to dance.

"No thank you. I don't know how," she says graciously. When he tries to explain the process, he's conveniently steered away by a fellow officer and her expression hardens. "Perhaps I shouldn't be here," she whispers, drawing closer. "Perhaps it was stupid my coming. This place is for your enjoyment."

"Yes," I say, and she holds my gaze.

"*Yes,* it was stupid that I came?"

"No. *Yes* it's for our enjoyment, and *yes* I'm enjoying your being here." Her eyes sparkle. Or is it the light reflecting off the crystal chandeliers, the band softly playing a rendition of *Fools Rush In,* by Tommy Dorsey.

"Your captain very much speaks his mind."

"That's an understatement. He's just a little worked-up over his meeting with the admirals."

"Yes…yes, I heard."

"Heard what?"

"That it didn't go over as well as hoped."

"What do you mean?"

She lowers her voice. "Please don't repeat this Michael. Doctor Hoffmann places a great deal of faith in my being discreet. I shouldn't even be mentioning it."

"I'll keep it on the lowdown," I say smiling.

"Well…Admiral Lance and particularly Admiral Greene aren't quite sure your captain is the right man for the job."

"What do you mean?"

"He's…well…as you say in the vernacular, *a little rough around the edges.*"

"Doctor Charlesworth, Oliver Canfield is one of the finest submarine skippers in the Pacific fleet. You can't get anyone more competent. Hess and Bennett know that."

"I don't doubt you."

"Well then?"

"If you mean by that, what decision has been made, it's very likely we'll see an ancillary commander attached to the project."

"*Ancillary?* What do you mean?"

"A second *skipper,* as you call it, attached to the mission."

"That's ridiculous. You can't have two skippers on one boat. It's the first rule of combat, chain-of-command. Conflicting sets of orders will get people killed."

"I don't know anything about military protocol Commander Murphy. I'm just telling you, they're considering-" Her attention is suddenly drawn to the front door as two very conspicuous men dressed in dark suits enter, scanning the room. She abruptly returns to her drink. "Drat. Have they seen me yet?" One of the men taps his partner and points in our direction.

"Yes. They're coming over."

"Here we go," she whispers, "…my shadows."

The men approach us at the bar. "Doctor Charlesworth, can you accompany us back to the laboratory? Immediately." She gives me a strange look before turning and addressing the men.

"Of course. Let me pay my bill." I lay my hand atop hers.

"On me Doctor." A thin smile emerges on her face; a face I've somehow known before.

"Thank-you Michael."

As unexpectedly as she arrived, she's escorted out between them. I stare at the night through the windows long after they've gone. The rolling surf of the mighty ocean hurls itself against the shore as it has done, true to its nature, for eons.

—

The crew re-converges at the bar, all except Canfield. He's nowhere to be found, his cap left hanging on the rack. It wouldn't be the first time. The crew, in fact the entire hotel, treated the man like the wayward uncle that shows up on the couch at irregular intervals.

The men continue to drink, talking about their wives, girlfriends, and distractions, deep into the evening; their merry banter filling the room. No matter how I try, I no longer see their faces, only her eyes, no longer hear their words or understand their chatter, only the echo of her voice repeating like a soft mantra in my mind.

I end up *tying one on*. The shore patrol is kind enough to dump me at the curb of the house. The front door is locked. I wander to the backyard upsetting the trellis and Butch, the dog, goes crazy. I hear Hildy from the window.

"Mike?"

"It's me Hildy, let me in." Once inside, I don't even shower but fall into a deep fitful slumber.

I'm dreaming. I know I'm dreaming but telling myself other. I'm in New York City, its granite skyscrapers piercing fog laden watery skies. We're walking together, Lucy and I, down lower Lexington Avenue. A soft tranquil rain coats us in a patina of tiny droplets. All about us is the vibrancy of the city. We laugh together, the miasma of the food and car exhaust upon the wind. She stops. I'm caught within her knowing gaze, deep and agleam. In words that pierce any unreality I hear the voice that is hers: *'Dear, fear not. I do love, and tis thee. My heart yearns for you. Surely you know we are one, forever and enon.'* With these words she turns and begins to disappear into the mist.

"Where are you going?" I call as she becomes more diaphanous. "Lucy." I try to follow her but can't make my body move. When I look at my legs, I'm treading water pouring into the compartment of a submarine. Men are screaming like banshees. They're closing the watertight doors, sealing me inside. As hard as I try, I cannot make my body move through the confluence, now up to my shoulders. "Lucy!" I shout, water hitting my mouth, stifling my cries. I'm drowning, being swallowed by an immense ocean pulling me under, water washing over me. Men scream horribly, clawing at the metal enclosing them, their fingers tearing and shredding against the steel, blood coursing from their hands, filling the compartment in a crimson hue, saturating my eyes, the dream turning a horrid blood-red.

Awakening in the darkness, perspiration pouring across my face and neck, I feel my way through the blackness, forcing open a window, taking in large breaths of air. The curtains dance under an aeolian breeze, waves curling along the midnight beach. A thin gossamer rain has started to fall, a quiet stillness enveloping the ancient sea, sitting silently on the edge of infinity, watching, waiting.

My shouting has awakened Hildy. "Mike, what on earth?" I'm floating within a vast tide of darkness; awash in the flotsam and jetsam of space and time.

"I–I was dreaming. Another nightmare about drowning."

"Who is Lucy?"

"What?"

"You heard me. I want to know who *Lucy* is." The dark ocean softly sighs, as if calling. "Mike, are you seeing another woman?"

"What? Hildy…"

"Just tell me, have the decency."

———

"Honey…it was just a dream."

"Mike, what's happening to you? You've been acting so strange, becoming so moody, so secretive. You've never kept secrets from me before. All this *talk* about the future, forgetting things about our life. You've become like a different person. I feel like I don't know you anymore." I stare at her sitting in the moonlight, confusion in her sad eyes.

"Alright, I'm going to tell you. I'm going to tell you what's been happening. This is going to be hard for you to understand but…the mission…this secret mission is…" I freeze remembering Admiral Lance's threat should I reveal any details to another person.

"What? What's happening?"

"Honey, I can't. I can't tell you. I've been sworn to secrecy. It's just another patrol." She takes up the water glass from the bedside table and smashes it across the floor.

"Stop it! I'm sick of hearing that same answer from you. It's not *just another patrol*. Besides, I'm not talking about the mission. I'm talking about you! The way you've been acting since your return. Forgetting things, things about our life together, as if it doesn't matter to you anymore." She's on the verge of tears. I take her in my arms, holding her tightly.

"Honey, I can't explain it, this feeling."

"What feeling?"

"Like…like I'm someone else. It feels like I'm another person, an invisible man inside." She's staring at me as if she's seen a ghost. "Honey listen to me. There's no doubt in my mind. For some strange unknown reason, this person, has travelled back in time to this place, for some important reason. If I could just remember, it would all make sense somehow."

"Mike, you're scaring me."

"Honey, I'm your husband, Mike Murphy, but I'm also…someone else. It's as if some silent power were preventing me from remembering." The expression forming on her face is unreadable. I take her shoulders. "I know this is hard to understand but…I know I'm from the future. I'm not imagining it. I think this person, *Lucy*, is someone I know from there, from the future. In fact, I'm certain of it." She throws the blankets aside and begins to dress. "What are you doing?"

"Going to Rue's."

"At this hour? Honey, just calm down, listen to what I'm trying to say. I need you. I need you to listen." She ignores me. "Hildy, come back to bed, let's talk this through." When I take her arm, she yanks it away.

"I don't take my orders from you *Commander*."

"Hildy you're being unreasonable."

"*I'm* being unreasonable?" she explodes. "Oh really *Mr. Murphy*, or *Mr. Whoever*. You're shouting another woman's name to the neighborhood and I'm the one being unreasonable?"

"Hildy-"

"Why not put up a billboard!" She leaves me sitting in a stupor. When I hear the front door open, I race out to the drive. She's getting into the Plymouth, starting the motor.

"Hildy, this is ridiculous. Let's talk this through." She engages the transmission grinding the gears. As I open the passenger door, she puts the car in reverse. I'm swept into the hibiscus bush gashing my hand on the fence. I pick myself up out of the mud and watch her gunning the Plymouth down the avenue.

The neighbor's dog howls relentlessly and the light switches on. I glance at the moon peeking through the slow movement of clouds, the pale light dancing across the wide Pacific. "Why? Why is this happening?" I ask out loud. The moon doesn't respond, merely plays hide and seek through the heavy storm clouds, her timeless nocturnal radiance cloaking the heavens and the earth in a translucent ephemeral glow.

The Carpenters emerge from their bungalow inquiring about the commotion. Standing there in muddy underwear, I assure them everything is fine and return to the house. As I enter, I hear Agnes Carpenter ask her husband *what's wrong*. "Young lovers," he mutters shushing the dog and closing the door. All goes quiet once more.

Within my vacant and lonely home, I seek sleep that never comes; wandering the house like a stranger in a strange land. The articles in the moonlight seem weird and foreign under the gray radiance of the light. A framed photo on the fake fireplace mantel stares from the shadows, the man etched in silver particles.

"*Lieutenant Commander Michael J. Murphy*, explorer, sea-warrior," I mutter, talking to the image as if it possessed consciousness, then throwing the thing across the room, shattering it.

I open the desk, pull out the pistol and stare at it in the moonlight. Inside the drawer is a box of bullets. As I sit and load the magazine the thought occurs to me, I could end this farce right here and now. For instance, what would happen if I shoot myself? I'm certainly not the first man to ask the question or explore the possibility. It's been asked and explored for centuries. What would happen is I simply pull the trigger? A quick advent into nothingness?

Sitting in the darkness like a scarecrow made of straw, I surmise my case must be a unique one. Any common man simply exits the world, but where do I go? Up or down? Forward, or backward? The *light*, or darkness? Do I follow this feeling, this notion of timelessness, someplace else? A place outside our feeble concept of the material world or the *afterlife*? Will I wake up as if from a bad dream, whole and united with my total self, a complete man? I fill the chamber with a bullet and hold the thing to my head. Again, as before, time stops, the silence crystalline. Sitting there alone, I wonder what happens to Mike Murphy? Will they find him dead across a cheap wooden desk, or does he too become free, free of the double man occupying his life? Destroying it. I drop the pistol, feeling a great weight forcing my shoulders toward the center of the earth.

In the ensuing quietude I hear a ticking; the old mantel clock. I hadn't noticed it before, how loud it sounds, each second ticking away, slowly increasing in its breadth. I try to force myself through the crevices of time, between the increments of each second; force myself to return to the man I was, hear his name spoken, see his face. It's then a quiet desperation floods me like ice water. I no longer remember my face, see it clearly in my mind. I've become an invisible man, lost in the past, living an invisible life.

The following morning is dark and overcast, an early morning storm scouring the vacant streets in a thin film of rain. Palm fronds are scattered the length of the boulevard and the ocean spits foam across the asphalt, unwinding inland like a gray snake stalking an empty city. The lonely street oddly beckons me, the rain falling on the stone whispering: '*Come. Follow me away. Walk out of this life and disappear into the world. Come.*'

I pay off the cab and knock on the front door of the Canfield's blue stucco near Diamondhead. Rue answers in a pair of black capri pants and a white chamois sweater, the letters *R-M* embroidered at the neck in fine black thread. Her eyes set firmly upon me, her taciturn expression speaking volumes.

"Hello Rue."

"Good morning time traveler. What brings you to this century?" I feel the stab of her words. She was as tough as the skipper, maybe tougher.

"Is Hildy awake?" She doesn't let me off the hook, blocking my way with her leg, then her body. Rue was a natural beauty, with the body and demeanor of a movie star.

"Gosh, I don't know Mike. We had a real wild party here last night. Just after midnight. Too bad you missed it. You were the center of conversation."

"May I see her please?" She stands there, blocking the entrance, like toying with a bug in a jar before stepping to one-side and gesturing.

"Entre-vous."

It's not even ten o'clock in the morning. Canfield already has a can of beer in his fist. The ribbing only continues.

"Hey, H. G. Wells. Have a seat, let's talk *stock market*."

I take the Lay-Z-Boy adjacent his recliner. "Very funny."

"You prefer the ponies? Either is a sure bet. We can quit our day jobs. We'll make a mint."

"Is Hildy awake?" He looks at Rue hovering over my shoulder. She relishes in my anticipation, toying with her compact, her lips ruby-red.

"Who? Oh, you mean our new boarder?" she says winking at herself in the tiny mirror; pursing her lips. It's breakfast for the rest of Honolulu. Rue looks like she's ready to hit the town.

"Is she awake?"

She snaps the compact closed and glowers. "I'll go check," she says coolly, strolling the hallway like a model working a runway.

"Is she still upset?" I ask, picking up the medal sitting atop the table between our chairs; his Navy Cross.

"Which one?"

"Hildy."

"Not any more than usual. You want a beer?"

"Coffee might be a better idea."

"That's Rue's department," he says, looking me over with a less than endearing expression. "Look, you can take this with a grain of salt, but I'd suggest you get a handle on this, right now. Nip it in the bud." The seriousness on his face brings home the gravity of my situation.

"I know. This is crazy and getting crazier. Am I losing my faculties Skipper? Is that what this is, some kind of war stress? Is my mind purposely trying to become another person to escape from this conflict?"

He lights a cigarette, mulling over the question. "You're not crazy Murph. You took a shot to the head. Those long-haired books are full of stuff about guys getting nutty from blows to the head. Are you hearing me Murph? Am I getting through this time?" he says with intent. I stroll to the front window to think.

There's a dwarf-lemon tree in the front yard filled to capacity with bright yellow fruit. Each globe looks like a tiny golden sun lost within a maze of deep-green foliage, heavy with rain. I pick up a framed black-and-white picture from the table beside the sofa; Rue and Hildy together, their high school graduation picture. Which of the two twins was younger? Hildy, Rue the *older sister*.

"Get it through your head Mike. You're Lieutenant Commander Michael Murphy. Get a handle on yourself boy. It's bad enough you're on the verge of throwing away a career, now you're putting your marriage on the line." I return the picture and stare at him. "You're walking a razor son. Buck-up and let's get back to work. I need you on this next patrol Mike. I'm with you, *all the way*," he says quoting our boat's motto. It was his motto, the three words a complete summation of Canfield's philosophy of submarine warfare, and it was true. *All the way*. Every submariner knew it from the moment they stepped aboard *his boat*. It was all or nothing. You were in it *all the way*, at least you better be.

Rue returns, picking up his pack of Lucky Strikes. We wait until she's lit one and had a puff, glaring at her husband the entire time. She shakes the match out, dispersing the smoke with a casual wave of her jeweled wrist and nods in the direction of the bedrooms. "End of the hall on the left Romeo."

She's on her side facing the wall. "Hildy, can we talk please?" When she turns, her eyes are red, and my chest tightens. "I'm sorry…I'm sorry." She embraces me softly, her lips to my ear.

"Oliver told me what happened. About the man hitting you; waking up and thinking you were a different person. Mike I'm worried." She begins to cry.

"Hildy, don't cry. Don't be worried. Things are going to be better from now on."

"You need to see a doctor."

"I am, tomorrow morning. I'm to report to the dispensary before going down to the boat."

"I'm talking about a psychologist Mike."

"A psychologist?" I gaze at the Canfield's tiny backyard. Palm trees cut across the back of the lot, etching dark jagged lines into an ominous gray horizon. "Looks like the storm is passing to the north."

"I'm serious Mike. I want you to see a doctor, right away." She looks so fragile.

"I can't Hildy."

"Why?"

"They'll ground me. It'll cost my career in submarines, probably the Navy."

"What does that matter? We can start over."

"What am I going to do, drive a hack? Bag groceries? Stock shelves at the local hardware store? I'm a career naval officer, a first lieutenant. In another few months I'll be a full commander. I've worked my whole life to get this far."

"What does any of that matter Mike, as long as we're together? I don't care about your *Navy career*…or this stupid, stupid war. I hate it. Hate it! I hate everything about it; the bread-lines, the rationing." I take her head into my shoulder.

"Honey, things will be fine, once hostilities cease."

"Hostilities won't cease Mike. Open your eyes. The world is falling apart around us. The world we knew is gone, forever."

"You're wrong."

"The world will never be at peace. How could you even think it? Men are incapable of peace. Men like Hitler and Mussolini. They won't rest until they've destroyed everything. Everything that's good, everything civilized. How can you not see that? And here you are, in the middle of it, waiting to be killed. I can't stand it Mike, wondering if you'll ever come back again."

"Hildy, it's not as bad as you-"

"What do you think I do all the time you're away in that, that ugly thing? I attend the luncheons, the USO gatherings…the funerals."

"Shhh, honey, don't."

"I can't stand it Mike. I can't stand it anymore. The waiting. I hear it all the time now. This submarine *lost,* that one *overdue.* This one *missing.* It's not fair. Why do you have to go out there again and again? Don't you see? This is your chance to get out, get away from it. Oliver has agreed to report on your condition. I'm going to do the same."

"What do you mean by that?"

"This is our chance to be free of it, forever. We can return to Vallejo, the house we're building, live a normal life together. It's our turn to be happy."

I take her face in my hands. Brush the tears from her cheeks. "Hildy, listen to me. I could never live with myself if I just walk away like that. What we're accomplishing out here is vital to the future, a future full of hope and promise, peace around the globe, the end of tyranny on the planet."

"Michael, wake up! There will be no end to this. Hitler has destroyed Europe. The Japanese have spread their armies across the Pacific. This war will go on and on until you're dead…and Oliver, all our friends. Just like Jim Hudgins."

She breaks, a deep anguish broiling from the center of her being. How can I argue with her? We were losing submarines; one, sometimes two boats a month now with no end in sight.

A strange feeling of vertigo takes hold, as if I were falling. Why not do as she says? Why not leave? Return to the town of our youth, be together as we always dreamed, since high school.

Memories of earlier years flood me like a torrent; school dances, picnics, sports events, the new music, big-band swing and the new dance steps; walking the halls with her, holding hands when the teachers weren't watching, the most popular girl in the school; our first kiss behind the gymnasium. Suddenly, the war, the attack on Pearl Harbor; all the boys enlisting. I recall our sad parting like yesterday; tears in the moonlight at Land's End in San Francisco. Then, her visit to her sister in Hawaii and the whole thing starting over again; this time a wedding.

Yes, why not leave this endless conflict behind and live as normal people, without the threat of death hovering? She was right. Why must I go out there again and again until I'm drowned alive? This *is* an opportunity, an opportunity to get away from the confusion, the doubt. My vision blurs, like a heavy rain across a windshield and it takes all my resolve not to break.

"Please. Please sweetheart, get out now. I can help. I'll get a job at the *five-and-dime* back home in Vallejo. Or better yet, Tiffany's in San Francisco. Aunt Ruth knows the manager of the boutique. Remember the day we went together? With Mom and Dad, Aunt Ruth and-"

"Hildy, don't do this. Everything will turn out all right."

She turns away. "No Mike, it won't!"

"In two more years, this entire conflict will be over. Japan and Germany will be defeated, and a new wonderful life will be there for the taking, especially in the Navy. The United States will own the seas."

She's incredulous. "How can you even think that?"

"Because it's true."

"How could you possibly think you know what will happen?"

"Hildy, I know what I'm talking about. I've seen that world. I've *felt* it. Freedom, liberty." Her expression is beyond my comprehension. There are no words for what is happening. I can't even tell her the reasons behind our next mission despite her constant asking. "Let's have coffee with the Canfields and put this behind us." She turns away on her side and it feels like a hole rips open in my gut.

"I need to be alone...I need time to think."

"Think about what?"

"Us."

"There's nothing to think about. Let's go back home."

"Please Mike, just...leave me alone."

As I stare at her I know in my heart that it's useless. The thought becomes a certainty in my mind, the mind of Michael Murphy...that I'm losing; losing her, my life, the whole damn thing.

That solemn afternoon we hold service for our fallen comrade, Lieutenant Jim Hudgins. When I see his photo, his cheery demeanor, I remember everything about the man. Jim was a good friend, one year my junior at Annapolis.

Every officer from the Manta Ray's wardroom is in attendance in full dress uniform; pressed white slacks and pure-white tunics. Our black and gold shoulder boards' cut a neat line along the path as we address the color-guard.

"Ten-hut!" Quartermaster Riley brings the guard to attention and a three-volley salute is fired into the air, the reports echoing sharply off the headstones staring out to sea. The guard is then brought to rest and *Taps* sounded, the bugle's melancholy notes answered from afar by another quieter, more mournful horn lost somewhere in the hedgerows lining the graveyard.

The officers stand at attention as the chaplain presents Lorna with a flag folded into a starry blue triangle. There is no body over which to mourn or reflect, only this neatly folded flag of the nation to represent the man she cherished. She holds it as if it were something immensely precious, and the person I least expect breaks, a deep sorrow emanating from the center of his being and the Manta Ray's wardroom feels the sorrow reverberate down the rank-and-file like thunder.

Chapter 6: The Refit

A warm steady wind snaps the USO banners.

I'm outside the medical dispensary. It's a fine summer morning. The air blowing in from the Pacific is like an old friend, nostalgia inundating the moment. The streets are filled with thirties and forties era vehicles; a nervous excitement playing hide-and-seek with the lazy morning sun. Despite the war with all its dark foreboding enterprises, a *lightness* fills the air that I haven't felt since I was young. The Pacific. Deep within its sun-washed brilliance lies an answer to an enigma.

Crossing the plaza that skirts a bombed-out theater, I pause to study the ripped and burned faces of forgotten stars and starlets. Weathered by the wind and rain, faded by neglect, they gaze imperviously through the broken glass into the cerulean landscape of a shattered dream.

Everywhere remains immutable evidence of the great attack of 1941, when Japan desperately surprised America and decimated her Pacific fleet. Bullet and aerial cannon holes–yet to be repaired–burn indelible marks upon the buildings and the faces of the sailors and nurses coming and going from the dispensary.

The old mercury thermometer, advertising licorice, reads 72 degrees Fahrenheit. These are the Trade Winds Robert Louis Stevenson lived, yet failed to divulge fully to the world in his adventures. It took this enormous engagement, a world war, to force *civilization* to the edge of the world, where primordial miracles meld with water and sand.

The blue and white ocean extends into a distant gray sky and the thought hits me gazing at the azure horizon that the *invisible* man, never knew this island. These memories exist solely within Michael Murphy, the man I must become again, if this charade is to be played-out for whatever mysterious reasons. *All the Way,* the motto of our boat, each man awarded a special pin with this motto engraved upon its face, twin dolphins treading white water against a solid blue background.

The old Plymouth trundles through the various security checkpoints down to *submarine row*, my rank getting me dockside where the provisioning has commenced in earnest on the boat. I study her from the distance, her sleek contours and ruddy complexion. A tough old craft, she had given our enemies more than a few bruises. Our boat. *'She who protects us whilst at sea,'* a more private motto the sailors whisper together when the ocean closes in. As I look upon this incredible machine, a strange feeling of warmth emerges within my chest, as if *she* were pulling me. I quicken my pace, nearly run to her.

Sailors in blue fatigues are swinging fresh Mark 14 torpedoes from the dock to the submarine, the men lowering the ordnance into the forward torpedo room hatch located halfway between *the sail* and the nose of the boat. Everywhere is the hum and drone of machines and aircraft as the bustling port conveys the materiel of war.

Crossing the forward gangplank, I side up to a perspiring Ned Binkershon and his sweaty torpedo crew. His biceps ripple under the sun, the name *Lily* tattooed in black ink across the sunburnt right forearm.

"Why are we loading torpedoes Ned? I thought they're going to cut through the hull?"

"They are. This hatch won't be here tomorrow. They're cutting through here to here," he says, pointing with a wrench. "We're stowing half our normal allotment of *fish* now."

"Why?"

"They have to be stowed before the generator, or coil, or whatever the hell you call it, gets placed. Then they plan to weld it shut. Seal it off to the sea. The emergency escape hatch too Murph." He gives me a pensive look before shouting at Jaeger. "Cleat your line Jiggs! Jesus-H. You trying to blow a hole through the bottom of the boat?"

"Yeah, and us with it," Lesky adds. "*Seaman third class*, yeah no kidding. You're lucky to even be on this detail Jaeger."

"Look who's talking? They don't call you *Easy* for no reason."

"You're cruising for a bruising Jaeger, the old five finger sandwich."

"Anytime fat-boy, anytime."

"Shut the hell up, both of you!" Binkershon blows. "Brother, I've had it up to my eyeballs with you two guys. The incessant bickering! *Pick, pick, pick*. I'm going out of my ever-loving mind!"

"It ain't me Binkershon. Yell at Jaeger."

"Keep it up Lesky. Keep flapping your gums. Wait and see what happens. Knuckleheads!" he shouts, grabbing their collars and knocking their heads together.

I use the interruption to head aft, winding my way through a maze of equipment and materiel sitting atop the deck; tanks of acetylene and oxygen, cutting torches and steel plating, boxes of welding rod and hardware stacked in every conceivable spot.

Electric cable, air, and water hoses are dangling over the water between the submarine and the dock supplying *shore-power* to the boat; the smell of burnt steel laces the salty sea air.

"Hey, look who decided to make the war," Stewart says to Taylor when I join them aft. "The number one wallflower of the fleet." I look down between the men and something tears inside me. They've commenced cutting a gaping hole through the deck into the after-torpedo hold. Sailors in thick leather aprons and gloves, their faces hidden behind welding masks, are cutting through the skin of the boat. "Well? What did the brain doctor say?" he asks, lighting a cigarette with his treasured Zippo.

"I've a concussion."

"Anything serious?" Bill inquires.

"Rest and relaxation. Don't worry, I'll be around for our little foray west."

"And meanwhile your share of drinking I hope, starting tonight," Stewart says, ruffling my hair, an annoying habit of his. "The Royal just isn't the same without you Murph."

"Where's Skipper?" Taylor points his chin behind me.

Canfield emerges with Bremer through the midship hatch at our feet. "I don't give a damn Chief those are the goddam orders. See that it's done," he shouts. Bremer immediately storms aft, cursing out the man on the torch about what he's not doing properly.

The skipper squares himself before us wiping sweat from his face. "Is that German purposely trying to bust my goddamn balls?" he bellows at Stewart and Taylor, both men conveniently *pleading the fifth*. It's my turn next. "That damn kraut is as stubborn as a Kentucky jackass, *stubborner!* Who made me the Navy's complaint department?!"

"Reporting for duty Captain." He glares at me.

"How was your little *vacation* to Honolulu?" he asks pointedly.

"Uneventful. A mild concussion."

"Anything else?" I shake my head.

He takes me aside so the officers can't overhear us and pulls a ruffled pack of *Camels* from his breast pocket. "You tell them about *the other guy*?" he asks lighting a cigarette.

"No. I thought it best to let it go. I'm moving on."

His eyes cut into mine. "Are you sure?"

"I'm fine, ready for duty." This news seems to lighten his mood.

"Good deal. I'm going to need you on this patrol, like I never did before." Something in the way he phrases his statement piques my curiosity.

"Everything all right?" He inadvertently breaks his cigarette, tossing it into the surrey collecting about the tail of the boat. He stares at the butt bobbing in the oil and dead fish.

"I'm sorry Mike, my recommendation to assign you command of your own boat was denied. You were probably expecting it, under the circumstances?" He averts his eyes toward the trucks coming and going along the quay; the sun a hazy dull yellow in the dust raised by their tires mixing with the smoke from the tugboats plying the harbor.

"It's fine Captain, I'm ready to sail."

"Well I'm damn glad you're back as my Exec. The old team back together…one more roll of the dice." I smile but feel *gravity* in his manner. Stewart interrupts us.

"Skipper, you better get another guy on the torch. Swear to god Chief's going to kill that poor guy."

"Goddammit Chief!" Canfield howls, joining the gaggle of men gathering about the hole. Chief Bremer actually has the man by the collar.

As I watch Canfield and the NCOs attempt to break it up, I mull over the captain's words, more importantly the look behind those words.

"What a crock of shit this is turning into," Stewart hisses behind clenched teeth, heading for the bow.

The following days are tense as the *push and shove* going on between the crew and the technicians assigned to the retrofit escalates. Parmalee and the electricians fare better but the torpedo crews are fit to be tied as their *neat and tidy* compartments are stripped and torn asunder by the inset of the two supercoils. A myriad of wires and cables lace through the boat like tentacles, probing every compartment; every free space becoming jammed with components, equipment necessary for the functioning of *the field* that will encircle the vessel.

The coils are brought in on my watch, on a precariously stormy evening, concealed under heavy olive-green tarps. They're lowered by crane, one at a time, and affixed within the narrow confines of the torpedo compartments.

The crew under my watch that night is getting soaked to the bone and miserable.

"When will it end?" Danny Dyer moans squeezing his thin arms around his skinny torso. Danny was a musician from San Diego and sensitive to cold, having grown up without it. "It rained this morning, again this afternoon. You'd think it would have rained itself out by now, but no, here's a little more just to keep things interesting."

"A whole lot more," Frank Stroup says flatly, the *Moten Stomp* by Fletcher Henderson playing on an old wooden radio behind his head, the only dry spot left inside the compartment.

"Who knows, maybe we'll get lucky, maybe just float to Tokyo on the run-off," Teddy Ritchie adds blinking at the gray sky looming large above the meager glow of the dock lights. Teddy was another card-carrying member of Tukey Collins' collection of *Brooklyn misfits*. Collins and Georgio grew up in Bensonhurst. Teddy was from Canarsie. Stroup, Flatbush.

"*Belch* turn that damn radio off," Binkershon says. "Happy music just don't suit the current mood," and Belcher unceremoniously kills the music. "So, the Dodgers lose again. Nice. That puts us effectively…a dozen games out of first place and counting."

"We wouldn't be in this predicament if Reese hadn't joined the Navy. What a dingbat."

"He was drafted idiot."

"No, he wasn't. I heard he enlisted."

"What difference does it make?" Collins interjects. "Reese couldn't save their season. At this point, you'd need a whole new ball club."

"I don't know Tuke, '42 was a pretty good year for Brooklyn at *short*."

"Wake up ding-dong. Pee-Wee Reese ain't gonna win you the pennant. Sure, he's a great defensive player. I ain't taking that away from the guy but the big game is what I'm talking about."

"What *are* you talking about loudmouth?" Binkershon inquires.

"I'm talking about the long-ball Binky, the home run wins pennants. If your club ain't got the muscle, take the pine."

"Aw, what do you know."

"Sorry but I beg to differ," Ritchie interjects. "Defense wins games Tuke, proven fact."

"How many times do I need to *reutterate* with you square-head? Sure, defense *wins* games, just not the season, the whole Stromboli. Take the cotton out of your ears Ted."

"You're bent," Binkershon says. "The heat is getting to you Collins. Or maybe it's all the fumes here in the *ass-end* of the boat," he laughs, and the *forward crew* manages a collective half-hearted smirk.

"What heat?" Collins says looking at the sky pouring into the hold. "Use your noodle Ritchie. What good is catching a ball if you can't put points on the wall?"

"What good is putting points on the wall if the other team does it more than you?"

"Exactly my point *Noodles*. The team that racks up the biggest score wins the most games, ergo, the long ball. The long ball brings the pennant home…back to Ebbets let us pray."

"Who died and made you commissioner of baseball?"

"I've played the game my whole life Binkershon, seen it over and over again. The home run buddy-boy. Got a name to prove it too."

"Crissakes please don't say DiMaggio."

"Not him…Babe Ruth."

"A lousy Yankee?! You're breaking my heart Collins!"

"Is it my fault he ended up on the wrong team?"

A near riot ensues, everyone talking at once. When Nichols and Belcher start a *shoving match* I whistle through my fingers.

"Fellas! Change the subject." The compartment goes quiet except for the dry-dock's hammers reverberating across the water, the constant pounding softened by the steady pour of the rain.

"What the hell are they hammering on over there?" Belcher asks to break the silence.

———

"My head!" Binkershon says. "To think I said *no* to Marge to be standing here with you mooks…swapping *facts* with the self-appointed commissioner of baseball."

"I'm crying in my beer…if I only had one," Collins rebuffs.

"*Marge?*" Jack Georgio echoes from inside the Maneuvering room door, the only dry spot large enough for a crewman still considered being *on-station*. "Marge who?"

"Did you go stupid again?" Teddy interrupts. "You know…*Slim*…the twelve-foot-tall redhead at *Matilda's Bar and grill*. The one packin' the eighty-eights. Where you been Georgie?"

Binkershon cuts him off. "Murph, you or Skip need to bust some skulls *a-sap*. It's the middle of the ever-loving night. This is inhuman." The remark instantly mobilizes both crews.

"Possibly against Navy regulations."

"Think we're breaking a few labor laws over here Lieutenant Murphy."

"Ditto. National labor-laws."

"Naval-code violations sir. Check the manual."

"You'd think the *Baron of Graymatter* woulda thrown-in the towel by now," Collins adds. "We're getting rained-out here Lieutenant, call the game, sheesh."

"It's not a ballgame Collins," I mutter from beneath my rain-skin. "There's a reason for doing it on a night like this."

"Says who Lieutenant? What for?" Belcher asks from the launch platform in the stern.

"I'll answer that," Binkershon interjects. "Secrecy dumbo, why else?"

"Hey what about that Lieutenant Murphy? Why us here doing this jazz and not a relief crew?" Dyer presses.

"Didn't you read the *non-disclosement* you signed meathead?" Collins interrupts. "You're on for the ride Danny-boy. They don't want just anybody knowing what we're doing." He looks around, palms to the air. "Who the hell am I kidding? *I* don't know what we're doing."

The sub slowly quiets, even the jackhammers take pause.

"Hey *Droop*, kick on the bilge pump," Binkershon says to Stroup standing beside the electrics bay. Frank Stroup didn't earn his nickname by eponymous connection. Stroup's demeanor never changed, not one iota. Ever. Whether joy or the fear of drowning, nothing seemed to register emotionally with Frank, at least not on his face.

"Why bother?" Nichols mutters, rain streaming down his beard. "At this rate, we'll be underwater in half an hour."

"No we won't Nicky," Collins says scratching his three-day stubble. "Their secret machine is gonna lift the whole sub right up over the Japs lousy heads and we'll drop a *Mark 14* down the stack of the stinkin' Yamato. Boom. Done. Back to Coney."

With the mention of the famous East Coast amusement park, everyone disappears into their own thoughts. Dyer tries, in vain, to light a cigarette with a pack of damp matches, eventually tossing both onto the grating beneath our shoes.

"Man, there's got to be a better way to earn a living."

We're standing amidst the rain to aid the technicians lowering the coils onto pre-aligned footings welded into the floor of the sub. The men work together with the civilian technicians to bolt the coil footings securely into massive shock absorbers and the night is long, wet, laborious, and uneventful; expletives notwithstanding. By dawn they're welding the hull back into place and by first light there's no outward indication that two very secret, mysterious machines are now within the extreme ends of the vessel.

A great deal of care is given these machines and the men of the Manta Ray take a strong dislike to them, and unfortunately, the persons in charge of them. It comes to a head when Chief Bremer actually throws one of the technicians over the side of the sub. The entire crew is brought before the brass and severely reprimanded with Bremer, Binkershon, and Collins excluded from any further involvement in the retrofit, gaining their *nightly updates* at the bar in the Royal Hawaiian Hotel.

When the heavy work is finished a team of physicists and engineers storm the interior of the boat like a swarm of locust. They commence ripping the insides out of the sub to make room for the new equipment and something inside me is deeply troubled by the sudden dismantling of our boat; this supposedly ignorant vessel that has so diligently served us, our home, and the nation's protector.

Along for the ride are Hoffmann and Charlesworth overseeing the entirety of the work. Lucy attracts her share of attention. I find myself chewing-out some of the deck crew for whistling or other minor infractions. I cite Admiral Bennett's order, but something deep and personal is stirring my inner state-of-mind, a profound compassion, as if I had known her for a very long time; know her thoughts, her mind, our growing attraction for each other. I also realize we will be sailing together, and this concerns me; a woman on a boat full of men under my watch and care.

I've direct orders to berth her in the senior officer's cabin, the compartment I normally share with Stewart and Taylor. I help secure her belongings and a strange feeling grips me when she chooses my old bunk as her own. I can't help thinking how out of place she seems–her feminine manner–as she begins the arduous task of retrofitting a boat filled with course salty men.

———

Unlike the other British scientists, Lawton and the others, it's clear that she harbors no preconceived, judgmental notions about Americans or sailors. Nearly all the men take on a caring and brotherly affection for her, doting about her like a pack of gooney birds on a roost. The only exception is Gunner's Mate Fitzgerald.

Fitz was a hardnosed, opinionated individual from Cleveland, Ohio, possessing a strong contempt for women and persons of color. There had been several altercations between him and other crewmen. Despite admonishments and threats to have him disqualified from submarines, Fitzgerald continued to possess a quiet seething contempt for persons outside his concept of privilege. He talked down to Coffee as if he were his personal servant and was covetous of Toles' senior ranking in the gunnery. He also possessed an obvious but unspoken disdain for command, a dangerous trait during wartime.

Most disconcerting of all was the relish he took in surface raiding; those unfortunate moments when the Manta Ray was forced, by the dictates of war, to fire upon smaller enemy boats and sampans; a detail endured by submariners during this loathsome conflict. For the other men of the gun crew the *duty* was obligatory; Fitzgerald reveled in it, once forcing Dave Cisco, our ex-gunnery chief, to punch him senseless for failing to follow an order to cease firing into a flotilla of Japanese sailors whose ship had been sunk and were left floating–unarmed–amongst the flotsam that had been their ship.

On several occasions I find Fitzgerald staring weirdly at her from a distance, the look on his face, disquieting. I approach the subject with Babineaux, the new gunnery chief. He confirms my observations have not gone unnoticed by other members of the crew.

"Why didn't we keep Cisco, or Vinny Prevoger? Why even bring Fitzgerald?"

"Prevoger had a blemish on his record; a stolen jeep. Dave Cisco was sent to Groton, to new construction. Why Babs? Do you think I should rotate Fitz out? It wouldn't be hard to do."

"Aw, don't worry about it, Mr. Murphy. I'll keep an eye on him. I'll punch his lights out if he tries anything funny." Wendy Babineaux was a tough guy with a big heart, an ex-boxer and a lawyer's son from Monroe, Louisiana. His father had championed issues of law for underprivileged farmers whose lands were being threatened by the misuse of old state-constitutional verbiage. As a result, Wendell grew up poor, and tough. "Fitz as much as touches that fine woman Murph, my boot will be ten feet up his ass."

The commissioned officers have been relocated to the petty officer's quarters. Duncan, Smith and the new NCO, Judesay, have been moved to *the Ritz*, the name christened the crew's bunkroom. Duncan taps on the bulkhead of his old bivouac, handing me several sheets of paper.

"What's this?"

"The crew manifest sir, in triplicate."

"Thank-you Ensign."

"Sir? You've only half our crew listed here. Is that an omission? How are we supposed to operate the boat efficiently with only half a crew?"

"You know *why* Duncan. We need to make room for the science team and the additional equipment."

"I realize that sir but forty-five seaman for a war patrol?"

"Off the record, it's not a standard patrol. We've orders to engage the enemy only as a last resort. Only if we're attacked or fired upon, which is highly unlikely."

"But Mr. Murphy, is that smart? What if we *are* attacked? How can you man a torpedo room with three hands and one chief? Or a deck battery with only three *rated* gunners?"

"Ensign, these are our operational orders from Pearl. This number is being hand-fed me directly from Command." He stands mute, apparently at odds with the idea of entering enemy waters with a skeleton crew. "Don't worry Eb, the likelihood of this boat firing even one torpedo *in anger* before we reach Tokyo Harbor is a thousand to one. Dismissed."

He salutes and leaves.

Duncan is right of course. The list of men is heavily pared down; orders to conform from the usual contingent of ninety sailors to no more than half. I look over the manifest, neatly typed, in triplicate; behind each man's name the number of war patrols he has completed.

Manifest: SS Manta Ray USN ComSubPac–classified
Captain of the Boat- Canfield, Oliver 7
Executive Officer- Murphy, Michael 6
Lieutenant JG- Stewart, Ellis 4
Quartermaster- Taylor, William 3
Ensign- Duncan, Eban 2
NCO- Smith, John 1
NCO- Judesay, Lynn 1
Warrant Officer/Yeoman- Wells, Winston 0
Chief of the Boat/Engineer- Bremer, Peter 11
Boatswain- Burlsley, Gil 5
Pharmacist- Cooper, Montgomery 2
Radarman- Herndon, Roosevelt 3
Sonarman- Goldman, Gallen 3
Hydrophone- Elder, Zigmund 3
Senior Steward- Porteru, Charles 8

Baker- Dover, Richard 5
Cook- McAnulty, Cyril 4
Steward- Romayo, Santino 2
Gunner- Babineaux, Wendell 6
Gunner's Mate 1st class- Toles, William 3
Gunner's Mate 2nd class- Fitzgerald, Kevin 3
Machinist- Lloyd, Earl 10
Machinist's Mate 1st class- Howard, Conrad 5
Machinist's Mate 1st class- Rawlston, Victor 4
Machinist's Mate 3rd class- McClatchy, Patrick 2
Electrician- Parmalee, Anson 3
Electrician's Mate 1st class- Torsch, Samuel 3
Electrician's Mate 2nd class- Ashburn, Bobby 2
Electrician's Mate 3rd class- Lawler, Sanford 1
Manifold- Szotsman, George 6
Manifold- Hintz, Henry 2
Forward Torpedo Chief- Binkershon, Ned 7
Forward Torpedo Mate 1st class- Nichols, Wallace 5
Forward Torpedo Mate 2nd class- Dyer, Daniel 3
Forward Torpedo Mate 3rd class- Belcher, Thomas 2
After Torpedo Chief- Collins, Thadeus 6
After Torpedo Mate 1st class- Stroup, Frank 4
After Torpedo Mate 1st class- Ritchie, Theodore 4
After Torpedo Mate 2nd class- Georgio, Joseph 3
Seaman 1st class- Sorel, Quentin 4
Seaman 1st class- Pendleton, Ronald 3
Seaman 2nd class- Wyatt, Robert 2
Seaman 2nd class- Lesky, Eric 2
Fireman 3rd class- Jaeger, Billy 1
Fireman 3rd class- Calhoun, Rupert 0

There's a tapping on the bulkhead. Parmalee arrests my attention, hovering in the doorway.

"We'll be pulling a lot of amps Lieutenant Murphy. I'm requesting we step up our feeder gauge to four-aught cable and include a neutral leg with the ground, just to play it safe."

"Whatever you think best Anson. Don't take any chances." On a whim I hand him the crew manifest. "Give this a once over, and your reaction."

He scans the document, pinches his chin then whistles. "We better stay clear of trouble. We'll be lucky to fire two fish at a time. Or man more than one gun."

"I'm more concerned about our electrics roster. It's thin and half your boys are green. Sorry but I couldn't get you more experienced men. Rick Thompson wasn't cleared for the mission and Artie Pitts was sent to Australia, to a new submarine. I don't know anything about Ashburn or Lawler except they're young, and green."

"No sweat Lieutenant. As long as you keep Sam away from the watch-rotation, I think we'll be okay. Sandy's my weakest link, Lawler. I've assigned him to babysit the scientists. Bobby can usually do what I tell him without hurting himself or someone else. But Sam's the main ingredient. I'm an *electrician* Mr. Murphy but Sam Torsch is a *juicer*. A true red, white, and blue, *made-in-America* juicer. We make a good team."

"He'll remain quietly in your detail Anson. I'll see to it."

Judesay interrupts us. "Commander Murphy? Dr. Charlesworth is asking for you. In private."

She's at the tiny desk in her quarters, writing in a ledger. I tap on the bulkhead although the curtain has been left open.

"Oh, Commander Murphy, do come in. Please sit," she says pointing to the edge of the bunk, the only viable seat besides the small wooden chair at her desk. We're suddenly quietly alone together. "Hello," she says smiling, her eyes oddly expectant.

"I heard you were requesting my attention to a personal matter?"

"That's a rather formal way of putting it but yes." She draws the curtain taut and sits beside me on the bunk, gazing into my eyes. "I wanted your unbiased opinion of the way I and my group are behaving aboard the submarine."

"Behaving?"

"I want your honest evaluation of my performance as a crewman, *no holds barred.*"

"I'm impressed. Your comprehension of the systems being installed is exceptional." She gazes over the lenses of her glasses. I wonder if the rims were possibly passed-down from a previous generation, perhaps a grandmother. Her eyes pulsate, lustrous and perfect.

"Go on."

"Well, frankly, I'm surprised by how well you communicate with the men on my crew. They're the ones *behaving* for a change. They're all quite impressed with you, your technicians assigned to the project as well, approximately a dozen glaringly tight-lipped men."

She rolls her eyes. "That's Lawton's doing."

"Your senior technician? Is something wrong?"

"Clinically, no."

"What's the matter?"

"Your men dislike him. Immensely. They've developed a very strong distaste for him, his iconoclastic manner. I'm somewhat concerned."

"What's the problem?" She takes my arm in hers.

"Brian's *British conceit* certainly, yet I sense his disdain for sailors and their…peculiarities, lies at the heart of *the problem*. I'm uncertain what to do about it." She leans her head against my shoulder, silently pondering; a noticeable warmth radiating between us.

"The ocean is a truly vast place Lucy, mysterious, ever-changing, unpredictable. There are long held traditions in the Navy, particularly in submarines, where superstition reigns."

"Superstition? I'm intrigued. Like what?"

"Certain posturing, rituals, ardently observed, so as not to incite the wrath of what is, in essence, an enormous living thing. It doesn't take a man long to adopt a sense of awe regarding the ocean's temperaments." She pushes a wisp of hair behind her ear.

"I remember things my father would do. Tell me about the submarine. What's *her* peculiarities?"

"Well, for example, it's protocol on the Manta Ray to make the sign of the cross, the four cardinal points, before our cooks dump garbage at sea. This gesture maintains the integrity that we're *feeding the fishes* rather than dumping filth. It's also common on the Manta Ray to give her gunwales a gentle pat, like stroking a pet. The men joke about *wearing a hole in her armor* by all this loving affection. Everyone does it."

"Tell me about crewman Dooley."

"Crewman Dooley?" Her eyes fix on mine. Green. "He's the only man killed on the Manta Ray."

"Yes, I know. Tell me about him."

"Porteru has been telling you stories again?"

"Of course. Tell me about his bunk Michael. It's directly affecting the situation."

"During her maiden war patrol, the Manta Ray became engaged in a surface raid on a Japanese trawler suspected of running ammunition near the straits of Bungo Suido. She was obviously a munitions ferry and fired back. A gunner's mate, a loader named Nick Dooley, was killed; the only man lost from the Manta Ray to date."

"I know all this already. Mr. Howard was kind enough to fill me in on every single detail. He was trying to frighten me I think, but it just made me all the more curious. Tell me about his bunk."

"Well, shortly after his death, the sailors reported seeing, and *feeling*, Dooley's presence in the submarine, in particular his old bunk. From that time onward that bunk has been Dooley's bunk, considered off-limits to anyone. Why are you asking me all this?"

Her eyes delve mine. "When Lawton found out about it, he purposely moved into the bunk despite the objections of your crew. Curious about the situation, I asked him why he chose to disregard tradition."

"What did he say?"

"Why don't you ask him yourself. They're having breakfast now."

"Are you daft Lieutenant? I don't believe in all that rot," he snarls over his meal of bangers and mash, foodstuffs brought in especially for the British scientists. "It's the bloody twentieth century Mate. That's all fluff. No such things as ghosts or spirits, all the imagination of primitive minds. That bunk is the best bed on the ship, hardly used; doesn't smell of sailor stink."

"You don't believe a man exists past his death?" I ask pouring blackstrap molasses over my pancakes; a condiment Porteru kept onboard.

"I do not," Lawton states. "It's obvious we *check-out*."

"Everything you are, or were, all your thoughts, experiences, moments and feelings, just disappear from existence, forever?"

"So it would seem."

"That *seems* a colossal waste, doesn't it?"

"That's life. Have you evidence? Proof to the contrary?"

"Just feelings, notions."

"*Feelings and notions* are hardly proof Yank. Why is there such scant proof? Because such things are mere fantasy. The answer should be obvious enough, even for persons of limited intellect," he says scanning the American crew. The machinists all rise en masse and loudly vacate the compartment.

"Perhaps it's the other way around Lawton?"

"I don't catch your drift."

"Perhaps it's the means of your *proof* that seeks reevaluation. Perhaps the truth, the proof you desire, is beyond the narrow senses of man. The five senses you hold so dear aren't adequate."

He stares blankly into space. "Excuse me but I've more important things to do than babble on about…whatever it is you're babbling about." He abruptly leaves and Hawkins rolls his eyes, reluctantly following him aft. As soon as they're gone, Coffee sides up to us, a serious expression on his face, wiping the stainless-steel with a cotton towel.

"That man's in for the time of his life if he keeps on with that bunk."

"Ya'll getting that old southern feeling coming on again Coffee?" Sorel asks through a mouthful of fried potatoes.

"Mr. Murphy's right. There is such things as haunts. Seen it with my own eyes, Dooley walking around like he's still on duty. Ya'll see it too if you'd quiet yourself down long enough to take notice." He redirects his attention to the new recruits. "Dooley comes and goes like he done in life; pokes around the engine room or the control room time to time. I'm doubting he'll be a'right with anyone in that bunk."

"You actually see him?" Calhoun asks wide-eyed, taking Lawton's place, a plateful of pancakes and eggs in his fist.

"Glimpses…time to time…when the boat quiets."

"Let's not go into that again Coffee," Wells says, the crew having already indoctrinated them about the phantom seaman. "I get chills hearing about that sort of thing," he says chewing on a piece of bacon and washing it down with powdered milk.

"Rightly so," Coffee presses on. "Sometimes they look just like you or me," he says directly to Wells and everyone readies himself for another *Cajun tale*. "I'll never forget the time back in Lafayette. We's all just sitting around jawin' when my aunt Phadrea comes walking through the front door like she done every day of her life for eighty-four year. She looks at us sitting there with our mouths open and says as clear as I'm speaking to you now, '*I want a new lock on this here door, this one don't work right. Sometimes I can't get in,*' then leaves for the kitchen. Everyone turns white and my aunt Neddy, her sister, faints. Aunt Pha had been dead close on to two year."

"Heck, you're putting me on," Wells says looking for agreement amongst the group. "There's no such thing as a ghost…right?"

"What he's talking about is true." Everyone turns and stares at Jukes in the corner smoking a cigarette. "I once saw a ghost, back in Scranton. It was the dead of winter. Bone-chilling freeze. I came in late to work because the bus stalled-out from the cold. When I walked in, I saw a rigger, a guy named Hough, standing at the end of a truss beam like he was in a daze. I didn't pay him no mind. I was sweating about getting to my station before the foreman jumped down my neck. They were all standing around taking coffee though it was early, way ahead of the break. I ask Lowery what was going on he says: '*Redfield Hough died this morning. We're taking a moment.*'"

"*Hough*? The guy you saw standing there?"

"I say, *'He isn't dead. He's standing down there at the end of the truss.'* Lowery informs me his wife had called. Red died in his sleep that morning. Man, I swear on a stack of bibles I spent the entire day looking for that guy. They all thought I was hung-over, or saw someone else that looked like Red. No way man, I know what I saw, it was Red Hough standing there as clear as I'm seeing you."

Later that afternoon I'm taking coffee in the wardroom, command central for the retrofit. The small stainless-steel table is stacked with blueprints, cathode tubes and switches. Lucy joins me for a cup of tea. I recap my conversation with Lawton, then question her about ghosts.

"Ghosts?" she laughs at my seriousness. "Michael, is Conrad putting you up to this?"

"Is there any scientific proof they exist?"

"Are you seeing disembodied spirits too Commander Murphy?"

"Perhaps I'm a ghost. Could it be possible?" She takes up my hand, her touch warm.

"You certainly don't feel like a ghost," she says smartly.

"Could it be possible? Could they exist in such a real state, that the person himself doesn't realize he's actually dead?"

"*Real state?*"

"Exactly like myself here and now. Is there scientific proof to back it up?"

"Are you being sincere?" She laughs. "Seriously, is our mischievous Mr. Howard putting you up to this? I'm *on* to you Michael. You two are cooking up something unsporting."

"Lucy…I'm being serious."

She studies me, growing reflective, her scientist's demeanor returning. "They would be a form of energy, free of the material body. So yes, I believe it more than probable they do in fact exist…just like you."

"*Just like me,*" I echo, suddenly very far away. She takes a spoonful of sugar from the lead-crystal bowl and slowly stirs it into her tea.

"I'm not sure what you're contemplating but I can assure you that you're very much a massive ball of energy Michael." Her eyes wander my head and shoulders. "A very handsome ball of energy," she says quietly before Hawkins interrupts us.

"Luce, Brian's in knots over this *intervalometer* business. Can you have another look love?" He lights a cigarette, sans holder. "Swear I'm going to throttle the bastard if he keeps it up."

"Keeps what up?" I regret asking when I see his expression.

"Being a bloody arse!" he spits, instantly collecting himself. "Sorry Lieutenant."

"Tell him I'll be right down Liam."

"Super. Cheers," he says and leaves. Her eyes return to mine.

"More energy than substance I should think Commander, all of us." She quiets her voice, her eyes seeing through me. "When I was ten years of age, I had an accident."

"What happened?"

"A moment of clarity actually. In that moment I saw life, existence for what it truly must be. Everyone was on fire. I saw what I believe to be reality. In its *true* state. Everything energy. Everything in constant motion."

"A vision? You were asleep?"

"Quite awake. That was the beginning of this path I'm on. This study of…*electronics*." She tops off her tea at the hot water decanter. "There really is no such thing as material constructs Michael. At the heart of all matter lies energy and at the heart of energy…"

"Consciousness," I say as if listening to another.

She studies me intently, her eyebrow elongating. "Yes…perhaps that's exactly it. Less a *Navy man* and more a philosopher kind sir?"

"*More energy than substance*, so a friend once told me. More a physicist, Doctor?"

"I'm not only a physicist Michael. I've a doctorate in electrical engineering, from Cambridge, so I've a vested interest in…*electricity*."

"When did it begin, all this…electrical obsessing?" Her eyebrow responds again, and she rejoins me at the table, loosening her coveralls.

"The *obsessing* started when I was fourteen," she says. "It was a lot of work but without the engineering it would be impossible to make this work. I mean for myself. I'm fortunate being assigned this incredible project, being young and…*a woman*…as if the title equated with being maligned." She looks at her hands, grease and dirt under the nails and quietly slips them beneath the table, looking into my eyes.

"You've been prejudiced against?" I ask, the question surprising her.

"The world of physics and electricity is a man's world, just as the military is a man's world. Or haven't you been groomed to this *fact* yet?"

"Yes, I suppose. However, a day will come when that phrase will be meaningless. Women will stand alongside men in these pursuits, not only this world but beyond."

"Do you know what you're saying? You're not feverish, are you?"

"Men and women will travel off-world together." She seems mesmerized. "What is it?" her silent trance-like stare concerning me.

"You're very different from the men you serve with," she breathes. "I don't mean to sound critical but not all your colleagues would say something so…inspiring."

"You think I'm a dreamer?"

"*A dreamer?*" she echoes deep in thought, propping herself on one elbow. "Yes. Perhaps that's it. You're a dreamer Commander Murphy?"

"Quite the contrary. I'm a horrible pragmatist."

"Dreamer or naught, you're very different from the men you command, even those above your station. As if…" Her eyes search mine, looking for something.

"*As if* what?"

"As if…" her voice thinning to barely a whisper, "…you don't belong here…in this time and place. Not at all." Her eyes continue to fathom mine, looking into me. The arrival of Dr. Hoffmann and several of his staff interrupt her gaze, or any further discussion on dreaming.

"Charlesworth, we're ahead of schedule, do you realize?"

"Yes Dr. Hoffmann, I'm quite impressed with our progress. Your staff has done an excellent job. You as well Commander, your people have been invaluable," she says graciously.

"Indeed Lieutenant, our thanks to you and your captain. Despite the differences early on we've made outstanding progress adapting the ship…excuse me, *the boat*."

"Thank-you Dr. Hoffmann. I'll tell the men."

"Commander Murphy, I'm curious. Are you free this evening by chance?"

"*Free* sir?"

"We've a small soiree planned this evening back at the lab. An excuse to drink some sherry really. Do you think you could manage say, eight o'clock?" I look at Lucy, her eyes expectant.

"Yes. I appreciate your asking."

"Very good. Ah, one small problem young man. Due to the sensitive nature of the project, I'm afraid you wouldn't be allowed a guest. I pray this doesn't dissuade you from attending?"

"No problem. Thank-you Dr. Hoffmann."

"Good, all set then. Carry on," he says leaving with his team to inspect the forward coil.

"Well, you seem to have bridged the gap."

"Oh?"

"Be prepared, scientists are oft-times the rudest people on the planet. They'll ask about your education at which point you'll be ostracized from further discussion and relegated to the wings the remainder of the evening," she says beaming then instantly changes her demeanor. "Forgive me. That was crass," she mutters, lacing her fingers across her throat. "I must be getting tired…all the diesel fumes."

"No apologies necessary. Thanks for the warning. You'll be there?"

"Indeed, kind sir. These occasions are perfunctory."

Chapter 7: The Net

*A*t twilight I'm knocking on the Canfield's door.

The darkened windows have me doubting my message to Hildy has gotten through. I'm surprised when the door opens, and Rue's sultry form is silhouetted within the frame of the door like the first act in a film-noir flick. I look past her into the darkness of the house.

"Is your sister awake?" She's sipping a gin gimlet, her answer, slow in coming.

"Come on in Mike. I've been waiting for you." She leaves the door wide. A few candles burn, coating the interior of the home in a soft amber glow, the radio quietly playing a Jo Stafford melody. I drop my cap on the end table, taking in the quietude of the house.

"Has everyone gone out?"

"I got your message. I'm glad you came."

"Is she awake?"

"She's not here Mike. Her and Oliver went to tonight's USO performance. They needed to get out of the house. She's done nothing but mope since she moved in. You look nice. Full dress uniform. I'm impressed."

"There's a meeting at the science facility tonight."

"You always look so sharp in your white uniform," she says scanning me head to foot. "You want a drink? Gin okay?" She starts to build a gin martini.

"Don't bother over it. I only stopped-by to speak with Hildy."

"Don't be a bore Mike." She finishes mixing, then hands me the drink, standing unusually close, actually playing with the insignia pinned to my breast. "Nearly a full commander now. You'll probably make captain soon according to the old man." I wonder if she's referring to her husband or someone else. She runs a finger along the edge of my shoulder board. I'm beginning to feel nervous about her mood.

"I have to get going Rue. There's a meeting at the science laboratory tonight."

"You said that already." She takes the La-Z-Boy, patting the sofa. "Relax Mike, we need to talk." She crosses her legs, her toenails painted a deep crimson.

"Talk about what?"

"Hildy…and you." I take a seat and wait while she sips her gin. "She's weak Mike, and needy. Sis never had much backbone. I've had to do all of the *heavy lifting* after Mom and Dad were killed. God, I wonder where she'd be today without me taking charge of things."

"Hildy's delicate, sensitive."

She laughs. "You can say that again. She was the same all through school. I had to do all the thinking for us while she stared at herself in a mirror."

"What are you getting at?" Mischief pulsates in her eyes. She takes the spot beside me on the couch, the length of her thigh against mine.

"That's what I like about you Mike. You're exactly like me. You don't mince your words. You come to the point and expect other people to do the same. Hildy must drive you nuts. She never comes to the point. If she's got an issue with you, you'll be the last to hear about it. I've had to deal with it my whole life."

"Are you getting at something?"

"Stop pretending, like it's going to go away. She wants you out of the Navy, out of submarines. For good. She's been crying about it for months."

"I'm aware that she-"

"I don't think you understand how serious this has become. Mike…don't go on this next patrol, stay home. If not for her sake, then mine." Her eyes are on fire, reflecting the candlelight.

"What are you suggesting? I couldn't possibly back out of my duties at this point."

"Why? Why not?" I'm uncertain if she's serious or creating conversation.

"This isn't just *another* patrol. It's…serious. The men are counting on me…and Oliver."

"You wouldn't be letting anyone down Mike, certainly not Ollie."

I stroll to the patio windows, to clear my head. She refills her glass at the bar, before joining me in the moonlight cutting through the blinds. Diamondhead sits radiant under a deep indigo sky, like an ebony jewel gazing out to sea. Despite the mandatory black-out, soft lights twinkle in the distance, the moon coating the hills in an ephemeral glow. Her body is wrapped in black and white bands of moonlight.

"You think Ollie has you on a pedestal, don't you?" She stirs the gimlet with her finger. Rue was always a mystery to me, a stormy, intelligent woman, sensual and driven. She shakes her head. "Afraid not. He's using you to make a name for himself; it's all smoke and mirrors."

"I don't get you."

"Wow. You're thick. Okay…why haven't you been given your own boat? Have you asked yourself that question lately?" Her eyes *hide* within the shadow cast by the blinds; just a pinprick of moonlight on the corneas.

"Because…just…timing." Her laugh drips sarcasm.

"No. Sorry…that's not it."

"Say what you're thinking. Let's not play games." She responds by taking my waist in her arm.

"You better sit down. You're not going to like what I tell you." She maneuvers me back to the sofa while she takes the La-Z-Boy. "Admiral Hess has had his eye on you for quite some time. Did you know that? He's spoken with Ollie on numerous occasions, usually their drunken all-night poker binges." She *toys* with my pant leg, pinching the cuff between her toes. "What do you think I do during their little get-togethers, cook?" She slides beside me on the sofa. "I listen to their conversations *natch*. I listen to everything. Sure, they think I'm reading, or talking to Marilyn, but I can tune out Marilyn Hess like tuning out a bad radio program." She snaps her fingers, the nails scarlet red. "The woman is vacant, rambles on to excess about the most useless vapid tripe. About the servants, the USO volunteers…blah-blah. All I need to do is nod or say, *'Oh really Mar?'* from time to time, while I listen to the juicy stuff Ollie pumps out of Carl like working a slot machine. Ollie's got a knack for that Mike, pumping *the brass* for information they shouldn't be divulging. So do I. It's the one natural talent we share."

"What was said about me?"

"That's the best stuff, *you*." She takes my bicep to her breast, her breath soft on my neck. "Because I like you, I like hearing about you. I like to hear the things they say…about the things you do. The way you run the boat, command men. It's exciting." Her dark eyes pulsate as she silently fathoms me. "They play their little games, moving men around like pieces on a chessboard."

"What was said Rue?"

She plays the moment out, like an actress on a stage, a sagacious grin emerging at the corners of her lips. The song on the radio changes; the soft melodic voice of Dinah Shore singing *Blues in the Night*.

"Did you know Carl Hess wanted you at the helm of your own boat after your *Jag* run with Oliver? Carl saw you were a natural submarine skipper even that early. Did you know that?"

"No. No I didn't," I admit, shocked to hear it from this source.

"Of course not, because the only way you could have known, is if Ollie told you." She's right. If it were true, it would come through my immediate commanding officer.

"Why wasn't I told then?" She looks at me askance, her eyes narrowing; the ring dangling from her ear, reflecting the candlelight.

"When did you ever grow up? Because Ollie chose not to tell you."

"Why wouldn't he tell me?" Her insipid expression is unsettling. She stares into the room as if collecting her thoughts, perhaps rehearsing a script.

"You want the *official* answer?" she asks, raising a thinly painted eyebrow.

"Yes, I would."

"*Officially*, you were too *green*. You needed another patrol with a *seasoned skipper*, someone to *show you the ropes*. Blah-blah, sound familiar?"

"That's not entirely off mark."

"Don't you think that's a decision you should be allowed to make? Or at the very least, be included in?" Her words sting. She traces the veins atop my hand with the tip of her index finger, feeling the blood flow. "Would you care for the unofficial reason?"

"Yes."

"I'm only speculating. After all, Ollie doesn't necessarily include me in all his *maneuvers*. Sometimes it takes guile."

"What reason?"

"It really goes without saying. He wants to keep you, as his first officer. Here you go again, a sixth patrol. Four as a first officer." Her words stab at me.

"A skipper should have a couple patrols as an X-O…it makes perfect sense. It's just the way it worked out." I break away to feign topping off my glass at the bar; to think. The night sky extends for millions of miles, the light of a billion stars entering the room.

She follows me over, studies me from the darkness cast by the moon seeping through the panes. In the distance, a party seems to be in progress, voices and laughter emanating from the hillside. She scissors her jeweled fingers between the blinds, peering into the night.

"Sure Mike, sure. The Navy needs experienced sub commanders, badly right? But why hurry it? After all, Lorna Hudgins' old man got a submarine and look what happened. Ollie probably saved your life." Her words cut me. However, like it or not, she's correct again. There *was* a dire need for qualified submarine skippers. The war was waging in the Pacific and America was getting a black-eye. The submarines had become the only effective means of attacking the enemy in his own waters. We were giving the Japanese a hard time, mauling her merchant fleet and creating serious loses amongst her men-of-war, all this in the utmost secrecy. Experienced submarine skippers were in demand. But why was Jim sent out before me, and the boat lost? A dark feeling begins to entwine my thoughts. "Yeah, you're probably right Mike. Decisions like that go with rank anyway. Command over other men's careers…where they go, what they do."

"Okay, he should have told me." I take a long draught from my drink; too much gin. She leans her hip into mine, the length of our legs touching, and strokes my back.

"Would you like to hear more?"

"More?"

"Of course. You think it ends there? You must have asked yourself, after you came back from the first patrol as his executive officer? Would he recommend you. What did he tell you?"

"That he'd look into it."

"And?"

"*And*…they would consider it after another run."

Her eyes are dark, piercing. "You know what your problem is Mike? You're altruistic…so you think everyone else is. You need to come to the realization that people are selfish, manipulative."

"Say what you mean Rue."

"He's never brought your requests forward."

"You're saying he lied to me?" She laughs, playing some kind of mental game. I take the drink from her hand and place it on the bar. "I think you've had enough." Her initial surprise dissipates as she relaxes her body into mine.

"Yes, Commander Murphy," she whispers, playing with my collar. I fold her hands together.

"Rue, you're inebriated. You need to get to bed and I need to get to my engagement."

"But we were just getting to the good stuff Mike. Don't you want to hear the good stuff?" Her eyes are in shadow. I gently force her face into the moonlight.

"Rue, I think you've said enough for one night."

"No. I haven't. There's more and you know it."

"What else?"

"Are you asking, or just indulging me?"

"Yes. I'm asking."

She stirs my drink with her finger, tasting it. "Hess asked Ollie to release you prior your last patrol. He wants you to command a new boat. Ollie told him you requested to stay on as his Exec." Her eyes reflect the moonlight, holding mine.

"Why would he? Why would he do such a thing?"

"Why do you think?"

"Say it."

"Because *your friend* is a selfish, heartless bastard. A man who uses people for his own ends," she whispers, then kisses me, her arms folding around my neck, her lips intoxicating, like fine wine; the moon watching us through the window.

"Rue…"

"Make love to me Mike." She presses her body into mine, pulling me like a magnet; taking my face in her hands. Neither mischief nor joy is set upon her countenance but a deep yearning. "I haven't made love with Oliver in months. He's become impotent." I'm stunned, my body reacting; she sees it on my face, slowly recoiling, quietly taking up her pack of cigarettes from the bar, the flame from the lighter coating her features in a hollow glow. When she turns, a cynical expression forms on her face. "Cute huh Mike? Me, Rue Morrissey, without a lover…how ironic."

"I'm sorry. I had no idea."

"Well…now you know."

"What's happened?"

"What do you think?" I have no answer. "Try *war stress* for starters. Hudgins and the rest are dead. You forgot who you were. Oliver can't make love. The *spoils of war*. Better than dying I suppose…well, then again, maybe not," she says acerbically, smoking within the moonbeams.

"Are you seeing a doctor about this?"

She laughs, a painful fragile laugh. "Sure. Why not?"

"And?" A Count Basie number starts on the radio and the tempo within the tune hardens her gaze. She tosses her hair back, snuffing out the cigarette in the ashtray on the bar.

"His psychiatrist is as old as the grave. I doubt he's been *laid* in over a decade." She leans the small of her back into the bar, her body fully to me. *"He'll get over it when the war ends,* quote-end-quote. Like that's ever going to happen." I wonder about the look forming in her eyes. "And just to compound our, *little problem,* Ollie's been diagnosed alcoholic, *under the table* of course. Were it official, he'd be taken out of submarines, probably the Navy." I set my drink down, clutching the bamboo rail of the bar, the gin clouding my thoughts.

"Why not do that? He'd be home. You'd be together, away from the war."

Her eyes go cold, nearly as cold as her next words.

"What, and have him hanging around here all day? No thanks."

"How can you say that?" She takes my hands in hers, caressing her body with them.

"Because I don't want him. I want you…like you want me." She kisses me, passionately, and I realize, I do want her, some part of me, wants to leap as if into an abyss. I gently break off our embrace.

"I've got to go." As I retrieve my cap, she blocks my path to the door, standing in the darkness like a phantom.

"Why are you doing this Mike?"

"Doing what?"

"Playing this little game of yours?"

"*Game?* What do you mean?"

"You know perfectly well what I mean." She takes me in her arms. "You want me. You've made it more than clear enough. So here we are, the others away." I try to leave but she holds me. "Mike, stop it. I'm telling you…I want you."

"What about Hildy? Have you thought about her?"

"Hildy's stupid. Look at the way she treats you, as if you were a child. A grown man, and at war. What does she do? Deserts you, the fool." She pulls me tightly to her body, heat radiating between us. "I'm not a fool Mike. I know what I want."

When she kisses me, passion sears my brain, suppressed feelings emerging from deep within my body. Memories flood my psyche like flipping through a photo album; a Christmas in Vallejo together, Rue in silk pajamas opening presents beneath the tree; a sunset on Waikiki, and yet another on North Beach; coffee together at dawn. I'm instantly awash with dozens of memories. What she's saying is true of course. I do want her, as any man desires a spirited, sensual woman.

As we embrace, my hands forming the contours of her body, I feel myself falling, as if into a quagmire. When Lucy's face emerges within my mind's eye, her tranquil gaze, something deeply profound takes hold. I gently pull Rue's arms from around my neck and step back from *the edge*, her expression impossible to read; anger or incredulity?

"I'm sorry Rue, this can never happen. I am sorry."

When I go to leave, she puts the freeze on. "Mike, if you walk out that door…you'll regret it." The tone in her voice stops me in my tracks. "I mean it. Whatever game you're playing, I'm not buying."

"*Buying*?"

"If you leave, I'll report everything to Simms and the medical board, everything."

"Report what?"

"How you woke up on the ship thinking you were some other man, *a man from the future.* That you think you know what will happen in the future, all of it."

"Rue, don't do this."

"I'm serious Mike. I don't want you out there, dead." She kicks over the end-table spilling its contents across the floor; the photo of her and Hildy breaking upon the tiles, the shattered glass reflecting the firelight. "I won't permit it Mike. I won't."

"Permit it?"

"I want you here…with me." She studies the look on my face. "I intend to have it my way, one way or the other; your own boat, or the psycho ward at Hickman." I'm stunned. "You know because of the mission you'll be put in isolation. Oh yes, I get what I want out of Oliver, when I want it. I know everything about the mission. The secret invisibility thing, the hush-hush, the scientists, all of it."

"My god, do you know what you're implying?"

"Hildy's leaving for San Francisco. Hess wants you on another boat. Fine, we'll let him know. While that happens, you're here, with me, and Ollie's off on another patrol, his great passion in life, sinking ships. But this time he'll be without you, and without you…he won't be back. I know it Mike. I can feel it. Without you…he'll kill himself and his crew."

Silence.

"You must be drunk. I can't believe you're serious."

"Dead serious. You can do it my way, or the hard way…and after all, what's so bad about my way?" She laces her fingers atop one hip and straightens her back to emphasize the point.

"What about Hildy? You think Hildy is going to just step aside and agree to all this?"

"Are you saying she hasn't told you yet?" She stares at me from the darkness, flame erupting in the pupils of her eyes.

"Told me what?"

"That little weakling," she curses through her teeth. "She's got no backbone. I can't count on her for anything."

"What are you talking about?"

She bites her nails, the color of blood. "Hildy's divorcing you Mike." She sees the shock on my face. "Apparently you haven't heard yet. She's at the end of her rope with it all. Being married to a Navy man isn't all it's cracked up to be. And Hawaii? Heaven forbid, *too hot, too small, too dangerous,* the Japanese hiding behind every palm tree, ready to invade any minute. I'm sorry I'm the one to tell you but…unless you throw away a brilliant naval career and start cleaning gutters for a living or washing cars, you and her, are on the rocks." She takes my shoulders. "On the other hand, I love a Navy man, capable of becoming an admiral," she melts into my body, her lips to my cheek. "I'll help you Mike. Together we'll get there. I have it all planned. Exactly how and through whom it will be done, but together, you and I." When her lips kiss mine, I shun them, and she turns on me. "I mean it, if you walk out that door, you're throwing away a career, for keeps."

All or Nothing at All, by Frank Sinatra, starts to play on the radio, the popular tune complimenting the gravity of the moment. At the door, I turn and look at her.

"Go to bed Rue. You just need a good night's sleep."

"Get out! Get out of here."

"You'll forget all this tomorrow." She follows me to the door.

"I hope you enjoy mopping floors for a living. I bet the Navy hires ex-submarine commanders to wait tables at the Royal."

I park the Plymouth beneath a stand of palms separating the science lab from the compound's motor pool and step into the cool caress of night. In the distance I hear the sound of a basketball game in progress. The smell of sweaty cotton jerseys and canvas tennis shoes on the breeze.

The moon hovers, coating the world in a deep nocturnal brilliance. The effervescent moonlight makes the base seem surreal, like a dreamscape. Staring into the vast indigo sky, I wonder if this moon is the one that I've always known. Or did it exist seventy years ago, within the eyes of another? The night beckons me, as if I were to walk into the darkness, simply step off this raft I think is my life, the darkness would absorb me whole, take me back into a world only a thin veneer away, like opening one's eyes from sleep. I close them and wait. When I open them, the same eternal moon studies me quietly from the heavens.

Sorrow tears into my heart like a freight train off the rails. I'm suddenly lost in worry about the tack my life is taking when I'm shaken by the sound of a gentle familiar laugh cutting through the sadness lacing my soul. The sound pulls me through the stand of palms to the edge of the break. I see in the distance, scientists and technicians laughing and drinking on the lanai, champagne in their hands; tuxedoes and sequin dresses, like watching a movie from afar.

From the shadows under the trees, I spy Lucy in a flowing azure gown, framed in the soft glow of the tiki torches. She reminds me of a fine crystalline doll I had seen years ago in the window at Tiffany's on San Francisco's Union Square; crystalline, serene, perfect.

I take the concrete walk to the guard station presenting my credentials to the Marine sergeant. He scrutinizes me closely, confirming I'm the man in the photo before waving me inside.

The soiree is bustling with the principle scientists and technicians assigned to the project, everyone looking dapper and festive. Dr. Hoffmann introduces me to the various men and women attached to his immediate sector. Many of the scientists, in particular the British, are apart from their families and no one seems wont in discussing details about *the work.* Most are enjoying drinks and conversation, others dancing to a twelve-piece band playing *swing* covers. The stage is adorned in red, white, and blue bunting and the color-guard sports the Union Jack perched beside Old Glory. The band starts a lively version of *Looking at the World Thru Rose Colored Glasses.*

Eventually I find Lucy in her stunning aquamarine dress; realize what a handsome woman she is when not draped in drab-beige coveralls with dirt and oil on her face and hands. She smiles, her eyes glinting under the torchlight.

"Good evening Commander Murphy. I was afraid you might not make it." She extracts a glass of champagne from the passing tray and places it into my hand.

"What gave you that notion?" I ask as we toast our glasses.

"Your state of mind of late. I think you've a lot on your mind lately. Like now, tonight, you're only *half* here. Part of you is…somewhere else."

We're interrupted by Lawton, Hawkins, and the bevy of scientists assigned directly to the submarine retrofit. They all seem pleased to see me, except Lawton. He's developed an evident dislike for me–a general banality at best.

It's quite obvious how appreciated Lucy has become by the American and British scientists, although a certain chauvinistic air imbues the men's words and mannerisms. I actually find myself taking offense at some of the things they say, the inferences they direct toward her gender. Is she oblivious to their ulterior meanings, or is she a more composed person than I? No, it's the times. I must not forget I'm a man *out of season.*

"What's it like?" Hawkins presses her, spilling rum atop Burke's shoes. "Those musty old halls at Cambridge…rather stuffy I should think. Not a place for a pretty girl."

"Who's *pretty* Hawk?" Burke adds. "This girl here is merely a photo double. The real Dr. Charlesworth is buried in a book somewhere."

"Or hooking up electrodes to lab rats."

"You're a *lab rat*," she rebuts, and they all share a laugh.

When Hoffmann *borrows* her, to meet an American senator in attendance, I'm left standing with Lawton and the other Britons. Dunwoody, the *manager* of the land team–those persons not involved directly with the submarine–is amongst the group of young physicists loitering about with drinks and cigarettes in their hands.

"So, Yank, surprised to see a sailor here tonight. What's your role in all this?" He lights a cigarette jutting from an ostentatious ivory holder clenched between his teeth.

"I'm the first officer of the Manta Ray. I report directly to Captain Canfield." For whatever reasons they exchange a rather cynical laugh.

"You mean the drunken sod that'll run the ship?" He exhales a stream of smoke into the air.

"Knock it off Dun," Hawkins says quietly.

"To what are you referring?" I inquire.

Dunwoody shares a look with his friends. "Everyone's heard about your captain." I've hardly a reaction to his meaning. "Your captain," he presses. "Word is he…tips the elbow, yes?" I decide not to answer the innuendo and wait as the discussion bantering between the Britons returns to me. "So then, tell us Yank, sunk very many bloody Germans?"

"Japanese," one of *the boys* says.

"Yes, yes. Sunk any Japanese lately Commodore?" I stare at the man wondering if the talk is simply drunken buffoonery.

"Bloody hell Dun, you don't just blurt out a question like that," Hawkins informs him. "He's an officer. Show some respect."

"Right-o Commander," he says imitating a salute. "*Done-in* any dirty Japs?" I decide to leave when Lawton arrests my arm.

"That's no way to get-on. The lads are just *pissed*."

"So…*Commander Murphy*," Dunwoody continues. "I've been hearing quite a lot about you lately. Tell me, what do you think about the mission?"

"What do you mean?"

"All this rigmarole." Before I can answer this vague question, he asks me about invisibility.

"I don't know anything about invisibility, the science or other." They have a hearty laugh at my expense. "However, there will come a time when we travel to the moon; send explorers into space," I say, to shut up their giddy schoolboy exchanges.

"Well, listen to the yank, off to the moon now."

"Men *will* travel to the moon, and Mars, eventually."

They all have a good laugh and slowly disperse, some of *the boys* deciding to throw darts, others refilling their drinks. Only Lawton remains.

"How do we get to the moon Commander? Please don't say in a spaceship."

"Rockets," I say and it's like ringing a bell.

"Did you say *rockets*?"

"Yes. Rockets will take men to the moon."

His gaze wanders before fixing on me. "What do you know about…rockets?"

"That they'll take mankind to the moon." He seems as if frozen.

"What have you heard? How much is known inside the States already?"

"*Known?*"

"About Cherrystone, the Jerries' program…their infernal super weapon, the vaunted V1?"

"Yes."

"*Yes* what?"

"There will be the V1…and the V2. It will be the foundation of the future American rocket program." He stares at me as if I were speaking backwards, taking my arm and gently maneuvering me further away from the others.

"What university are you working with?"

"I graduated from Vallejo High School. I did two years at the Naval Academy in Annapolis and another year in the New London submarine school."

"Come now, what program are you attached to? It's all right, I'm not as loose-lipped as my cronies."

"Program?"

"Are you purposely making me out a fool? With knowledge of this sort, you expect me to believe you're not inside OSS? Or at least American Naval Intelligence?"

We're interrupted by his friends returning with mugs full of brew. "So how goes the good fight Commodore? You blokes getting things done out here?" Dunwoody interrupts.

"Steady but sure."

"Not as we hear it. We hear back home you yanks are getting a good sound thrashing. Pretty much in retreat every corner."

"It's not over, not by a long shot. Give it two more years."

"Two more years?" Lawton asks. "For what?"

"For the end of the war," I say, and they laugh. "What's so humorous about that?"

"We doubt it'll take two years, bit less we wager. Should things go as planned."

"What do you mean?"

"What do I mean lads? Should we let our *American friend* in on it, our little secret of secrets?"

"Shut your gob Lawton, you're pissed."

"Let him go Dun, it isn't work hours," Hawkins mutters, lighting a cigarette.

"I'm just saying he's pissed, and he better watch his mouth is what."

"Forget 'ol Woody. Go ahead Lawton," Hawkins presses on valiantly. "It's your neck. Have your say." Lawton becomes suddenly quiescent.

"Go ahead, fill the yank in Lawty. He's along for the bloody thing isn't he?" Burke slurs. "He's a right to know."

"*Know* what?" I ask in the ensuing silence, their schoolboy tittering clearly masking something important left unsaid.

"This little foray to the East..." Lawton mutters, deep in thought. "It's very precarious..."

"You're going west, silly old duffer."

"Get stuffed Burke, I said *the* East."

"Well you got to go bloody west to get bloody east, eh?"

"Bollocks, you haven't a clue which way you're going Burke, you filthy drunken sod," Hawkins says dropping into a chair and crossing his gangly legs. His pinstripe suit sports cuffs sewn into the pant legs, his shoes black and white wingtips. "Now shut your trap and let old Lawton hang himself. Have at it old boy," he says toasting Lawton, everyone becoming uncomfortably reticent; no one speaks.

"Why not go bloody east first? You could stick your torpedo up Hitler's arse on the way through," Dunwoody says to break the tension, and they all have a good laugh.

"Ah, why put my head on the block for this bloke?" Lawton says. "Ask him where he went to school lads." True to Lucy's warning, I'm grilled about my education, suffering blank stares when I confide about my limited exposure to advanced education and soon, after a *good-hearted* ribbing, I'm left standing alone with a drink in my hand.

While staring out to sea, I feel a soft touch on my shoulder and she's there, resplendent in the muted light of the room.

"Hello sailor." She dons a coquettish grin. "I just heard all about your extensive education," she informs me, smiling from behind her champagne.

"Very funny."

She laughs at my response. "I told you," she chides under her breath. "They can really be snobbish about that sort of thing, downright nasty in fact. As if being British weren't enough."

"I'll manage." She takes my arm and we stroll the room, watching the couples dancing to *Someone's Rocking My Dreamboat.*

"Michael look. Aren't they lovely? The couples dancing together. So gay, despite the war…and all the pressure…"

"Would you like to dance?"

"Oh…no…I…" she blushes. "I can't dance," she whispers in my ear. "I've never learned how."

"There's nothing to *learn*. You don't use your mind Lucy. You use your…your body," I say inadvertently canvassing her womanly form. She blushes further. "Wait here a moment."

When the band finishes, I tap the alto-sax player's sleeve.

"Excuse me. Do you fellas know *Moonlight Serenade* by Glenn Miller?" He glances at Lucy waiting near the wall.

"We do it. That's in the next set." I slide him a five. He takes the bill, snapping it. "Actually, think that number's up next Admiral." The band has a quick impromptu huddle, taking their positions, the saxophone and clarinet players all standing.

The dulcet tones of the reeds penetrate the room and several couples immediately converge upon the floor. I take her hand, gently pulling her toward the dancefloor. It's nearly like dragging a boat anchor across beach sand.

"Michael, stop it. I really don't know what to do," she whispers. "Michael…"

"It's easy. Take my hand…now put your arm around my shoulders. Now…just let go."

"I don't know how."

"Lucy…trust me. Let go." She melts into my arms and we sway to the soft melody of the music. The eyes of the other couples follow us, smiling.

She puts her cheek to mine. "Everyone is watching us," she says into my ear.

"I know," I say, lost within the tranquility of her embrace. She lays her head against my shoulder and we sway, becoming invisible together, the rest of the world disappearing like smoke in a breeze. When the song ends, we stroll the lanai under the moonlight.

Her dress glows under the lunar radiance, the color melding with the nocturnal tones of the Pacific. She takes the full of my arm, breathing in deeply, the ocean waves sighing with her breath. For just a fraction of an instance, I feel it, peace on earth.

"Lucy...how is it that you've ended up here, on *Shadowfox*, such a dangerous project?"

"Meaning?"

"Well, you're so young and...well...a woman." Her eyes silently fathom mine. She nudges me under the moonshadow of the palms rimming the lanai. We're alone together, within the gentle embrace of night, the ocean radiant above the trees and darkened rooftops.

"My mother has a doctorate in mathematics, became involved with British Intelligence, one of several female mathematicians solving certain mathematical problems at a tiny place in Buckinghamshire you've never heard of."

"Bletchley? Bletchley Park?" She seems to go numb

"How on earth...? How could you know about Bletchley Park? That's a complete secret. Have you been talking with Dr. Hoffmann behind my back?"

"I remember it was a place where they employed a lot of British women, mathematicians. It was where they created Colossus, wasn't it?" She places her hand tightly across my mouth, waits for the couple to stroll pass us under the moonlight before pulling me further into the shadows.

"Michael...for god's sake...how? How could you know about Colossus? Why the mere thought of it is...fantastical."

"I remember something about it...from years ago."

Her eyes dilate wildly. "Michael...I'm sorry but I'm extremely uncomfortable discussing this. Colossus is highly secret, and very, very new...why the mere thought...? If I didn't know better...I'd think you were a government agent."

"No. I'm the person you think I am Lucy."

"How could you know these things?" She waits.

"I don't know." Her eyes narrow. "Let's return to the subject we were talking about, how you became involved with the experiment. You were talking about your mother."

She shakes her head, as if waking from a dream. "Yes. Mum. Right. She's brilliant, however, she was shunned by the scientific elite of her day. I pray this doesn't sound bitter, but women are often relegated to the back-row in English scientific aristocracy; plagiarized, men taking credit for their work. Mum was such a casualty. Fifteen years of highly detailed work, stolen out from beneath her by a male colleague…and this was allowed, considered acceptable, because of her gender."

"That's awful. I'm sorry to hear it."

"I believe that's the reason she pushed me so hard to exceed. Mum was obsessed with my becoming successful in the field of physics. All this, *desire,* was compounded when they discovered my intelligence quotient was off the charts," she says without the slightest air of hubris.

"She wanted you to be a physicist?"

"I was being groomed to follow in her footsteps, taken out of public school, away from my friends, sequestered with a bunch of crabby old men who resented my presence. I'm sorry Michael, I'm blathering. I doubt you want to hear all this." I gently brush strands of hair from her cheek, touch the fine contours of her face. She takes my hand and we continue to walk under the shadows.

"Please. Go on."

"Well…I was tutored in physics and chemistry, inundated is the better word. Mum wanted me to be a physicist, but I wanted to sail. Dad took me often. Something about the sea, its mystery, pulling me."

"You learned how to sail?"

"I can navigate a two-mast ketch…the *Theodora*. She had a main and a mizzen-sail. Dad even rigged a spinnaker."

"I didn't realize you had a love for the sea."

"Either it was Dad or…the freedom from those drab old rooms, the smell of chalk and body odor replaced by the scent of the ocean. Those moldy monotonous voices replaced by the sounds of the sea." She turns and our eyes lock. Timeless. I want to take her in my arms, need to, desperately.

The moment is interrupted by Lawton. "Lucy, the party's gone horribly dull. The lads are stealing off downtown for a bit of fun. Care to join in?" She looks into me, contemplating something deeply. "C'mon love, it'll be fun," he presses.

"Alright. In a moment."

"Grand. We're leaving in just a few minutes. Cheers," he says to me smugly, sauntering back to his colleagues loitering at the makeshift bar; white linen sheets laid across a series of desks butted up to one another.

"Well, you get to go back to your wife Mr. Murphy. Tell her we appreciate lending you to us for the evening." Her eyes penetrate mine. She sees more than I had hoped. "What's that look?"

"Nothing."

"Hardly *nothing*. Mr. Murphy, if we're going to have a successful working arrangement then it needs to be based upon trust." Her gaze is unrelenting. There's no avoiding the question.

"We're separated. She's staying with her sister." I decide not to elaborate further.

"I don't believe it. Why, just the other day I saw you and her-" She catches herself. I realize she must have seen me kissing Hildy in the reception area at Naval HQ.

"This branch of the service can be a little rough on marriages." Her eyes penetrate deeper into mine. "She's asked me to leave the service. Quit the Navy."

"Michael...I'm sorry." I see the concern form on her face, pure, like looking into something beautiful or sacred.

"Come on then Lucy, we're off!" Lawton beckons and the young technician's intrusion brushes aside any further conversation. Before she leaves, she extends her hand, the color of porcelain beneath moonlight; our grasp longer than I expect.

"Take care Mr. Murphy," she whispers, an inner radiance within her pupils. Or is it the moon's reflection casting a brilliance on the surface of her eyes? They descend on her like ants, wrapping her shawl about her shoulders, steering her toward the door and she's ushered off into the night. After they leave, Hoffmann joins me on the lanai wearing a strange smile.

"You know something Commander? I've grown very fond of that young lady. A singularly special person, unlike any other woman I've known. Please don't repeat this. She would dislike my saying it openly, but despite her keen intellect, there's something I find innocently charming about her that sets her apart from so many women with their fanciful ideas, expectations and selfish pursuits."

"She's a very unique person." He smiles anew. "What is it sir?"

"That's a perfect word, *unique*. Well, good evening Commander."

Soon, I'm alone, everyone having either left for Honolulu or retired to the bungalows adjacent the laboratory complex. The band is quietly wrapping out. An old janitor is asleep in the corner with his broom while the catering team is pouring drinks from vagrant bottles of whiskey and gin.

<hr>

The moon gazes down from her soft billowy firmament; night clouds sprinkled with silver stardust. The caterer cranks up an old portable Victrola, setting the needle to the platter; *They All Fall in Love* by Will Osborne and his orchestra. He pours a shot from one of the derelict bottles and hands it to me. I raise it to the moon, peering at us through the windows.

"Your Highness." I tip my cap to the barmen before wandering through the chaos left of the party back to the car. The parking lot is eerily quiet, glowing under the radiant moon. As I open the door of the Plymouth, I hear a familiar voice emanate from the darkness beneath the stand of palms.

"Spare a light?" I step into the shadows, my eyes adjusting to the dark. A tall thin Briton juts a cigarette out between us. "Spare a light *Yank*?"

"Hawkins? Sorry. I don't smoke."

"Bloody Yank," he curses pulling a lighter from his pants pocket and lighting his cigarette.

"What are you doing here?" I ask. He scans the entire lot before closing the distance between us.

"Don't go home tonight Commander." I'm speechless. He draws hard on the cigarette before tossing it into the bushes. "Don't go home tonight. Go anywhere else. Get a room. Find a bar or an all-night diner. Just…don't go home." With those words he climbs behind the wheel of a Packard and tears off into the night. I'm left standing there like a kid jilted on a prom date. I climb into the Plymouth, inadvertently grinding the gears, and set off into the night, the derelict streets eerily vacant.

That night, I'm dreaming, a contentious dream. I'm fighting with several men, fighting for my life. When I fully awaken, it's all too real. The dream is imitating a stark reality. I'm being forced from my bed by MPs in plain white uniforms.

Two of the men pin my arms behind my back while a male nurse is preparing to inject me with a hypodermic needle. I kick this man in the gut. He doubles over dropping the hypo, causing the sailors to trip me onto my stomach, one of the men shoving my face into the floor with such force I think he's going to break my neck.

"Don't fight us Commander Murphy. Come along quiet-like and you won't get your arm broke." They attempt to tie my wrists with a rope. I twist free and slam my fist across the master-sergeant's jaw, drawing him off. However, the other man holds on as if his life depended on it.

The sergeant catches blood in his hand, cursing. "You son-of-a-bitch!" he shouts, kicking me in the side and I feel a rib snap. They land on my back, a knee across my neck and the two men tie my hands, pulling me to my feet. The last thing I see is Hildy in the doorway, her hand over her mouth, a military police captain pulling her away. I feel an impact at the base of my skull and the lights go out.

Chapter 8: The Squeeze

*B*lack turns to gray then into a painful brilliant white.

"Commander Murphy, do you know why you're here?" keeps repeating in my head until the fog clears, and fear takes hold. I'm in a shoddily padded room, locked in a bleach-white straight-jacket. Everything is the color of snow, except the olive-green uniform of the Army colonel.

"You've placed me in a psycho ward?"

"This isn't a *psycho ward* Commander Murphy, rather an interment room."

"Interment, interrogation, whatever you choose to call it, let me out of this jacket. Let's talk like civilized men."

"Civilized? You broke the jaw of my guard."

"He was trying to crack my vertebra. Why not send someone who knows how to knock on a door?"

"My name is Karnes. You can call me *Colonel* or *Sir*. State your name for the record."

"My name? Delano Roosevelt."

Karnes glares at the master-sergeant beside him. "Leave him until his head clears." The lights are turned out. I'm left sitting in a silent blacked-out room without food or water for hours.

Day two, they remove the jacket. "You've no right to keep me locked-up like this. What is this some kind of puppet court?"

"We've every right to keep you as long as we deem necessary."

"How? Why?"

"Your wife, Murphy."

"My wife?"

"She's reported you insane."

"That's not true and you know it."

"Commander, have you ever been anyone else?"

"*Anyone else?*"

"Another person?"

"You mean like in a play, on a stage?"

"On a patrol, when you impacted your head."

"You know about that. It was reported. I was treated and released."

"Who were you while in this other persona?"

"I don't understand the question."

"Didn't you tell others, including your wife, that you know about things that will happen in the future, things based on a firsthand knowledge of such a place…isn't that so Mr. Murphy?"

"I had delusions after the concussion." He scans the files on the desk. "What people are you talking about? Who?"

"Did you not tell pharmacist Cooper, and other members of your crew, that you had travelled back in time and knew about…" he flips through some papers on the table, "…*television*…and *advanced wireless technology?* Didn't you tell your wife and her sister, you were from the future? That you know about future events before they happen?"

"Okay, I read a few of Connie Howard's comic books. Just some post-patrol fun and games…that's all it was."

He closes the folder and smirks. "That's all it was." He slams his palm atop the table and glares. "We got all the time in the world Murphy. All the time in the world. However, you don't. You're going to be our guest for a little while. Let me know when you're ready to talk."

He collects his papers and exits the room with the sergeant. The lights are switched off and a black, absolute silence follows for the next several hours, the room void of light, food, or water.

Incredibly, I'm back onboard the Manta Ray, the submarine not allowing anyone near me. They curse and rail, spitting obscenities from the dock until she races her engines growling like a wild animal, blasting her airhorn and the men onshore scatter like roaches. I touch her gunwales and the boat purrs, the sound similar to the purring of a large predator cat; a lion or tiger. In the middle of this comforting dream they shake me violently awake.

"Rise and shine Murphy. We want answers." It's Karnes with two of his sergeants. They shine bright lights into my eyes and the questions are renewed in earnest. I'm peppered relentlessly with a rotating series of questions about *Phoenix.*

"Again, Commander Murphy. What do you know about the Phoenix project?"

"I've already answered that question. Nothing."

"Phoenix, Commander Murphy, attached to Shadow-fox. Tell me what you know about it."

"As I've already said, repeatedly, we've no program attached to us by that name."

"We're not speaking about maneuvers Commander…the Phoenix program. Your program."

"Get to the point, you mean Shadow-fox, the Manta Ray retrofit."

"I *mean* Phoenix, attached to Shadow-fox, the advanced weapons component of the mission. Tell me everything you know about it."

"There is no *Phoenix* attached to us, to Shadow-fox."

"We've got all night Murphy if you want to play it that way? We got all the time in the world."

"You keep reminding me of that. There is no *Phoenix* attached to us. I'm sorry but you're mistaken."

"I'll say it again. We've got all the time in the world; days, weeks, months if I deem it necessary. I own you Murphy. Own you. I'm going to squeeze until you either break or come clean." He repeats the same series of meaningless questions over and over again, until they feed me bread and water before turning out the lights and I'm left to ponder my dilemma in total darkness.

Early day three, I'm violently awakened by Karnes and his sergeants. A Briton sits with the colonel this time. I can't make out his face clearly due to the light they shine in my eyes, but his voice sounds familiar somehow. Did I chance to meet him that night at the party?

"Commander Murphy, is it true you told several of the British scientists that America possessed a rocket program, that was in essence, a space flight program?"

"Who told you that?"

"We've sworn statements already in our possession. Answer the question."

"I told your man Lawton that I thought one day man would travel to the moon."

"Based on what technology?"

"The obvious."

"Explain."

"We'll attempt it by any *expedient* means at our disposal."

He shuffles through his stack of notes. "Did you not tell the British science team that mankind would arrive by what you referred to as *a rocket*?"

"How else would you assume it done *expediently*?"

"What do you know about rockets Commander?"

"Nothing, except the Germans will be bombing London with them soon." There's a pause as the Briton whispers with Karnes.

"Why would you think that?"

"Because it's inevitable. Hitler is a sociopath, and a murderer."

The two men speak together, and the Americans reluctantly vacate the room before the Briton readdresses me, his voice nearly a whisper. "Commander Murphy, what do you know about project *Candlewick*?"

"Nothing."

"Nothing?"

"Yes. Nothing."

"What about operation *Cherrystone*?"

"I heard Lawton, use that phrase for the first time the other night."

"What do you know about it?"

"Nothing."

"Come now Commander, please be forthcoming."

"The party was the first and only time I've ever heard that phrase."

The man in the powder-blue suit stares at me through the glare, silently contemplating something before pressing a button and the colonel and his sergeant reenter the room; the entire series of questions repeated. After a third and fourth round of exhaustive inquiry, the man exits the room. Karnes gathers his papers and another extensive blackout ensues, eventually followed by a fifth, sixth and seventh round of the same senseless questions, the constant glare of white light burning in my eyes, the drone of their voices echoing like a hollow empty wind through my soul.

That night I have a lucid dream, at least I think it a dream; Lucy beside me in the darkness. *'Michael, I'm going to get you out of here. I don't care what it takes. I won't leave you alone in this place.'* Due to my exhaustion and depleted state, or perhaps the caress of her fingers, imaginary or other, I can't hold onto consciousness.

Day five? I'm interrogated by Karnes, for hours. "Murphy tell us more about the delusions you suffered after your fall. Let it out. Get it off your chest and we can get you back to your life again."

"I've told you, repeatedly. There's nothing to tell. I suffered a concussion which-"

"Murphy, it'll go better for you if you tell us the facts in detail. Start at the beginning. If you cooperate, there's a roast beef dinner with baked potato and sour cream waiting in the commissary. Probably even a cold beer. How about it?"

"There's nothing else to tell. As I said yesterday, and the day before that, I had delusions, a few bad dreams, nothing new in my line of work."

"Murphy, what is your other name?"

"My name is Lieutenant Commander Michael J. Murphy, the 'J' stands for…for nothing."

"What about your other name? Your name from the future?" Like a bad movie, the questions repeat themselves over and over again, ad infinitum, until the lights are turned out and I'm left to sit silently in the dark with my bread and water, my feeble thoughts and rapidly fading memories. In the darkness, my mind dreams of Lucy, her gentle ways, until sleep frees me of the torment enclosing me from all sides.

"Murphy tell us about Phoenix, the Phoenix program, start at the beginning." Day five, or six? I can no longer remember.

"What do you know about these weapons systems? How do they work? What technology? Who has told you what? It's better Murphy if you come clean. Clear your mind of all the details. It'll feel good Murphy to get it off your chest once and for all. You can return to your home. Go ahead, start from the beginning." More bad dreams…

I'm asleep in the darkness when the lights come on and several persons are suddenly filing into the room. How long has it been? I can feel my beard growth. I squint at the men lined before me. A solemn group of civilians, flanking Rear-Admiral Hess.

"We don't recognize your authority in this matter Admiral. This is no longer a Navy concern, or even a military matter. This is about national security."

"You're suggesting a goddamn presidential summons Colonel?"

"I can only accept orders from the State Department, on State Department letterhead."

"I'll deliver your letterhead up your ass Colonel. Hand-fed!" I can hear his teeth grinding from ten feet away.

"Are you threatening me Admiral?"

"This is the only time I'm coming over here. Release this man immediately or come hell-or-highwater I'll have your ass in a sling."

"There's no reason to get violent Admiral. This matter doesn't concern you."

Hess stations himself staunchly before Karnes. "There's a war on you dunderhead! You think we've time for this bull? Release Commander Murphy immediately, on my direct order, or by thunder soldier, I'll keelhaul you alive!"

"Admiral Hess, this man knows too much. He's a national security threat."

"Dammit man, he's a goddamn submarine commander and one of the project's senior officers. He's been cleared. Read the goddamn order!" Hess shakes the letter at Karnes.

He peruses the form. "I can't accept this."

The Admiral blows. "Get your commanding officer's ass down here soldier before I personally rip your guts out! And it better be the boss. I'm not leaving without Commander Murphy and we're leaving, now," he says gesturing to the civilians. "Pack him out gentlemen."

Karnes picks up the telephone at his station. "Get me Brigadier General Haddow."

Haddow is a severe, heavy-set man of sixty-plus years, perhaps older. "It's a simple question Carl, *who* is requesting his release?"

"Besides Lance? The director of the OSS."

"OSS?" Haddow paces in thought. "It's out of my hands Carl. Colonel Karnes is indicating the man is possibly schizophrenic."

"Because he had a marital spat? Wes…"

"If he's become schizophrenic, it could jeopardize the security of the mission. Now be honest, why take the risk? The Navy is brimming with fine young men Carl, all eager to take the helm of your ships. Pick up the phone, make a call."

He leads Haddow away from the others, inadvertently nearer to me. "Wes, if Murphy's not on that boat…Dr. Charlesworth is refusing to continue with the project."

"You can't be serious? On what grounds?"

"Security."

"The entire project is dark Admiral. There's been no leaks. Our cover stories are making the curious look stupid. Security? Ridiculous. We're taking the utmost precautions."

"I'm not talking about *project* security Wesley. We're talking about *her* security."

"*Her* security? What about it?"

"She's stated emphatically to the upper echelon that Murphy is the only one she trusts. She won't *go transit* unless he's reassigned."

"She can't do that. Have the woman arrested."

"She's a civilian, and a British national. We've no jurisdiction over her other than a sworn statement of silence, which she's abiding to. She simply will not go transit without Commander Murphy onboard that submarine."

"Carl, this is highly irregular."

"Incarcerating an officer on my staff is *irregular* General."

"I admit Karnes is a little aggressive, but there's supposedly good reasons they've taken it to these lengths, based on the information."

"Dammit Wes, your people have had this man locked up here for days. Not one shred of evidence indicates a crime has occurred, or that he's unfit for duty."

"Karnes thinks-"

"I don't give a rat's ass what Karnes thinks. This is no laughing matter. Dr. Charlesworth is stating, in no uncertain terminology, she will not leave port without this man onboard and she's submitted a rather blunt statement to the British ambassador as to why."

"It'll destroy her career."

"She knows it. She's accepted that consequence."

"Have her discredited and replaced."

"Neuman and Hoffmann have made it clear. Without Dr. Charlesworth remaining with the project the launch will be delayed, possibly months."

Haddow silently rages. "Stupid frivolous...*woman*."

"Is a genius, indispensable. Without that *woman* aboard, this entire mission is delayed, potentially scrapped."

"It's ridiculous. He's just a submarine commander. Have her superiors held accountable."

"Even if we did, we're in the same situation. We're in too deep at this point. She's the linchpin of the project. We're only days from a launch."

"But Carl, this man needs to be diagnosed properly."

"A bump on the head Wesley, we've a few dozen affidavits on our end. Your people have come up blank. Sign the release." He stares at the form on the table.

"Split personality Carl? You think you know all about that too I suppose?"

"He saw double for a few hours, a concussion. Goddammit General. I've sent three subordinates over here and they came back empty three times. I'm not coming down here again. Wes, you do understand, this is a *very special man's* pet-project? No one upstairs is laughing…all the way to the top. Sign it before this goes any higher." He waits out the expected duration of time, giving us all a thorough *looking-over* then starts to sign the document.

"General, you're not authorized to sign that letter."

Haddow glares at Karnes, then the master of the guard. "Major Cook escort the colonel out. I think he'll be going on vacation soon, very soon…minus several bars of his rank!"

"This isn't over yet Murphy," Karnes shouts, vacating the room. Haddow hands the form to one of the civilians loitering near the Admiral; glares at me then abruptly exits the room.

Hess takes my shoulder. "Let's get a cut of Filet Mignon down your throat son. Put this fiasco behind us."

I'm helped into the Admiral's car with the assistance of his adjutant. "He can barely walk Admiral. Shall we take him to the infirmary?"

"What and let those parasites get ahold of him again? Take him to my home Cortland. He doesn't need a doctor he needs a pot of navy beans and a fifth of bourbon."

The twilight car-ride up the mountain is like driving to heaven; fresh air and the smell of tropical fauna coursing through the opened window of the black Lincoln Continental. The sudden rush of oxygen makes me pass-out during the drive. When I awaken, I'm being helped into an elegant home high up in the hills overlooking Honolulu. Despite the blackout, the city twinkles in the darkness, sporadic lights, up and down the coast, cut across an absolute black shoreline.

Marilyn Hess walks me into her stately home and helps me into a soft velvety bed still wearing my shoes. I can hear her through the door of the bedroom. "My god Carl. He must have lost ten pounds. What are those people doing there?"

"Wasting the taxpayer's money."

"Well do something about it."

"I just did!" Silence. "I'm sorry Meg. I promised not to drag the job home and here it is, in the next room. Dammit."

"It's fine dear. What should I do about the dinner sitting on the table?"

"Just leave it. Let him sleep." The doorbell sounds. I hear the soft muttering of voices inside the home then the sound of Admiral Lance entering the living-room outside my door.

"Hope I'm not interrupting anything?"

"Phil, what brings you out? Meg, will you mix Phil a drink?"

"Bourbon on ice Admiral?"

"Just a half. Thank-you Marilyn. How's he doing?"

"What kind of shoddy operation is the Army running Phil? The man looks worse than a POW."

"Did he say anything?"

"He could hardly walk. He's passed-out. Apparently starving a man to death is the Army's idea of interrogation. When was torture by starvation put back on the docket?"

"Get him moved to the *Prometheus*. Better yet, have him berthed directly in the Manta Ray. Let's not take any chances at this point. We're only days from a *go*."

"You got it Admiral."

"What the hell happened Carl? I want it from the beginning." They're interrupted when Marilyn arrives with Lance's drink.

"Meg, could you give us a minute? In private."

"And run the risk of being interrogated by Colonel Karnes? I'll be in the bath dear. Goodnight Phil." I smell Hess light a cigar.

"What happened Carl?"

"I arranged a little party at the compound, for Hoffmann and his people. They've been working their tails off. I thought a little booze session with some music might smooth out a few nerves. There's a lot of tension over this launch."

"So I've heard."

"Anyway, for some hair-brained reason Hoffmann invited Murphy, without my permission. While at the party, Murphy told the Limeys a bunch of cock-and-bull stories about spaceships or some such garbage. One of their boys went straight to Haddow."

There's a pause in the room. "What's all this about his wife Carl, and her sister? I heard she called it in. Care to elaborate on that point?" I can hear Hess pace the room, his voice quieting considerably.

"Dammit to hell Phil…how do I know how a woman thinks? I've been married to one for forty years and I still don't understand them. They say one thing…then do the opposite. It's a goddamn shame." Another drawn out pause, I can hear Lance light a cigarette with a Zippo.

"Carl, I'll be honest with you. I don't like this assignment. Off the record, I think this whole crazy scheme is a waste of valuable time and money. Scientific hoopla. But what am I supposed to do about that? Say no? I take my orders from the top. Those people back in Princeton and London say this crazy idea will work. So, my job is to see the President's wishes through successfully, regardless how I feel about it."

"But we *are* having success Phil. Hell, this little setback is nothing to get-"

"Murphy talked about rockets with the British. How do you suppose he knew anything about rocket technology?"

"You got me Admiral. Any ideas?"

"It had to come from your desk Carl. Canfield conveniently overheard something that was said, and Murphy got it from him."

"Negative Admiral. Not a chance in hell. I don't talk about that, and certainly not with Canfield."

"How could Murphy know about our emerging rocket program, the intelligence we're getting out of Germany? Hell, he knew about the German V1 *and* V2 buildup, and what they're intending to do. How do you suppose a Navy submarine officer gains access to this kind of information?"

"I don't know, but I can guarantee it didn't come from my desk. Guaranteed." Silence.

"How in hell could a lieutenant commander know about the Nazi rocket program? It's the craziest thing I've ever heard." I hear Hess refilling his glass.

"Have him ordered to the Manta Ray Carl. Keep him assigned. Have a warrant officer attached to keep an eye on things."

"Already done. Hell, why soil your shorts over it? When the *Krauts* start dropping rockets on London, the world will know all about it."

"Construction was halted on the *Kentucky* and the *Hawaii*. Have a guess as to why?"

"They're too big. The reign of the battleship is over."

"That's the cover story. We've suspended work on these ships because they're intending to add rockets to their armament. In a few years, the rocket will become the Navy's principle weapons system. The *Kentucky's* sixteen-inch guns are scrap-metal Carl. In the *not-too-distant-future,* the United States Navy will be using guided missiles with exceptional range and accuracy to counter enemy carriers. Everything's changing Carl…we're older than the ships under our very own feet."

"*Phoenix* is a rocket program too?"

"Not exactly."

"Well what the hell is it? Why am I being kept in the dark?"

"*What is it?* An opinion."

"An *opinion?*"

"The opinion of the President…that atomic energy not be limited to merely defensive concerns but be tested offensively in the field. This little foray in the submarine is an experiment."

Silence.

"What can I do for you Phil? Or should I step aside? Hell, if I'm becoming a briar under your rump, I'll gladly get the hell out of the way."

"Carl...I brought you in as my second on this because you're an excellent judge of men. I backed you on the situation regarding Canfield but now, in lieu of these new developments, I'm considering a new skipper."

"I smell Greene."

"He's making it an issue. Threatening to take it over my head. This nonsense with Haddow shows how serious it's become."

"It would be a tragic mistake. Greene knows nothing about submarine warfare, what's actually going on out there. Look at his choice of skipper. John Bradshaw? A goddamn monkey with bars on his sleeve, a *yes* man, everything by the book. Well *the book* doesn't always work in the battle-zone."

"Greene doesn't trust Canfield."

"I don't trust Greene."

"Let's not start that over again. He thinks Canfield is unpredictable. Frankly, so do I."

"You're right Admiral. He is. Canfield's a sonofabitch Phil, why do you think I want Murphy onboard? But that *sonofabitch* is the only sub skipper I know that might, just might, weasel his boney ass through the Uraga Strait, deliver *the baby* and get out alive. They're writing off Hoffmann and Charlesworth, the whole damn boat, but I intend to get those people back home, alive. I'm making it a personal matter."

"Then it's settled. We'll assign two skippers to the mission. *Transit*, and *deployment*, just as Greene wants it."

"Another of his brilliant ideas. Phil, the man's as dumb as a mule with balls! You can't have two skippers on one boat. That's just asking for trouble."

"I'm juggling a lot of pieces here. Greene's responsible for the success of Phoenix. He can have it. The weapons component on the mission is...weird...psychotic."

"And there's another load of horseshit Phil. How the hell can you take out an entire carrier task force with one torpedo? Only some cockamamie scientist could think that one up. The idea is ludicrous."

"Carl…"

"Those people in New Jersey are out of their minds. I get the invisibility thing, sort of. That's why our boat will be packing a dozen Mark 14s when she crosses the strait, but *Phoenix*? Horseshit. Let me top off your glass. Phil, what's behind all this *crazy scheming* as you call it? Whose horn is up our ass? What's Chet saying?"

"It's MacArthur. That egotistical fool is trying to get our plan shelved. The *good general* is dead set on a run through the Philippines."

"And a run for the presidency."

"It'll be costly. We could lose over a quarter million men, possibly more. They're predicting over a hundred thousand US casualties in the Philippines alone, and for what?"

"So some narcissistic ass can have his cake, relive a former glory. Backup a handful of words he blew out of his *patoot* when the Japs kicked his butt off the island two years ago. Is the President onboard with our plan or not?"

"*Galvanic* is a go. Spruance hits Tarawa in a month."

"Hot damn. Good. What then?"

"Follow the plan. Press through the Marshalls. It won't be easy, but a lot more economical than slugging our way through the New Guinea and Borneo jungles."

"They're saying the nips are proving to be true jungle fighters. They know how to live off the land. Our boys will catch hell by the yard."

"The Nimitz plan will end all that. We'll cut off Japan's entire southern garrison. None of those soldiers will fire a single shot."

"The Navy's right Phil. Japan's overextended. Our submarines are proving it. The Army's got its head up its ass, wasting valuable time…and people."

"Exactly the sentiments from above. *Shadow-Fox* is an even more direct application of the plan; small, quick, and quiet, the potential pay-off…immeasurable. Should this *crazy scheme* go as hoped, they think we'll have the Japanese at the table before MacArthur has his boots on the ground in Manila."

The following morning, I'm moving out of the tiny house that had served as my home. Burlsley parks the jeep and squints at me in the morning sun.

"You want I should help you pack out Mr. Murphy?" He's armed with a Colt .45 strapped to his hip; the sleeves of his fatigues rolled up over his biceps. *Anywhere. Anytime. Pacific,* another of our boat's mottos, is tattooed on his arm in cursive. Our Bosun carefully scans the entirety of the boulevard. I see it clearly in his manner, the seriousness of what has happened; his assignment, get me to the Manta Ray, unconditionally.

"No thanks Gil. I'll be right out."

"Take all the time you need Commander Murphy. I'm just itching to shoot someone. Especially if he's Army."

'*Take only the smallest, most important items.*' Marching orders from the Admiral's staff. Strangely, very little seems of import at all, as if the idea of being suddenly free of these material objects is a blessing in disguise. I'm going back to live within the Manta Ray, the twin sides of my nature pulling me in opposite directions yet again. I'm saying good-bye to a deep, personal part of my life; realize when I step outside, I'll never be returning to this house nor the life that was contained within it.

A hollow feeling opens up inside me, from my very center. I realize, if I allow it to grow, it will consume me.

The various objects sitting about in the dull lazy light wandering in from the ocean look strange and foreign. I feel as if I'm standing on the very edge of the world, about to set sail into the complete unknown; how to let go? Upon the divan sits the shattered remains of the photograph. I stare at the man contained within the bent frame; her husband. The man she once knew.

"It's happened. What I feared most. I've ruined your life," I say to the picture. He smiles, unknowing. I quickly pack my duffel and exit the house as if it were on fire.

Outside, the Carpenter boys are standing at attention on the front stoop in proper rank and file, saluting. I set my satchel down and despite the pain in my ribs, take a knee.

"Where you going Mr. Murphy?" Jason inquires, concern coursing his young face.

"To my boat fellas," I mutter, clearing the lump in my throat.

"Golly, already?"

"Pretty soon Jace."

"Where's Mrs. Murphy?" Alex inquires.

"She's at her sister's house."

"Why?" The wind caresses their hair, the color of beach sand.

"It's a little bit complicated fellas."

"When will you be back?" Jason interjects. I stare at them, the blue in their eyes not altogether different than the color of the Pacific on a clear day. We're interrupted by the voice of their mother from across the hedge.

"Come along boys. Mr. Murphy has to report to his ship."

One last wayward look over his shoulder; Jace's eyes filling with water.

———

After she's directed the children back into her home, she looks at me, the wind off the ocean blowing thin strands of hair across her pale blue eyes, the same hue as her children's, only more faded, like a worn pair of dungarees.

"I'm sorry to hear you're leaving. You and Hildy have been such good neighbors."

"Thank-you. I appreciate you saying it." She looks sad. Somehow, she knows. A tightness forms in my chest. "Well, take care." As I head for the jeep, she stops me.

"Mr. Murphy, please be careful. Please make it home safe and sound, wherever that might be in the future." Her eyes grow misty. "I pray for you every day you're at war. You're all so very young, and so very far away."

"Thank-you Agnes." There's nothing more to say. She watches while I pack the jeep. As we drive down the boulevard, I can see her in the mirror solemnly waving.

At the front gate of the base, Burlsley is belayed by the MP. "End of the line Commander. They'll take you down in a shuttle. I'm heading back to Honolulu." He lowers his voice. "Skipper's AWOL again. Third time this week." They transfer my bags to a truck, and we trundle down to the waterline.

When I make dockside, I'm stunned. The sub is nowhere to be seen. In its place is an escort destroyer. An odd *emptiness* saturates me; the icy fingers of loneliness. Have they left without me? I grab the arm of a passing sailor.

"Where is the Manta Ray?"

"The what?"

"The Manta Ray. Have they left port already?"

"She an escort or a tender?"

"The fleet-boat that was berthed here."

"You mean the submarine going through refit? Between the escort and the sub-tender." He points to a gangplank abaft the destroyer's superstructure. "Don't bother Lieutenant. No one is allowed over there." I thank him and present my credentials to the guard. As I cross athwartships, I'm stopped by one of the ship's petty officers.

"Hey buddy. How'd you get in here?" I present my credentials. "*Commander Murphy*. We were told to expect you. Follow me sir." When we make the starboard side of the ship, I'm shocked. Berthed between the destroyer and the *Prometheus*, our flotilla's submarine-tender, floats the Manta Ray; every inch of the boat painted a deep flat-black, her sail, radar, guns, everything."

"Why is she painted black?" I ask the young officer beside me.

"Sir?"

"Never mind. Thank-you Ensign." I salute him and take the ladder-stair down to the deck of the submarine. They've suspended dark screen netting between the Prometheus and the escort obscuring the submarine from all sides and above. When I make the deck of our boat, two Navy MPs with batons and a petty officer, guard the entrance to the hatchway below. The petty officer looks over my credential.

"Welcome back aboard Commander Murphy," he says amicably. When I attempt to descend into the boat, they present me with a blindfold.

"What's this?"

"A blindfold sir."

I stare at the man. "You're joking of course?"

"No sir. Admiral Bennett's orders." I'm incredulous, reluctantly allow them to blind my eyes and direct me to the hatch. "Climb on down Commander. I'll bring your duffel."

When I make the bottom of the ladder, he steers me through the boat in the direction of the officer's cabins.

"Ensign, is this necessary? You do realize I'm assigned to the mission?"

"Yes sir. I'm well aware of that sir...just a little further. Watch your head." He shoves my head under the port leading toward the wardroom. "Here we are," he says, untying the blind. "Surprise Commander."

I'm suddenly surrounded by the salutations and smiling faces of nearly every man on the crew, everyone crowding the gangway and officer's billets. They've laced the wardroom with pink bunting and there's an enormous cake with white cream frosting on the table.

"Welcome back Mr. Murphy," Porteru says, pointing at the cake. "Red-velvet, your favorite." I'm assailed by the crew; pushed, shoved, poked and prodded by nearly every man assigned the detail. Coffee pinches my waist. "Skinny as a heron. We'll be getting that baby-fat back on soon enough you bet." He cuts into the cake, sailors vying for position to get the first piece.

"Gosh Lieutenant, we wasn't so sure we was gonna see you, from what we was hearing and all."

"What's the deal Pat, that the new English?" Lesky asks, and a minor scuffle ensues, Binkershon breaking it up.

"Recede gentlemen, give the man room to breathe." Binkershon steers me toward the petty officer's cabin. "Gangway ladies, move aside, officer on the deck. Murph, we got your sack all made out in ribbons and bows." They've stuffed my bunk with soap, deodorant, a fruit basket and mouthwash. "Take a look. Toiletries, perfume, nothing but the best," he says slapping my shoulder and the whole crew gets a good laugh. Collins jams a fifth of rum into my chest.

"To the best *Exec* in Uncle Sam's ever-loving Navy," he says, punching my shoulder and Stewart ruffles my hair.

"Thanks fellas. I appreciate it. More than you realize."

"We figured we wanted you to feel at home Murph. As much as, well…you get the picture." I gaze at the faces gathered around me. Faces of all colors, from many different places; like brothers.

A sudden profound silence hovers over us, when Chief Bremer's voice thunders through the compartment. "Okay girls give the Exec some space. Let's go, clear the compartment," and the crew crowding the rooms and hallway slowly disperse. Only Stewart and Taylor loiter.

"You all set here? You need anything?"

"I'm all set Bill, thanks."

"Mike, we heard about what happened. Let us know if you need anything…need to talk."

"Thanks, but I'm putting it behind me for now."

"Good deal," Stewart says ruffling my hair again. "We got a boat full of crap to get sorted Murph. Skipper's fit to be tied. He's chewing everybody out left and right. It'll be good to have his old *punching bag* back."

"I'll be up in a minute."

Taylor lingers. "Did you see Dr. Charlesworth since you arrived?"

"No, I haven't. Why?"

"She was pretty concerned about you…very concerned. I suppose she'd appreciate it if you checked-in. They've a lab set-up over in the Prometheus, in their machine shop. Poor kid, she's surrounded by dirt and filth. A sub-tender is no place for a lady."

"Bill, did she miss any of her calls? I mean, was she absent…for a period of time?"

He cocks his head. "*Absent?*"

"Away on leave? Any trips into Honolulu…or over to Hickman?"

"I don't think so. Fifteen hours *on,* every day. That gal is tougher than she looks. They're making great progress on the installation. We may be sailing in a day or two."

"Good…thanks." He hovers in the doorway. "Is there something else?"

"You hear the news Mike?"

"What news?"

"It could be just sailor scuttlebutt, but I hope and pray it's true. The *fly-boys* are saying they shot down Admiral Yamamoto's plane last month. They're saying he's dead. It's probably too good to be true."

"No. It is true," I say growing distant. "He's dead. 1943…Isoroku Yamamoto, Japan's most treasured son. Shot down near Bougainville…"

"You did hear about it then?" he asks snapping me back.

"Um, yeah, something like that. Thanks Bill. I'll be right up." He looks at me strangely then leaves.

On the bunk sits a framed black-and-white picture of the crew proudly presenting our boat's battle flag. It was taken just before we set sail on the last patrol. Dead center, surrounded by the men of the crew, is a tall dark-haired officer. His cap possesses a slight jaunty tilt and his bent smile curves to one side.

"Lieutenant Commander Michael J. Murphy," I whisper softly as if to someone else in the room. "The 'J' stands for…" I hang the picture on the hook normally used for the daily rotation clipboard and adjust my cap the way the man in the photo has his. "How's that *Commander Murphy*?" We smile at each other. I adopt his peculiar grin and make my way up onto the deck, taking the catwalk over to the sub-tender lashed to our starboard beam.

She's inside the workshop of the Prometheus, at a tiny desk, writing in a ledger, those ugly glasses perched on the end of her nose. The light from the grimy bulb in the desk lamp coats her face in a soft alabaster glow, her delicate features a stark contrast to the welding torches, acetylene tanks and greasy tools piled about.

When she sees me, she freezes, closing the ledger and holding it tightly to her chest as if it contained some kind of secret. "Michael…you're back." She rises, her slender form like a specter in the dirt and darkness of the room.

"I heard you wanted to see me."

"Yes…of course…I…" She looks me over, concern shrouding her surprise. "My god, you're thin." I take her hand and we embrace, her arms tightening around me. When we part, moisture rims her irises. The following silence is deafening, nearly overwhelming. I fight the desire to take her into my arms and kiss her, searching my mind for something to say.

"Why has the Manta Ray been painted black? There isn't a millimeter left untouched." I instantly regret the question, the emotion in her face dissipating, replaced by her *scientist's face*, the moment lost, forever.

"We're exploring the blackbody theory. It should aid us in our effort."

"Blackbody?"

"Hardly theory. It's physical science really. The theory predicts a *true* blackbody absorbs all electromagnetic radiation."

"Radiation?"

"Light, radio waves, sonar and radar, all sources. The right *temperature* of black minimizes reflection regardless of the frequency or angle of incidence."

She stares into my eyes, her pupils dilating; dark pools of wonderment. "Would the pupils of a person's eyes be considered a blackbody?" I ask and she becomes wordless, looking deeply into me. Her head gives a slight shake as if recoiling from a single thought, perhaps its opposite.

"Shall we get back to work Commander?"

"We've finished wiring the two supercoils fore and aft and meticulously isolated the electric circuits feeding the machines," she informs me. "The external antennae array is in place and the control cables that transmit the data signals necessary to send and receive the command functions have been carefully isolated." Although the technology is beyond my comprehension, a part of me is amused. "What's so funny?" she asks, blowing wisps of hair from her face as she wrestles with an electronic relay box too large for the bay station designed for it.

"In the future all this massive technology will be sent and received by a machine referred to as a computer." She freezes on the spot and stares.

"Here we go again. Did you say *computer*?"

"Yes, that's the word in my head. An *electronic brain* might be the more adequate description." She gazes into my eyes before asking me to help her wrangle with the unit.

"Hold this." We're shoulder to shoulder as she begins to wriggle the apparatus into place. "Mr. Murphy, how do you know about that sort of thing?"

"About what?"

"Computational devices. Do you read science journals perchance? Perhaps technical manuals while you're sunbathing?"

"No."

"How then?"

"How do I know about computers? Hmm, I'm not exactly sure."

She stops working and glares. "Please don't be dismissive with me Commander. I'm being quite serious."

"So am I." She sees the conviction on my face.

"How do you know about these devices?"

"I don't know. However, they will run the world. I know it somehow."

"Mr. Murphy, you're a very strange man."

"Not really. I just have…moments."

"You're very odd."

"What do you know about computers?" I ask and she actually shushes me.

"I wouldn't be talking about that if I were you."

"Why?"

"Well, in addition to what's happened to you recently…that subject is off-limits. Top-secret," she whispers directly into my ear, her breath warm on my cheek.

"Oh?"

"What do you think is the *brains* of the attenuator?"

"You."

She pauses in her labors to study me. "Mr. Murphy…you astound me."

"I don't get you."

"I might be the operator, per se, but the mathematical calculations required, per second, to attenuate and maintain the field is, well…off the charts."

"There's a computer onboard?" I ask and she places her fingers over my mouth.

"Please. Lower your voice Michael." She scans the compartment. "We shouldn't be talking about this. This is top-secret equipment. My god, how could you even know these things? Incredible," she mutters, returning to the work.

———

"In the future they'll become handheld devices. I'm certain about it." I look into the palm of my hand. "I can still feel the touch and weight of the thing."

"I should argue the point but somehow, it must go that way mustn't it? These enormous computers they're putting together, like Colossus. They're too massive, they'll fill entire laboratories."

"I remember something about that…large first machines." We're interrupted by Lawton.

"Lucy, there you are. I've been looking all over for you."

"Well I'm never too far away Brian. One end of the boat or the other."

"Dr. Hoffmann is requesting you on deck. An adjustment to the RF antennae."

She brushes moisture off her brow with the back of her wrist. "Tell him I'll be right up," she says coolly, the tension between the two, noticeable. He gives me a flat look, and leaves.

"We'll discuss this at another time," she says formally.

"It's a date." She stares, her eyes shifting between mine.

"*A date,*" she echoes strangely, her gaze lingering before leaving the compartment, just as Ensign Duncan enters.

"Lieutenant Murphy?"

"Go ahead Duncan."

"Can we speak sir?"

"What is it Ensign?"

"Sir, they're seriously scaling back the crew for this mission."

"We spoke about this Eban. They need extra room in the boat for the equipment and technicians. Have they said how many men they intend to cut?"

"They're indicating by half. That's clearly inaccurate, right sir?" I see the worry on the young officer's face.

"We'll see what the Navy gives us Ensign. How's the family back in Ames? Did you speak with your mother by telephone during the break?"

"They were at church the one chance I had to call."

"Sorry to hear it. Wish it were easier to make contact with the mainland. Perhaps in the future."

"I read a story in *Mystery Tales* about a guy calling around the world anytime he wanted with nothing but a tiny little box in his hand. He didn't even have to be hooked-up to the telephone lines. Pretty farfetched," he says, and I think about the dreams recurring in my sleep.

"If we're lucky, we might be home for Thanksgiving. Your family usually gets together right?"

"Always. They come from all over Iowa. Mom makes both turkey and ham because we're pig farmers and Dad has to have ham, but Mom's side is traditional, stuffed turkey, taters and pumpkin pie, cranberries, squash, pecan pudding. Aunt Beulah always brings her gelatin dessert and Grandma makes a three-bean salad that'd make your mouth water."

My stomach begins making noises when we're suddenly interrupted by Sorel, Pendleton and Ritchie grilling Lesky as they make their way through the compartment.

"Whyn't you shut your trap and go play with your torpedoes Ritchie. Who made you quality control officer, Li'l Abner?"

"Lesky, you're a piece of work."

"Commander Murphy tell these meatheads. I'm the hardest working seaman in the whole Pacific fleet. Sooner you clowns admit it, sooner you can get back to your circus."

"*Easy*, you're the biggest goldbrick in this man's Navy."

"Listen to this guy," he says to Sorel, already shaking his head.

"Eric, ya'll put more work into ducking duty than just doing what you're told. You're driving Chief nuts."

"What are you talking about? I do what I have to do."

"Exactly their point," Pendleton adds. "You do exactly just enough to squeak-by."

"Get lost Pendleton, who's asking you? Our first-string cheerleader," he says, pulling his pants up several inches. "How about it Commander Murphy? Do I rate on this ship-of-fools or what?"

"*Easy*, you're a walking piece of art," Ritchie interjects. "When the good lord made you, he wired together a classic. A piece of junk, but a classic."

"Go polish some brass square-head. Who are you, Sigmund Freud?"

"Who?"

"Sigmund Freud. The psychoanalyst. Okay, to make it clear to a dumb-head like you, a *headshrinker*."

"What boat is he assigned to?"

"Forget about it."

As the work culminates, the crew gains a steady and determined fondness for Lucy. While installing an electrical component to the rear coil–the *Boswell Sisters* singing acapella over the radio–the fun and games continue.

The men are complaining about Lawton again, his arrogance. "Don't take it so personally guys," Lucy says brushing wisps of hair from her cheek, leaving a line of dirt. "There's always a healthy tension between the science and engineering on any project. He's science, we're engineering."

Torsch slaps Howard's back. "You hear that mutton-chops, you just got promoted. You're officially an *engineer*." Howard winks to the others behind her back.

"Hey so Professor, word is you're from Jersey. True?"

"New Jersey you mean?"

"Yeah, yeah, *Jersey*."

"Well, I'm not *from* there Conrad, but yes, I do live in…*Jersey*."

"No kidding? Hey, maybe we're neighbors. What part you from Prof?" He winks again.

"*Part?* What city in New Jersey?"

"Yeah, yeah, what part you from? Maybe we're neighbors."

"I doubt that Conrad. I reside at the university…at Princeton."

"Princeton huh?" he says stroking his moustache. "That anywhere near Paterson?" Her expression is one of total confusion until he punches Torsch in the arm and the sailors all laugh, Torsch rubbing his shoulder. She grins; her sideways grin.

"Yes, Mr. Howard, not far from Paterson. Oh, and by the way, if you ever *short-sheet* my bunk again, I'll get even." The men laugh and Torsch returns the punch.

"Cripes," Howard mutters, rubbing his shoulder.

Chapter 9: Voyage

*T*he sun thunders across a vast cerulean horizon.

Dolphins are in our wake, running abeam. Lucy stretches in the sunlight, the golden globe framing her in silhouette, tinting her hair a deep chestnut brown. "Good news Commander, we're ready to set sail," she says just as the alarm bell erupts and tranquility melts under the press of panic.

"Lieutenant Murphy? You awake sir?" It's Petty Officer Judesay. I'm in the officer's wardroom. I've fallen asleep with a cup of coffee in my hand. I expect the worst, but the boat is silent. The alarm bell merely a dream. *Jumping at the Woodside* by Count Basie is playing over the boat's PA.

"What is it Lynn?"

"Message from Top. We're *green* for *go* sir." I brush my hair back and straighten my shirt.

"Copy, thanks. Where's Skipper?"

"Rumor has it, the *Hawaiian*."

"He's at the Royal? Again?" I ask, checking my watch.

He shrugs. "Check with the rotation. Burlsley was assigned *wingman* tonight."

I wash my face in the tiny foldout sink in my quarters, run a comb through my hair and don my cap and jacket. As I head through the sub, I spy Lucy in her cabin pouring over some notes, the lamp on the desk coating her features in a soft amber radiance.

I study her, the moment extending. She seems frozen, like a painting set in oil, a soft veneer of amber light coating the contours of her head, set against a dark chiaroscuro background. She turns and looks at me. Timeless.

"Why hello," she says, removing her glasses, noticing my jacket. "Where are you off to?"

"The Royal."

"An impromptu bon-voyage party?"

"In a way. I've just heard we're *green*."

"If that means what I think, the answer is yes. Dr. Hoffmann has informed your command we're prepared to sail. We'll continue deploying the machine during the voyage but, as they say, *all systems go*."

"How about you? Have you packed everything you'll need?" The look on her face immediately answers my question. "Lucy, I told you to spend time with your pack. Once we leave landfall we won't be turning around." There's no masking the concern forming on her face. "Listen, I've a jeep dockside, and time to take you back to your apartment…I mean, to the science compound."

Her eyes pulsate. "Wait for me Michael. I'll only be a minute."

I drive her to the science residency, right up to her tiny atelier, framed by palms and a vast swath of bird-of-paradise flowers, a blue moon silently watching us through the vines.

She stares at me in the darkness. "You're not coming in?"

"I wasn't planning to."

"How will I get back?"

"I would think the same way you always do."

She adopts a strange expression, gazing at the darkened bungalow. "I'm being ridiculous."

"About what?" She turns, her wounded gaze filled with a sudden inextricable sadness. "Lucy. What's the matter?"

She looks through me. "Why am I feeling this way? I'm leaving here, this tiny place, that has been my home." She averts her eyes. "I can't possibly tell anyone."

"Tell what?" She turns away, avoiding the question. "Answer me, tell what?" I take her cheek in my palm, gently forcing her gaze.

"I've been so absorbed with the retrofit. Now that we're leaving...I'm afraid."

"It's all right. I am too."

Her eyes seek mine. "You're saying that solely for my benefit."

"No. I'm not. It's the truth. The responsibility we're about to undertake, to go to war, and underwater no less. It *is* frightening. Trust me, we're going to be all right. I promise." These words are not my own, but a conviction spoken from somewhere deep inside. I see her face change in the moonlight.

"I know it. As long as you're here, everything will be all right," she whispers, as if to another. "Look at me, carrying-on like a schoolgirl. My god, what would everyone think if they saw me? Conrad Howard would have a field day."

"Every man on the boat feels it, *the fear*. Some of us are just better at hiding it." Her pupils expand in the darkness, the moon painting a pinprick of light atop the corneas.

"Thank-you Michael. Thank you for being here," she says strangely. The wind lifts the finer tresses of her hair and, again, I fight the urge to take her in my arms. "See you back at the boat Commander Murphy," she says and starts to leave.

"Lucy..." She pauses, returns and kisses me. I feel it in her kiss; the passion. "Lucy..."

"Go find your captain," she says softly, melting away from my touch, becoming invisible in the darkness.

———

I'm sitting with Canfield and Burlsley at the Royal Hawaiian when Ensign Duncan arrives fully dressed in his beige officer's uniform including black tie and cap. His shirt is newly pressed, the collar and cuffs starched.

"What, no life-vest?" Burlsley mutters; the look from me quieting him.

"Reporting on the boat sir."

"Go ahead," Canfield says, addressing Duncan's salute.

"Boat fully stocked and provisioned Skipper. *Step-one* of the retrofit complete. All hands and science teams ready to get underway sir."

"Very well," Canfield mumbles without further acknowledgement. The young officer looks at me dejectedly. Eban was a product of Annapolis, and the New London submarine school.

"Thank-you Ensign," I say saluting. When he leaves, Canfield orders another drink. "What's bugging you tonight Skipper? You're not usually so short with Duncan."

"That damn cornfed kid. You'd think he was born with the manual up his ass." When the captain's drink arrives, he downs it by half.

"Easy does it Skipper. We depart at twenty-two hundred." Canfield just looks at me, his gaze unsettling. "What's wrong?" I ask lowering my voice while Burlsley converses with the barmaid.

"I got a bad feeling about this one Mike," he says below the din, the bar filling with the crew of another boat just in from patrol; the rotation of the guard.

"Like what? What kind of feeling?"

The look in his eyes contrasts dramatically with the boisterous chatter of the sailors filling the room. "Like I'm never going to see my wife again."

Silence, louder than the hubbub inside the bar.

"It's probably just nerves. All this secrecy…and weird equipment onboard."

He downs his drink, tossing some bills on the bar. "Yeah. That's probably it." He takes up his jacket and heads out the door, Burlsley following like a faithful hunting dog.

An hour later I'm standing near the quay with Hildy. We embrace under the dull insipid glow of the dock lights and she begins to cry, the moon touching each tear.

"Don't cry Hildy. I'll be home soon."

"I don't like this Mike. There was such little time for us. There's never enough time anymore."

"Don't worry. Everything will be fine," I say but she's crying quietly, painfully. "I'll be home soon. We'll sort everything out then."

"No, we won't. I won't be here Mike, when you return. Not this time." My insides congeal and the ground beneath my feet seems to give way, as if I'm falling; floating in a thick viscous fog. "I'm going back to California, stay with aunt Ruth in San Francisco."

"Hildy…you're saying good-bye."

"I can't stand it Mike, the waiting; wondering. I won't do it anymore. I can't. I've made up my mind. Aunt Ruth is wiring me the money. I'm leaving in two days." Time stops and the world freezes.

Burlsley's pipe pierces the silence, sounding the imminent departure of the boat. I feel like a man on a tightrope beginning to lose balance. Which way will I fall?

The pipe sounds again, forcing my mind to surface from the depth of my despair. "The Bosun's whistle," I say to the night. "I have to go."

"Of course. I know the drill. I've been through it enough times." Her words cut into my heart. I can't look in her eyes. As I begin to leave, she calls to me. "Mike, wait…I almost forgot." She reaches into her purse, pulling out an old, well-loved photo. I study it under the glow of the lights. The photo of her in the flower-print dress. "Your good-luck charm."

I can barely choke out the words. "Hildy…please, don't go. Please wait for me."

Silence. Shouts, ribbing from the boat. "Your boat is calling you. Time to *fulfill your duty*," she says, her words cold; or is it the wind blowing off the Pacific?

"Hildy…"

"Mike, please, go."

The whistle pulls me like a moth to a flame. I look back from the gangplank, she quietly waves, holding her stomach. As I ascend to the bridge, she's already driving away.

The Boatswain's pipe calls the crew to attention, the sailors lining the deck. A brisk wind rattles our battle flag and the world stands on edge. Canfield gives his crew a long stoic look, each man patiently awaiting his command. This was our captain's style. His eyes often saying more than the words of his mouth.

He starts his slow methodic walk down the rank and file, a quietude steeping the air, louder than the roar of the surf in the distance, the hammering of steel from the drydocks.

The wind blows the scent of the ocean through the rank-and-file. He takes in the moment, extends it for his crew, the seriousness of the mission; the magnitude of the task. We're standing at the edge of the world, about to set sail into a maelstrom; a world at war.

"Men, this is Manta Ray's ninth war patrol. *Lucky nine*. Some of you have been with her from the start," he says squaring before Bremer and Lloyd, both men grinning broadly. "We're half a crew, so work twice as hard. I expect every man to fulfill his duty to the very highest of his abilities. Understood?" The entire company responds with one voice. Canfield heads down the midship hatch. "Mr. Murphy, take the boat out."

"Aye sir. All hands, man your stations, standby to cast-off." Organized chaos ensues as our well-oiled crew prepares to depart. I climb the rigging to the bridge. One last lonely look for her; she's gone. I order Burlsley to cast-off all lines.

"Aye-aye Mr. Murphy. Lines away boys!" Jaeger and Sorel cast the fore and aft lines clear of the submarine. We're cutting the umbilical. We're on our own.

I hit the toggle on the *squawk-box*. "Bring motors one and two on-line, all back one-third, left standard rudder." The Manta Ray growls, her exhaust manifolds belching smoke. The boat shudders under the thrust of her diesel engines, growling like a panther pulling on a leash. Stewart and Duncan join me on the bridge, wind rattling their collars. "Rudder amidships, all ahead one-third. Steady as you go," I order into the phone and the night closes in.

"You'll make a fine skipper your next time out Murph."

"Thanks, I appreciate that Stewie."

He tightens the collar on his jacket. "Damn, it sure got cold tonight," he says as Duncan calls down to the watch crew. "I heard something about in olden days, folklore, that it's a bad omen, the weather turning cold starting out on a night voyage." I study the man, not used to such rhetoric from him. Ellis Stewart was nearly one hundred percent Scottish.

"I didn't know you were superstitious."

"Not me…my family."

His parents were from the old country, Aberdeen, but Stewie sure as hell grew up in Chicago. He was something of a conundrum. One side extremely pragmatic, the other side, as he put it himself: *'One ear to my grandmother.'* We'd gone through Annapolis together, graduated in the same class. I was second from the top. Ellis was 29th; played football for Navy, an outside linebacker. He had been all-conference in high school.

The port glimmers in the night like an onyx jewel, the dock lights casting undulating bands of gold across the shimmering water, black as oil. In the distance, small craft and tugs meander the harbor and the dry-docks rage on, gnashing their teeth, metal clanging on metal, sparks spitting into the night; the insatiable jaws of war.

As quiet and lonely as a shadow, the Manta Ray slips under the lights of the harbor into the darkness of the restless Pacific; a black gaping maw set against a proscenium of storm clouds.

The pilot ship that escorts us from the harbor into the womb of the great ocean looks like a phantom, beckoning us into the darkness. Her name is unknown to me, but I pray it isn't *Tisiphone*, one of the furies that would lead men astray, lure them with visions of gold and opulence only to be cast upon the rocks and drown.

"Stewie, we'll cut the pilot loose thirty minutes out. I want to dive the boat at twenty-three hundred hours."

"Aye. You going below?"

"Skipper wants an alternate course plotted." I give Duncan the *thumbs-up*. "Get 'em in the sail Mr. Duncan."

"Aye sir," he says saluting and shouts over my shoulder as I descend into the conning tower, the sailors nervous but excited. "Lookouts to the bridge. Move it guys."

I drop into the conning tower, the boat pulsing under the thrust of her diesels and a feeling washes over me, swallows me as if in cotton. We're on our way, her first patrol after the retrofit; anticipation so heavy in the air you breathe it. We think ourselves separate but we belong to her, each man a part of this machine and its desires. I study the men, boys really when you came right down to it. Especially Duncan and the NCOs, kids in men's clothes. I look at our *radar team*, the *eyes* and *ears* of the boat, young but more worldly. It was their third time out as a team. They were proud of their rating and doing their jobs well. Their talk together was about almost anything except regulations and the base functions of the boat. These guys had been to college before the war, Zig and Goldy both intelligent and witty, Herndon also, but in a different way. Herndon talked a tough game but inside I knew he was wounded emotionally, probably from growing up in the ghettos of Detroit during the depression. He possessed a silent rage, something he kept bottled-up tightly. His achieving status as a radar technician was a credit to his tenacity. It was also a credit to the submarine service, *the silent service* offered opportunity to men of steady consistent character. Every man that served onboard a US submarine was a volunteer.

"Everything operative gentlemen?" I ask and the *'eyes and ears of the boat'* air out their collective concerns about the state of the equipment.

"Don't listen to the complaining. We're all set Commander," Goldman says. Gallen was a fourth-generation shipwright before enlisting. His grandfather and great-grandfather were both skilled wooden-boat builders from Nantucket Sound and one of his uncles had scrimshaw artwork in galleries up and down the New England coast.

"They did a top-down overhaul of every piece of equipment in *the tower* Lieutenant," Herndon declares. "Even added a few new bells and whistles."

"We'll get there with these relics," Elder adds, pinching his earphones to his head. We were still several thousand miles from enemy waters. However, Elder knew, as did every man on the sub, there always loomed the threat of an *Axis* submarine attack. *Anywhere. Anytime. Pacific.* It was a known fact our boat never slept. This patrol was going to tax them severely. No third tiers to cover their positions, or seconds really; it was going to be a tough rotation on a very uncertain voyage, many of the details about the actual mission kept hidden from the crew.

I drop below, the control room pulsing; sailors tweaking instrumentation, men moving stores and equipment through the boat. As I remove my jacket, Taylor hands me a hot cup of coffee.

"Relieving you as officer of the deck."

"Thanks. Where's the old man?"

"In his cabin."

Exiting the control room into the gangway that berths the officer's cabins, I find Lucy and Dr. Hoffmann stowing their personal affects. I squeeze past the men filing through the narrow hallway.

"How are you two *sailors* getting on?"

"Splendid," she says. "However, Michael, I insist you move me."

"Move you? Why? This is our commissioned officer's cabin. It doesn't get any better than-"

"I'm at odds about taking a room with three beds; displacing two other persons when space is at such a premium. I never dreamed how cramped a submarine becomes when everyone is aboard at the same time."

"This cabin has been designated for you, for the entire voyage. Admiral's orders."

"I hate to think I'm displacing two other persons. There must be a single room somewhere?" I point over my shoulder.

"The Captain's cabin is the only *single*." She covers her mouth with her fingers.

"Oops."

"Charlesworth, Bennett made these arrangements," Hoffmann interjects. "In the Navy, it's considered bad form to contradict an admiral's orders. Tell the young man thanks and let's discuss our next plan of action over a cup of tea."

"Agreed," I add, making suggestions regarding securing their things. "This is an unstable platform, especially on the surface in rough seas. Or if we have to crash-dive."

"Crash-dive?" she echoes. "That sounds ominous."

"If the boat is attacked on the surface." I see the questions forming in her eyes.

"I mustn't forget how dangerous this business is," she mutters. "Dr. Hoffmann if there's nothing pressing, I think I'll retire for the night. It's been a rather taxing day."

"There's nothing that can't wait. Goodnight Charlesworth." We share a look, before she slides the curtain taut. "Commander, I know it's late, but I could use a cup of that coffee you're holding."

We seek out the forward galley attached to the officer's wardroom. Santino, the young Filipino steward, fills one of the bone-china cups and hands it to him.

"What's next Commander Murphy? What's protocol leaving port?" he inquires amicably.

"We'll stay with the pilot another twenty minutes, until we're safely out of harbor, then dive the boat."

"To properly test the new welding," he says to no one in particular. I look at my watch.

"Better check in with the captain," I say, the doctor becoming silent, absorbed in his thinking.

Canfield's curtain is drawn. I tap on the bulkhead. When my second tap brings no response, I slide back the curtain. He's sitting at his desk staring at a photo.

"Captain? You said to inform you before we cut the pilot loose." He just stares at the photo. "Captain?" I gaze over his shoulder. It's an older photo of Rue in a white nurse's uniform. He snaps out of his reverie and looks at me.

"What?"

"We're cutting the pilot loose in a few minutes." He returns his attention to the photo. "Is that Rue? When she was a nurse?" he puts the photo away inside the desk drawer. "You wanted to be notified when-"

"Yeah, yeah, I heard you. Standby to dive," he says returning to the papers on his desk. As I leave, something pulls me back.

"You okay?" I ask and he stares through the bulkhead.

"I'll be up in a few minutes."

Back on the bridge, the sub penetrates the great ocean stretching before us like an ebony wilderness. The expanse of black rolling water pulls us inexorably into the unknown. Where will she take us now, the *Queen of Battle,* her armor gleaming under the moonlight?

The boat slices the waves beneath her bow and the sound she makes, *the eager huntress,* is well-known to these ears. We are the wolves of war, her hungry pack. The night air becomes energized; undines dancing white atop the dark waves, crowd her bow, beckoning us ever onward into the hunt. The battle phone jangles, breaking the lure of the midnight sea.

"Bridge." I hear the captain's request to dive the boat. "Aye sir." I hang-up and peer into the blackness before us. Within minutes there will be nothing above the water to belie our presence. She will disappear from the world, go blindly to meet her lover, *Aqueous Invictus*, the deep enigmatic underworld. "Lookouts below," I shout to the men in the shears. They drop like leaves in autumn, disappearing into the hatch like rainwater after a storm. I scan the deck, checking that no one has been left behind before I too melt into the boat, taking one last look at the moon; a thin alluring smile from the heavens.

Inside the conning tower, I pull on the hatch lanyard and Sorel doggs the wheel tight. I pause a moment, absorbing the womblike quietude of the closing of the main hatch. Above us soon, the mighty ocean will wash over, swallowing us whole, taking us forever downward into her nautical abyss, her resplendent playground, filled with treasure, mystery, and the corpses of thousands of ships, scattered across the depths of a lonely abysmal plane.

"Hatch secure Lieutenant," Sorel says bringing me back. He follows me into the belly of the boat, taking his position at the *bow-plane*. I join the captain and other officers loitering in the control room.

"Bridge is secure Captain. Pilot is away. Boat ready to dive."

Canfield cuts off his conversation with Hoffmann. "All ahead standard," he says. Ashburn echoes his command rotating the *engine order telegraph*, relaying his order to the maneuvering room. "Diving officer," the captain says directly to me, "dive the boat."

"Aye sir." I flip the toggle on the Com. "Dive," pull twice on the klaxon. *Aarugah-Aarugah* the boat bellows, the men massaging her brass and steel controls.

"Flood all tanks. Close main induction. Rig out bow-planes. *Ready* for silent running."

"Induction closed, green board," Bremer responds from the *Christmas tree,* the tiny green lights indicating the *closed* condition of the orifices leading in and out to the sea.

"Open the vents. Silent running. Make my depth one-double-zero," I say, asking them to lower the boat to one hundred feet. "Ten degree down bubble." Sorel, manning the diving plane, echoes the command like listening to a recording and the boat takes on a downward pitch. We cut into the deep, the boat wrapped in a velvety silence, the pressure from the sea squeezing the air in the compartment.

"Approaching one hundred feet Mr. Murphy."

"Level off. Zero degree down. Blow negative to the mark."

"Aye sir," Szotsman says from the diving manifold and the boat hisses.

"Negative to the mark and vented," Bremer informs me. "Depth, one-zero-zero." There's a slight rise in the bow.

"Forward trim, give me a thousand pounds."

Hintz twists the brass knobs on his board. "Flooding from the sea Commander, one thousand pounds, aye." The boat levels nicely. Bremer gives me *the nod.*

"Boat is trim Captain. All ahead standard."

"Deeper Murphy."

"Bow-plane, take her down." Sorel spins his wheel and the boat leans into the deep, Bremer watching the depth.

"One fifty. One-seventy-five. Two hundred feet," his voice echoes like a mantra. "Two-twenty-five." The boat creaks and groans. "Two hundred and fifty feet," he says with emphasis, looking at Canfield. "Two hundred and seventy-five feet." The boat moans from the pressure of the sea against her hull.

"Level off at three hundred," I say. When the boat levels I address the captain. "Boat is at *emergency depth* Captain." Canfield shoots me a dour look and surprises everyone in the control room, his voice barely above a whisper.

"Deeper." I look at Bremer and Stewart; sweat.

"Mr. Sorel, take us to three hundred and fifty feet, two-degree down bubble." He glances at Bremer but knows he need not wait for Chief's reaction.

"Aye sir, going to three-five-zero, aye." He carefully turns his giant silver wheel, watching the diving gauge closely. The boat tilts and groans.

"Three hundred and fifty feet," Chief exhales running a hand through his silvery hair.

"Fifty feet below regulation depth Captain."

Canfield's eyes lock with mine. "Deeper Murphy." You can nearly hear the men perspire.

I nod to Sorel. "Quentin, go to four hundred feet." He carefully turns the wheel. The boat violently shudders, a clatter echoes through the hull. Lucy enters through the watertight door clutching her robe tightly about her neck.

"What's going on?" she whispers to Hoffmann who takes the opportunity to expand his voice.

"Captain Canfield is testing the new welding."

"Three hundred and eighty feet," Chief says to add pith to the doctor's statement. Cork insulation pops off the ceiling from the pressure the sea places on the skin of the boat. I actually think I hear a scream, a small infinitesimal shriek as the boat lowers herself into the depths.

"Level off," I say, and they do so expediently.

"Four hundred feet," Bremer informs the crew.

"Boat is trim Captain. We're a hundred feet below emergency depth," I say. For a moment I think he's actually contemplating taking us deeper.

"Get the torpedo chiefs on the horn."

I ring-up the forward torpedo room. "Ned, how are the welds doing?" We hear expletives through the speaker.

"What the hell are you doing Murph?" he says. Canfield wrenches the Com from my hand.

"Binkershon, the Exec asked you a question!"

"The welds are fine, but the boat's having kittens, sir."

"Keep your personal comments to yourself," he shouts. "Collins, report on conditions aft."

"The welds are sweatin' bullets Skipper but holding." Canfield slams the Com down and gives us a fierce look.

"Let's get something in our heads right now. We're at war goddammit. Last time I checked, in war, those who prepare survive, those who don't, drown." The control room freezes from the sudden intensity of his voice. "If we have to crash-dive this boat, I wanna know the new work is up to snuff. Any of you yahoos disagree, say so now." No one breathes. He squares himself before me. "Lieutenant Murphy, this crew and their deportment is your responsibility."

"Yes sir, absolutely sir."

"Are you running an attack submarine or a coffee klatch?" He glares at me, then the crew and scientists in the control room. "I have to know right here and now if this boat can take it, not in Empire," he barks. "You think this is a goddamn dog-and-pony show? We're at war people. You screw up, you bury your dead at sea…if you're lucky."

Silence.

"That's all for today. Executive Officer, take her up, let's head west," he says and leaves for his cabin stopping to shake his head at Lucy in her robe and slippers.

I grab the Com. "Surface. Full rise on planes. Blow all tanks." Hoffmann and Lucy exit the compartment, concern indelibly etched upon their faces.

"What the hell was that?" Stewart asks immediately at my elbow. "Chewing us out *and* the science team?"

"Stewie, prepare a deck crew. Take the first watch, three lookouts." He doesn't acknowledge my order, heading for the Ritz. "Chief, standby to put primary engines on-line. Helm, come to two-six-zero."

"Aye, coming about, two-six-oh laid in sir," Wyatt says adjusting the helm to these new coordinates. Bremer doesn't say a word, just gives me *that look* and heads for the engine compartment.

The following morning both torpedo crews are in the after-torpedo room, closing out our rotation meeting when Stroup emerges from the aft-hold with the stainless-steel pots and copper tubing they use for their still.

"What's this?" I ask, freezing the men. Stroup's face never changed, not one iota, ever.

"Sir?"

"You heard me Stroup. What is all this?" Stroup just stares at me like I'm speaking French. The rest of the torpedo crew slowly converges, staring fixedly at the collection of pilfered pots and tubing in the torpedoman's arms

"You lose consciousness during the dive?" Collins squints. "You know what this is, equipment for our still."

"Get rid of it." They stare at me like I'm the local priest.

"Are you trying to be funny Murph?"

"Throw it over the side Binkershon."

You could hear a pin drop.

"Commander Murphy, you know Skip gives us permission to make this stuff."

"Do I need to repeat myself Dyer? Take it topside and throw it overboard, all of it."

"Aw c'mon Murphy. You must be kidding around," Collins says. "You know this thing doesn't make enough hooch to cause any harm…just enough to take the edge off."

"*And* it keeps the freeloaders away from our torpedo *gilly*," Binkershon adds, referring to the alcohol necessary to propel the torpedoes.

"Ergo, it's essential materiel for the proper functioning of the torpedoes, ergo the boat. Done."

"I won't say it again Tuke, get rid of it. Right now." Collins stares dejectedly at Binkershon who slides his arm across my shoulders.

"Murph, no one's gonna know. We'll keep it on the low-down. Trust us."

"Everyone's going to know, and you'll keep it off the boat Chief."

"Aw for the love of Pete! When did you get baptized?"

"Gentlemen this isn't *just another* war patrol. Washington *and* the OSS are onboard. If I find this stuff sequestered in the after-hold there'll be serious repercussions. Now get rid of it immediately." The men gather, staring at their gear like the dearly departed at a funeral. "Someone read it its last rites and commit it to the deep. We'll commence fire drills at oh-ten-hundred." I leave them with their charge and make for the radio shack. Stewart loiters at the door of the radio room with a handful of telegraphs.

"Jukes, did you radio in our new course to Pearl?"

"Acknowledged Mr. Murphy, switching to radio silence here out," he says lighting up again.

"Roscoe, do you ever take time out between cigarettes to breathe oxygen?" Stewart inquires. The radioman squints, scratching his stubble.

"I don't getcha Lieutenant Stewart?"

"Why did you join the submarine service? Why not the surface fleet where there's more air?" he says and leaves.

"Want to know why I joined the subs Commander Murphy?"

"Why Jukes?"

"If I was in the infantry or even regular Navy for that matter, I'd be in the slammer, sure as I'm looking at you."

"Why do you think that?"

"I'm no good with authority Mr. Murphy, never was…saluting and posturing and all that baloney. I couldn't even make it through high school before they threw me out. The submarine service doesn't give a shit about whether a guy can scrub toilets with a toothbrush. It's about results. And staying alive. That's me Mr. Murphy, staying alive."

He was right. The submarine service wasn't as regimented as the surface fleet, where a man's career could be compromised by a slip of the tongue or some minor infraction or omission. Enlisted men weren't expected to salute officers or even necessarily address them by rank. Each boat was different, some stricter than others. Canfield had established protocol early. If you covered your job and did it well, you were golden on the Manta Ray. There were no issues if an enlisted man failed to salute or address an officer in normal military fashion. As long as you were contributing to the proper functioning of the boat and its primary objective, sinking enemy ships. As long as you did what was expected and did it efficiently, you were on for the ride. *All the way*. As a result, our boat was a happy and content boat, eccentricities aside. It was more like one big happy-go-lucky family, each man adding his own particular flavor into the mix.

Breakfast is in the air, bacon and hotcakes covering the smell of the diesel fuel. When I check on the men in *the Ritz*, everyone has settled in for the voyage. The scuttlebutt ensues, an eclectic mix of stories, hopes and vacant desires, the science team listening-in. Seaman Wyatt hands Sorel his beaten old *Martin* guitar.

"Play us a tune Quent, one for the road." Every man in the room rolls onto his stomach and quiets. Quentin Sorel was from a famous Tennessee *bluegrass* family. Many of his relatives were involved with the Grand Ol' Opry, several employed as studio musicians in Nashville.

While he gives the thing a quick tuning, Lucy joins me at the port, a smile on her face. She takes my arm to steady herself from the gentle pitch and roll of the boat and our bodies gently sway together, a quiet invisible dance.

When he's finished tuning the Martin, Quentin clears his throat and the instrument fills the compartment accompanied by the tones of his deep rich voice.

'Once upon a time lived a man named Mike Murphy
'He lived outside another town called Albuquerque
'Blow ye winds of morning, blow ye winds high-oh
'Blow ye winds of morning, blow, blow, blow

'Now Michael fell in love with a pretty, nice, young girl
'First three letters of her name were Lucy Annie Pearl
'Blow ye winds of morning, blow ye winds high-oh
'Blow ye winds of morning, blow, blow, blow

'Just as they were about to wed, her father did say no
'And consequently she was sent beyond the O-hio
'Blow ye winds of morning, blow ye winds high-oh
'Blow ye winds of morning, blow, blow, blow

'Michael heard of this sad news he knew not what to say
'He had a mind to jump into, the Sesquehan-i-ay
'Blow ye winds of morning, blow ye winds high-oh
'Blow ye winds of morning, blow, blow, blow

'Now Michael went away out west, to seek his fort-i-an
'But he was caught and scalped by a bloody In-di-an
'Blow ye winds of morning, blow ye winds high-oh
'Blow ye winds of morning, blow, blow, blow

'Lucy heard of this sad news she knew not what to say
'She wept and wept and wept her poor sweet life away
'Blow ye winds of morning, blow ye winds high-oh
'Blow ye winds of morning, blow, blow, blow

Chapter *10*: *The Package*

*S*econd day into the voyage we're hit by a vicious storm.

The tranquil blue Pacific dons a coat of angry gray. It continues unabated for days and our speed of advance rapidly falls below plan.

The waves coursing the bleak horizon are mind-numbing, rogue swells approaching the height of a two-story home, the mighty Pacific showing her tooth. Huge rolling swells like enormous gray pyramids lash at our boat, the ocean pounding the bridge like the hammer of Thor.

The men of the watch are brought down out of the shears and locked behind the fairweather with belts and lanyards; the watches heavily taxed, the necessity to travel on the surface, not only at night but also during daylight, imperative to stay on schedule.

Our crew is put to the test early as the new recruits work to find their sea-legs, the boat severely rocked by the angry sea. The entire science team becomes bedridden and the galley becomes lonely except for the most-hearty sailors.

When we finally make the island of Midway, the Port Master refuses to grant us permission to enter the channel due to the severe weather. We *hove-to* eight hundred yards south by southeast from the mouth of the channel, the sea so rough, green-water is washing over the bridge cowling and draining into the conning tower, the control room *taking a bath*.

The men of the crew are miserable.

"That's it? Midway? That's what all the fighting was about, that piece of dirt?" Judesay studies the atoll from his station on the bridge, the island ducking in and out of the rainsqualls blowing in from the northwest. "It sure don't look like much. I thought it would be bigger."

"Maybe not Lynn, but that tiny piece of sand changed the outlook of the entire war." He's lost to my meaning. I realize, once again, I'm speaking from a place outside my immediate timeframe, the truth about the attack on Midway heavily veiled in the secrecy surrounding the breaking of the Japanese military codes. "Stay sharp fellas," I shout to my team in the shears. "Keep a sharp lookout for enemy periscopes. Mr. Judesay you have the bridge." They all acknowledge. I head below, shaking the sea from my body and extracting myself from my foul-weather parka, taking a moment in the conning tower to question the radar and sonar teams.

"Nothing Mr. Murphy, all quiet, as best we can tell in these seas," Goldman informs me, looking paler than usual. Below, in the control room, I join the men gathered about Jukes' station in the radio room.

"What's the poop Whittle, yes or no? Are we in or not?" Canfield barks over the short-wave.

"At least twenty-four hours," the crusty voice on the other end says. "*Lay-to* Manta Ray, we'll call you," and the line goes dead. Canfield slams the Com down, cursing.

"Twenty-four hours? Before we can make port?" Calhoun asks, incredulous. "Is he crazy Skipper?" Canfield scowls, vacating the compartment. "What did I say Mr. Murphy?" the novice seaman inquires.

"They can't chance us being washed aground Cal, getting hung up on the rocks. It would shut down the channel, the island's lifeline."

———

213

"Oh." Calhoun was from a tiny New Hampshire town of about eight hundred souls, including the animals. He was as green as an apple in June.

After thirty minutes of deliberation, the captain informs me the refueling stop planned at the island–to relax, top off our fuel reserves and take on additional provisions–will be bypassed in favor of sticking to our transit plan.

"Is Skipper losing his bearings?" Stewart asks returning from the bridge-watch soaking wet. "So, we *lay-to* a day Murph, so what? It's better than battling these seas. What if we break a rudder, or yank a screw?"

"Lieutenant Stewart, how long have you been with this boat?" Chief Bremer inquires, tipping his cap back and crossing his tattooed arms, the look and color of tanned leather.

"It'll be a year next month, why?"

"You're in shark's water kid. No one knows that better than Canfield."

"*Shark's water?*"

"You should know by now *Jag,* hoving off the mouth of Midway Island is just asking for a Jap torpedo in the ribs. Or am I speaking out of line Mr. Murphy?"

"Put two engines on-line Chief, all ahead standard," is my response. A look goes around the men in the control room as the sailors comply, Bremer ringing-up the *engine order telegraph* like a ten-cent slot.

"Lesky, come about. Two-seven-five degrees true. We'll resume original course in thirty minutes."

"Aye Mr. Murphy. So long Midway," he moans. "Next stop Tokyo Harbor." The entire crew groans as we readdress the ocean head-on, the churning–and nausea–renewing in earnest.

"*The Pacific*," Jukes says through his cigarette after radioing our departure to the island. "What brain-dead moron called this washing machine *the Pacific*?"

Our new young recruits show their tender undersides while even a few of the saltier veterans barely muddle through. It's a couple of tough days and nights. Lucy disappears into her quarters while the rest of her team wallow in their bunks with acute seasickness. Only Hawkins seems to *weather* the storm.

Since a few of the younger officers are knocked off their feet, the rest of the crew is left to tough it out, working double shifts on an already demanding rotation. Of the scientists, Lawton fares the worst. He's incredibly sick and vomiting. He also awakens screaming; plagued by unrelenting dreams about seaman Dooley.

"I told you," Porteru says to the few of us that answer that night's dinner bell. "Dooley won't have nothing to do with that man messing with his bunk. Ya'll best get him berthed in another. It don't pay to mess around with the *other side*," he says and I contemplate these words.

"Coffee give it a break. We'll move him. As soon as we get the chance," Connie Howard says dumping his plate. "Screw this. I'm heading topside Mr. Murphy, to cover Jaeger's watch."

"Coffee's right. He's running Cooper ragged," Parmalee adds before heading topside with Howard. "Every time he finally goes to sleep...Dooley."

I'm eating with one hand while holding onto the rim of the table with the other, the pitch-and-roll of the boat making it impossible to eat without sliding. Romayo has laid a rubberized cloth across the tables to keep our plates and cups from sliding and toppling. He smiles at his handiwork. The young man had a perpetually sunny disposition.

"Why doesn't the captain take us under?" Wyatt asks, unable to eat his beef stew.

"Because he's the boss," Babineaux says, sopping up gravy with a piece of bread, completely unaffected by the conditions. "He knows what he's doing."

"Climb down off it Babs," Fitzgerald interjects, barely able to eat. "There's no reason not to take us under, even for a little while. What's he trying to prove? I'll tell you *what*. He hates those eggheads so he's torturing them, and us, just to prove what a tough guy he is."

"It figures," Earl Lloyd says lowering his fork. "Fitzgerald, only a greenhorn like you would wallow around at two hundred feet making four knots for the next three thousand miles. If you were in charge, the war would be over before we make our area of operation."

"Climb off my back Earl," Fitzgerald snarls and Lloyd drains his coffee and stands.

"Sure Gunner. Watch," he says and leaves.

"Fitzgerald, if you have any personal comments you'd like directed toward the senior members of this boat," Babineaux interjects, "you go through me. You copy?" He glares at his second gunner and Fitz mumbles something incoherent and returns to poking at his food.

Wyatt lays his head in his arms and belches. McAnulty takes up his untouched bowl of stew.

"If you're going to throw up Wyatt, go do it in *the head*, not here. I'm done cleaning up after you rookie seamen. First it was Ashburn, then Lawler. You'd think I was you guys mother." Collins finishes his bowl of stew wiping his mouth with his sleeve and shaking the young man's shoulder.

"Pretend you're on the world's longest coaster ride Bob, and you're riding all day for free." These words–and the shaking–are hardly medicine and Wyatt makes for the head.

––––

Szotsman looks at me deadpan, crumbs adorning his scraggly beard. George could never really grow a full beard and had even less hair on his balding pate.

"What's the deal Mr. Murphy? Where's the Navy getting these kids these days, Woolworth's?"

Coffee taps my elbow, his voice in my ear. "Mr. Murphy, you got a minute?"

"What is it now Charles?"

"I'm concerned about Miss Lucy."

"What's wrong now?"

"She ain't eating in a normal fashion."

"*Normal fashion?*"

"Three squares a day. I'd say it was more half a square." Porteru was the boat's senior steward, assigned to her as well as the officers.

"Coffee, you're like a mother hen," Dover says having overheard us. "She's tougher than any you chowder-heads give her credit." He returns to the kitchen, the smell of fresh baked bread covering the scent of diesel fuel and vomit.

"Don't listen to Dickie, somebody ought to check," Porteru has a cup of hot chamomile tea in his hand, the smell of herbs mixing with the *perfume* of the boat.

"Have you tried knocking *Chief Steward?*"

"Sure, I knocked. She ain't answering. You're the Exec. How about it?" he asks, nudging me with the cup.

Tapping on the bulkhead brings no answer, nor calling through the curtain. Reluctantly I press through the muslin into a dark and muted compartment, only the tiny bulb left burning above the lavatory. The desk has gone bare, her binders and ledgers thrown to the floor by the rocking of the sea. I sit on the edge of the bunk and she stirs.

"You're worrying Porteru to death. He insisted I check on you." She slowly sits up. I can see plainly she's very ill. "He asked me to bring you this." I place the cup carefully in her fingers, holding them until I'm certain she won't spill.

"I'm being remiss in my duties," she mumbles.

"You and half the boat." She sips the steamy liquid and the flavor and bouquet seems to have a rejuvenating effect, her demeanor brightening. "How are you feeling?"

"Awful. I thought I was something of a sailor. Apparently not."

"This is a terrible storm Lucy. I'm fortunate to keep a watch team on the bridge and enough men in the control room." She looks into my eyes. In the dim light I see her delicate, vulnerable side; possess the strongest desire to take her face in my hands and kiss her again; the kiss we shared beneath the dulcet Hawaiian moon.

"How much longer will it last?" she asks, and I return to myself, my position and duties as first officer of the boat, and her protector.

"Not much longer. Clear skies ahead. We can see it on the long-range radar. We should be back to normal by tomorrow, drink-up." The floor is littered with papers filled with equations and statistics. Her silk robe, adorned with vibrant color-images of Japan, hangs beside the small stainless-steel mirror above the pop-out lavatory. I reach over and tighten the faucet that drips the potable water so precious to the boat. "We'll have waves for a bit, probably some rain, but not this rocking and rolling."

"Couldn't Captain Canfield simply submerge the boat and we would be free of this constant heave-ho?"

"Yes, but he's trying to stay on schedule."

"What schedule?"

I've no answer to her question. The experiment's launch date was already set, our transit offering ample time to rendezvous with the Athena–the fleet's new submarine-tender and *point of contact* in Empire water–one-hundred kilometers west of the Bonin Islands where the experiment would be tested before commencing the operation. I didn't really understand his insistence on battling the storm on the surface considering how much fuel we were expending.

"I don't know how to answer your question. There could be a variety of reasons, but I would be speculating. He's keeping aspects of this mission very close to his chest."

"I asked Dr. Hoffmann too, but he's acting so tightlipped. It's very uncharacteristic of him."

"Oh?"

"Dr. Hoffmann shares everything with me Michael, or at least he used to. Lately he's become preoccupied with something he won't share with me. It's quite odd." Because of her concern, perhaps the tone in her voice, I become quiet and detached, until she asks, "How do you do it? How can you be so tall and straight?"

"Tall and straight?"

"Unaffected by the storm. It's as if you were still on land. What's your secret?"

"Funny you ask. I remember being seasick, my whole life…a part of me, deathly afraid of the water, the mystery underneath the surface…afraid of the idea of drowning. Luckily the part that's here, is a sailor." She puzzles over my words but she's too ill to pursue it. "Don't think about the *heave-ho* Lucy, the motion of the boat. Accept it. Move with it."

"That's the big secret?"

"Keep your mind active on what you're doing. Surrender to the motion of the sea."

"That's exactly what I'm doing. *Surrendering*."

"Stay focused. You'll feel a change."

"Easier said than done," she mutters, sipping the drink. "Oh, this is splendid. What is it?"

"Who knows, don't ask. That Cajun is forever bringing herbs and spices aboard. I'm sure he's violating a few hundred Navy codes. But honestly, he's a better doctor than the various pharmacists we've had come and go. He told me once: '*Everything a man needs to live a hundred years grows right under his nose.*' I think those were his exact words."

"Well, nothing *grows* on this ship, except mold," she says, and I laugh. "Would you like to know something else Commander?"

"What?"

"You're very handsome when you smile."

I awaken, violently lashing out, the dream I'm experiencing a contentious one, my cabin filling with water, a man with no mouth, trying to drown me. I come to my senses and realize Wells, the new warrant officer, is in my cabin, a look of terror on his face.

"Wells what are you doing in my cabin?"

"My apologies Mr. Murphy but you failed to answer your bell. The OD sent me to wake you."

"What is it Yeoman?"

"S-J contact sir."

Rubbing my face, I check my watch in the gloom, the phosphorescent dial indicating the late hour.

"Thanks." He immediately vacates the compartment. I fill my lungs with diesel-tainted air, remembering the horrible nightmare, before climbing into my uniform and exiting the cabin.

The passageway is vacant and still, nearly serene in the dim light, the red surfacing lights have been activated. As I pass my old quarters, I pause before the muslin curtain, its green hue, black in the red light. On the other side of this thin sheet of cloth, she lies sleeping. I see her face clearly in my mind, feel the strongest desire to step inside; hold her again. When Nichols and Belcher exit the forward torpedo compartment, I continue into a blood-red control room, all white light extinguished. Quartermaster Taylor is scanning the compass.

"We've stopped Bill?"

"We're getting a read on the S-J radar. Radio contact too, signaling friendly. Radar is barely getting a read Mike. She's too small to be a destroyer."

"What's her range and bearing?"

"Forty degrees off the port bow, about two miles out."

"Who is it?"

"Not sure. We're getting strange transmissions."

I stare at the man. Is he purposely being obtuse? Not Bill Taylor. I push past him to the *radio shack* and stick my head into the tiny room filled floor to ceiling with radio transmission equipment; knobs, toggles and dials. Jukes–patented cigarette hanging from his mouth–is listening intently, the headset pressed against one ear.

"What's shakin' Jukes, one of us?"

"Sorry Lieutenant, I'm not sure."

"What do you mean *not sure*? Jukes, is that or is that not a United States naval craft out there?" I ask, unable to mask my irritation with his response.

"That's what's got me sir. It's a Navy frequency but…"

"But what?!"

"It's way off the current operational bandwidths. Why?"

"Jukes look at me. What are you talking about?"

"They're using one of the older frequencies. I don't get it, why Commander? It's wacko."

"You been sipping *gilly* again?"

"No sir," he says indignantly. "I don't know Mr. Murphy. It beats me." I give him a long look before heading back through the control room and grab the ladder to the conning tower.

"Heading topside Bill. Is the old man above?"

"Negative. In his bunk." This information freezes me a moment before I climb into the sweat-drenched confines of the conning tower. The *surfacing lights* coat the room in a blood-red glow, essential for protecting the boat from detection above at night. Smith, has the periscope in the *high* position, locked on the coordinates.

"Got 'em John?" I grab a pair of night-goggles designed to expedite the production of deep purple within the retinas.

"It's pretty dark out sir."

"What's he doing Rose?" Herndon is glued to the radar; moisture beads on his forehead, as if the man were sweating blood.

"Nothing. Just sitting there. What the hell's going on Mr. Murphy?" I stick my head into the hatchway to the bridge, rain finding my face.

"Permission to come above?"

"Granted."

Stewart has doubled the watch, the lookouts in the *sail* scanning the sea three-hundred-and-sixty degrees around the sub, engulfed in darkness. Sporadic flashes of lightning cut through the vast ebony sky like glass shattering under the tempo of thunder. A nor'easter is blowing thick evil clouds across our track and the dark ocean is heaving.

In the dark heavy rain, I'm surprised our watch team can see anything. I recheck my wristwatch, the green glow of the phosphor the only light in a near absolute gloom. 0200, the dead of night. Waves crash against her foredeck like ghosts raging in the wilds. The new moon is invisible, the ocean as black as obsidian.

"What's going on Stewie?"

"Forty port, just on the horizon," he says handing me his binoculars. I scan the area with the glasses. I can just make out a grim horizon, black on black but nothing else.

"It's pitch-black. I don't see a damn thing."

"He's there Murph, and he knows we're here."

"How do you know that?"

"Just keep looking." Suddenly a thin beam of light flashes from the vessel and is gone.

"A transom-light?"

"Every three and a half minutes on the nose."

"What the hell is that?" He shrugs. "Why isn't Skipper up here?" he shrugs again. "Has he been notified?"

"Of course," he expounds indignantly. Another close study, another pulse of light. "There, exactly three and half minutes on the nose." He spits into the wind.

"I'm going below," I say returning his binoculars and I'm down the ladder knocking on Canfield's cabin.

"Come in *Murph*," I hear from behind the muslin. He's at his desk, an official *'Captain's Eyes Only'* file in his hand. "Grab a seat." He sees the look on my face and smiles. "The engines have stopped. There's a ship sitting out there in the drink. She's solid black, except she flashes a beacon every three minutes. Close?"

"What's going on Skipper?"

His expression is eerie, unreadable. "What's going on? History."

The alarm bell shatters the moment, the boat thrown into chaos as men rush to their battle stations. Racing from Canfield's cabin, I smash into Romayo with a tray of dishes from the officer's wardroom. Cups and saucers bound and break the length of the gangway. No time for apologies–and none expected–I'm instantly back in the control room, Taylor relaying Stewart's orders from the bridge.

"Flood all tanks, emergency dive!"

"What the hell's going on Bill?"

"Bogey vessel closing." I'm immediately on my way up the ladder into the conning tower where the lookouts are dogging the top hatch.

"That has to be a Japanese sub-killer," Stewart curses, "they're heading straight for us."

I grab the Com. "All hands, battle stations," and hit the collision alarm. *Bong-bong-bong-bong,* the speaker cone spits, the entire boat exploding into action. "Bill bring us to periscope depth. *Approach team* to stations." I feel the boat pull out of its crash-dive. We quickly level off, the tumult of the ocean replaced by a soft embryonic quietude.

"Coming to sixty feet Mr. Murphy."

"Sonar, what's his range?"

"He's a mile and a half out, closing."

"John, get the scope back up." Smith helps re-raise the silver shaft of the attack periscope. I ride it up. "Bearing?"

"Two-sixty-two."

Training the scope on the indicated bearing, I see nothing but water. "Bill, level her, we're dipping our scope. Dump a thousand gallons from the forward trim." I hear the control room respond. When the scope breaks the surface again, all I see is a dark rolling ocean barely visible in the gloom. "Talk to me Gallen, what's his range?"

"Coming on Commander. Two thousand yards and closing." Scanning the scope, I find only a vast emptiness, the intruder entirely dark. The new moon adds nothing to the situation, hiding the very moment I need her most.

"Dammit, I can't see a thing. Hydrophone, you got him?"

"He's there. Coming on, screws getting louder."

I work the scope, gritting my teeth. "Dammit, I can't see a…wait, got him. Not a damn light burning…range?"

"Fifteen-double-oh."

"Sons-of-bitches," Stewart curses, spitting. "Using our own frequency to lure us in."

"What if she's one of ours?"

"Are you stupid Smith? She can't be one of ours. Why wouldn't she signal?"

"They did signal Lieutenant Stewart. The transmissions were clear."

"Proper transmissions Ensign! It has to be the Japs Murph. They don't know the proper frequencies, they're trying anything."

"They better hope I don't get my hands around their skipper's yellow neck, the dirty rat bastard," Fitzgerald says in the control room below us.

"Shut-up Fitz," Babineaux shouts from the hatch below my feet. "Standing-by to arm our guns topside Commander Murphy," he reports, buttoning his foul weather parka.

"Acknowledged, standby Gunner." I work the scope in the deplorable conditions, locking it on the dark silhouette on a direct course toward our boat. "He's heading straight at us."

"What the hell you going to do Murph? We're under orders not to engage the enemy. That's direct from Pearl." All the men in the conning tower freeze at their controls. I look at them, see the fear in their young faces. They're waiting on me for the right orders.

"Prepare forward-tube three." The men erupt into action, the order echoed to the forward torpedo room, each crewman implicitly knowing their respective tasks. "Standby to fire on her at two thousand feet." Each man becomes a cog in a wheel set into motion by the words of my mouth, the words formulated from two years of continuous submarine warfare.

"Forward torpedo room responds Commander Murphy."

"Very well. Approach team standby to fire. Smith on the TDC, Stewie take the plot."

"Aye-aye," Smith says but his eyes say something else.

"One-triple-zero yards and coming on."

"Bill, steady the boat, we're still dipping." There's more shouting from below. Stewart is instantly at my elbow.

"Are you out of your mind Murph? You're going with Smith? You're not putting Bill on the TDC?"

"Bill is the diving officer Stewie. John has been assigned *approach*."

"John is the *approach* officer because we're not supposed to be engaging the enemy. He's never run the real thing Murph. This isn't a goddamn exercise. This is for keeps."

"Lieutenant Stewart, take your position at the plot." Smith has obviously heard the argument. "John set up. I want a two-degree spread on a forty-degree angle. Set your torpedo depth to ten feet. Speed, thirty knots. Standby for further orders from me."

"Aye-aye Commander." I struggle to see in the maelstrom of dark roiling sea, wishing like hell I had a full moon above. When the boat steadies, I have him in the crosshairs.

"Come on in sucker, come and get it," Lesky mutters from the helm.

"Dirty slant bastards," Fitzgerald says beneath our feet.

"Quiet men," I say training the scope on the target.

"He's at seven hundred yards and closing sir."

"Mr. Smith, reset your torpedo to fifty degrees port, depth seven feet." He looks like he's ready to vomit. "John. Remember your training. We'll fire at two thousand feet."

"Yes sir."

"He's at five hundred yards Mr. Murphy."

"Flood tube three."

"Forward torpedo ready to fire," Stewart responds. Suddenly Goldman turns abruptly.

"Sir, bogey slowing…coming to…eight knots."

"Eight knots? Are you sure?"

He checks his gear. "Yes sir. Bogey vessel slowing to eight knots." I question Herndon bent over his screen, sweat rolling down his temples like a river.

"Confirming. Bogey slowing to seven knots, relative."

"What the hell? What's he doing?" Stewart curses. "More games? To hell with him, I say we fire Murph, do it!" I grab the battle-phone.

"Radio room…Jukes, any further transmissions from that ship?" I look at Stewart, rain–or sweat–dripping down his face. "Let me know the second you hear anything."

"What are you waiting for? Fire Murph, before he does. If that's a Jap torpedo boat he's getting the bead on us now."

"Easy Stu. Goldy what's his speed?"

"Unchanged. Bogey maintaining seven knots steady. He's like a sitting duck out there, sir."

"For Christ-sake shoot," Stewart presses, sweat soaking his collar.

"Easy Stewart, easy."

"Where's Skipper?" he shouts.

"Never mind."

"Well what are you going to do Murph, just sit here?"

"What I'm trained to do Ellis. I'm going to put a Mark 14 into the belly of that son-of-a-bitch!"

"Belay that order." Canfield is suddenly in the hatch at our feet. "Stand-down, prepare to surface the boat." He ducks below. I'm right on his heels. Below in the control room, I grab his arm.

"Dammit Captain, what's going on?" An instant silence permeates the room, the men freezing at their controls. Canfield stares at his arm until I release it.

"You'll learn soon enough First Officer. Surface the boat." Everyone springs into action, Taylor engaging three blasts on the klaxon signaling *rise*. Sailors twist knobs and pull air-pressure levers. The boat hisses, Canfield scowls. "What are you standing around for Murphy? Prepare a deck crew, now."

Minutes later the boat is rolling on top of the water, the interior of the conning tower inundated with red light, the color of blood. Some of the men wear night-goggles to better prepare their eyes for the darkness waiting on the surface. Everyone is cramming into the control room including doctors Hoffmann and Charlesworth. I see the confusion on her face; Hoffmann, however, seems strangely impatient, constantly checking and rechecking his watch.

"Secure the blow. Gunnery crew, standby to go topside." I climb the ladder into the conning tower, following Burlsley armed with a Thompson submachine gun. We wait for the signal to open the hatch. When it comes, he spins the wheel and the rain and sea pour in atop us, drenching our shoulders as we pull ourselves into the night waiting above.

The wind howls through the hatchway seeking the insides of the sub, crammed with the wondering faces of the scientists and crew.

Ascending the ladder, my men quickly take their firing positions; Burlsley on point from the bridge, Babineaux and Sorel on the *Bofors 40 mm*. Toles and Fitzgerald prepare our four-inch gun with McClatchy filling in as loader. These men were not afraid to scrap with an enemy. They had exchanged *lead* with the best on previous occasions. *'Our boat, she who protects us whilst at sea.'*

I'm training my binoculars on the target, now barely a hundred yards off our port bow, the sea rolling, at least five-foot swells. Stewart and the captain join us on the bridge. The dark intruder ship–what looks like a tender, void of running lights or insignia–maneuvers abeam. Canfield grabs the battle-phone.

"All back one-third. Steady her up Chief. Amidships."

The Manta Ray races her engines, reversing our position to align us better with the dark stranger on our portside. The boat rumbles beneath my feet, like a black panther growling in the night. Perhaps she senses danger, the boat vibrating with nervous tension.

"All stop," Canfield barks and all goes quiet except the great sea, whipped into frenzy by this weird nocturnal rendezvous. It throws itself relentlessly against our gunwales, spitting salt into the recesses of my nose and mouth. Our men, in drab-gray sou'westers, file up the hatch and fan-out along her foredeck, locking themselves into the guidewire with hooks and lanyards.

"Completely dark," Stewart says. "Not a mark or a number on her. How do you know she's one of ours Skip?"

"She's one of ours."

"She's too small to be a sub-killer," I say. "I can't make-out any guns or ordnance on her decks."

"Research vessel," Canfield responds.

"Oh? You have an identification?"

"S.S. Arthur O'Malley. Old Coast Guard tender." I stare at the captain in silhouette, black as coal, like a Balinese shadow puppet.

"Brother, I sure wish she'd signal," Stewart says checking the clip on his .45 automatic. As if on cue, the vessel flashes several dots and dashes. "It's Morse code."

"You get it?" I ask him and Canfield cuts me off.

"It'll be her name and number. They're requesting to come aboard."

"That's what it says. S.S. Arthur O'Malley…requesting permission to come abeam."

"Copy them and grant them permission," Canfield says, turning to Burlsley. "Bosun, standby to take on passengers."

"Aye Captain." He climbs over the cowling and drops to the deck below handing his weapon to Fitzgerald who assumes his *point* position on the bridge. Stewart and I share a look. Canfield sees it on our faces.

"Do you have a question Mr. Murphy?"

"No sir." I twist the toggle on the squawk box. "Chief, run up the ship-to-ship wire rig. Standby to take on passengers."

"See that's it done," he says. I stare at him a moment, considering the request to oversee the order nearly ridiculous.

Below, the boat is erupting with tension and curiosity. Bremer and Conrad Howard are scratching their heads, waiting for Torsch and Parmalee to extract the wire rigging from the electrician's stow.

"*Passengers?*" Chief queries me, a frown etched into his grizzled face.

"That's what he said."

"Like who?" Howard interjects.

"How would I know seaman?"

"What are we now, a floating brothel?" Chief says. I ignore the comment. "Connie, grab my raingear."

"Aye Chief."

"And my 9mm."

"Aye." He disappears aft, his spot replaced by Taylor.

"He's running a line in this weather? The sea is five feet."

Returning topside with the rigging, they're *talking* back and forth via the Aldis lamp, Wyatt operating the device bolted to the bridge cowling. The wind and rain lashes at our faces; anticipation thicker than the atmosphere.

"They're sending over a launch," Stewart says lowering his binoculars.

"Bosun, get 'em aboard," Canfield shouts to Burlsley.

The launch makes its way alongside, bobbing in the surf. Our crew secures their craft helping the men up onto the deck. I'm surprised by the sudden appearance of Hoffmann on the bridge buried within someone's sou'wester.

"Dr. Hoffmann, what brings you to the war?"

"Are they aboard yet Captain?" Canfield points toward the men carefully filing onto the submarine, our crew taking pains to lock them in, securing them against the advent of slipping or being washed into the turbulent ocean. We watch a lean severe man climb the ladder and join us on the bridge.

"Permission to come on board," he says to Canfield.

"Granted. Welcome aboard the Manta Ray."

"Commander John Bradshaw," he says saluting.

"Oliver Canfield." He extends a handshake, Bradshaw ignoring it.

"Hello Dr. Hoffmann."

"Good evening Bradshaw. How was the journey?"

"Uneventful."

"Is Professor Brauer with you?"

"He'll be coming over with *the package*."

"Good. I believe we're ready for the inclusion of the Phoenix system components."

"He'll be pleased to hear it."

"Meet me downstairs in my cabin. This isn't my environment up here," he says clutching the rail of the cowling like a kid on a roller coaster.

"I'll tell him," he says. Hoffmann makes for the hatch.

"Head below Bradshaw, my boys will stow your gear."

"No thanks Canfield. We'll take care of our gear ourselves thanks."

"Suit yourself."

Bradshaw barks orders and his men begin to unload gear from the launch taking exception when the Manta Ray crew attempts to help.

"Skipper, what gives?" Burlsley shouts from the deck, at odds with this unusual approach to seafaring protocol.

"Stand-down Bosun. Secure their craft until everything is safely aboard."

"Aye-aye," he grumbles. Bradshaw jumps in with his men and they commence lugging several heavily laden boxes onboard. Canfield gives us a dour look, shaking his head.

"Keep an eye on things," he mutters, heading below.

As soon as he's gone Stewart is at my elbow. "What the hell's going on Mike? Why weren't we briefed about this?"

"Quiet Stewie, there's men above," I say referring to the lookouts in the sail and he closes the distance between us.

"Well what goes on Commander? Why weren't we briefed?" he spits, waiting for an answer.

"I don't know," is all I can say, as much at odds with what's happening as he. "Get below and prepare for our *guests*. Prepare a station to receive their gear." He doesn't acknowledge me, just disappears below but his words remain with me topside.

"We're ready to run the wire Mr. Murphy," Burlsley shouts from the deck.

"Very well. Standby Bosun. Make fast."

"Aye sir."

Silence clouds my mind. Even the roar of the sea disappears from my thoughts. Why wasn't I, at the very least, included in what's happening? Why this weird nocturnal rendezvous? Obviously, this is why the captain had me lay-in the alternate course, contrary to the one originally plotted, effectively circumnavigating *the lanes*. It was designed to take us here, this very spot at this very time, and during a new moon, the ocean as black as coal. Why? And why this lone phantom ship, as dark as the ocean that surrounds us? Bradshaw climbs the sail and is suddenly at my side. He gazes about, bewildered.

"Where's Canfield?"

"Below."

"He's not overseeing the transfer of the package?"

"What is it you need Commander Bradshaw?"

"Someone in command to oversee the transfer of the package!"

"I'm Lieutenant Commander Murphy, first officer of the boat. I'll be overseeing the transfer."

"Well, get at it, *Lieutenant*," he barks purposely emphasizing my subordinate title.

"Our men have been standing-by." I gesture to my crew waiting patiently on deck. "The wire rig is prepped and ready to go on your order."

With the assistance of the O'Malley's crew we rig a guide wire between the vessels and begin the dangerous process of moving men and materiel between the two craft. When *the package* arrives on deck, I'm surprised by how small it looks considering the banter regarding its handling.

It looks about the size of a *Cutie*, the misnomer given the Navy's recent secret weapon; a homing torpedo, released from below that rises from the deep, exploding under an enemy ship's hull. The *Cutie* won her nom-de-plume as the only effective weapon for a submarine pinned on the ocean floor by surface raiders. However, this thing being transferred from the O'Malley to the Manta Ray is too small and light to be a Cutie. What is it? And why won't they let my crew anywhere near it?

During the equipment transfer, one of the O'Malley's crew catches a wave and goes over. Fortunately, he wears a life-vest. However, we quickly realize that despite his efforts, the man is being taken by the tide.

"Lieutenant Culver, why wasn't that man locked in?" Bradshaw barks to his second in command.

"He couldn't release the load mechanism Commander, not without disengaging his hook."

"Get that man aboard sailor, right now."

"How sir?" Bradshaw goes blank, incapable of a response to his lieutenant's question. He then defers to me on the spot. Before I can ask for a volunteer, Burlsley is stripping off his jacket and boots.

"I'll get him." He grabs our emergency line tying a bowline knot with one hand and slinging it over his shoulder across his chest. Burlsley was a well-seasoned sailor, brave; he cared about the men he served with, whatever rank or boat that man happened to be assigned.

"You're going into the water after that man without a boat or a life-vest?" Bradshaw asks belaying Burlsley.

"I can't reach him soon enough in a vest sir."

"Sailor, you put that vest back on."

"Commander, way I figure it, we got exactly twenty seconds to reach that guy before he's headed out to sea for good." Bradshaw, amazingly, just stands there mute. Burlsley looks to me. "Commander Murphy?"

"Go ahead Gil." Burlsley takes a look back at Lesky and Jaeger manning the line.

"Don't you guys let go of that rope," he says and dives into the oil-black sea.

"Pay-out the line carefully," I shout to the men on the deck. We watch as Burlsley makes his way into the blackness of the ocean. Seaman Wyatt is on my left. "Wyatt, train our beam on their man in the water."

"Aye sir," he responds, switching on the sea-lamp mounted to the cowling wall. As soon as the light flashes across the turgid water, locking on the sailor in the vest, Bradshaw is spitting at me from the deck.

"Get that light off Murphy, are you stupid?"

"Commander, we've two men in the water. My man can't locate your man without-"

"Murphy turn that light off right now! What if a Jap airplane spots it?"

"We're too far out for enemy aircraft sir. There's no moon. It's too dark."

"Then a Japanese sub or whatever. Sailor, turn that light off now!" Wyatt has the man firmly in the beam. I see Burlsley making for the spot.

"Sir?" Wyatt says from the side of his mouth.

"Keep the beam on until our Bosun reaches him Wyatt, that's an order."

When Burlsley reaches the man the worst happens, the sailor panics, clawing at him, pulling him under despite Gil's shouts for him to relax. We watch this horrific scene unfold from the boat, helpless.

"Oh my god, he's going to drown Burlsley," Wyatt exhales. Fitzgerald engages the magazine of the Thompson.

"Shall I shoot him Commander? I can hit their guy from here."

"Take a powder Fitz," Connie says from beside Chief. "You can't shoot that guy. He's on our side."

"He's drowning Gil. I say we shoot him. Commander Murphy?" He actually takes aim with the Thompson.

"Stand-down Gunner, that's an order."

"Lieutenant Murphy! You let that man leave this ship without a life vest," Bradshaw screams from the deck. "If those men drown it's your fault!"

"Commander, permission to pop that loudmouth in the chops," Babineaux says from behind the 40mm. At the point I decide to order the men to pull in the line, effectively abandoning the rescue, Burlsley manages a solid right hook and knocks the sailor unconscious. He gets him turned over onto his back, atop himself, and signals.

"Get them aboard fellas," I say, going over the cowling and dropping down to the deck, assisting with the line.

"Steady boys," Chief shouts joining in, "don't rip his arms off."

When they reach the side of the sub, I tell Wyatt to switch off the beam. We help the sailors onto the deck, blood running from the unconscious man's mouth. Burlsley sprawls across the deck's teakwood planking, gasping for breath.

"The dumbass. He was going to drown me Mr. Murphy," he says squinting at me, the saltwater burning his eyes. "Had to give him a shot in the mouth."

"You did fine Gil, just fine. Head below and get some hot coffee in you," I say. He manages a weak salute as Jaeger helps him to his feet.

"We'll never live this one down," Lesky adds, taking the other arm. "You forget how to walk Burlsley?" I realize how close the Manta Ray has come to losing her second man. When we attempt to move the injured sailor, Bradshaw again belays my order.

"Leave him. Tie him to the deck." He turns to his second. "Unload the equipment first Culver, then return him to the O'Malley when we pick up Professor Brauer."

"Sir, we've a pharmacist on board. We'll have him checked out while-"

"Did you not hear me Lieutenant Murphy?" he nearly screams. "I said leave him."

"Are you out of your mind?" Chief Bremer shouts from his sou'wester. "This man is unconscious, and bleeding."

"So what? It's his fault for being careless. We've a job to do sailor, so do it!" He turns away, shouting at his men and they commence unloading the launch.

"To hell with him and his parade," Chief snarls. "I'll be below Murph." He joins the men helping Burlsley down the hatch just as Stewart emerges from it.

"Our boatswain got their man back onboard?" he asks looking at the man being tied to the deck with lash cable.

"Yes, thankfully. That was close."

"Relieving you as OD," he says pulling the collar of his pea-coat up tightly around his cap.

"Thanks, heading below." I gaze back at Bradshaw shouting at his men. "Stay out of trouble."

He nods, watching the chaos on deck. "Yeah, thanks."

We're shaking off the wet and cold when a portly silver-haired man squeezes through the hatch in the ceiling and joins us in the control room.

"Brauer, how was your *cruise*?" Hoffmann says with alacrity. The man is cloaked in a bulky foul-weather parka, looking very ill as he begins stripping away the jacket tied about his neck. I extend one of the foldout seats and help him sit. For a moment I think he's in the throes of a heart attack, or about to vomit.

"Are you all right sir?" I ask.

"Hoffmann, some men are made for sailing. I am not."

"How are you feeling Professor?" Lucy asks taking his wrist and actually checking his pulse.

"Leave it Charlesworth, I'm just seasick, I'll be fine. Let me sit a moment." He glances at me. "Thank-you Commander," he says noting the insignia on my collar and tapping the chair beneath his rump.

"No problem sir, take your time."

"Brauer, this is Commander Murphy, the first officer," Hoffmann says, and we shake hands.

"The pleasure is mine," he says. "Hoffmann could I have some water?" I gesture to Duncan and he heads for the mess. "I tell you Hoffmann, sailing is not my cup of tea. I've been sick the entire trip. I can't keep food down."

"That will change when we submerge Professor Brauer."

"When will that be Commander?"

"Daybreak. Tomorrow we cross into Empire water. We'll ride above during darkness to charge our batteries, submerge at dawn, or if we're buzzed by aircraft or patrol boats."

"Brauer, forego the water. Join us for a cup of tea in the officer's mess-hall, our *command central* for the project." We assist the professor in removing his foul weather gear and maneuver him to the wardroom.

"All in all, we're very close to ready. This is a very able crew," Lucy says. I place a cup of black coffee on the table before the professor.

"How long do you estimate the installation of the new components Brauer?"

"Not long Hoffmann. We've wired all the *Phoenix* bay-stations and boards prior *the cruise* as you state it. It's merely a matter of plugging-in and calibrating to the *Shadow-fox* system. Charlesworth, what about the power source? Are we getting what we need?" She defers to the young sandy-haired seaman listening-in at the doorway.

"You're tied-in to our mains Professor. Your transformers are in-line as well and functional, we tested them yesterday. Surge suppression is being fine-tuned. We're sending you three-phase power down three legs of four-aught cable. I've included a *neutral* with the *ground*. Each leg is carrying 119 to 120 volts per leg per your requirements."

"Hoffmann who is this young man?"

"This is Anson Parmalee, the ship's electrician."

They exchange a firm handshake. "Where were you schooled in electricity Mr. Parmalee?"

"I did my undergraduate work at Caltech, sir."

"Outstanding young man."

"Professor Brauer, the mains will feed the coils while the external counter-array will be tied-in to the boat's auxiliary batteries. Each circuit is isolated from the other, effectively separating the system's two energy reserves as per our operational directive."

"More than sufficient. We should be all right." We're interrupted when Canfield joins us, water dripping from his rain slicker. He pours a cup of coffee, pushing his cap back from his forehead.

"How's it going up there?" I inquire.

"Slow," he says to Hoffmann. "They won't let our boys touch their gear."

"There's a good reason for that Captain. One you'll know eventually."

"That's not my concern Doc. Sitting here like a duck in the crosshairs is."

"I understand Captain. It won't be long. Captain, have you plotted our next course?"

"Yeah…why?"

"We may be diverting from it."

"What do you mean?"

"It'll be discussed. You'll be briefed."

"*Briefed?* By who?"

"Whom. Commander Bradshaw."

"Bradshaw? That wannabe Navy regular, says *whom*?"

"Admiral Greene, your orders should have arrived by now." Canfield sets his cup down and immediately heads for the radio room. I'm right on his heels.

"Jukes, anything off the wire just now?"

"Hot off the press Skip, priority message. Encoded." Canfield snatches it and shoves it at Bill Taylor hovering over my shoulder.

"Quartermaster, have this deciphered immediately."

We're sipping coffee in the crew's mess when Taylor returns with the deciphered message. Canfield crushes it in his fist. "Those bunch of yahoos back at Pearl."

"What is it?" I ask. He shoves the note at me. "Says we're to convene closed session upon *our guest's* arrival. He has sealed orders signed by Greene."

"Something tells me I'm not going to like it."

Half an hour later we're gathered in the wardroom. Canfield, Bradshaw, doctors Hoffmann, Charlesworth, and Brauer all crowded into the compartment hovering over a nautical map spread across the stainless-steel table.

"We'll head directly west at full speed and rendezvous with the Athena here," Bradshaw proclaims, pointing at a tiny dot on the map. "Exactly one hundred kilometers due east of this island, *Hachijojima*."

"And conduct the experiment from the Athena's deck," Hoffmann says.

"Once the experiment is confirmed, we'll sail due north two hundred kilometers straight into Tokyo Bay." He looks up from the map. I already see the expression forming on Canfield's face.

"Who drew up this approach Bradshaw?"

"Myself in fact."

"It figures, a deckhand like you."

"Meaning what?" Canfield looks hard in my direction.

"Sir, the Japanese are placing their submarines on north-to-south pickets, here, here, and here." I point out several long sweeps across the massive body of water between our position and Japan. "They'll anticipate a westerly intercept on those coordinates. We're bound to make contact." The man stares at me, as if I were speaking Greek.

"So what? If they're there, we'll go under them." He looks at Hoffmann. "Or perhaps straight by them, invisible."

"Sir, each screen is composed of seven to eight submarines, lying in wait. They're trying to cut off our supply route to the Gilberts, close off Empire to direct incursions. We've lost a boat or two trying to *thread the needle*."

"Didn't Pearl tell you this when you submitted this lousy scheme?" Canfield interjects.

"Not even Pearl will know our movements. This is a top-secret mission Canfield and this piece of paper from Admiral Greene gives me complete control over this vessel and where it goes." Canfield takes the form, perusing it.

"This piece of paper?" He rips it in half, crumpling it in his fist and throwing it across the compartment.

"That's insubordination Canfield!"

"These dolphins say otherwise," Canfield says thumbing the submarine commander's insignia on his collar.

"I'll report this to Admiral Greene."

"You'll be talking to him through a tube!" Canfield snarls, the two men literally nose-to-nose.

"Gentlemen, please. Please control yourselves," Hoffmann says. "Fisticuffs will not help our situation."

"He's never commanded a fleet-boat Doc. He'll get us all killed."

"Commander Bradshaw, Captain Canfield is correct. After all, he's a fully experienced submarine captain. Let him command until our rendezvous with the Athena. At that point we commence *Phoenix*, the operational aspect of the mission, as per Greene's order. Agreed?"

"But my orders from Admiral Greene gave me control of this boat. I'm responsible for the Phoenix mission."

"Exactly the point. The *operation* begins when we reunite with the Athena team and commence the actual experiment, and of course the subsequent deployment."

"But his directive, in that letter. I suggest we radio him."

"You don't have the rating. You've never commanded a fleet-boat in a war-zone," Canfield presses.

"I'm fully trained Canfield. I did a year at Groton."

"You're a lousy desk-jockey, admit it." They're nose-to-nose again. I fear they'll actually go to punches. I'd seen it before. Canfield had a wicked left-hook and liked to use it.

"Bradshaw," Brauer interjects, "Greene isn't top command on the mission, Lance is. Are you actually suggesting we radio these men to dispute our disagreements with them?" There are no clear responses.

"Excellent," Hoffmann says, taking the initiative. "While Captain Canfield takes care of the boat, we'll prepare for the field tests."

"Field tests?" Canfield inquires. "Doc, we're at war. You think the Japanese are on a joy-ride out here?"

"Captain, surely you were briefed. The process is theoretical. The equipment must be attenuated in transit until the proper frequency levels are ascertained. Once the footprint of the ship is locked, we expect to achieve the desired results." He lights his pipe and the compartment goes silent.

"What does that mean Dr. Hoffmann, *the footprint* of the boat?" I ask. Both men defer to Lucy.

"Well, Commander, the boat is comprised of steel and electrical systems, giving off their own electromagnetic fields. We must attenuate the particle field to synchronize seamlessly with the boat's magnetic signature or we'll fail to effectively stabilize the platform."

"I don't get all that mumbo-jumbo lady," Canfield says indignantly. Lucy looks to Dr. Hoffmann.

"Captain, electric current creates magnetism," Hoffmann says relighting his pipe, filling the compartment with a gray haze. "Likewise, magnetism creates electricity. We'll be creating a counter-field, an interference pattern, tuned to interface with the particle field around the exterior of the submarine. If properly tuned, we hope to achieve *negative light*." Canfield's expression speaks volumes, confusion coursing his grizzled face.

"Captain Canfield," Lucy says, taking his wrist, "perhaps it would be better for your comprehension if you didn't think of the coils as electronic devices but rather perhaps enormous magnets, per se, designed to literally bend light."

"For what purpose?" His question dumbfounds her.

"You know the answer to that question," Hoffmann says. "To deliver our ordnance package undetected."

"Through the Uraga Strait," Canfield mutters, becoming suddenly distant. "Into Tokyo Harbor…no-man's land. A place no fleet-boat has ever gone. Invisible."

"Right under their noses," Bradshaw sneers. "In broad daylight. It'll make history."

The following hours turn into days, the scientists readying the boat, tweaking instrumentation, calibrating and re-calibrating electrical components, testing relays and circuits. Lucy becomes preoccupied with the new devices, wiring them into the system with the science team and electricians, testing and retesting the system components while my duties–the daily maintenance and operations of the boat–absorb my attention.

The electricians clamor out from under the after-battery's floor plate. They're topping-off the boat's electric batteries with fresh water. Parmalee wipes sweat from his brow with his sleeve while Ashburn and Lawler cough and spit.

"Take a break you guys, go air out your lungs," he says. The young recruits beat a hasty retreat to the bridge. There was always the threat of toxic gases being emitted by the batteries. I help Parmalee out of the hold and he sits on the floor. He often sat crossed-legged and even meditated.

"How are the batteries handling the extra load of the experiment?"

"Batteries are fine Mr. Murphy but they're going through water like no tomorrow. We may have to cut back on the showers again, at least the crew."

"I can't cut back on the crew. I've already lowered the allotment from five minutes a week to three minutes every ten days. Anything less would be inhuman."

"Then the scientists will have to step up to the plate, go to bat for us."

"Anson use any other metaphor than baseball. I've been inundated with the Brooklyn Dodgers since the retrofit."

"What about surfing then? Ask them to step on the board and ride it out."

"Surfing? You said *surfing*. I know about that sport."

"I doubt it Lieutenant. Surfing isn't *a sport,* it's a brand-new thing. I've been doing a little on Waikiki when we're off duty but the place to be is North Shore. Man, you should see a couple of these Hawaiian guys ride those big waves up there on the coast. It's off the hook."

"I thought you grew up in Berkeley?"

"San Diego. We moved to the Bay Area when I was sixteen, but San Diego is where I first learned about surfing. You get a large board, big but not too big, the lightest wood you can find and round off the edges. Pick up a wave and try to ride it to shore. I spent hours doing it. That's a lot of swimming and dragging a waterlogged board around."

"I heard you're a good swimmer, that you had a boat shot out from underneath you, same as Lloyd. The fellas said you swam over twenty miles before you were rescued?"

"My first boat. But we didn't hit a mine like Earl. We had a torpedo lock on a circular run. By the time they figured it out it was too late. Our own torpedo struck the sub and sank it. We were on a surface approach, attacking a trawler. I was on the bridge, saw the whole thing happen. I'll never forget watching that fish start on its end-around. A real sinking feeling, no pun. We tried to dive but didn't even get the top hatch closed before the boat was struck and sank."

"How did you survive?"

"Funny Mr. Murphy…I don't know."

"What do you mean?"

"I don't know how I got out of that sub before she went down. It happened so fast. I guess I swam up through the top hatch but honestly, I don't remember doing it, I was just there, floating."

"Anyone else get out?"

He shakes his head somberly. "No one. Every man was killed or drowned except me, floating in the middle of the ocean. The ship we were attacking spooked. I didn't have any choice but to swim, hours of it. It gets discouraging but I didn't want to just give up and cash-it-in."

"What did you do?"

"Swam. When I got tired, I floated on my back, to rest, then swam more…always toward the North Star, the only fixed position to guide me. That star took me to an island Lieutenant."

"What island?"

"No idea. It was about half a square mile, maybe less. I got through the reef-break and holed up for the night. In the morning I started figuring how to survive. It wasn't as tough as you might think. There was a small mountain with a freshwater spring, and coconuts on the island…and a weird sort of fruit I don't think I've ever seen, before or since."

"Weren't you afraid of being poisoned?"

"I started slow, just a nibble at a time before I was eating them whole. The days were hot, but the nights were wild."

"What do you mean *wild*?"

"I mean wild. The island got strange at night, the stars dipping and diving into the ocean. The sea around the island glowed at night, the water phosphorescent from the marine animals. The reef break made it really light up and sitting there on that beach under the moonlight was like being on another planet. Everything glowed, everything. The plants, even the mountain glowed."

"Fascinating. The Navy rescue you?"

"No, natives, from another island, a day's canoe ride away. They saw me somehow, were just suddenly there on the beach. I really had no choice but to go with them. They paddled that canoe all night, following the stars. I figured my head was destined for the end of a stick, but they were great. Beautiful people, peaceful. The children and the women walked around naked on the island."

"Which island was it?"

"No idea Lieutenant. I ended up with a fever. While I was out of it, they paddled me to an atoll under a flight path where I was spotted by a Navy PBY. You know, someday I want to revisit that island, those people, if I could ever find it again, or if they're even alive any longer."

We're interrupted by Cooper. "Mr. Murphy, do you have a moment sir? In private?"

"Are we good here Anson?"

"We're topped-off Lieutenant. All set for now."

I walk Cooper to the wardroom, closing the curtain. "Private enough?" Something serious is on the young corpsman's mind. "Sit down Cooper. What's bugging you?"

"Dr. Charlesworth."

"*Dr. Charlesworth?* How is she bugging you?"

"Sir, she came to my station for a headache, something to help her sleep. While I was fishing my kit, she noticed I had some painkillers, asked if she might have a few of those instead. I inquired further and she…very reluctantly, showed me bruises on her arm she didn't explain very well."

"She's been doing some pretty strenuous work. It probably was-"

"Commander Murphy…the bruises were caused by another person."

"You mean by accident?"

"I've seen this sort of thing once before. The bruises on Dr. Charlesworth were caused by someone shaking her violently."

I'm stunned. "Are you certain about this?"

"I recognize the pattern of the grip, the finger imprints."

"Who Cooper? Who did this?"

"She wouldn't tell me sir…but I think someone should ask her about it."

We're having coffee in the mess when the alarm bell screams, the sub rapidly filling with water. Water is pouring through the oval doors, green-water snaking through the compartment like a river. I race to the control room reaching for the hatch to the conning tower when I awaken in bed, my hand grabbing the bunk above mine; only a dream.

I'm in *the Ritz* with the enlisted men, having been displaced again, this time by the new commander. It's a quiet sleeping boat, sailors playing cards, some throwing dice.

"Hey Vic, let me have another one of your *Luckies*."

"Why you always gotta put the bite on me Easy? Do I got the word *sucker* tattooed on my forehead? Go put the bum on someone else for a change."

"Excuse me for asking! One lousy cigarette."

"That's the problem with you Easy. One turns into two, two turns into ten, ten turns into another pack."

"Alright already! Forget I asked. Sheesh. *Anty-in* losers. Let's see what Lady-Luck has in store this go-a-round." He deals the deck. "It's your lead Connie."

"I know…I'm thinking."

"Well think faster."

"What's your problem Lesky, can't wait to get back to scrubbing saucepans?"

<hr>

"Save me the lecture and play willya? The only guy in the fleet who can make a career out of a game of cards," he says to the others mulling over their hands. "Sheesh."

"Why does *she* get a five-minute shower everyday if she wants while the rest of us get a lousy three-minute shower once a week?" Fitzgerald's voice again, the familiar negative tack.

"Because she's a woman you creep, and a lady," Howard says. "Hit me Easy."

"And a pal of Admiral Bennett's," McClatchy adds. "Reason enough?"

"I say it should be the same as for us, once a week. What makes her more special than us?"

"Fitz change the channel. The program is getting monotonous."

"What makes her more special than you or me Babs? Or even Lesky for that matter."

"That a rub Fitzgerald?" Lesky was from Philly, forever on the defensive.

"A *rub* is when the innuendo has no basis in reality," Chief Bremer chimes-in from behind his book, smoke from his pipe caressing the bulb over his shoulder.

"What's that supposed to mean Chief?"

"Try to figure it out before the weekend gets here."

"Why're you always riding me Chief?"

"Because you're always screwing up."

"You go soft on Jaeger Chief. He screws up more'n me."

"*Easy*...you're hopeless."

"Shut-up and play your cards," Babineaux interjects. "Try and keep your mind on the card game hot-shot, okay?"

Lesky tosses the cards aside and pulls his pants up several inches, formally addressing the group. "Who was the first guy flat on his back when the big storm hit?"

"You," Toles declares.

"Flush your head out Gunny. Ol' Jiggsy there, flat on his back, boom."

"Then shortly thereafter, you, *boom*."

"You're always thinking aren't you Toles. That brain up there always grinding away despite the rust…it was hours later smart-guy."

"It was fifteen minutes, ask Cooper." They *bum rush* Cooper.

"How about it Coop?"

"*Hours and hours,* or fifteen minutes?"

"Guys, leave me out of it."

During the commotion, I roll out of my bunk and head into the crew mess area where I'm surprised to find a lone and weary female scientist sitting before a cup of coffee, her head in her arms. I quietly pour myself a cup from the dispenser bolted to the countertop and join her.

"Hello," I whisper. When she raises her eyes, they light.

"Why hello."

"You're drinking coffee? I thought you only drank tea?"

"I needed something stronger, and we're out of my flavor of tea, drat it all. You were right. I should have smuggled more onboard before we left."

"Smuggling tea onto a United States fleet-boat? Why Dr. Charlesworth, I'm aghast." This garners a genuine smile, her dulcet eyes looking deeply into mine.

"How are you Michael? There never seems time for our visits anymore. Are things well?"

"As *well* as can be expected with two commanders onboard."

She rolls her eyes. "That's all fubar."

"*Fubar?*"

"Forget I said that. It's better I keep my nose out of where it doesn't belong."

"Why don't you sleep Lucy? You seem tired."

"I am, but what can be done about it? There's too many things, too many details to be ironed out before tomorrow's test."

"So, it's a *go* then, *stage-one*, tomorrow?"

"Oh, indeed kind sir," she says. "We're not ready. Our induction test went negative. We had to isolate and re-calibrate all data relays on the RF system. We just now finished," she says covering a yawn with her fingers.

"I've no idea what you just said." We share a laugh.

"Re-adjustments, re-calculations...a lot of complex mathematics." I take her hand and gently pull up the sleeve. Her beautiful smile instantly disappears. "Michael, what are you doing?"

"You're bruised. What happened?"

"Nothing." There are clear indications Cooper is correct.

"Who did this to you?" The following silence is unbearable. "Lucy, tell me. Who did this?"

"I told your pharmacist...I...I bumped it...I fell during the storm." I see it, in her eyes.

"Why won't you tell me?"

"It's just a bruise. It's over and done with. Please...just, let it go." She takes her arm from my grasp, straightening the sleeve. "Do you mind topping off my coffee? Please."

"Will we be ready for the final test when we rendezvous with the Athena?" I ask from the dispenser, the intent in her words changing the subject.

"Who knows...yes, of course. Commander Bradshaw is pushing us so hard. I'm worried. Hard to sleep thinking..."

I sit beside her. "About what?" She becomes quiet, reflective, pulling closer to me.

"This whole thing. The experiment. It's more dangerous than you think. We're like children with a lit match."

Silence.

"How do you figure that Doctor?" She starts to answer, then instantly checks herself.

"Never mind. It's nothing. Nothing a good eight hours of sleep couldn't fix…even four or five." She's not complaining, simply stating a fact.

"Lucy, why push yourself so much? You work twice as hard as anyone else."

"Isn't the answer obvious? I wasn't supposed to go on this mission. *Not a job for a woman.* Actually, they used the word *girl*. That's basically the reason."

"What reason?"

"People risked their careers for me Michael, don't you understand that? Important people. I…I mustn't let them down."

"But you're running yourself a little hard, don't you think?" Her face darkens and I instantly regret my words, a patina of tears glossing her irises.

"I must be quite a sight."

"You know I didn't mean it that way. I mean you guys have really been burning the midnight oil." She stares into her coffee. We're interrupted by the rotation of the night watch, the men clamoring into their sou'westers as they pass. "A storm must be blowing through."

"Yes," is all she says.

"Look, Dr. Charlesworth, I'm just a sailor. I wasn't trained at Princeton, but can I ask what we're wrangling with here? All the gizmos…the whole crew's on edge. They don't like these machines." I see the answer to my question in her eyes. "My orders are to assist you and not ask questions but…I'm having trouble sleeping too."

Her face changes. "It's just electronics."

"That's right, you said that before." Her eyes shift over my shoulder, canvassing the mess-hall.

"There is a danger, certain risks, if we don't do our jobs properly."

"What dangers?"

"It has a lot to do with waves."

"Like out there?" I say pointing through the bulkhead.

"Well, I'm referring to light of course. Light is both a particle and a wave, depending on how you look at it."

"*Look* at it?"

"Yes, *look* at it, understand?"

"I'm not sure. What do you mean?"

"Everything is waves Michael, everything. Once you understand this fact, energy and matter, life itself really, takes on a whole new perspective. We're just now beginning to realize the complexity of things, and the simplicity."

"Waves. Yes. Somehow, I know what you're talking about. How? I've never studied physics. How could I know anything about waves?"

"You're a sailor, you know it intuitively. You sense it within your...your body."

"Tell me Lucy. I keep hearing you and the scientists talking about *transverse* waves, a key aspect of the experiment. What are they?"

"Well, take this submarine, floating in the surf. As a wave goes by, we move up and down, or the water around the boat does, but the wave moves toward shore. This is called a *transverse* wave. If the medium moves in the same direction as the wave, then the wave is *longitudinal*." Her silent gaze forces my shoulders to rise and fall. "Let me put it this way, a wave is characterized by its frequency, wavelength and speed."

"Right. I'm aware of those terms."

"Being a sailor, you already know a wave has a crest and a trough. In context of physics, or electronics, the frequency is the number of crests per second, the wavelength is the distance between crests and the speed is the velocity of a single crest, understand?"

"Will there be a test?"

"Okay, never mind all that. The main point isn't so much the waves themselves but a unique quality of the wave phenomenon that's referred to as *interference*."

"I've heard you and Dr. Hoffmann talking about that."

"Right, *interference,* you understand?"

"Not at all."

"Okay…sticking with the nautical theme…when a ship travels on the surface you get waves, the wake trailing the ship. What happens when two ship's wakes intersect?"

"You get bigger waves."

"Well, yes, that's correct but you also get…?" The look on my face apparently answers her question. "You get interference Michael. The big waves you mentioned are two crests doubling but imagine if the crest of a wave arrives exactly to that of the other's trough?"

"The water goes flat. They cancel each other."

"Yes…*the water goes flat*…I like that analogy. This is what's referred to as *destructive interference*. Two cycles canceling at a precise point can produce the total absence of waves. If the waves are light waves, then the destructive interference results in dark spots."

"Dark spots?"

"With proper frequency calibration, the twin oscillating fields create an effect resulting in the negation, or bending, of reflected light."

"Invisibility."

"Yes, or so the math indicates."

"So, these coils create a wave around the boat?"

"A field, twin fields. A series of interlaced wave patterns would be the best description of it."

"How does that make the boat invisible?"

"That's where the RF array and the attenuation equipment come in. It sets up a counter-current, a counter-field. The counter-field creates the interference."

"The dark spots."

"However, it must be controlled, attenuated, to create the necessary bending of the cycle or the ship would just appear as a dark shadow moving over the water."

I shake my head. "This is beyond me. Question though…field or no, the boat is still here, we can touch it?"

"Nothing changes inside the field…or so we pray," she says cryptically. We wait while Santino passes through with a plate of sandwiches for the officer's wardroom.

"How does the boat disappear?"

"*It* doesn't," she says, noting my surprise. "What are you actually seeing when you look at your boat from a distance?"

"Three hundred and twelve feet of US Navy fleet-boat."

"No."

I wonder if she's being flip. "No?"

"No," she repeats. "You're seeing light reflected off the ship's hull. What you're actually seeing is just light. Reflected light waves, photons."

"Create an interference pattern, and the reflected light is changed, diverted."

"The point isn't to make the thing itself disappear-"

"But the light around the boat, reflected off from it."

"You have a brilliant mind Mr. Murphy," she says, looking deeply into me. "It will serve you and your crew well."

Our fingers lock. I gently pull her to me, refusing to stop it this time. The moment our lips touch, all hell breaks loose, the collision bell blaring over the boat's PA.

"Crew to general quarters, this is not a drill." We're instantly in the control room. Canfield enters in his t-shirt and boxer-shorts.

"OD, what's the skinny?"

"SJ contact Skipper, multiple readings, three-forty north," Stewart follows Canfield up the ladder into the conning tower. Bradshaw enters buttoning his shirt.

"What's going on?" he asks Lucy standing near the diving manifold.

"Something about *SJ contact*," a nervous tone escalating in her voice.

"Crew to battle stations. Approach team to the Con," blares over the speaker, the whine of the battle siren putting the boat into a sheer chaotic state. Bradshaw scrambles up the ladder to the conning tower and Lucy covers her neck with her fingers as if struggling to breathe. I study her; only a moment ago, her eyes glowing. Now she stands as if buffeted by a storm, rocked about by the sudden and instantaneous eruption of men scrambling for their battle stations. I pull her to the forward portal.

"Lucy, get into your bunk, keep the curtain drawn. I'll be down in a few minutes. Don't worry, it's only a passing convoy." These words have a soothing effect and she squeezes through the portal toward her cabin. I join the men crowding the conning tower.

Canfield has the periscope in the high position to better see in the distance. Stewart is at the stadimeter, Taylor the TDC. Herndon is shouting from his position at the radar.

"Three-thirty north Skipper." Canfield inches the periscope left then right, setting solid on the coordinates.

"Got 'em…masts…it's almost dawn boys. The last dawn of a man's short life," he whispers. "Right standard rudder. Ahead two-thirds." His order is echoed below. The boat pitches with the new direction.

"What are you doing Canfield?" Bradshaw interjects into the flow, the captain ignoring him, shouting down the hatch to Bremer still holding his pipe and book.

"Chief, we're still on patrol! Steady the goddamn boat."

"Canfield, I asked you a question, what do you think you're doing?"

The captain returns to the scope. "There's three of them. A troop transport, a big one…and a tanker. Moving fast. The lead ship is a set-up, a decoy, running point. They're steaming fifteen knots maybe." He hastily scans the periscope 360 degrees about the boat. "I don't see any escorts. I'll wager they're trying to sneak a few thousand soldiers ashore somewhere in the Marshalls." He stares at the battle phone, as if considering something deeply, then picks it up. "Forward torpedo room. Binkershon, prepare tubes three and four, all hands to battle stations."

Bradshaw grabs his arm. "What do you think you're doing?!" All eyes are on the two commanders.

Canfield jerks his arm free. "What I'm paid to do Bradshaw, sink enemy ships."

Bradshaw grabs him again. "You're actually planning to attack those ships? You have no authority to jeopardize this mission."

"Let go of me."

"You know your orders Canfield. We're not to engage enemy shipping."

"Get your hands off me," Canfield snarls through clenched teeth.

"Canfield, I'm warning you."

"Get your hands off me or I'll have you slapped in irons!" The remark draws off Bradshaw.

"Have you gone insane? I'll have you court-martialed."

"Bradshaw, I don't expect a desk-jockey like you to understand but I intend to prevent those Japanese soldiers from getting ashore."

"If you attack those ships you could jeopardize this entire mission!" It's a standoff, all eyes and ears on the commanders.

"Mr. Murphy, escort Commander Bradshaw below." Another moment that extends seemingly into eternity. "Mr. Murphy, did you hear my order?"

"Yes Captain, but in this instance Commander Bradshaw is correct. Our orders from Pearl are explicit." Canfield erupts, spitting fire.

"Damn his orders! Are we not a United States Navy fleet-boat at war?!"

"Yes sir, but-"

"Are the orders not perfectly clear Mr. Murphy, from the outset? To take the fight to the enemy, punch him in the mouth, sink his ships?"

"Yes Captain, but-"

"That's a desperation move up there Murphy. An unescorted troop deployment. I know it by smell. I intend to remove the threat right here."

"But Captain, it doesn't change the fact that-"

"Do I need to remind you Mr. Murphy? The United States attack submarine is all that stands in the way of the enemy running roughshod over our troops and our possessions, the whole goddamn Pacific! Every one of the Mikado's ships we sink sends a message back to Tokyo."

"Captain, I understand that, but it doesn't change the fact that our operational orders state implicitly that-"

"Mr. Murphy, you are relieved of your command! Lieutenant Stewart, escort the X-O and Commander Bradshaw below. Clear the conning tower!"

"Aye Captain," Stewart gestures toward the hatch. "Gentlemen." Bradshaw heads below in a huff but I descend slowly, as if falling into a bad dream.

In the chaotic environment of the control room I listen as Bradshaw rails at Jukes in the radio room, shouting at the top of his lungs.

"Put that cigarette out sailor, now! Get on that thing and open up a channel to Pearl Harbor. Submarine Command."

"No can-do Commander."

"You heard me Radioman. Get me a line into Pearl Harbor right now."

"No sir."

"Are you purposely being insubordinate? That's a direct order!"

"We're under strict radio silence. Marching orders from the boss."

"Dammit man, I'm *the boss*. I'm giving the orders here. Radio Pearl Harbor immediately."

"Sorry sir, those are our operational orders straight from ComSubPac. '*Strict radio silence after delivery of the baby, Lance.*'"

Bradshaw curses and steams through the control room apparently on course toward Hoffmann's cabin for he brushes past Brauer emerging through the port.

"What's Canfield doing up there?" he questions me.

"Attacking a Japanese troop transport."

"That's a violation of our orders."

"I know."

There's nothing to be said. Brauer follows in Bradshaw's footsteps.

"Full ahead Chief," we hear from above. Bremer rings up the command on the *engine order telegraph*, the device jangling under his fierce grip. "Helmsman bring her about, zero-two-zero," Canfield shouts. "Approach team standby to fire." A sickly feeling overtakes me as the boat readies to attack the transport.

"Angle on the bow?"

"Starboard sixty degrees."

"Forward tubes standing-by Captain."

"Range?"

"Thirteen hundred feet."

"You're firing on the lead ship Skipper?"

"Negative, she's high in the water Stewart, a decoy, we'll put one fish into the transport and one into the tanker. Set depth at twelve feet Bill. Speed…thirty-five knots."

"Plotted."

"Bearing…mark."

"Oh-twenty."

"Set."

"Fire one." I listen to the rhythmic cadence of their voices as they release the torpedo and reset on the second.

"Bearing…mark."

"Zero-one-niner."

"Fire two." Again, the familiar *swish-bing,* the air pressure changing in the boat.

"Both *fish* away Skipper. Both running hot, straight, and normal."

"Bill, what's the time on the lead torpedo?"

"Thirty-five seconds. Twenty seconds. Ten seconds. Five, four, three, two…" An enormous concussion rocks the boat, followed by another thunderous clap; accolades are shared.

"Hit on both ships. The tanker is on fire," Canfield says from the scope. "Excellent work boys."

A horrid sound, like moaning–the screaming of metal tearing apart–obfuscates any exchange of accolades as their bulkheads twist and collapse. I swear I hear the sounds of men screaming.

"They're breaking-up Skipper."

"Dive! Emergency dive!" Two blasts from the klaxon suddenly penetrates the sub. Canfield comes flying down the ladder–Stewart right behind him–panic on their faces.

"Face dive! Get us low Chief. Jap *tin cans* right on top of us."

"Flood tanks! Bow-plane hard down!" Bremer shouts and Sorel spins his giant chrome wheel. Plates of food, cups of coffee, hit the floor as the boat angles sharply downward.

"Twin screws Captain," Elder shouts from the hydrophone. "One bearing oh-ten the other zero-two-niner." It's then we hear it, the sound every submariner fears. The destroyer starts *pinging* us, their sonar penetrating the sea, searching for our position in the depths, the echo-ranger seeking our hull, a *look* circles the control room like wildfire.

"Sonofabitch…ASDIC."

Hoffmann enters disheveled, half-dressed. "Commander Murphy, whatever is happening? What is that sound?"

"Brace yourself Dr. Hoffmann, we're under attack."

"Three hundred yards and closing," Elder shouts from his station and for the briefest moment I wonder if I'm reliving a dream, each word as if rehearsed. The pinging gets louder, shorter; the intervals closer together. Men look up, as if in prayer, the sound of the Japanese propellers slicing the water.

"Helm, hard left!" Canfield barks and Jaeger *spins* the wheel. The boat shudders as if terrified. He glares at Hoffmann standing beside me. "I got cocky Doc, distracted. Got impatient and made a mistake. Here it comes. Payback."

Elder sticks his head in the hatch above us, I don't like the look in his eyes. "They're right on top of us Skipper." I know the exact words he'll say next, the phrase indelibly implanted in my psyche. "I hear splashes. Depth charges on their way down."

"Get back to your bunk Dr. Hoffmann," I say pushing him toward the forward port. "Hurry."

The concussion of the first charge is so horrendous it takes out the lights the entire length of the boat, emergency backups kicking-in moments later. The second explosion is in such close proximity the boat lists nearly forty-five degrees. Men are slammed against the bulkheads and the glass faces of nearly every control dial bursts, smoke and seawater spraying the compartment from the air ventilation pipes, masking the screaming of men as they race to shut off every valve they can reach. In the ensuing chaos, Canfield yanks my arm, snarling.

"Mr. Murphy, you've been relieved. Clear the control room!" I stare at the man, the steel-gray eyes spitting fire through the smoke and spray. Is it hate or some other emotion on his face? He's correct of course. I've been relieved of my command by the captain of the boat. I've no longer any authority to issue commands of any sort. Technically, I have no right to even be in the control room. "I said clear control! Now!"

Reflex turns me *forward,* toward the officer's cabins, my old bunk. When I realize my mistake, I'm already in the passageway, the watertight doors slamming shut, standard procedure in preparation of flooding.

For whatever reasons–or perhaps a thousand reasons–I'm alone before the doorway of my old cabin. I stare at the green muslin veil that separates us when a volley of charges rocks the boat, a shockwave rippling the length of the sub.

I'm shoved through the fabric onto the cabin floor. She's in my old bunk, her hands over her ears, terror on her face.

The boat lurches, forcing us together, her arms pulling me tightly to her body. As if the submarine herself were twisting, seeking the depths, it forces us closer together. We hold each other as if we might come apart, or the opposite, be crushed to death in an instant. I see her fear, yet also a deep passionate yearning. She pulls my neck to hers, our lips finding each other, our desire exploding like the depth-charges around us. When my thoughts push me to return to the control room–the captain's order bordering on the insane–she won't let go.

"Michael don't leave me," her lips to my cheek. "Don't leave me here to drown alone. I've been alone my entire life," she cries. "It was always work. There was never time for life…for living. I know nothing about love. I don't know how to die."

We're shaken by depth charge after depth charge. I caress the features of her face, the tips of my fingers seeking the mystery within. "Lucy…how can this be happening?" Her response is a deep passionate kiss and the worries clouding my mind dissipate into a flowing not unlike the great wide ocean that surrounds us, a vast primordial sea, filled with life.

As if we might perish within the next moment, I take her, kiss her, passionately, my hands flowing across the contours of her body, each concussion forcing us closer, tighter, until we become one; gently rocked within an endless series of explosions and silences.

Chapter 11: The Experiment

*T*he first sailor I run into is Gil Burlsley.

"It's been four hours Mr. Murphy, the depth charging."

"I know that Gil. I'm asking you for a damage report."

"The after-torpedo room is flooding. We got water in the engine room, through the exhaust manifold. The mess-hall hatch was nearly sheared right-the-fuck off. They've rigged a block-and-fall. It's pretty ugly back there."

Inside the mess-hall a horrendous scene, water pouring into the sub through the hatch–held tenuously in place by a brilliant bit of seamanship, the men shackling the block-and-fall between the hatch and floor-plate dogging it tight. Despite this cavalier effort an enormous amount of water is flooding the engine rooms, both compartments becoming inundated with seawater. Desperation begins to take hold.

"It has to be fixed Chief."

"Murph, the only way to fix it, is to surface the goddamn boat!" He's soaking wet, water dripping from his beard. "At this rate of intake, unless we surface now, both compartments will be flooded. We'll be too heavy to get off the bottom." The look on Bremer's face goes straight through me. "We're drowning Murph."

"We can't surface Chief, you know that. We'll be shot to pieces. It has to be fixed down here. How?" I don't like the look forming on his face. "How Chief?" A volley of depth charges motivates his response.

"There's no guarantee it'll work. It's a crap-shoot."

"How?"

"The only way to fix it down here on the bottom, and it's a longshot, is for someone to take this here bar, snake their body twenty-feet up the goddam manifold pipe, reset the flapper that's been rent loose…and pray to the *holy sister* it doesn't fail while the poor sonofabitch is in there. That'd be one godawful way to die."

The pipe is twenty-five feet long, barely wide enough for a man to inch his body through. I take the prybar from his hand and glare at the gaping maw of the pipe; black as night. The thought of squeezing my body into it is terrifying. If I don't go now, I might not muster the courage again. As I begin to climb into the pipe a hand grips my collar and I'm face-to-face with Earl Lloyd.

"Sorry Mr. Murphy, you're not *rated* for this assignment. This is machinist's territory, step away from the pipe."

The men gather around Lloyd as he strips off his shirt, his torso covered with scars. He takes in large breaths of air and starts into the pipe with the spanner, the men tying a rope around one ankle.

"What goddam good will that do?" Bremer says into Connie Howard's ear. "If he drowns in that pipe it'll take Mare Island to get him out of there."

"At least he's not up the damn pipe alone."

"Give it hell Lloyd," Chief shouts as Earl inches his way into the darkness. Another series of charges rocks the boat and the water worsens, more seawater flowing from the pipe. We hear Lloyd cursing and spitting from the darkness.

"He's drowning. Get him out of there Chief!" McClatchy shouts, grabbing the rope and Bremer has him by the collar.

"Pat, if he doesn't fix that goddamn seal, we'll all drown. We'll never get off the bottom. Start praying." Every man in the compartment is left to face his own mortality when we hear a knocking, like someone at the door of a house.

"Earl, pounding on something with the bar," Chief says like a kid telling ghost stories around a campfire. The flow slowly ebbs to a trickle. Eventually, two dirty boots emerge, and the men pull Earl Lloyd back into the world like birthing a child. He's completely ashen with soot, only his eyes unsoiled. We all stare at the manifold pipe, only a trickle of seawater seeping from it.

"You sonofabitch," Bremer says grabbing him by the back of his neck, the two men, the boat's engineer and its mechanic, inseparable. "You dirty, raggedy old sonofabitch!"

"That goddamn thing wouldn't budge by prying it, not one inch. Hard as I tried wrenching on it, the rascal wouldn't budge. What the hell am I supposed to do, turn around? So, I beat the living hell out of the fucker and by thunder she set firm." Another volley of charges has the crew looking at the pipe. He glares at them. "It's fixed! Get back to work. This ain't over yet." I take his shoulder.

"Well done Mr. Lloyd. Well done."

"Aw, piece of cake Mr. Murphy. We were poor as all hell when we was kids growing up there in Plattsburg. Dad bet on the ponies. The bookies got everything. First the tools, then Mom's silverware, then the car, then the whole goddamn house. We didn't have a pot to piss in. I used to climb through sewer pipes tighter than that on a two-bit dare." He puts his shirt on, over the soot and wades aft, shouting for his toolkit.

"What happened to you *first-half?*" Stewart doesn't really expect a response to his question. His hair hangs in his eyes, his shirt soaked and covered with oil splatter. The cigarette hanging from his lips slowly extinguishes from the water dripping from his nose.

"Anything new to report?"

"The boat is fucked Murph. Sonar and radar smashed and broken, the machinery inundated; the equipment and circuitry of the experiment a total wash."

When the pinging finally ceases, the concussions tormenting us stop and the cat-and-mouse game begins. We know they're above, waiting for us to make a mistake.

"Right standard rudder. Coast to 320 feet then level," Canfield whispers as the men continue their attempts to allude our pursuers. "Gotta hand it to that Jap sonofabitch up there. He knows what he's doing." I *cough*. He looks at me like looking at a bug on his sleeve.

"Captain, I'm sorry but we need to run the bilge pumps. It's critical that we do so."

"Have you lost your mind? It'll give away our position."

"Captain, we have to clear the seawater before it swamps our batteries."

His expression is like ice. "Did you not hear what I just said Murphy? They'll hear us and the whole goddamn thing will start all over again."

"Sir, if we don't remove several thousand gallons soon, saltwater will breach the battery bays, the sub will fill with chlorine gas. It could kill over half the crew." He doesn't need me to state the obvious. "We've taken on a serious amount of water. We're too heavy and getting heavier." Canfield scans the faces of the men, his grim expression conveying our situation all too clearly.

"Very well," is all he says and returns to hawking Zig's shoulder. "Anything?"

"Just the faint sounds coming from zero-nineteen Skipper. A repetitive noise. Something loose, a lanyard in the wind, something not tied down. Maybe a school of herring. Heck I don't know."

"Bill, ring-up flank speed. Silent running. All-ahead, come to 200 feet. Mr. Murphy…run your pumps."

When we begin moving again, we're pinged and depth-charged mercilessly; Canfield and the wardroom locked in a life-and-death game of hide-and-seek while we scramble to get as much water expelled from the boat as possible.

We're kept at three hundred feet for three more hours, most of it a steady consistent pounding, Canfield wiggling and turning the boat enough to keep *the death-charge* off us, the dreaded closely placed explosive that could rip a hole in the hull, the sea flood the boat and drown everyone. It's grueling and men begin to buckle under the strain.

When the boat quiets again we spend several hours licking our wounds and *listening*, sure that the Japanese destroyers are silently prowling above, waiting for us to resurface. When we finally make sixty feet to *take a look* the dark ocean is empty, only the burning hulk of the transport in the distance, seemingly void of men. I find it apropos that our twisting and turning leagues beneath the ocean has brought us right back here to the scene of the attack. The burning hulk of the ruined ship illuminating the distant night like fire on a lonely midnight prairie.

"Why doesn't she sink Skipper?" Eban Duncan asks his captain, lowering the periscope; his tie long removed his normally starched collar steeped in seawater and sweat.

"Same reason we didn't Ensign. Mr. Stewart, surface."

The first thing that happens, against all advice, is Bradshaw has Culver establish radio contact with Pearl Harbor about what's happened. Canfield is instantly stripped of his command by Hess and restricted to quarters for the remainder of the mission, facing a possible court-martial. I've been re-assigned my duties and Bradshaw is now fully in command of the boat.

Once we stabilize, the machinists are pitted against the rising of the sun to repair the damage to the engines and weld the newly machined parts to secure the breaks, all this with a skeleton crew, the seamen falling-in with the machinists to help expedite repairs.

Howard takes a moment to light a *Camel* with the welding torch. "If there's a Jap sub around he'll see that pile of sparks for miles," he says pointing the torch at the burning hulk and handing his smoke to Rawlston. He dons his mask and resumes welding the new hatch-doggs sheared off during the attack. The seamen surrounding the machinists, glow within the golden light of the torch like men around a campfire. They hold up blankets to douse the light of the welder. A thin moon crawls along a somber western horizon, the night nearly absolute. Stars like diamond dust are scattered across the heavens, stretching into infinity. Something aboard the Japanese transport explodes sending a ball of flame into the night, the concussion reverberating across the water.

"Head below Mr. Murphy," Rawlston says, cigarette smoke issuing from his nose. "We'll take care of this. Go grab some chow while you got time."

Because of the demands of the situation, I see nearly nothing of Lucy. When I finally get a minute to speak with her, Burlsley takes that moment to update me on the repairs.

"Chief thinks we took in over ten thousand gallons, it's hard to tell Mr. Murphy. They're pumping the rest out now. There's acid in the water. Parmalee, Torsch and Lawler are securing the rear batteries but it's dangerous. Ashburn bridged the electrodes and lost a finger. What a dope, he's too stupid to listen to directions. Coop is running nonstop." She laces her fingers across her neck. I see the shock on her face but there's no avoiding the next mandatory question.

"What's our current injury report Bosun?"

"Two men are down with broken limbs, Calhoun and Wells, and one of the scientists, Burke, got spooked. We have him tied down and doped up. Wells has a broken leg, but Calhoun took the worst of it. The bone is sticking right out of his arm. I told that rookie seaman not to brace himself against the hull Mr. Murphy. Does he listen to me? One well-placed depth charge will snap a man's arm in half," he says directly to Lucy and she turns pale. "I'm not kidding Lieutenant. You should see it. The whole damn bone is snapped in half. His arm is hanging there like a wet noodle."

"That'll be all Gil. Check on the after-torpedo hold. I want a full report on repairs."

"They've tightened that down pretty good sir. We won't be taking on any more water there."

"Well, check anyway."

"Yes sir," he says saluting and heads aft.

She looks ready to collapse. "Are you all right?"

"Michael, I should be seeing to those men, not parading about, doting over our damnable machine. The men are suffering."

"You're not a medical doctor, you're a physicist." Emotion surfaces on her face, the chaos swirling around us. I fear she's about to faint, or worse.

"Michael...I...I..." A tear cuts the length of her cheek.

"Lucy, come with me." I take her hand and lead her to the crew's mess; ask Porteru to make a cup of herbal tea.

"This here isn't just any tea Miss Lucy. This here's a special one-of-a-kind concoction my aunts taught me is good for a woman's disposition, when they're feeling stress." His smile is infectious. "Now young lady, if you'll excuse me. I've breakfast to serve this crew in one hour."

In the control room, Szotsman, Hintz and Wyatt are replacing broken valves and Taylor is assisting Jaeger removing and replacing gauges and crystal dial-covers, the repairs necessary to maintain diving integrity. We thread our way to the wardroom. The scientists are sitting with Bradshaw mulling over the damage to the cloaking system. Lucy takes a seat, a dazed look on her face. Hoffmann's wild hair is amazingly wilder and Brauer sports a large bruise on his right cheek.

"Good timing Murphy," Bradshaw interrupts. "Have a seat," he says not attempting to make any room for me. "What's the condition of the boat? Give it to me straight."

"We've removed the block-and-fall that secured the mess-hall hatch. The machinists are repairing it now."

"How long to repair it?"

"It has to be finished within the hour or we can't submerge." The man stares at me. "The Japanese patrols will be here soon. You can set your watch to a probable 0500 visit."

"How do you guess that?"

"No *guess* sir. Sunrise." The scientists exchange concerned looks.

"What else?"

"We took in well over ten thousand gallons of green-water. We were able to divert most of it into the ballast tanks, but some got into the batteries and shorted out several banks, the electricians are working to restore the situation to normal but it's very dangerous. When saltwater mixes with battery acid bad things happen."

"Was any of the damage permanent Commander? If we lose even one of those banks it could offset our electrical requirements to successfully complete the experiment."

"I can't answer that question at the moment Dr. Hoffmann, but Parmalee gave me the impression he thinks it remediable. If anyone in the fleet could save those contaminated banks, it's Anson Parmalee."

"Agreed, the young man is exceptional. Only two years of higher education Brauer. Imagine where he could be today if he were schooled more thoroughly."

"Tell him it's critical he fix those banks," Bradshaw interrupts.

"He knows that sir."

"What else?"

"Radar and sonar were knocked out, will require twenty-four hours to repair. The diesels were flooded, the number four engine has thrown a shaft and will be off-line, perhaps permanently and number one needs an entire overhaul. However, the remaining two diesels should be operative. There was leakage in the after-hold that's being tightened now. Other than that, a lot of in-board gauges and valves need replacing. That's the bulk of the damage. Could've been worse I suppose."

"Well see that it's done," Bradshaw barks. I'm uncertain if he's dismissing me or stating the obvious.

"Michael…Mr. Murphy, what is the overall condition of the men?" Lucy asks.

"They're pretty frazzled. That was a severe pounding. It's a miracle the boat wasn't crushed. What's the condition of the experiment?" Her silent response answers my question.

"We're set back days," Hoffmann says. "The entire system has to be overhauled, re-calibrated. Rebuilt technically speaking. It could require weeks."

"*Weeks?*"

"Which we can't afford," Brauer says leaning back and massaging his neck. "We'll never make the assignment date."

"We must stay on schedule Charlesworth."

"I know, Dr. Hoffmann," she whispers. I see the water forming at the edges of her eyes and feel a deep concern for her wellbeing. She lifts her shoulders, forcing a weak smile. "We'll manage. We have to."

"That's the spirit Charlesworth, we'll throw every available person we can muster into the overhaul. We can't continue to count so heavily on your talents."

"Thank-you Professor Brauer, we'll manage."

"Damn right," Brauer says slapping the table. "And the best way is to get at it," he says excusing himself from the room, Hoffmann choosing to follow him.

Bradshaw gathers his papers. "Keep me informed of progress Murphy."

"Of course." He exits the compartment closing the curtain tightly as per his secretive nature. We're suddenly alone. She stands, touching my chest. "Are you all right?" I whisper. She lays her head into my shoulder. When I raise her chin to look into her eyes our lips meet and we kiss, and her kiss sends me someplace else, someplace faraway, someplace peaceful and serene. The sudden swish of the curtain behind me shatters the moment.

"Murph, I wanted to-" We turn to see Stewart's head through the gap in the curtain. "Um…sorry." He closes the curtain and the look on Lucy's face freezes my heart.

"Forgive me," she says, leaving the room.

The lookouts in the shears are scanning the night. There's already a sliver of pale-yellow dawn creeping along the eastern horizon like a gossamer golden thread. Stewart is on the cigarette deck smoking. He offers me his pack. Despite the fact I don't smoke, I take one and light it with his Zippo. The ocean is sedate, nearly serene; waiting the dawn.

"Nice night," he exhales. "Hope it's not our last." I think about these words. How true they really are.

"We're in a precarious spot," I mutter.

"*You* sure are."

"Stewie…"

He holds his palm up between us. "Murph, we've been friends for a long time. You don't owe me any explanations."

"It has nothing to do with explaining anything. I…"

"Murph, you're more than just a *friend*, you're like a brother. I don't harbor any ill-will about that down there." I toss the cigarette overboard and grab the railing, bowing my head. When I resume our gaze in the darkness he's waiting.

"Stewie…I've fallen in love with Lucy Charlesworth."

"You just figured that out?"

"What do you mean?"

"Come off it son, the whole boat already knows." I freeze.

"Knows what?"

"That you two are in love. A blind man could see it. Everyone except a numbskull like you." He laughs at my blank expression. "Come on Murph, we've all been working together for weeks. Everyone sees it. When you're not around she's…*all business*, I guess is the way to say it. But the moment you walk into the room…"

"What?"

"Hell, I'll say it…the woman is beautiful. Not exactly my type, being so damn brainy. I get intimidated around intelligent women. That's why I married Sally. But if I ever saw two people that should be together…"

An explosion ripples across the water; an enormous fireball extending toward heaven as more ordnance heats and blows on the broken ship.

"Aw, for Christ sakes. I sound like one of those cheesy radio programs on RKO. Let's change the channel before I start crying in my towel. We got worse problems on our hands anyway."

"You're referring to repairs?"

"I'm referring to command."

"Go on."

"We're in serious trouble Murph," he says, glancing at the men on watch.

"Say your piece Stewie, it'll stay between us."

"That popinjay Bradshaw is out for blood."

"I know. He's pressing for a court-martial."

"That's not what I mean." I wait for him to elaborate. "Something in my gut says this paper-hanger is going to get us all killed. I know it."

"How do you figure?"

"Come on Murph, shake the webs loose. The guy's out to make a name for himself, at any cost. I got a sneaking suspicion the price will be our skins."

We stare into the vast Pacific, the ocean rolling for miles in all directions. The thin moon cuts a yellow ribbon across the water like a two-lane blacktop, rolling into infinity.

"He's reckless Murph, and inexperienced, even worse, stupid. Like when we surfaced. The first thing that desk-jockey does is break radio silence. Great. Let's broadcast to the entire Japanese fleet the Manta Ray is still in the war. The man's an idiot." Stewart spits downwind. "Damn cute little arrangement, don't you think? The minute *the big ball* hits that horizon, this spot will be swarming with Jap aircraft."

"I know."

"Canfield's reckless too. What's happened pretty much confirms that. But he isn't stupid. That's why we're still alive. But Bradshaw…"

"What? Speak your mind Ellis."

"He doesn't care about people. He doesn't give a damn about this crew. That makes him extremely dangerous."

"You're right. But what can we do about it? Pearl calls the shots. Admiral Greene has put him in charge."

"He's never commanded a fleet-boat Murph."

"I know that."

"Then do something."

"Do something? Like what?"

"Get on the horn to Pearl. Hess will bring Greene and the rest of the brass to their senses."

"That's impossible. I can't ask them to replace a full commander with a lieutenant commander. It's ridiculous."

"Then *take* command. We'll back you up, *all the way*."

I freeze at these words, their meaning going through me like ice. "*Take* command? You can't be serious?"

"Absolutely serious. We're all behind you."

"*We?*"

"The entire wardroom. Chief and the enlisted men too. Hell, I bet even that egghead Hoffmann will back you up…and your lady doctor there."

"Stewie, you better change the subject."

"We've been talking. Bill, Dunc, Chief, the NCOs, everyone to a man, we're all-"

"Stewie, this conversation is over right now." I'm surprised by the intensity in my own voice.

"You're going to just walk away from this? It's your duty to do something about it. That joker is going to get us all killed."

"Lieutenant Stewart, check on the men below." He takes one last drag off his smoke and tosses it into the wind.

"Think about it, *Commander*. Think real hard about it." He slaps my shoulder and heads below.

He's talking about mutiny of course. *Mutiny*. I repeat the word in my mind as if it were a curse; laugh about the irony of it. It's exactly what's happened. Bradshaw wanted the boat and got it, putting the vessel and its contingent of human beings at extreme risk in doing so. Now the men want her back and see me as the answer. The problem is, I agree with them. Stewart *is* right. He's used the exact right word, *stupid*. Bradshaw was arrogant and stupid, a bad combination, yes, and very, very dangerous. The situation we were in was evidence of it. If we survive the dawn, what will I do?

Moments later I'm in the engine room where I find the machinists sitting with their heads in their laps. Rawlston is asleep, a dirty filthy rag for a pillow. I kneel next to a prostrate Earl Lloyd, gripping a greasy C-wrench and realize he's out. I nod to Connie Howard.

"Earl, asleep?"

"He's been at it for seventeen hours Mr. Murphy," McClatchy says. "He fixed two of the diesels. He just dozed off." I carefully extract the wrench from his oil-black hands and give the spanner to Conrad.

"You look like a Cub's fan on a Sunday," he says. I quietly wait for his report. "The boat's repaired Mr. Murphy. We've welded the machined parts for the hatch and sealed leaks in the exhaust manifold and the after-hold too. All burst pipes are either fully repaired or temporarily bypassed. Chief is still working on the radar and sonar. They're going to take more time, but the boat is ready to dive."

I look at each of the men, each one's weary, oil-encrusted smile. Sorel is passed-out with the machinists, his fingers cracked and bleeding, the same fingers that just days ago strummed the most beautiful notes I had ever heard played on a guitar.

"Well done gentlemen," is all I manage to say, a tightness in my throat stifling any further words. Their grins broaden, McClatchy's minus his four upper front teeth; long departed. "Get some food fellas, you may need it in five minutes when we dive, who the hell knows." They smile and nod, but no one seems to have the energy to move. Lloyd starts to snore.

Minutes before sunrise we submerge without incident and head north by northwest with our ears on. Barely a mile from our last position, Elder picks up a series of explosions emanating from those approximate coordinates.

"I think they're bombing our last position," he mutters to the officers gathered about the hydrophone station. Herndon is listening at Zig's shoulder.

"Either that or somebody's getting one hell of an ass-kicking."

The vessel becomes a beehive of activity as further repairs are performed on the sub and the science team commences the arduous task of resetting and recalibrating the cloaking system.

At fifteen-hundred hours, one hour before I report for bridge-watch, I rise and share a splendid dinner with the crew in the mess hall, the science team joining in. Nobody knew how he did it, but Coffee always seemed to manage something special after a depth charge attack. Tonight, it's turkey, homemade stuffing with real mashed potatoes and gravy, even cranberries.

"Coffee why don't you move in with us in Bakersfield after the war. You cook better than Evie," Rawlston says, a rare smile visible through his stubble.

"Where you and McAnulty keeping these goodies Coffee? In your bunks?"

"Don't give away no secrets Coffee," Cyril says refilling the gravy caddy. "If you say, these mugs will just get at it. So don't even be asking that stuff."

"They aren't going to tell you anything Toles. It would incriminate them. These men are professional food smugglers," Jukes says snuffing his cigarette out in what's left of his coleslaw.

"Don't be slingin' no allegations mister high and mighty radio-operator," Porteru says. "I's a fully decorated war hero." Everyone agrees, this being his fifth patrol with the Manta Ray. It was a well-known fact that Canfield *stole* Porteru from another boat where he'd served his additional tours; something about a poker game.

"What's the secret ingredient in the stuffing Coffee? Come on, give."

"Nutmeg. But it don't do no good if you don't know what you're doing." He turns to me, lowering his voice. "Where the Skipper at Mr. Murphy? Captain don't eat no more?" He already has a plate loaded and in-hand. I decide to bring him the plate, not having had time to visit him since the debacle.

"Keep mine warm Coffee. I'll be back in a minute."

"I gotcha covered Mr. Murphy," he says, covering my plate with a piece of cheesecloth and placing it on the warmer atop the tiny stove that served, so adeptly, the Cajun's culinary talents.

As I wind my way through the control room, each and every sailor takes a moment to stop and smell the food. Sorel salivates and Szotsman's stomach starts to rumble.

"Aw, that's brutal Commander," Lesky says. "Chief, requesting permission to be relieved."

"Relieved? Why?"

"To go eat." The look on Chief's face should be framed in gold.

"You know what your problem is Easy?"

"What Chief?"

"*You.*"

No answer is heard at his cabin. When I part the curtain, I'm surprised to find him at his tiny desk with a fifth of bourbon, obsessing over the picture of Rue.

"Am I'm disturbing you?" Nothing. I'm left standing there with a plate of food in my hand. "Coffee asked me to bring you this. It's turkey and mashed potatoes." He doesn't move an inch until he lifts his glass to sip the liquor. I set the plate beside him on the desk and sit on the edge of the bunk. "Skipper?" Nothing, until I touch his shoulder. "Captain, do you hear me?" He gazes at me, a strange disquieting look.

"Yeah I hear you." I don't expect his next words. "I'm never going to see her again. One way or the other, it's over."

"Rue, you mean?"

He looks at me strangely, as if confused by my question before his face hardens.

"She's behind what happened to you Mike, pulling strings she should've never had her hands on to begin with. It's all my fault, the whole goddamn mess." He reaches into his desk drawer and procures another shot glass, fills it and hands it to me. I decide it best to join him despite my dislike of hard liquor. He looks at me, an utterly *lost* expression that goes through me like a knife. "I killed Jim Hudgins, the entire crew, all those men, they're dead because of me," he says, unable to mask the pain bottled-up inside.

"Captain…"

"That was supposed to be your boat Mike. Jim was supposed to be your X-O. I pulled strings last minute to keep you onboard the Manta Ray. Jim was quietly promoted to lieutenant commander and took himself and eighty men to the bottom of the ocean."

He tightens his fists, trying to control a deep inner pain. "Say it with me Murph, the names...*Dick Song, Phil Wheatley, Billy Diggs, Nino Branch, Danny Childs, Arlo Curtis, Ken Custer, Harley Dent, Bobby Eldridge, Lou Fonteneau*...say it goddamn you!" He slams his fist on the desk. "Call muster Murph, your crew! I killed those men, every one of them." He nearly doubles over from the intense pain consuming him.

"It's over Captain. *Water under the bow* as you say it."

"*Over?* It's just goddamn starting," he spits, seething.

I wait; and wonder.

"They're taking her from me Mike, the Manta Ray. It came from Pearl, right from Carl's desk." Moisture rims the edges of his hardened gaze. He strokes her bulkhead, nearly lovingly. "She's not just a chunk of steel Murph, dumb and stupid like my last boat. She's a living, breathing thing." He's looking at me but seeing something else. "Don't ask me how but this boat has a mind, a soul. It feels, thinks and feels, as if every man who has come and gone has left a piece of himself."

"Skipper..."

"She's alive Murph, don't you feel it?" A lump forms in my throat, choking off my words. "You want to know why we've been *lucky?* Because this boat is alive...she feels, has moods, just like a real woman. And she loves her boys Murph. Each and every one of these rag-tag bunch of...fine young men. Go ahead. Tell me I'm crazy. That metal and wire can't think and feel...and love." He waits.

"Yes sir. I do think it possible."

"She's alive Mike, this boat, alive. I follow *her* orders, not the other way around. I can no easier control her moods than a man tame a wild beast. She pulls me to the attack scope. I see through her eyes and it's like we become one."

"I know."

"I do what she tells me, go where she takes me. Nothing else matters. When I'm home…all I can think about is *her*." He tops off his glass, downs it neat. "I could feel it. When this whole crazy thing first came down. I could feel it when they started ripping her insides out. None of us were coming back alive. Not this time."

"Skipper…"

"We failed her Murph. We just stood there and watched, while they cut her open like a gutting a goddamn fish." There's nothing to say or do but drink. "You don't agree with me, do you?"

"About what?"

"Attacking those ships." I stare at the floor.

"It wasn't my decision to make Captain."

"I'm a submarine skipper Murph, not a goddamn schoolboy. I never got farther than the ninth grade." He glares into me. "I sank those ships because not to do so would be a crime against the fighting men of this nation." He slams his fist on the desktop. "Our boys are dying out there!"

"Yes…I know."

"Every one of those *oilers* that gets through fuels the enemy's planes, greases his tanks. Every transport full of enemy soldiers kills American GIs."

"I understand that Captain."

He collects himself, somewhat.

"Hell, all I ever had was the Navy. I was just a dirt-poor kid from Kentucky," he says taking up the picture of Rue. "Times were tough. When Dad broke down and left, I was ten. The farm went to pot and maw hit the bottle. When she got drunk, or mad…she'd beat me and my older brother Donny with a leaf-rake. It was just the way it was."

"I'm sorry."

"I always had hope with Donny around. He brought light into the world. When he got killed…he was just…eighteen. Think about that Murph, only eighteen years old, and gone from the world. Gone. My brother. The best part of me, and my family. Something broke inside. It wasn't long after that maw was dead too. She drank herself to death. None took me in except the Navy. I was seventeen, lied on my application. Joined the submarine service and now I sink enemy ships. That's it, all I got. If they throw me out Mike…I'll shoot myself in the head."

He becomes lost in the photo again, like a man entering into a silent world, immoveable. When I get up to leave, he turns, a most profound expression on his face.

"Murph, I'll go out on a limb for you, only you." I'm compelled to sit again, his voice quieting to a thin whisper. "If anyone finds out I told you, they'll put me on the hard-rock pile at Leavenworth for the rest of my borne days."

"What is it?"

"Our mission isn't to sink the *Yamato* and the *Musashi*." I stare at the man. Has Oliver Canfield gone insane?

"I don't understand Captain."

"This whole invisibility thing, all the secrecy, haven't you asked yourself?"

"Sink the two great battleships." Canfield shakes his head. "What then?"

"The meeting with the admirals, after the briefing, you thought was an ass-reaming…"

"Yes?"

"They're planning on setting off a new weapon. Something beyond your wildest imagination. A sort of…super weapon, a super bomb."

"What do you mean Skipper?"

"We're not to torpedo the battleships at all, but deliver this, *dirty bomb*, as they refer to it. Blow the whole damn port, right off the map. Take Tokyo Harbor out of the war."

I stare at the man, his steel gaze unflinching.

"Skipper, what bomb could do something like that? It would be huge, too big to fit inside the boat."

He shakes his head. "It's *the package* that came in on the O'Malley. It's with the Mark 14 torpedoes in the nose of our boat." These words cut to the core. Time stops. Crystalline. He suddenly grabs my arm. "Ask that guy, the guy you said you were when you *came-to* in the sub, from the bump on your head. He's from the future, right? He'll know. It's got to be the reason Murph. The reason you've become two people. Hell yes, I believed you. Everybody thought you were cracking-up, buckling under the strain, but the voice over my shoulder said otherwise."

"But Skipper…I…I am Mike Murphy…right?"

"He'll know what to do, he'll know, because if what they said is true, this thing is *the devil*…the devil in the form of a bomb. Hell, on earth, the end of life as we know it…the green earth, the blue ocean…all beauty, gone." He looks up, completely lost expression on his face. "Mike, I wanted you to sink the O'Malley, send it to the bottom of the sea. I just sat here and almost let it happen." He crosses his arms on the desk and lowers his head as if being forced down by a great weight. "Now get out of here and leave me alone."

The box containing *the package* is sequestered in the forward torpedo room where a Marine sergeant sits guarding it. When I enter, heading straight for the box, my men drop their tools, snuff out their cigarettes and quietly join me. The sergeant looks at me deadpan.

"You want something?" he asks impertinently.

"Open it." He slowly rises to his feet, puffing out his chest, a man apparently proud of his physique.

"Can't do that Lieutenant. Commander Bradshaw's orders."

"I said open it." He sticks his thumbs in his belt and ripples his biceps.

"No disrespect to your rank, but I take my orders from Commander Bradshaw."

"I'm not going to ask you again Sergeant. Open that box, right now." He takes a step forward and exhales into my face.

"Make me." Binkershon slaps my chest with the back of his hand, forcing his way between us.

"I don't think you heard the Commander right. He said open it, so open it."

"Not a chance."

Ned starts to roll his shirtsleeves over his biceps. "You know what tough-guy? I didn't like you the minute you stepped aboard our boat and I'm liking you a whole lot less now. I'll tell you what chum, you open this lousy crate for the Commander here…and I'll let you keep your teeth. Sound like a deal?"

"You're going to fight me?" he says, incredulous.

"It won't be a fight. I'm gonna take your ugly puss right off at the shoulders." The men are nose-to-nose and the rest of Ned's crew flank him on both sides. I'd seen it before. They didn't go looking for trouble but never walked away from it. They were in it together, *all the way*. Suddenly Lieutenant Culver, second in command from the O'Malley, steps between them.

"McCullum, Commander Murphy is in charge. Open it."

"But Lieutenant, you heard Commander Bradshaw."

"Yeah, I heard him. Open it up."

When we pry the lid off, I'm hardly impressed. Sitting inside the weird plastic packaging is nothing more than a small torpedo, less than a quarter the size of a Mark 14. It's painted a drab gray and has several numbers and odd designs stenciled on the housing.

"That's it? That's what all the hullabaloo is about?" Binkershon asks. "Posting a fulltime stooge to guard it?"

"Looks like a Cutie," Stroup mutters.

"Too small to be a Cutie, Droop," Nichols says.

"What is it Culver?"

"I don't know Commander Murphy. Bradshaw doesn't say a thing, just that we're not supposed to let anyone near it." I stare at it; the thing stares back.

"Seal it shut. Everyone…forget what just happened."

"Thank-you sir," Culver says looking relieved as they proceed to reseal the box. When I start to exit the compartment Binkershon grabs my shoulder.

"Murph, I don't get it. Is this someone's idea of a gag? We thought for sure it was gold in that box, the way they lord over the thing. What do you make of that, a tiny little torpedo? This some clown's idea of a joke?"

"I don't know Ned…but stay away from it."

That night I see it in my dreaming, the face of the devil, cloaked within the fire of an enormous mushroom cloud ascending over the sleeping city. He's laughing, laughing at us, and at me. When I awaken, I strike my head against the metal tubing of the bunk above me. I'm in *the Ritz*, the men are joking and laughing over a game of five-card stud. I see their faces shining through the cigarette smoke as they banter back and forth. They don't realize I'm awake, or perhaps they've forgotten I'm even there.

"Deal me in Easy, and make sure somebody cuts the deck this time."

"What are you getting at? You think I'm cheating?"

"*Think?* Easy, when no one cuts you win, when someone cuts you lose, figure it out."

"You got a big mouth Burlsley."

"Oh yeah? You want to find out how big?"

"What's with you guys?" Babineaux says. "Give it a rest. Easy deal the cards, Burls break. Now shut up so I can think." During the ensuing silence someone farts.

"Belcher, can't your asshole take time off?"

"Hardy-har-har."

"I'm serious. Jesus lord…"

"What's next on this crummy mission?" Belcher asks to change the subject. "Someone going to fill us in on what we're doing? This so-called *war patrol* is giving me gas."

"*Belch*, every patrol gives you gas."

"Hey Parmalee, you're chummy with *the top*. What do you make out of this crazy mission?"

"Don't ask him, he's in a fog. He's gone nutty over the lady scientist."

"Yeah how about that Anson? Making any time with that dame yet?"

"Wouldn't you like to know."

"Not him. She's sweet on the X-O. You see the way she looks at him? Brother what I'd give to be in the Exec's shoes, even for one day. Mama-mia. That's a fine-looking woman."

Chief Bremer is cutting through on route to the engine room, overhearing their conversation. "You ladies got nothing better to do then gossip? I've a US Navy submarine full of wet stainless-steel in need of polishing. Any volunteers?" You could hear a pin drop. "Nothing to say now, huh? *Heroes*…" he huffs and heads aft.

"What's with Chief? Why's he staring down my neck? I ain't as much as looked at that broad."

"And you sure as heck better not Eric," Duncan chimes-in from his bunk. "You heard Admiral Bennett's orders, *hands-off*." Connie throws his comic book him.

"Listen to our beloved Ensign here boys. I bet this kid hasn't even seen a woman naked yet. How 'bout it Eban?" They converge on him, a playful roughing-up, rolling him in his mattress and pounding on it.

"Look boys, a pig in a blanket," Burlsley declares. "Just like being back home in Iowa right Eb?"

"Lay-off you guys! I'm going to report this to Lieutenant Stewart."

"Hear that? He's *going to* report us. We're shaking in our shorts Duncan." There's another round of friendly drubbing, the men pounding on the mattress with their fists.

"Okay, give it a rest," Babineaux shouts, quieting the group. "I'll be glad when this patrol is over. When we make the states, I'm grabbing a plane back to New Orleans, see Polly, make up for lost time…and shouting at her before I left. What fool shouts at his girl before going to war?"

"Let it go Babs. You'll see her again, make things right."

"It's just this damn patrol. It's keeping me up nights. You work close with them Connie. What's your take? The doctors on our side or what?"

"Who knows, all them boneheads think about are those crummy machines."

"I won't turn my back to the thing after what happened to Nichols, that's just plain bizarre."

"Yeah, what about that? How can it turn on by itself? Right out of nowhere? Gives a guy the willies."

"My hair stands on end when I'm around the thing. Literally. Is it me, or the dang machine?"

"It ain't you, the damn things are giving the whole crew the bejeebies. You been hearing the rumors. Spooksville."

"It ain't the machines that's bugging me," Fitzgerald interjects. "That lousy hack Bradshaw isn't making things better, walking around like Mussolini, barking orders that don't make sense. Somebody needs to tell him how it is. I say we give the bigshot an ultimatum. Either he gives command back to the skipper…or he has an accident."

"Who's going to cause the accident Fitz, you?"

"If it's for the good of our boat, yeah."

"How would you do it? Shoot him in the back when he isn't looking?"

"How do you think it's done Connie? He slips and falls over the side. They'll never find him. Unless the sharks leave something."

"Save it Fitz," Babineaux says. "Shut up, all of you. Not another damn word about anything from anybody. Deal the cards *Easy* and keep your hands where I can see 'em."

I close my eyes, returning to the dream. Is it possible, something so enormous, so horrid? Canfield's words keep reverberating in my head. *'Ask the guy from the future, he'll know.'* Have I forgotten? Have I become so enmeshed within this life I've forgotten who I really am? I am from the future, and the horror I've just witnessed in my dream is real.

The following days are filled with the methodic drudgery of repairing the damage sustained by the attack and dodging Japanese surface ships encountered on our precarious excursion into *Empire*. The only break in the monotony is a weird event that transpires the day before Chief's forty-seventh birthday. I'm called down to the pharmacist's bunk where I find Cooper sitting with Burlsley, Torsch, and a very nervous seaman third-class Hintz sipping a glass of whiskey.

"What is this a cocktail party?" I ask Cooper.

"Sir, this is Hintz, it's his first patrol with us."

"I'm quite aware of that Corpsman." I wait for someone to elaborate. All eyes are on Hintz who seems to be in shock.

"You better sit down, Mr. Murphy."

"Cooper, I'm a little busy at the moment. Can this wait?"

"Please sir." I take the bunk across from Hintz and realize the man is in a near catatonic state, staring into space. Cooper takes the drink from his hand and gestures at me. "Go ahead Hintz, tell Mr. Murphy exactly what you told me." The man seems incapable of speaking. Is it shock or terror I see in the young sailor's expression? Whatever the emotion, it's unnerving. "Go ahead Hintz, tell the Exec what you saw."

"I…" He goes blank, sweat teeming his forehead.

"Let's have it seaman. What's this all about?"

"Sir…I…" He covers his face with his hands.

"Hintz tell me what's happened, that's an order." The words seem to wake him from his delirium.

"I…I don't know what I saw." The men exchange a strange expression.

"Hintz let's have it. Start at the beginning. Where were you when…this thing or whatever happened?"

"In the after-torpedo room."

"What were you doing in there?"

"I brought some equipment down…for the work they're doing on the coil." He goes blank again, staring into space.

"Parmalee asked him to check the electric feed with the amp probe," Torsch interjects. "There'd been random pulses in the circuit."

"Go on Hintz."

"I was just about finished when the machine turned on, all by itself. No one started it. The torpedo crew were just standing around talking…Danny, Teddy, Georgie…then they were gone."

"What do you mean *gone*?"

"I mean gone sir," he says weirdly and returns to a near-catatonic stare.

"What happened next?"

"After, maybe a minute, they came back…like nothing happened." He rubs his face, his hands visibly shaking. Cooper hands him the glass of liquor.

"Here Henry, finish this. It'll calm you down." He tries to drink but I can clearly see something very unusual has taken place, at least in his mind.

"I'm seeing things, right? Coop? Stress fatigue, right?" he asks, desperation escalating in his voice. "They say the submarine service can do that. They call it *claustrophobia*. They say it can happen to a guy real easy like."

"Just relax Henry, drink up," Cooper says actually raising the glass to his face, the man downing it, coughing.

"Hintz, you say the men disappeared?"

"It was *real* Mr. Murphy. There was this humming, then a sort of…bluish light. Then they all just…faded away…then…came back, like nothing had happened."

"Do you think perhaps it was a delusion?"

He suddenly grows agitated. "What's going on Mr. Murphy? Why was I just standing there alone? It was like I was on the sub but everything was…different. Like I was somewhere else…like I was somewhere very far away."

"Hintz, I want you to report to Parmalee. Tell him I'm taking you out of the *electrics* rotation, while we look into this. I'm restricting you to your bunk for now, just for a little while. Take it easy, catch-up on some reading." His eyes go blank, then suddenly he becomes nearly violent.

"What good will that do? We have to get out of here Mr. Murphy, right now! Get back to Pearl Harbor," he starts, the two other men instantly restraining him.

"Whoa, Hintz, calm down."

"Get us out of here!" the man repeats hysterically over and over again until Burlsley punches him in the jaw and he goes silent.

"Take him to his bunk Bosun, keep an eye on him."

"Aye-aye sir." When the men leave, I stare at the medic.

"What in hell's going on Cooper? What was that?" He's aghast the situation exceeding his understanding.

"Heck Mr. Murphy, I'm a corpsman not a psychiatrist."

"You think that man is suffering from stress?"

"Heck, it beats me sir, could be but…" He stares into space.

"Speak up."

"When I first treated him…he…"

"What? Speak up Pharmacist." He shakes his head.

"Nothing Mr. Murphy. I think we're all a bit overworked." I can see clearly something is being left unsaid. Perhaps due to my lack of sleep I decide not to press it.

"That'll be all Cooper. Keep me informed of his condition."

"Yes sir."

I'm diving into the deep, descending along an old hemp rope down into a dark aquatic abyss, the depth marked off with linen strips tied-off in fathoms. Down, deeper I go into the misty sediment-laced water when I spot a dark shape in the distance, approximately twenty meters further below me. As I approach, I realize it's a diver in a Navy wetsuit. The man seems immobile, his arms and legs hanging in a bizarre manner, his suit oddly bloated.

As I near him, I begin to suspect he's a corpse floating amid the water, unmoving, his body hidden under layers of black rubberized suit. I carefully approach, cautiously peer into the facemask, stunned to realize its Hintz; unconscious.

I shake him gently. He seems as if sleeping, his eyes closed, peacefully floating in the endless deep. As I try to wake him the cables of my diving suit become entangled in his arms and legs. In my frantic action in trying to free myself, the ascent rope becomes wrapped around his body forcing us closer together. I'm breathing faster, harder, attempting to untangle the lines when the face behind the glass transforms into a garish skull. In my panic, our arms begin to entwine as if he were pulling me, his ghastly skeletal face forced next to mine. I shove the apparition away with all my might, clawing for the surface until I come to my senses and realize I'm in my bunk, Burlsley restraining me.

"Crissakes Lieutenant wake up!"

"What are you doing?" I inquire, barely containing my anxiety.

"Sorry sir but I think you were having a nightmare."

"Let go of me. What are you doing Gil? Why are you waking me?"

"Lieutenant Murphy, Hintz is missing."

The crew becomes obsessed with the search. The boat is scoured top to bottom. Stem to stern. We investigate the holds below all the compartments, the battery stores, even the bilge. The man is completely absent from the submarine.

I'm sitting with my officers and chiefs going over the thing detail by detail. No one has seen him leave his bunk and the watch crew insist they never saw him up on deck.

"There can't be any other explanation," Stewart says biting into one of Dover's blueberry muffins. "Somehow Hintz managed to make his way topside undetected and…jumped overboard."

"But why Lieutenant? Why would Hintz jump off the boat? That just don't make no sense."

"You said it yourself Burlsley, he was on edge. He became disoriented, whatever, and jumped. End of story. People do crazy things in war."

"Why? Why would he?"

"The depth-charge attack probably got to him," Chief says stroking his beard. "He cracked, lost control."

"He was fine after the depth-charging. He's been through it on his last boat."

"Then why'd you punch him in the mouth? I'll tell you why. He was becoming unstable. Look, it's happened before. It wouldn't be the first time a guy's jumped."

"No sir, not Hintz. He was young and stupid but not suicidal. He just got married a couple months ago."

"Well what then?" Bremer says and Burlsley looks at me.

"It's that damn machine back there Mr. Murphy, that's done this, somehow, someway."

"Burlsley, are you going nutty?" Stewart interjects. "Hintz jumped, end of story. Get it through that Polish head of yours." Burlsley is right at his nose.

"How could he jump without any of us knowing?" I realize the entire group is becoming extremely agitated.

"Alright knock it off. Everyone stand-down. Bosun, that'll be all, thanks for your report."

"Mr. Murphy, he was just a kid. There's no way he would up and jump. I don't believe it, not for one damn second."

"Look Gil, I know you were close. Just…take a break. We'll look into it further. Dismissed. All of you, dismissed." As the men disperse, I request Cooper to remain.

"Cooper, I'm going to ask you point-blank. I want a direct answer. Do you think Hintz jumped?" He takes a long time to respond.

"I don't know what to think sir, he just didn't seem the type. He was an optimistic person. Joyful. It doesn't fit."

———

"Did he say anything strange, last time you checked?"

"No sir. He was quiet, nervous, but quiet. I'm sorry Mr. Murphy but I'm stumped."

"What's your gut telling you Coop?"

"That something weird is going on…something to do with those machines."

"Explain that remark Corpsman."

"I can't explain it sir, but I can tell you this. The entire crew is becoming morbid."

"*Morbid?* That's a tall word Cooper."

"The men are becoming afraid of those things. Weird stuff has been happening. A couple guys have said things that are…out of this world."

"What things?"

"I better not say."

"Dammit Cooper, I'm ordering you to say."

"Weird things, happening around the machines. They turn on by themselves, without anyone doing it. How Mr. Murphy? Weird things have been happening. Lawler was shocked, burned actually, when the coil was turned off. They still can't figure out how? But that's nothing compared to what some of the guys have been seeing."

"Like what?"

"Well, without using names…during one of the tests, one of the men said he saw his mother standing there, trying to tell him something. She died three years ago."

"Go on."

"Another man said he was at his station when the machine started running on its own. He said he distinctly saw dark shapes, kind of in the form of human beings but more…*blob* shaped. Completely black, he said they had no face, no eyes, and they moved around in a weird manner."

"What happened?"

"The things moved around the compartment then disappeared. I had to give him a sedative, promise I wouldn't report it. He's still having trouble sleeping."

I mull over this shocking news. "What else?"

"A few other reports, strange things, lights moving around in the cabin. Couple of the men complained about chills coming on suddenly, feelings of foreboding. *Dread* was the word one guy used. This is only my second time out with this crew, but the change is noticeable." He runs a hand through his golden hair, staring dejectedly at the floor.

"Okay Cooper, that'll be all." He goes to leave. At the portal he turns and studies me. "Is there something else?"

"You asked me about my gut Mr. Murphy."

"Yes?"

"Sir, I've no rational basis for this feeling, but I don't think he did it…Hintz."

"Did what?"

"Jumped."

We sift through Hintz's personal affects in an attempt to decipher the mystery, nothing is amiss or evident to shed light on the mystery, all his belongings intact; his credentials and Navy manual neatly stowed. His beloved Buck knife is where he always kept it and his billfold holds only a driver's license and two dollars and fourteen cents.

Amongst his personal belongings, mostly letters and photographs from home, are a wooden yo-yo and a hand-carved figurine of an old man holding an adz. I turn the carving in my hand, the quality of the artist, exceptional.

"Those were carved by his grand-pap," Chief Petty Officer Smith says from my elbow. "Apparently woodcarving is a passion in his family. So he told me once."

Buried deep within the young man's papers we find a stack of letters, mostly from a woman named *Maudy Clare*, post-marked Charleston, South Carolina. I decide to read the most recent.

Dearest Henry,

I pray you're well. Forgive my leaving for Charleston so abruptly. Your mother has written me of your decision to return to Hawaii and continue with the submarine. Henry, why must you persist so? Your mother and father have made it more than clear their disdain of such a dangerous endeavor. Why volunteer for such an arduous and terrifying pursuit? Was it what Cully said, concerning your manhood? Hen, you mustn't worry over the trifles of a jealous heart.

Dearest, I cherish you, but your dear mother's visions continue unabated. Doesn't her thoughts, our concerns upon the matter carry any weight with you whatsoever? You're being selfish and cruel. All your kin are at odds with your decision, contrary your mother's grieving.

You know I love you truly, but Henry, it's become intolerable, simply intolerable. I'm sorry to inform you in this manner but I shan't be seeing you off, nor waiting upon your arrival home. It's best I move on to other things than pine away my life for a man who doesn't value the convictions of his loved ones.

Blessings,
Maudy

Stowed neatly amongst these missives is a dog-eared letter addressed to him from his family. The letter is folded and bent as if reread a number of times.

Henry,

'Maw sayd yall relistd in submrine. Son I sayd it afor Im ded set agin it. Yer poor maw caint slep for wory yall in so dangris sircumspecs. Alls sayd I reckon a man gots be tru to hissef. All a man rely gots when ded an gon is peple sayd he wert a good an holy man an tru to hissef an his morls. I seen ded men son an nun I knowd leff wit nun cept emty hands. Looks thay tol maw yall not gitin tis heer letre afor shipin out. All hops an purpus yall dus I soor over wut I sayd last time yall wus hom son. Im hopin prayer thus heer boat ar betre tis time out. Provdencel purvid. God bless son git hom saf yer patre
Pugh Hintz Jr

Smith is looking over my shoulder, reading the letter. "McClellanville," he mutters pointing out the return address and postal code printed across the stamp.

"South Carolina. You're from Carolina John. Do you know this place?"

"McClellanville is just a shot up the road from Charleston, rural fishing village. I reckon this here man is a fisherman. Hintz's pap."

"How do you suppose that?" He points to the writing.

"*Hintz* doesn't sound like a French name, but it must be. His use of words like '*patre*' and '*betre*' look French to me. Maybe there's some Creole in his family; New Orleans rubbing off. There was a migration of fishing clans from New Orleans a century back. I'd reckon Henry's family is poor. It's fairly obvious."

"Did you get to know each other?"

"I tried but Henry…how do I say it without sounding high-tone? I'm from an old well-to-do Charleston family."

"Clarify that."

"I reckon he felt divisions still apply, even way out here. My family's history dates back to the war, the Civil War. I'm from a seventh-generation military family Commander Murphy. I had a great grandfather and several great-great-uncles fight for the South. All highly decorated officers. All West Point graduates."

"I recall it."

"Those are big shoes to fill Mr. Murphy."

"I'd like to discuss your family's history with you sometime John."

"I'd enjoy that sir." He turns the letter in his hand, a look of resignation on his face.

"What is it?"

"I should've made a stronger attempt to bridge the divide with Hintz, after all Mr. Murphy, his pap is right. We're born with nothing and we die with nothing. All your fine trappings, all your silver and china…even the medals they pin on your chest don't amount to a hill of beans when you're looking at your grave."

"Lucy, is it possible, in theory, that this experiment, this equipment could make a man disappear?" She looks up from the work on the table, her eyes thinning above the rims of her glasses. It's my thought she understands the question implicitly.

"That *is* the point of all this Michael, making something invisible."

"I'm not talking about bending light. I'm talking about a man physically disappearing from the boat."

Her eyes shift. "I wouldn't know what you mean."

"Lucy, some of the men feel that the coils could have had something to do with Hintz disappearing."

She's incredulous, or is it shock? "Are you trying to say…that the technology was responsible for the young man's disappearance?" Our eyes lock. I can actually see it, the answer to my question. She slowly, robotically gathers her notes. I can't tell if she's thinking or numbed by the audacity of my question. At the door of the compartment she stops. "Michael, what you're suggesting, what you're alluding to is…" She leaves. I'm left pondering the half-statement.

Chapter 12: Lost Island

I'm in the Yeoman's cabin, typing on the *Underwood*.

With Wells injured, the senior officers have been tasked with the drudgery of filing the necessary paperwork for the proper functioning–and recording–of the patrol. Somewhere between the lines and numbers, my mind drifts. I'm in the future again, the street of a large modern metropolis full of modern cars and people. Cooper taps at the door bringing me back. "Mr. Murphy, do you have a minute sir?"

"I'm pretty busy Cooper. What is?"

"It's about Wells, more importantly Calhoun."

"What about them?" He takes the old wooden chair beside me in the corner. I'm not excited about the expression on his face. "Coop, I'd appreciate it if just once you came to me with some good news for a change." His face is unmoving, like stone. Something very serious has occurred. "What about Wells and Calhoun?"

"Sir, we need to get them ashore, to medical attention, immediately, at least Calhoun."

"Cooper, that's impossible and you know it," I say returning to the typewriter, the thing seems ancient, like some relic from a bygone era.

"Mr. Murphy, if Calhoun isn't taken to a doctor, and soon, he'll be out one left arm."

I'm stunned. "Are you being flip? Explain that remark Pharmacist."

"The bone was broken so severely, it's impossible to avoid it."

"Avoid what?"

"Gangrene." The word goes through me like electricity. "It may have already started. The bone breached the skin. It's become infected. There's no doubt about it. If he doesn't get serious medical attention soon…we'll be forced to amputate the arm at the elbow, maybe at the shoulder."

I stare through the man. "I see."

"Mr. Murphy, I'm just a pharmacist, not a surgeon. I'm not ready, or even capable of taking on a situation like this. In three more days, four at the most, we'll be through the boat's stock of morphine. When that happens…" he stares dejectedly at the floor.

The wardroom is packed; Bradshaw, Lucy and my officers. Chiefs Bremer and Lloyd have been asked to sit-in. The *wardroom* stares solemnly into space, fully assessing the gravity of the situation. We're pouring over a map of the western Pacific.

"It's outside our operational orders Murphy," Bradshaw drones on again. "We're not to approach land until Tokyo. Our orders are perfectly clear."

"Sir, do you understand death by gangrene?" Cooper asks. "The body literally dies piecemeal. It's slow, agonizing. We'd be better off just…giving him a little extra morphine," he says, looking me in the eye.

"We'll do it Cooper. We'll put ashore. Somewhere."

"That would be taking a gigantic risk don't you think, Murphy? Can't we wait until the mission is completed?"

"Sir, there isn't time," Cooper says. "We have to get Calhoun ashore to a surgeon. Immediately. It's gangrene. If he's not taken to some kind of…doctor or hospital…"

"Where? Out here in the middle of the Pacific Ocean? It's absurd Corpsman."

Silence coats the compartment.

"Chief? Earl? Any ideas?" I say to our veterans loitering with the NCOs. They exchange a look. Chief nods.

"You could head north Murph. Try to locate the *Lost Islands*." For a moment I think Bremer is playing some sort of mariner's joke. No one is laughing. He tugs on the navigational map. "We're about here, approximately. There's a string of tiny volcanic islands not exactly on the *Navy's* map, about here." Bremer points to an area of water northwest of our current position. "They're small gooney-bird islands, too tiny to shit on. But one is large enough to host a garrison…right about here I reckon. Give-or-take a mile or two." Bill Taylor marks the exact spot with a pencil. "Anyone know anything about *Lost Island?*" he queries my officers, all resolutely mute.

"*Lost Island?*" I echo.

"It don't have a proper *Christian* name Mr. Murphy," Bremer says with aplomb. "As far as anyone knows, they're called the *Lost Islands* because they keep showing up at different navigational points on the map."

"What do you mean?"

"They seem to move around, change places."

"How? That's absurd Engineer," Bradshaw interjects.

"They're full of cannibals," Earl says. "Headhunters and voodoo."

"There isn't any *voodoo* in the Pacific Isles Earl," Chief says matter-of-factly. "Out here they call it *Mana*. And yeah, those islands are ass-full of it. I could tell you stories that'd make your nose-hairs curl. Mana-magic fills those places. Islands appear from nowhere then disappear back into the sea. Could be the action of the volcanic rift but the natives-"

"An island can't just move itself Bremer!" Bradshaw barks and Chief grimaces.

"Use your head. There's an ass-load of them. One boat sees and charts an island here, another boat sees supposedly the same damn island over there. They all look the same. Sheer volcanic cliffs, no beach. Completely useless," Bremer says, looking Bradshaw over, top-down, to emphasis his choice of words. He returns his hardened expression on me. "All except one Murph. One has two volcanoes with a volcanic runoff between the mountains. The Japanese built an airstrip on it. Any of you *girls* feel the urge, chime-in," he says pointedly. The men all shake their heads. "Lloyder, you remember that reconnaissance patrol, a year and a half back, right? Maybe it was two years?" Earl takes up the map, holds it to his nose. It was a well-kept secret on our boat that Earl Lloyd, the boat's beloved motor-machinist, was almost blind.

"Yeah I remember Chief. A habitable island, but more over here," he says pointing and Bill Taylor marks this spot too. "Sure as hell. The Japs were dug in like ticks. The sonsofbitches were tunneling along the low ground, placing mortar and machinegun ports right into the rockface. We watched them through the periscope."

"The ocean drops right off the coastline Murph," Bremer mutters. "The *one-hundred-foot curve* barely a thousand feet from shore. We got in pretty damn close. We might be able to wiggle the Manta Ray in there and make landfall in the inflatable. We reconnoitered two small ports, one east, another on the western side. They have a small airfield between the ports. I remember we radioed that in. I don't think anything was ever done about it."

"How do you know all this?" I ask, amazed.

"We got assigned a reconnaissance patrol, just before Canfield became skipper," Lloyd says. "Barlow was the skipper then, and not a very good one," he says to Bremer.

"As useless as tits on a nun."

"Chief!" Burlsley interrupts, surprising everyone. "There's a lady in the room." All eyes shift to Lucy. Bremer pinches his cap down over one eye.

"Begging your pardon Ma'am…old habits."

Lucy cocks a sideways grin. "She's your boat Chief. At the moment, I'm just ballast," and the entire group dons a smile except Bradshaw. Bremer shifts his gaze back to me, his expression flipping.

"Pearl sent us doping around the eastern edge of Empire, to stay out of trouble. Barlow didn't have the backbone for submarine warfare, or the brains. Think they figured he'd lose the sub."

"No way Chief, we never got close enough," Lloyd declares. "He'd fiddle around positioning the boat for hours but always manage to lose the angle of attack. We'd watch the Japs sail away every time. Remember the mission up the Macassar Strait?" Chief holds up his palm.

"We could paddle in there by raft Murph. Leave Calhoun with a local doctor, or the Japanese, I guess. They're human beings, right? They wouldn't kick a guy when he's down, right?"

"Leave him with the Japs?" Stewart asks. "There has to be an alternative."

"What alternative Stewart?" Chief says. "We'll be lucky if we find the damn island, let alone a civilian doctor on it."

"Leave our man with the enemy?"

"Lieutenant Stewart, if Cal doesn't get medical attention and soon…it won't matter who we leave him with." Cooper doesn't need to press his point.

"Okay. If that's our only option Murphy, see that's it's done. I'm putting you in charge of the mission." Bradshaw closes his folder and vacates the compartment.

"Goddamn idiot," Chief hisses through his teeth. "Useless. Completely useless."

"Bill, vector a course *in*. Inform Herndon to set the SJ to thirty miles out. Tell the bridge-watch to keep a close eye out for floating mines. If we find it, we'll surface at zero-hundred, put our raft into the water…and leave Cal and Wells with the local medicos."

"That's taking a huge chance isn't it Murph? Going ashore at night? What are we going to do? Go running around an island in the dark looking for a hospital?"

"Hold on a second Stewart. Earl…didn't we drop spotters on that patrol?"

"Nah, the next patrol, first one under Canfield."

"That's right. Brother did the new skipper pitch a holy fit about that! He wanted to head straight to Japan, sink ships, not screw around with *the little fellers*, think he called them."

"They weren't any shorter than him," Lloyd declares. "In fact, one was taller."

"Spotters?"

"We dropped four Filipino guerillas ashore, little guys, spotters, and enough food and gear for the first month. Those guys are trained to live off the land."

"Might they still be there? With a radio?" I ask the group. "In fact, if the Manta Ray executed the drop, their radio frequency and call letters, everything, would have been recorded in our boat's log…wouldn't it?" A *look* circles the table.

"Why don't we find out Mr. Murphy?"

We're gathered around Jukes' station like a tied ballgame in the ninth inning. He twists the knobs and taps out the Morse code signal.

"'*Anybody out there with ears on?*' That's your message Roscoe?" Stewart inquires. "What you send a bunch of Filipino natives?"

Jukes' cigarette dips to half-mast. "What do you want I should say Lieutenant? *Manta Ray here, how's by you?*"

Incredibly, fifteen minutes later, our message is confirmed. "Holy mother Jesus, those sonsofbitches are still there." Bremer says pushing his cap off his forehead. "What a piece of luck."

"*Luck* is if we actually hit the beach without getting our asses shot to hell," Burlsley adds.

I'm having coffee with the crew in the mess, everyone gathered around like Christmas at an orphanage. I've a solemn choice to make, who goes ashore.

"How do we do it? Who leads?" Stewart asks, his expression pensive.

"I'll lead."

"Not you Murph, someone else." He scans the men in the compartment. None of the officers seem excited about the idea. "I'll do it. I'll go," he says as if he just drew the death-card.

"Stewie...you're too big of a target," I say, and a chuckle ripples through the fellas.

"You'll give away the whole outfit Lieutenant Stewart," Burlsley quips.

"We can't send in Murph," he persists. "I, Bill or Eban...Smith or Judesay will go. We'll draw *lots*." I see the fear indelibly form in their eyes. Kids in men's clothing.

"It's my call Stewart. I'm making it. I'll lead the detail." All hands quiet, in silent meditation over these words.

"Okay," Stewart sighs. "Who goes with you?"

"I'll ask for volunteers. Since everyone will volunteer, I'll take Burlsley, Babineaux and Toles."

The men exchange smiles. "Damn good choices Lieutenant," Babineaux says nodding.

"I'll go too."

"No Cooper."

"You'll need me sir, moving Calhoun. He's in constant pain now. If we find a doctor, I can get him up-to-date quick." We're interrupted by Sorel entering the compartment.

"Commander Murphy? *Land-ho*. Lost Island on the starboard beam."

I look at my team. "Suit up."

I'm in the Yeoman's cabin, preparing for the mission, the sound of the curtain turns me around. I stare at her face, as if carved in the finest alabaster stone. She doesn't say a word, closing the curtain and embracing me, unwilling to let go.

"Lucy, I need to get ready." She won't let go; her arms locked tightly around my body. "Lucy."

"Why Michael? Why do you have to go ashore?"

"Lucy…"

"Why must you go? Shouldn't the commander of the boat stay onboard?" I gently *pry* her from my chest.

"Bradshaw is in command." She's already resigned to the fact. "Besides," I say taking her shoulders. "How can I ask Stewart, or Bill Taylor, or Eban Duncan to do this job? How can I ask another officer to risk his life?"

"You order them," she says as if her heart were breaking. I stare into her sad verdant gaze, tears glossing the corneas.

"I wish it were that easy." She covers her eyes with the palm of her hand. I take that hand and kiss it, and her, passionately; as if it were my last day on earth.

"Dope him out good Coop. We can't have him crying out. It'll give away our position."

"Already done Mr. Burlsley."

The men have donned all-black garb and applied soot to their faces. The gunners are armed with Thompson machineguns, all the men except Cooper wear Colt .45 automatic pistols with extra ammo clips. Fitzgerald has also volunteered to go. For some reason his enthusiasm concerns me. I'm in the forward battery of the submarine with Babineaux, my chief gunner.

"Leave him behind. We'll manage just fine without him."

"But he's an extra gun Wendell, and volunteering. It's a tough call to say no."

"You asked my opinion. I gave it to you. It's your call."

Santino interrupts us. "Commander Murphy? Permission to join the landing team going ashore."

"Damn it to hell! Another *volunteer*. What are you talking about Romayo? This isn't a damn beach-party."

"Sir, the guerillas put ashore were Filipino. I'm Filipino."

"So what?"

"So, you're going to need someone to communicate with them. They speak Tagalog. I speak Tagalog sir." I stare at the young man, his smile in stark contrast to the content of his request. I look at Babineaux, solemnly nodding.

"He's right Lieutenant. We'll need him. I bet those guys speak more Jap now than English."

"Goddam it…" I sigh, squeezing my fist so hard my knuckles crack. "All right Santino. Gear up." His infectious smile lights the dim hall of the gangway.

"Thank-you sir."

"Don't thank me. Not until you're safely back onboard."

"Yes sir." He leaves to find a pair of black slacks and a black pullover. I glower at Babineaux.

"Tell Fitz to suit up. Let's get this over with."

We're hovering around the periscope like a pack of wolves; scanning the placid sea, nearly tranquil under a phosphorescent moon.

"All quiet. The sea is calm. Prepare to surface. Chief, we'll approach decks awash."

"Aye-aye Mr. Murphy. Switch on the surfacing lights," he orders, and the entire sub is inundated in blood-red light.

The island looks like a postcard, framed beneath an endless indigo sky stretching into infinity; its silhouette coal-black in the eye of the periscope. I scan the ocean 360 degrees about the boat. Northeast, out to sea, a tiny light is bobbing on the waves. I switch to high-power; a small fishing dingy is sailing northward on a gentle breeze blowing from the southwest. I slap the scope's arms closed.

"Surface," and the Manta Ray quietly breaks the waves a mere thousand feet from shore.

With the red surfacing lights on, the compartment seems womblike. We open the main hatch—seawater pouring upon our shoulders—and take the bridge, anticipation in the air heavier than the smell of the jungle on the wind.

"Mr. Duncan, get the lookouts in the sail. Station Sorel on the 20mm, McClatchy the loader."

The Pacific night is hot and muggy, the air hanging heavy like a shroud. Stars pepper the horizon for miles. As the submarine inches inland, tracking her depth by sonar, I scan the coastline nestled between the two volcanoes towering to the north and south like black ebony jewels. The box squelches: "Depth-sonar reading Mr. Murphy. Approaching the one-hundred-foot curve."

"Very well. Full surface," I say into the wire and the sleek and slender body of the Manta Ray slowly rises from the bosom of the ocean, her battle armor glistening under the moonlight.

In the distance we can hear the soft sound of music. The mountain to the south is dark and craggy, like a vast misshapen monstrosity, entirely black. The volcano rising to the north is younger, tall, sleek and conical shaped. The sloping mountainside twinkles with sporadic lights; torches or campfires.

"Depth approaching seventy feet Mr. Murphy," Duncan informs me from within his life-vest.

"Very well Ensign, all-stop. Drop anchor, quietly." I breathe in the night. "What do you think Stewie?"

"Who knows? The coordinates they transmitted puts them exactly due west of this position," he gestures with the length of his arm. "Right next to a Jap camp? I don't like it Murph, not one bit. What if it's a set-up? What if the Japs are sending those messages? What if the guerrillas are dead and the enemy has their radio?" I've no response to these disturbing possibilities.

"Well, now or never," I say and call down the hatch. "Let's get the raft in the water fellas, quietly." My team of *frogmen* fix their packs, checking their weapons.

"No one speaks a word here out," Babineaux says. "Hand gestures only. No one smokes, coughs or farts. Clear?" The men acknowledge. Wyatt and Lesky secure the raft while my team assembles on deck. Chief hands Babineaux and Burlsley each a grenade.

"Just in case boys," he says, and they pack them inside their jackets.

"Gentlemen, lock and load your weapons."

"Aye-aye Mr. Murphy," they answer with one voice, engaging the bolts on their Thompsons.

"Romayo and Cooper, you're on Calhoun," I say to the men on deck, black as shadows. "Burlsley, Babineaux, Toles and Fitz on the oars."

"Aye," they say as one voice.

"Gil, position yourself on the forward oar station. One hundred feet from shore, take point. When we hit the beach everyone except Cal walks the boat into the tree-line. When we're *all clear*, we'll radio the guerillas. Any questions?"

We're helped down to the water, our black inflatable bobbing gently in the surf, the ocean amazingly calm. They lower the injured man into the raft.

"Wells isn't coming Stewie?"

"He declined the invitation."

"He's missing the adventure of a lifetime," Burlsley says.

"Should any of us live long enough to enjoy it," Toles adds cryptically.

"Willy, you're a pessimist. This will be a cakewalk buddy," Lesky says, and a heavy feeling hits me in the gut like a brick.

The landing-team takes their positions. On my command, they begin rowing toward shore, the night instantly closing in. Halfway to shore Romayo scans the immensity around us.

"It's beautiful," he says quietly, "the island and sea. It's like paradise."

"Santino, not another word," Babineaux says grimly.

"Yes sir. Sorry sir."

Exactly per my orders about a hundred feet from shore, Burlesley takes point, scanning the shoreline with a pair of 7x50 binoculars; the Thompson slung across his back reflecting a sliver of moonlight. Calhoun moans as the raft hits the waves.

"Keep your eyes peeled fellas. See anything Gil?"

"Negative. All quiet."

As we near shore, we spot a small contingent of Japanese soldiers milling about what appears to be a concrete wharf, barely two hundred yards to the south.

Burlsley gestures his fist into the air and the men on the oars halt in their labors. The quietude of the omnipresent night is broken by sporadic shouts and laughter from shore. The great ocean gently sighs.

"Commander, there's a bunch of nips crowding that dock. I say we veer right, make land further to the north, near that dark patch of palms." He gestures with his arm.

"Affirmative. Make it so gentlemen."

We paddle the float through the waves, Calhoun crying out when the boat hits the beach break. I place my hand across his mouth, withdrawing my .45 from its holster, worried there might be enemy soldiers under the shadows cast by the moonlight.

When we hit shore, Babineaux and Burlsley leap into the water, pulling the raft onto the beach. I gesture for silence and the team freezes, Cooper quieting the wounded recruit.

We take position behind a fallen palm tree and I borrow Burlsley's binoculars. Japanese soldiers are moving about in the meager light of their campfire. They seem to be celebrating, drinking sake from clay pots and I wonder if perhaps it might be a holiday back home. They laugh, talking loudly and playing board games, as if the war were over, or perhaps nonexistent for them. I gesture to my team.

"Move out." We drag the float with its wounded sailor into the shadows beneath the trees. The immense jungle swallows us like wading into ink, the only sounds–other than the soft pulse of the surf–is the rapture coming from the wharf. "Leave the raft here. Move out."

The jungle absorbs us, casting phantasm before each step. Birds, or monkeys, shout hollow calls from the darkness, the moon, a shimmering silver chariot, ascending up the side of the volcano.

We stake a basecamp beneath a grove of coconut palms, the night nearly absolute. I extract the radio from Toles' pack and station Romayo behind a tangle of fallen trees; the radio, pre-set to the designated frequency.

"Have at Santino but quietly." I post the men on a small perimeter. "Toles take the north, Burlsley west. Fitz cover our rear. Babs stick with me and keep an eye on our neighbors." Each man follows the order without a word.

"*Romeo-Foxtrot to Mindanao. Romeo-Foxtrot to Mindanao, come in Mindanao,*" Santino repeats softly like a mantra, first in English then in Tagalog.

"The Japanese camp is louder than I thought," I mutter to Babineaux.

"Man, this is insane," shaking his head. "The Japs are right there. You could spit and hit one."

"Look at 'em, whooping it up," Fitzgerald hisses, suddenly behind us. "Celebrating their conquests. We could take out the whole rotten mess right here and now Commander Murphy. Just lay right into them. Let's do it. Let's kill them all."

"Fitz, keep that weapon quiet until I say otherwise."

After several minutes of silent waiting–the stillness of the jungle broken only by the soft cadence of Romayo keying the mic–he informs me he's getting no response. I check over the unit. It's functioning properly. Babineaux attempts to raise them, then Burlsley takes a turn. After several minutes he looks at me deadpan.

"No soap Mr. Murphy. They're not answering."

Toles joins us from the bush. "But why? It's the same damn frequency we used on the sub."

I had put Toles in charge of the radio, double-checking with Jukes that the proper frequency settings were locked.

"Are you sure you set the right bandwidth?"

"I think so."

"You *think so*?" Fitzgerald spits. "You got it wrong Toles. We're on the wrong channel."

"Shut your mouth Fitzgerald, you just along for the ride. No one's asking your damn opinion. I know what I'm doing. It's the same goddamn channel Mr. Murphy. I swear it."

"Well where the hell are they then? Why aren't they answering us?" Fitzgerald says and the team goes silent. This moment was inevitable. Why should I think otherwise? That they would be waiting for us with open arms, cracking cans of beer like old friends at a luau? "You've no choice Lieutenant Murphy," Fitzgerald says. "You're going to have to leave Calhoun here."

"Where?" Burlsley asks.

"Here, or back on the beach."

Babineaux grabs Fitz by the collar. "I ought to bust you in the chops."

"Well what other choice do we got? Let's leave him on the beach and get out."

"Let go Babs, let me have the first punch," Burlsley nearly shouts, attempting to grab Fitzgerald and I'm forced to physically intercede.

"Stand-down Bosun. All of you, not another word." I realize my team is getting extremely antsy. "Just cool down. Let's think this out." The following silence is filled with the sounds of insects and frogs; a cacophony of tropical creatures singing praise to a primordial night and an invisible *source*.

"We could take a little *walk* up the road," Babineaux whispers in my ear. "Maybe they got a honkey-tonk." I quietly mull this over.

"Men wait here. I'll shadow the Japanese camp for a bit. There might be a medical facility, a tent. Something."

———

"I'll go with him," Babineaux says dropping his pack and Burlsley is instantly mimicking him. "Fitz, give us your extra magazine clips."

"You out of your mind?"

Burlsley is instantly in his face. "You heard your Chief. Give fucker, now!"

"Why should I?"

"Oh brother, Fitzgerald, you're just asking for it. Go ahead, say that once more. Do it."

Babineaux grabs both men by their necks. "Knock it off."

"I need my ammo myself," Fitzgerald says, rubbing his neck.

"Fitz, not another word or I swear I'll punch your lights out and leave *you* on the beach," Babineaux says. Everything quiets. I huddle my men.

"Listen up. Toles, Fitz, stay here with Cooper and Calhoun. Romayo come with us. We'll scout the perimeter for a medic. Willy, if there's trouble and you hear shooting, wait as long as you can before returning to the boat."

"Commander Murphy…"

"If we chance upon a doctor, or a native, we'll bring him here, to Calhoun. If we find a medical tent, we'll bring Cal there, leave him with the Japanese. He'll be taken prisoner but at least he'll get the medical attention he needs to save his life. Shoulder arms." I recheck the clip of my .45 and load the chamber. "I'll take point. Babineaux behind me, Romayo then Burlsley covering our rear. Let's move out."

We slowly, methodically, penetrate the living jungle. The air itself seems colored an absolute black. I can barely see a foot before me, the moon erased by the jungle canopy. The stifling miasma of the foliage creates phantasmagoria in the blackness before me, death behind every tree and limb.

We're careful to keep an eye to the south, watching the Japanese soldiers come and go from their tents ingeniously camouflaged under palm fronds and banana leaves. Several hundred meters in, we're stopped dead in our tracks. Two young Japanese soldiers, with rifles and bayonets at rest, are drinking sake under the moonlight. My men quietly huddle.

"We'll have to go around them," I whisper but Babineaux is shaking his head.

"No way Lieutenant. We can't leave them. They're sure to hear us."

"What can we do?" His response to my question is to withdraw his knife, extending the blade between us. The weapon glints, reflecting a thin shaft of moonlight. With simple hand gestures he indicates Burlsley is to take out the man on the right while he dispatches the man on the left. He gestures for me to remain. Burlsley soundlessly drops his rifle, withdrawing his blade and evaporates into the jungle.

Like watching some weird nocturnal cinema, my men simultaneously attack the soldiers, covering their mouths while piercing their spleens from behind with knives. Not a sound issues from the dying men as they're carefully lowered to the ground, as one might put a sleeping man to bed. When they return, no one says a word. We move further into the black. As we pass the dead soldiers, I see their faces in the moonlight, their bleak eyes staring from the darkness, a chill coursing my body despite the tropical heat.

Several hundred meters into the gloom we halt. In the distance sits a house made of bamboo, with *shoji*-paper doors. It sits in the utter darkness like a prop, a toy house perched just this side of infinity. A dull yellow light escapes through the open windows, sheltered by overhanging eves.

"A doctor's office Commander?"

"I don't know. I don't think so…think it's a private residence. Let's take a closer look."

My body pumps adrenaline like sweat, my heart racing as we approach the hutch from under the shadows. There's a break in the canopy and the slender white moon coats us in an unearthly glow, like phantom soldiers. For a moment I feel like I'm not even on the earth but some other more mystical planet, where light is infused with silver and phosphor; death waiting on all sides.

We make the side of the building, my heart pumping like a tom-tom. I gesture for the others to wait while I peer in the window. When I kneel back down my men are huddling around my next words.

"It's an old man, sitting cross-legged on the floor reading a newspaper." While I watch the edge of the jungle, they each quietly take a look.

"You think he's a doctor? It'd be too good to be true."

"No. I think he's some sort of government person, a councilman or clerk."

"How you figure Commander?"

"All the papers stacked about in piles. He must be a local government agent. Public works probably."

"He could get our guy to a doc I bet," Burlsley whispers.

"I'm sure of it."

"What do you want to do Commander Murphy?"

"Gil, cover the back of the house, Wendy take the front with Romayo. I'm going in a side window and walking out the front door with him. We'll head back to basecamp, same way we came in." They don't speak, simply do it, instantly and efficiently. I take a deep breath stare at my gun hand shaking in the moonlight before quietly slipping inside the house through one of the open windows.

The bamboo room I enter is apparently for storage, filled nearly to capacity with books, ledgers and papers tied in stacks with thick woolen string. The moon casts a surprising amount of light through the open window. I can see the contents of the room quite clearly. There are numerous boxes and a collection of framed photographs. Contained within these photographs of mostly men in suits are several of women in beautiful flowery kimonos, geisha women, poised and elegant, their faces painted white.

The last photo I pick up is of the man in the next room. Albeit younger, I clearly see it's the same man, surrounded by a woman in a cherry-flower kimono and two young children. I realize he's an administrator. He's been brought to this remote island to enact some form of government oversight, most likely under the auspices of the Japanese army. Like me, he's a long way from home.

Through the crack of the door, I gaze at the man in the room. The floor is made entirely of wood planks and there's a fire-pit framed into the flooring in the exact center of the room. A small flame heats a cast-iron kettle hanging on a hook.

He's motionless, only the smoke wafting from his cigarette and the soft gentle métier of my watch ticking away the seconds portends anything is moving in real-time. He's absorbed with a newspaper, the headlines in Kanji, oblivious that there is a man in the next room with a gun.

Not a sound can be heard, not even the shouts and laughter of the soldiers in the distance intrude upon the scene. We seem as if locked in space and time. I, staring at the man, the man staring at the paper, the smoke curling toward the ceiling, the ticking of the watch on my wrist, the birds–or monkeys–howling from the darkness outside; the insects buzzing.

There doesn't appear to be anyone else in the home. I'm preparing to move-in and present my .45 to him, when he slowly gets to his feet and pours a cup of tea from the kettle. He just stands there, contemplating something, gazing blankly into space; drinking tea.

After a minute, that feels like an hour, I worry he's considering leaving the room, possibly the house altogether. I think about Calhoun and the men I've placed on-station and before I know what's happening, I'm in the room pointing a pistol at his head.

Incredulity is not a strong enough word to describe the look on his face. The cigarette falls from his mouth, burning his hand causing him to drop his cup, the vessel shattering across the floor. He stands there as if frozen, his eyes the size of the moon outside the window. I gesture for him to sit. He does, expediently. I don't want to be seen from outside standing around like a mannequin on display. The air is hot and oppressive, the mood tense and electrified.

"Just relax," I say scanning the domicile, ascertaining whether we're truly alone. To my right sits a small kitchen, a series of rice balls set neatly atop the counter on a ceramic plate. A handpump feeds a large tub in the corner, large enough for a man, filled with steaming hot water, a coal fire smoldering beneath it, heating the water. I point. "Bath?" He shifts his eyes, back and forth several times. I mimic washing myself. "Bath?"

"Hai. O-furo…dozo…dozo," he says gesturing, apparently more than happy to have me take a bath. Nothing would please me more than to hang my holster on one of the pegs and soak in the thing for an hour.

"Thanks, but I'm a little short on time." He hasn't a clue as to the meaning of my words. It's obvious he speaks no English whatsoever.

Opposite the kitchenette, I see a bed covered over with mosquito netting. Beside the bed sits a small table with a book and a kerosene lamp burning softly. There's nothing *military* about him or the home, nothing to indicate he's a soldier, or even involved in military affairs. I ask him his name. He's completely lost to my question. Sweat begins to bead-up on his brow. I point to my chest. "Murphy," I say and point to him. Nothing. I repeat the operation again, exactly the same way.

He taps his chest. "Mura-fee..." he echoes. I shake my head.

"Murphy," I say tapping my chest, then point at him again. "You?"

He grasps my meaning. "Noburo," he says pointing to himself. I echo his name back. He nods–and sweats–profusely. "Sato Noburo," he emphasizes, bowing so low his forehead actually touches the floor. I point back and forth between us.

"Noburo. You, me...walk..." I mimic the process with my index and middle fingers, *walking* them across the back of my gun hand.

"Honto...?" he murmurs, neither a question nor a statement but more a nervous acknowledgement. I gesture toward the door.

"Let's go." With a nudge from the pistol, he implicitly gets my meaning and very cautiously we exit the building together, my gun tucked tightly under his arm.

"Sonofabitch Commander Murphy, nicely done. You walked right in and right out like you owned the place."

"Save it for the boat Gil, take point. Move out, quietly." We silently retrace our steps back to the others waiting at basecamp.

He studies Calhoun's arm, speaking in a language none of us can understand but the message gets through clear enough. Calhoun is in serious trouble.

"What's he saying Commander? You get any of that?"

"Not really, but it doesn't matter. *He* understands." I point to him then Calhoun. "Noburo. You…him…" I join both hands together in a ball. "You…him…"

"Hai," he says, nodding grimly. "So desu," he responds realizing we have no choice but to leave them behind together. A sense of relief floods his face. "Hai, wakari masu, Mura-fee san."

"Fellas, he understands the seriousness of Calhoun's condition. We can leave Cal here with Mr. Sato."

"*Mr. Sato?*" Fitzgerald spits and everyone freezes. "Our new friend *Mr. Sato* huh? You're going to leave Calhoun with this lousy slant?" We're all stunned, everyone staring at the man as if he had just jumped off a bridge. "Look at him. He ain't no doctor. I say we kill him."

"Fitz, are you losing your mind? What little you have." Babineaux says. "This guy will see that Calhoun gets treatment before the gangrene kills him."

"I don't trust him. I don't trust his eyes," he says glaring, the man growing nervous under Fitzgerald's menacing stare, the tone of the words emanating from his mouth.

"Fitzgerald go check on the boat. Prepare to depart the island," I say, and he huffs.

"Taking the easy way out huh, *Commander?*"

"Fitz two minutes ago you wanted to leave Calhoun on the damn beach," Babineaux interjects.

"Yeah so? Better than leaving our guy with this lousy slant-eyed bastard."

"Seaman Fitzgerald, I've given you an order. Check on the raft. Standby to depart."

He huffs at my order, loping off toward the beach.

"An ape with a gun," Burlsley mutters.

"When we get back to the boat, he might as well keep rowing. He's gonna wish he was never born when I get through with him," Babineaux growls. I can actually hear his teeth grinding. "I wish like hell it was Cisco that was here. I better keep an eye on him Lieutenant." He heads off into the dark, Romayo right behind him.

"Mr. Sato, thank-you," I say, and he bows, nervously. We begin to pack out. The last man I talk to is Calhoun. "Cal, I'm sorry it had to be like this, leaving you behind. There just isn't any other way. You need help, badly. They're the enemy but they're still human beings. There's no other choice left us."

"I understand Commander. It's better this way. I'll be okay. After the war is over, we'll catch up over beers, okay sir?" He smiles, winching, holding his arm tightly to his chest. I look at our old man and he looks at me, nodding solemnly.

"Ko-man-da-san…Mura-fee-san…daijobu…*okay*," he says making a circle with his thumb and index finger. "Daijobu." He manages a weak but nervous smile.

"Okay, Sato-san…thanks."

Just as we start to leave, "Ko-man-da." He holds his hands before himself, loosely bound, nearly in prayer and bows his head. "Gomen-nasai," he says remaining prostrate, his head bowed.

"What the heck is he doing Commander Murphy?" Burlsley asks from beside me.

"He's apologizing."

"Apologizing? For what?"

"The war."

It's with an enormous sense of relief–perhaps disbelief–when we finally break for the raft, the magic carpet that will sweep us away, spirit us off *Lost Island* and back to the safety of the Manta Ray; away from the claws of this dark, tense place. However, as we approach the beach, the impossible happens and gunfire erupts ahead of us shattering the quietude of the night. Chaos explodes all around. When we make the beach, Babineaux is punching Fitzgerald senseless.

"Stupid, stupid sonofabitch, why? Why?!"

"What happened? Babineaux, answer me. What's happened?"

"This stupid redneck opened fire on the Japanese camp. For no reason." He punches Fitz in the jaw again, blood finding my face. Burlsley restrains him, Romayo grabbing his other arm. "Fitzgerald, if we get out of this alive. I swear I'm gonna kill you. I'm gonna beat your face into a bloody pulp before I shoot you and throw you to the sharks."

"Babineaux, get ahold of yourself."

Burlsley grabs his collar. "You knocked him out Champ. He's done. Let's get the hell out of here buddy. C'mon, let's blow!" He races to the fallen trees to watch our flank.

"There was no reason to shoot Commander, why? Why? You stupid sonofabitch!" He kicks the unconscious man in the gut and Toles restrains him. Slowly the rage within the sailor dissipates. "Stupid redneck hick sonofabitch…why? Why shoot? Why?" There's no answer to his question.

"What do we do with him?"

"Leave him," Toles insists. "It's what he damn well deserves."

"We can't just leave him Willy."

"The hell we can't! We're doing the world a favor. Let's get the hell out of here." I'm suddenly on the spot.

"Guys, we got company," Burlsley shouts from his position, his Thompson at the ready. "Somebody make a decision, fast." In the distance I see them, like tiny toy soldiers moving across the lunar-white landscape of the moonlit beach.

"C'mon Commander Murphy, let's get the hell off of this island," Toles says discarding his pack and shouldering his weapon.

"Fellas, as much as I want to, I can't just leave Fitzgerald here. Get the raft in the water. I'll carry him down." Suddenly Burlsley opens up, spraying the beach. I can see men falling to the sand as we join him at his position. Babineaux opens fire and suddenly the entire beach seems devoid of men, at least any in sight.

"The ones that drop are the survivors. The ones that linger then fall are hits," Burlsley informs me, spraying the beach once more.

"Let's grab Fitz and get out of here," I say and Babineaux looks at me and laughs, a weird bizarre laugh reverberating under the moonlight. I see it, the look of irony on his face.

"I'll do it Murph. I knocked the bum out. I'll carry the bum out." Gunfire erupts from the jungle behind us. I hear tiny bits of metal scream through the air millimeters from my head. "Get going Commander," Babineaux shouts and opens up to our rear. Men cry out from the jungle and his gunfire is answered from the darkness. He empties the clip and reloads. "Go! I'll cover you."

"Everybody grab the raft. Move!" I shout.

Burlsley *dusts* the beach once more then joins the rest of us as we drag the inflatable down the sand and into the surf. We're protected, somewhat, by the lava rock formations and several felled palms scattered by a recent typhoon.

The waves pound against our chests as bullets careen into the surf inches from our bodies. Babineaux sprays the jungle with his Thompson in long fluid sweeps then tosses his grenade. The tree line erupts in a violent crimson turbulence, the screams of men shattering the night. At the waterline Burlsley peppers the soldiers coming up the beach.

"C'mon Babs, move it!" We watch as Babineaux takes up Fitzgerald's limp body and zig-zags down the beach making for the boat. The men call him onward when horror strikes and machinegun fire from the jungle makes his body wobble and contort in a sickening way. I watch as if in slow motion as he falls, motionless in the sand; the color of snow.

Time stops. Crystalline. Burlsley empties his entire clip into the spot where the enemy fire had issued and the jungle goes oddly quiet. "Goddamn sonofabitches!" he rails into the darkness, racing for the fallen men.

"Gil!" I shout but he's already on his way to the men. To the south, the soldiers are getting back onto their feet. I fire a few rounds from my .45 at the bravest. They duck back into the sand. "Toles!" I shout. He's suddenly beside me coating the beach in sporadic bursts.

Cooper is at my elbow. "We got to get them to the raft Commander." I restrain him.

"Don't Cooper. You'll be killed. Stay here, you and Romayo get ready to paddle."

My sojourn up the beach is insane. Men firing blindly at each other in the tropical night, the near mystical landscape a stark contrast to the horror we're living. When I make it to the men, Burlsley is lying there, crying.

"Gil..."

"He's dead Mr. Murphy...Babs...he's dead." I stare into Wendell Babineaux's ever-gentle eyes. They're open, staring intently at the moon above, as if fathoming an enigma.

Burlsley drops his head…and cries.

"Gil, let's go." I attempt to pull him to his feet. It's as if the man were stuck in quicksand.

"It's no good Mr. Murphy, they shot up my legs…I can't walk." The moment lingers as if we were mired in glue, the shouts and rifle fire dying-out to thin whispers.

"Gil…" He rolls onto his side. I see blood, black as oil in the moonlight, seeping from his legs and abdomen. "I'm going to get you out of here." I try to lift him, but he pushes me away.

"It's no good Mr. Murphy. Take Fitz, I'll cover you. It's the only way you'll get off this beach alive." I stare at the two men prostrate upon the sand, the good son, and the bad.

"Gil…I can't leave you here to die like this."

"You can't take us both, sir. Get that lousy piece of shit out of here. Good riddance!" he shouts, spitting on the prostrate sailor and begins firing into the tree line in short repetitive bursts. I grab his shoulder.

"Gil, I can't leave you here. I won't." He reloads his clip.

"It don't matter anyway Mr. Murphy. I'm a dead man either way."

"What do you mean?"

"Get the hell out of here Mr. Murphy! Get the boys back to the Manta Ray and get the hell out," he shoves me. "Go!" I sit there mute while he peppers the tree-line with fire. He then withdraws the grenade from inside his jacket and pulls the pin. "*Grab and go* Mr. Murphy. Tell the boys back on the boat they better get this mission right. This better all be worth it." He heaves the explosive into the trees and the darkness erupts with fire and screaming. "Go dammit go!"

I don't remember doing it but somehow, I have Fitzgerald on my shoulder and I'm running for the water. I hear Burlsley's Thompson coating the jungle behind me.

Toles is tattooing the soldiers pinned down on the beach. A few dozen yards from the raft I feel a round pierce my shoulder and the impact makes me falter. I manage to stagger forward, the men shouting. When I hit the raft, the men are instantly manning the oars.

"Paddle like hell! Paddle like all hell," Toles repeats over the roar of the surf, or is it the gunfire exploding around us? I grab the fourth oar and put it to the water.

"Row fellas, row with all you got," I shout, each man pulling against the waves fighting us, trying to force us back toward the beach. A searing pain wracks my shoulder as I pull on the oar. A mortar round explodes on the beach. Shards of steel cut through the ether like tiny whistles.

"I see the sub, dead ahead," Cooper shouts. Bullets pierce the air, ripping into the raft. I hear it deflating. "Keep rowing guys or we're swimming the rest of the way."

"Why don't they fire Mr. Murphy?" Toles shouts, water dripping from his mouth.

"What?"

"The goddamn sub! Why they just sitting on their ass?" Toles is right. We're halfway to the submarine, well below their line-of-fire. Why weren't they covering our retreat?

Suddenly Romayo cries out, dropping his oar. As he turns, pain wracking his young face, we see the moment of his death; the instant he dies. We all see it, the pain and horror replaced by a strange sudden calm, and he quietly slips into the sea, the ocean gently taking him.

"Romayo. Santino! Fellas, we have to go back."

"Too late Mr. Murphy, he's gone! Keep rowing sir. Keep rowing." Gunfire pierces the raft and the water erupts around us, bullet rounds cutting the air and sea. "Goddammit why ain't you firing?!" Toles screams into the night like a crazy man.

As if the sub could hear him, someone opens up on the 20mm cannon, firing into the beach and the gunfire plaguing our retreat falls off dramatically.

When we make the boat, a dozen sailors converge to get us onto the deck and below. I see Quentin Sorel manning the Oerlikon 20mm, firing without pause, the canon's tracers cutting neat clean lines into the edge of the jungle.

Once everyone is below, they secure the hatch.

"Get us out of here Chief." Stewart shouts. "Reverse engines. All-back full! Standby to take her down."

The crew and science teams are crowding the mess-hall. Tension electrifying the air. Blood flows from my wound across the stainless-steel table, finding the floor. Lucy, her fingers coated in crimson, helps Cooper arrest the bleeding; Porteru nervously doting over them.

The men from the landing party, what's left of us, are in a collective state of shock. Fitzgerald enters the room, followed by Bradshaw. The compartment goes silent, all eyes on the sailor. You could hear a pin drop. He scans the faces of the entire crew crowded in and around the compartment.

"So, while we were standing around waiting for Murphy to finish screwing around in the jungle, talking to that Jap like they were old buddies, a couple slants walked up the beach straight for us. I had no choice but to shoot them Commander Bradshaw, what would you have done sir?" Bradshaw stares blankly in my direction while Lucy and Cooper stuff bandage into the wound.

"How's his arm Corpsman?"

"We're lucky Commander Bradshaw, the bullet went clean through the fleshy part. I've applied antiseptic. The wound should heal without infection."

"I'll make a poultice for this," Porteru interjects. "It'll pull the poison out. We'll be okay Mr. Murphy, you'll see. You'll heal right up."

"Well Murphy, do you have any more questions for Fitzgerald?" I stare at the man, incredulous.

"Yes, I've questions, plenty."

"Like what?" I wonder if Bradshaw is truly that stupid or simply barely alive.

"Why did Babineaux say repeatedly you shot blindly into the Japanese camp? Why would he say that Fitzgerald?"

"Beats me Lieutenant. I figure Babs was kind of losing it, falling apart. I was doing my best to keep us all focused."

"You were doing your best to compromise the integrity of the mission. You consistently-"

"Commander Bradshaw, you should've been out there with us instead of Lieutenant Murphy. Things would have gone a whole lot better if you were in charge."

"You lying sack of shit!" Toles unloads. "You shot into the Japanese camp for no reason. Why'd Babineaux punch him out?" he says directly to Bradshaw.

"You tell me seaman."

"Because he had to! He had to stop Fitz, giving away our position and lousing up the mission. Now Babineaux is dead, Burlsley and Romayo..." Tears well up in the gunner's hardened gaze. "Mr. Murphy, even now I can hardly believe it. They're gone...and he killed them."

Bradshaw glares at Fitzgerald. "Well seaman? You have an answer to that charge?" Fitzgerald adopts a cynical smile and for a moment I have the strongest urge to take the pistol from my hip and just shoot the man.

"Typical Commander Bradshaw, guys like Toles."

"*Guys like Toles?*"

"He's jealous of me."

"What!" Toles exhales.

"He wasn't even there. He was hiding someplace. Toles is always trying to make himself look good at my expense. I'd be second gunner if it wasn't for how chummy he's with Babs and Murphy. He's always talking garbage behind my back." Toles goes for his throat and Smith and Judesay are forced to intercede.

"That's enough Mr. Toles, you're relieved. Everyone, this inquiry is over."

"Over?" I say incredulous. "Cooper, you've nothing to say?" Cooper stops winding the bandage about my shoulder.

"Gee Mr. Murphy, I was over by the raft, closer to Willy covering the north. Santino was with Fitz when the shooting started."

"Well, Romayo is dead. Babineaux too," Bradshaw says like summing up attendance at a picnic. "The only men who could really say what happened, except Fitzgerald." Everyone stares at Fitz; that same cynical smile.

"Like I said Commander Bradshaw. Couple slants walked right up on us in the dark. I did what any true American would do. I shot the bastards. What would you do, if you were there? Ask for directions?"

Bradshaw closes his folder. "The proceedings are over."

"Over?"

"I told you it was a bad idea Murphy, but you chose to do it anyway, against my advice. Now three crewmen are dead. It's your fault those men were killed."

Lucy suddenly slaps him, my blood across his face. "How dare you! How dare you say something so utterly vulgar to these brave men." In the absolute silence that follows, he wipes the blood from his cheek, staring at the rag, as if transfixed by the blood, or numbed by it.

"Dr. Charlesworth…you're restricted to your quarters until further notice. Lieutenant Culver, escort Dr. Charlesworth to her cabin. Post a guard."

"Commander Bradshaw, you can't be serious?"

"Now Lieutenant! Or I'll have you incarcerated as well."

"You needn't *incarcerate* anyone," she says exiting the compartment, Culver reluctantly following.

"Everyone dismissed!" Bradshaw bellows and leaves, the crew slowly dispersing. I stare at Fitzgerald as he rises from the table. He sees my attention upon him. His response is a sneer that curls the upper lip, that same cynical smile, the *smile* he's worn since first stepping foot on the boat.

"This is going to sting a little Mr. Murphy. Some guys prefer to look away."

"Cooper…I've just been shot. I think I can take a needle without fainting." He injects me with morphine and covers the pinprick with cotton.

"Get in your bunk Mr. Murphy, you'll be checking-out in a few minutes. Once you're out, I'll sew the wound shut." He leaves. Only Stewart remains, his silence filling the room.

"Stewie, call Sorel in. I want to commend him for saving our lives. We were like ducks in a shooting gallery out there." His expression goes grave. "What's the matter?"

"You didn't hear?"

"Hear what?"

"Sorel is being restricted to his bunk, pending a court-martial."

"For Christ's sake why?"

"For disregarding Commander Bradshaw's order."

"What order?"

He looks me square in the eye. "To stand-down. Maintain silence."

"What are you saying?"

"Quentin Sorel is being court-martialed for firing at the Japanese that were going to kill you and the landing party." He slams his fist upon the table and exits the compartment.

When I awaken, the incredible has happened. I'm back. I've returned. All about me is my life, the house well-known, the family loved. Standing with me is Lucy, a glass of wine in her hand. She's older, worldly and mature, the same smile in her eyes but wiser, more *knowing*. The voices and laughter of our friends fill the room. The television is blaring nonsense and they're laughing about a meme on our son's smartphone.

At the precise moment I'm thinking I've truly returned, become free of the burden of my life and responsibilities onboard the Manta Ray, Burlsley, in neat clean blue fatigues, his white cap buggered in his fist, enters the room and salutes.

"Commander Murphy, Bradshaw is going to conduct the experiment, with all the guys still onboard. That's a really bad idea, right sir?" He pulls his cap on, slightly to one side, the way he always wore it, and slowly becomes invisible. I fall headlong into a deep sleep.

Chapter *13: Invisible*

"*C*ommander Bradshaw?"

"Not now Murphy, we're getting ready to conduct the experiment."

"What experiment?"

"Murphy, you've been thoroughly briefed."

"I'd appreciate it if you would state it."

"The invisibility experiment, the point of the mission."

"You're not going to rendezvous with the Athena first?"

"There's no reason to delay the invisibility test. It's an offensive tactical weapon I intend to use. We're commencing immediately."

"You're going to experiment with the lives of this crew?"

"That's insubordination! You'll assist with the success of this mission or stand aside."

"Our *mission* is to rendezvous with the Athena, then proceed with the field test without our compliment of men aboard. I've done my homework."

He's silently raging. "Well, I'm changing that. I'm in command of the Manta Ray now Murphy. We'll commence a full test with our full complement of crew at their battle stations, just as if in war. Understood?"

"On whose authority?"

He pounds his fist on the compass bay. "On the authority of this country. Get with the program Murphy, there's a war on, or hadn't you noticed?"

"Yes, I've *noticed*. I've been in it for two solid years."

"Then buck-up Murphy. Let's get it done."

"But sir, you're potentially endangering people's lives, and the approach you've plotted is taking us deeper into Japanese pickets."

"Dammit Murphy! We don't have time to go lollygagging around the Pacific. We'll proceed directly west toward the enemy at eighteen knots. Those are my orders First Officer and we'll test the equipment tonight at oh-two-hundred if Hoffmann says we're ready. Is that clear?"

"But Commander, it's imperative you understand-"

"Damn it to hell Murphy! We don't have time to screw around. Hitler has taken over the whole of Europe. France has fallen and Britain is next. When that happens, there'll be no hope. Japan will knock us out of the Pacific then move on the American mainland. We don't have months or even weeks to waste." I see it clearly in his face, paranoia. "We need to attack now Murphy, not next week or next month."

"Sir, I understand the necessity for action, but we owe it to the officers and men of this crew to proceed in an intelligent and determined manner not to just gamble needlessly with-"

"Gamble? Did I hear you say *gamble*? Quartermaster Taylor!"

"Yes sir."

"Quartermaster, I believe the X-O is still suffering from his wounds. Please escort him to his bunk. Have the paramedic examine his head. I think he's become delirious."

"That's not necessary. I'm perfectly fit for duty."

"Well I want another checkup. Dismissed."

"Did pharmacist Cooper report to you on my condition?"

"What about it?"

"Was his prognosis not satisfactory?"

"It was but-" Hawkins ducks his head through the portal.

"Commander Bradshaw, Dr. Hoffmann indicates we're ready to start."

"Thank-you," he says saluting the civilian who awkwardly salutes back. Hawkins flashes me a very pensive look and is gone.

"Okay Murphy let's get to it then. Let's take the bridge," he says ascending the ladder topside. I share a look with Taylor and follow him, careful not to aggravate my shoulder.

We join Duncan on the bridge, scanning the dark rolling ocean, two lookouts in the shears, one aft. "What's the word Ensign?" Bradshaw asks.

"*Word* sir?"

"Do you see the enemy anywhere about?"

"Negative, all quiet."

"Carry on Ensign," he says, and Duncan returns to his binoculars. I gaze at the dull yellow moon directly above. Dark clouds like knife blades cut through it like thin black fingers. Two of the scientists in foul weather jackets are checking the antennae array. Brauer emerges from the hatch and calls these men in.

"Better get your men inside Bradshaw," he says and disappears below.

"Bring your lookouts down Ensign," Bradshaw says.

"Lookouts below," Duncan shouts and the men drop from the sail, counting off as they disappear into the hatch.

"You too Duncan," I say.

"Belay that order. The Ensign will remain."

"You're having Duncan stay topside?"

"He won't be alone, you'll remain also." I'm shocked.

"Is that wise?"

"Those are my orders! We won't have a spotting vessel. I want a report from here on the progress of the experiment."

"With all due respect sir, I specifically heard the doctors say it was ill-advised to have any crewmembers outside the-"

"Goddammit Murphy! I've just about had it with your insubordination. If you're afraid, then replace yourself with an able-bodied seaman."

"It has nothing to do with being *afraid*, and everything to do with my responsibility for the safety of the crew."

He's seething. "Stand-down Murphy, that's an order," he says through clenched teeth. The battle phone jangles. "Bridge!" he shouts into it. "Yes…confirmed, standing-by." He hangs up. "It's a green-light. Standby to go." I look at Duncan, gloom wracking his face. Bradshaw rings the control room. I take one more look at the moon directly overhead and it's neither a grin nor a smile this time, more a dull mustard-colored frown. "I want a two-minute countdown over the speaker Taylor, copy me?" Bradshaw says into the phone checking his watch and hangs up. "Well men, here we go. History in the making." He grabs the railing of the bridge cowling, gazing across the foredeck like a kid about to take his first rollercoaster ride. There's nothing to do but wait as Taylor counts the seconds over the Com in ten-second intervals. At zero-fifteen, his voice intensifies.

"Ten seconds…five, four, three, two, one, ignition."

A painful piercing sound erupts, just on the edge of human hearing, followed by a high-pitched whining. It morphs into a loud whirring with a pulsating throb that I *feel* more than hear. A strange bluish mist begins to surround the exterior of the boat, the moon becoming opaque.

"Look!" Duncan shouts arresting my attention back to the deck. Sparks begin to dance about the superstructure. Balls of St. Elmo's fire roll across the deck and a loud pulsating throb forces us to cover our ears. A bluish fog envelops the craft and the ocean and sky can no longer be seen.

"How long?" I shout to Bradshaw at the top of my lungs.

"What?"

"How long will they run it?"

"Several minutes."

An eerie unworldly mist encapsulates the boat and the metal begins to glow, becoming phosphorescent; bursts of lightning and static electricity spark through the ether.

"Ensign call the control room," Bradshaw shouts and Duncan picks up the phone shouting into the receiver. "What do they say?"

"Nothing. There's no response."

"Keep trying Ensign." Suddenly a sonic boom rocks the boat and Bradshaw actually ducks, sparks dancing through the sail like Christmas at Macys.

"Shut it down!" I shout into Bradshaw's ear.

"What?"

"Shut it down, before the sparks ignite our ordnance!" He hesitates a moment, realizing the gravity of my statement, before grabbing the phone from Duncan's hand.

"Shut it down! Tell doctor Hoffmann to pull the plug!" he repeats into the phone until there is a slow reversal of the process. Eventually the high-pitched whirring subsides, the sparks and mist fade and the ocean returns. We breathe a sigh of relief until Duncan's voice shatters the quiet.

"Look, the moon has moved!" I'm momentarily numb. Staring down at us is a deep bluish moon without clouds in a different place in the sky; astern us, farther to the east.

"What are you talking about Ensign?" Bradshaw growls.

"The moon. It's changed position."

"That's impossible."

"Look!" he shouts pointing. Bradshaw goes dumb. "How can that be Commander Murphy? It's gone east."

"What in Sam Hill is going on?" Bradshaw mutters as reality sets in. "How could the moon move?" he asks me.

"Maybe *it* didn't."

"Explain that comment." I wonder if he's in denial.

"The laws of physics. The moon can't move backward."

"What are you getting at?"

"The moon is in a different position, further east."

"My god he's right." Duncan says. "How can the moon move backward in the sky?"

"That's absurd," Bradshaw says. Duncan looks like he might actually throttle him.

"Then explain that!" he shouts.

"I don't know, but there has to be a logical explanation." The battle phone cuts him off. Petty Officer Smith's voice.

"Commander Murphy?"

"Go ahead Smith."

"Sir, you better get down here, on the double."

"What's wrong?" There's a pause, then Stewart's voice comes on-line.

"Murph, you better come below, right away."

"What is it?"

"You better come below." The line goes dead. As I start below, I'm belayed by Duncan.

"Commander Murphy, is it me, or does the sea look really flat?"

"One thing at a time Duncan. Maintain the watch."

I descend the ladder into an eerie silence, the scientists and crew gathered in the control room in an apparent collective state of shock. "What is it?" No one answers; Lucy, Hoffmann and Brauer wordlessly staring at each other. "Stewie, what is it?" He points forward, his eyes weirdly dilated. "Lieutenant Stewart, I asked you a question." His eyes are looking through me.

"Forward torpedo room."

What is the look etched upon their faces? Shock? Fear? I duck through the watertight door and make my way to the bow. Sailors are staring in the direction of the forward torpedo room as if some horror lurked behind the door. At the bulkhead Pendleton and Wyatt stand mute.

"Open it."

"Don't go in there, sir," Pendleton says. He's terrified.

"Open it Ron." They twist the wheel and the oval door is flung back into a misty, darkened chamber. "Why are the lights out?" I question the men gathered around me like a funeral. No one answers. "Bob, give me your light." Seaman Wyatt hands me his flashlight. As I begin to probe the room another beam follows mine. Bradshaw has mustered the courage–or curiosity–to shadow me in.

The first thing I notice, besides the mist laden darkness, is a peculiar acidic smell similar to burnt wiring but different. The next critical realization is a shocking absence of men.

"Binkershon?" I call out, my voice ringing off the vacant hull. "Ned answer me." Absolute silence permeates the room, not a soul to be seen within the flashlight's beam. Bradshaw pushes past me and begins to frantically search the room as if the men might be hiding under their bunks or sequestered between the torpedoes stacked along the hull. The box containing the package sits without its guard.

"Culver? McCullum, report!" he bellows; to no one. When he turns into my light, I see the sweat across his forehead. "Murphy…where are your men?" I turn to my quartermaster.

"Bill, where is Binkershon and his crew?" He shakes his head, as if in a trance. "Answer me. Where's the forward torpedo crew?" The man is incapable of answering, slowly shaking his head side to side.

Stewart enters, scanning the compartment, shock cut into his face. "Stewie, commence a full search of the boat." He stares blankly into the empty compartment. "Now."

"Aye…aye sir." He turns to the men plastered about the portal. "Search the boat, shears to keel. Move." The officers continue to gawk into the compartment. My beam locks on the large vibrating coil. It looks weird in the dull light of the hand torch. Suddenly Taylor shatters the silence.

"Well Commander Bradshaw, how do you explain this?" Bradshaw is scanning the empty room with his flashlight.

"There must be some explanation. They must have walked away from their posts, vacated the compartment."

"*Vacated?*" Taylor echoes and laughs, an odd unsettling laugh. "Maybe they went for a swim? They're gone you idiot! The whole damn crew!"

"Take it easy Bill," I mutter, surprised by the man's sudden outburst.

"Take it easy? Where the hell are they Mike? They were at station. Binkershon, Nichols, Belcher…where are they?"

"Just calm down."

"It's that thing!" he screams pointing at the coil. "That thing did this. That thing!"

I look at Stewart. "Get him out of here." Stewart grabs Taylor by the shoulder.

"Easy Bill, let's get some coffee."

"Coffee? Yeah sure Stu, let's have a goddamn tea party." He snarls at Bradshaw. "This tin-plated submarine skipper can be the guest of honor!" I shove Taylor toward the door and Stewart and Torsch quickly pull him aft. "He killed them! He ordered them to stay in here with that thing. He murdered them! Murderer!" After he's gone the silence can be cut with a knife. Bradshaw shoves past me, exiting the room.

As I scan the compartment with the flashlight, something on the floor reflects my beam. I extract a gold chain with a golden amulet, holding it in the light.

"What is it Lieutenant?" Judesay asks from my elbow.

"Ned Binkershon's gold medallion. Saint Christopher. His wife Lillian gave it to him the day we shipped out of New London. He's never taken it off…except today."

I'm summoned back to the bridge. Nothing within my training as an officer or within my experience as a man prepares me. For miles around the boat, the sea is as still and unmoving as glass! Not a ripple breaks the quietude of the immense sea, nor a wind breaks the stillness; we're frozen in place, nothing but a thin blue moon watching us solemnly from above.

"Commander Murphy, this can't be happening," Duncan stutters. "This…this can't be real. The ocean can't be still like this…can it?" I've no practical answer for him.

"Keep your wits about you Eban, remember your training. The crew is counting on you, your leadership. Do you understand me Ensign?" His expression changes dramatically. I see his old *self* reemerge on his face. He stands at attention and salutes.

"Aye-aye Commander. Thank-you sir."

"Keep an eye on things up here Mr. Duncan. I'm going to get us some answers."

The atmosphere in the officer's wardroom is as stagnant as the ocean, the doctors visibly stunned. Hoffman broods while Brauer smokes his pipe. Lucy just stares into her cup as if it were a tiny portal into another world, a world beneath the surface of her tea. Stewart joins us pulling the curtain closed. I don't like the look on his face.

"Surely there's some explanation?" Bradshaw says yet again, less a question than a revolving statement followed by another solemn pause.

"Mr. Stewart, have you *re-ascertained* our coordinates?"

"Everything's knocked out Dr. Hoffmann, all electronic navigation, but our sextant indicates we're a thousand nautical miles due west of our previous position."

"Are you insane Stewart?" Bradshaw declares. "That's impossible. Your stars are off. Check it again."

"He doesn't need to," I interject. "Chief has already confirmed the information. Smith also."

"And the Athena? Have you located it?"

"Negative."

"You've tried to radio her of course?"

"Repeatedly. Pearl as well. Nothing. Radar. Sonar. Hydrophone. All systems are nil. It's…weird." Hoffmann and Brauer exchange a look, some kind of silent acknowledgement. There's a rap on the bulkhead and McClatchy slides the curtain aside.

"Mr. Murphy, reporting on our search of the boat."

"Go ahead Pat."

"No dice sir. Not a thing." He gives Bradshaw *the eye*.

"Keep looking," Bradshaw barks at the sailor.

McClatchy pauses, his mouth half open. "Yes sir," he says vindictively, salutes and exits. McClatchy was a good sailor. Despite his tendency to openly speak his mind–often in the worst possible moments–he implicitly followed orders. It was important to him not only as a rated seaman but as a person. Pat grew up poor in Dothan, Alabama, a sharecropper's son, one of fourteen children.

"Dr. Hoffmann, what's happening to us? Do you even have a guess?" I ask to break the ensuing silence. The doctors share a solemn look. The moment hovers.

"Dr. Hoffmann, he deserves a response don't you think?" Lucy whispers. Hoffmann silently reflects before clearing his throat, his fingertips finding each other, as if in prayer.

"Gentlemen, as remarkable as this will sound, we believe in our attempt to create the invisibility screen, we've created some kind of…warping."

"Warping? What do you mean?"

"Perhaps *phasing* might be the better word. Yes, we're out of phase."

"Could you elaborate on that sir?" A silence permeates the moment, the doctor collecting his thoughts.

"The experiment's principal science involves frequency modulation, the bending of light waves. Light by its very nature involves us inextricably with the concept of *space-time*. Technically, I believe they are the same. Three aspects of the same phenomena. The concept of the *space-time* continuum still seeks exploration. There are many questions, many questions, regarding the nature of light and more importantly, its relation to subatomic particle behavior. These particles create forces that coalesce into aggregates that compose *reality* as we perceive it, the nuances of our observable universe if you will."

"We both graduated with a two-year degree in seamanship," Stewart interjects.

"Mr. Stewart, how many dimensions to our world, this world around you?"

"Three. Height, width and length."

"Incorrect. There are four, arguably five, that are readily self-evident. Your example can be embellished. You must consider the single point as the first probable dimension; after-all, it's more than nothing yet less than *something*. Thusly, the line forms two dimensions, *here* and *there*. The triangle forms the third point effectively creating the *plane*."

"Exactly. Height, width and length."

"Ah, but here is where it gets more complex. The fourth coordinate forms the pyramid or prism and of course you must include time, *the space within*, as the fifth."

"Five dimensions…" I mutter.

"In all probability Mr. Murphy there are more, millions, perhaps an infinite number." He stares through the table. "My god, the possibilities."

"Sir?"

"*Time* Mr. Murphy. You must include *time* in your concept of *space*. They are intrinsically the same phenomenon. What has happened confirms it in my mind."

"Explain," Bradshaw says. "Time is past and gone."

"Do your best to comprehend this. A light photon travelling at 186,000 miles per second will take four years to arrive from our nearest star neighbor. The light we perceive is four years in the past. We are in actuality seeing backward in time. Space and time are relative to one another."

"I'm not sure I get that. *Seeing backward in time?*"

"The German physicist Albert Einstein has been concerned with the concept of acceleration. What we've just experienced confirms, in my mind, his theory on Special Relativity is in truth correct. The coils work as magnets, the magnetism is creating, in essence, gravity. Gravity is distorting space…and time. You're correct Charlesworth, we've accelerated."

"What does that mean?"

"The theory predicts that the speed of light in a vacuum is independent of the motion of other things, other states of being, regardless of their trajectories or velocities."

"Scale it down Hoffmann. The gentlemen are sailors not physicists," Brauer says from behind his pipe.

"I understand him Dr. Brauer. Time and space are relative…to the observer."

"*The observer*…yes…excellent Mr. Murphy. When we activated our particle accelerator, we created a powerful magnetic field that interacted with the earth's magnetic field. These currents are in motion as the earth itself is in motion."

"Yes, the math would be astounding," I hear myself say, as if listening to another, an inner voice, and Lucy looks up from her teacup.

"*Astounding* is hardly the word Mr. Murphy," Hoffmann presses. "The earth is moving at a fantastic rate of speed, what is referred to as *velocity*. We are revolving around the sun, which in turn is revolving around our galactic core that is revolving around a super galaxy we postulate may be rotating around the center of the universe."

"Yes. I understand."

"There is every probability there is more than this one *singularity*. We're contemplating potentially vast properties."

Stewart–loudly–relinquishes his seat at the table to refill his coffee.

"Go on Doctor."

"Remember, the gravitational force is an absolute mystery to us." He glances at Brauer.

"The point here gentlemen, is we believe we may have vibrated out of our fixed position in space-time. Merely by chance, or perhaps the luck of terminating the experiment prematurely, the shift was miniscule, a mere 2000 kilometers. Thankfully, the medium was uniform."

"*The medium* Professor Brauer?"

"The ocean, as opposed to rematerializing in uneven terrain like mountains for instance. We're speculating, but it's our assumption that-"

"Why are we just sitting here talking? What about the men that disappeared?" Stewart interjects. "Where are they?" Hoffmann and Brauer exchange a serious expression.

"This is more complex Mr. Stewart, requiring further consideration, much further."

"Do you have any idea at all?" I ask. The men go strangely silent. Lucy looks up from the table.

"Professor, they deserve to know. Trust them to understand, in spirit, what we think has happened."

Hoffmann nods. "I'm afraid I agree with her Brauer." The rotund scientist shrugs. "Gentlemen, it is pure speculation, but we believe they're still here."

"Still here?" Bradshaw mutters. "Where?"

"Perhaps standing next to you Bradshaw, or the very spot you currently occupy," Hoffmann says, and Bradshaw actually studies the space about his person.

"I don't understand Dr. Hoffmann. If you think they're here…why don't we see them?"

"Don't use your rational mind Michael," Lucy says. "That illusive quality we term *intuition* might serve you better in this instance. It is very possible the men wander this submarine looking for us, as we likewise look for them."

"You think they're in some kind of alternate dimension?"

"Or vibrational state, we're purely speculating."

"But how? Why them and not the rest of us?" Bradshaw blurts out.

"Proximity," Lucy says, the remark directed at the senior scientist. "It must be the reason different men were affected in different ways. The forward coil is the primary, the nexus of the field. The up and down molecular spin pulses at a slightly accelerated rate…and with the increased ionic discharge inside the compartment from the warhead-" Hoffmann gestures and she stops. Hoffmann shakes his head.

"Go on," I urge her.

"We think it probable the men within the compartment were affected differently."

"It would have been better had we cleared the compartment prior the test," Hoffmann says, removing his spectacles and pinching his eyes. "The oversight was my own. I bear the responsibility for the missing men…for conducting the experiment without proper precautions."

Silence.

"No…no Dr. Hoffmann, it wasn't you," Bradshaw says. "I pushed too hard." Hoffmann looks up, his eyes wet. "I ordered you to move forward despite your reservations. I even ordered those men to their stations contrary to your request, all your requests," he says looking at the three principle scientists. "They're not here. Quartermaster Taylor is correct. I–I killed those men. I killed them."

A profound silence fills the room. We silently watch Bradshaw robotically gather his papers then fumble them across the floor. He stares blankly at the forms before exiting the room without them, the silence broken only when Stewart slams his fist on the table upsetting his coffee cup.

"Dr. Hoffmann, is there anything we can do? Anything at all?" I inquire. Hoffmann seems resigned. "Professor Brauer, there must be something you've considered?" Brauer nods looking to Hoffmann who shakes his head.

"No Brauer, I don't think so."

"What? Tell us."

"We attempt a momentary pulse…a reset would be the best way to describe it."

"A reset?"

"Yes. We bring the ship back up to the same *molecular excitement* prior the arcing, then abort, precisely as per our calculations."

"You think it will work?"

"We've no practical idea, however, the math indicates a strong probability. It's difficult to explain, but we've speculated a return to our original vibrational state."

"Return of the missing crew you mean?" Stewart asks.

"I mean us Mr. Stewart."

"*Us?* What do you mean sir?" I ask.

"Haven't you wondered Commander? Why we've been unable to establish contact with the Athena, or the O'Malley, or even Pearl Harbor…anyone or anything?"

"The thought has crossed my mind."

"It is completely within the realm of probability that we're not *in the world,* as you know it. As Hoffmann said earlier, we've accelerated. We're out of phase."

"That's crazy," Stewart exhales.

"Perhaps."

"What is being *out of phase*?" I inquire.

"Atomically shifted, just enough to put us out of molecular phase."

"*Out of phase?* What the hell is he talking about?"

"Easy Stewie. Dr. Hoffmann, we're real men, flesh and bone, not electricity."

"Actually Michael, that's debatable," Lucy interjects. "We consider ourselves matter, material, but what is mass in reality but energy, a form of energy; an aggregation of molecular forces that form this veneer we call *matter.* Your body, your brain, even your mind is a form of energy. It's evident we've affected these fields, these states of being in ways we couldn't possibly fathom at the moment, not without further research and experimentation. This is what is meant by *out of phase.*"

Stewart suddenly becomes anxious. "Mike, I'm going topside for a cigarette, air-out my head."

"Check on the men Ellis. See if there's been any contact, with anything." He exits without a word.

"You probably think we're cold heartless beings, or we've gone insane. Please speak your mind Mr. Murphy."

"Dr. Hoffmann, what you're talking about is the least crazy thing happening at the moment."

He manages a weak smile. "So, what do you want to do Commander Murphy?"

"Me?"

"Your captain has been relieved of his command, restricted to quarters pending a court-martial. Bradshaw has just collapsed mentally, effectively walking away from his responsibilities. You're in command now. What would you propose we do?"

I'm in the mess-hall with my officers and senior crewmen when Stewart joins us from the bridge.

"How are things topside Stewie?"

"The same. Nothing but miles of ocean still as a pond. It's crazy, giving everyone the creeps. I had to relieve Smith and send Rawlston to the pharmacist for a sedative."

"Are lookouts still posted?"

"Of course, Duncan's on watch, with Lesky and Wyatt. Lesky's too stupid to understand what's going on. Bob…Bob Wyatt is next in line for a sedative."

"How's Taylor doing Rose?"

"Coop's with him. Not good. He just keeps mumbling the same shit over and over. It's nuts. He can't wrap his head around this. Hell, what sane man could?"

"Anything on the radio yet Jukes? Anything at all?"

"Zilch Lieutenant, not a thing, I mean nothing. Not even background noise. It's weird man. I mean, there's always background noise, always. This is…nothing. Flatline."

"Well keep trying Roscoe," Stewart says.

"Mr. Stewart, there's just nothing out there."

"I said keep trying. Go do it." Jukes extinguishes his cigarette and leaves for the radio room.

"Nothing over long-range?"

"Radar, sonar or hydrophone either," Elder says. "Everything reads flat. I've never seen anything like it. It's not natural."

"It's just like those eggheads were saying in the wardroom," Stewart says to me. "Maybe we're in some kind of…limbo." The look in his eyes is disturbing.

"You talk to Bradshaw Chief?"

"Bradshaw's done Murph. He can't look the crew in the eye. Everyone on the boat knows he ordered those men to station against Hoffmann's wishes. Hell, the whole damn predicament we're in, shoving the experiment down our throats. The man's a jackass. He's finally admitted it to himself. He's afraid to come out of his cabin."

"We should have rendezvoused with the Athena," Goldman adds. "What was he thinking?"

"He wasn't thinking, thus the shit we're in. You talk to Skipper again Murph?"

"It's over Chief. When Hess took the boat away, it was like getting stabbed in the back by his best friend."

"But it's his chance to get back in the saddle. Doesn't he see that?"

"We'd never get him sober soon enough. He's down the bottle again."

"Then you're the ranking officer Mike. What do you want to do?" Stewart inquires.

"Hell, what do you think Mr. Stewart?" Herndon shouts. "You turn this goddamn boat around and head for Pearl! No one gives a damn about the goddamn mission."

"Herndon…"

"In case you haven't looked, we're just sitting here. There hasn't been a breeze for hours, the sea's like glass, there's no sound. What the hell does it mean?!"

"Stand-down Herndon that's an order," Chief shouts. "Just take it easy. What do want to do Murph?"

"We have three choices gentlemen. Go ahead with the mission and pray the Athena is where she's supposed to be, return to Pearl, or try the reset. Those are the options."

"You think it'll work, the reset?"

"How the hell would he know? This whole goddamn thing is nuts!"

"Herndon, I'm not going to say it again. Calm down. You've a job to do sailor."

"Well, whatever we do Chief we better do it soon. People are losing it," Herndon says lighting up, his hand shaking.

"What would you do Chief, if you were in my shoes?"

"Well, I sure as hell wouldn't go any further into Empire, that's for damn sure. We got enough trouble on our hands than risk tangling with the Japanese navy. If they're even out there." He takes a moment to think. "It's pure gut Murph, but you asked, so…yeah, I guess I'd do it. I'd try their reset."

"You would?"

"Yes, I think I would." He scowls at the others. "Don't be shy ladies, chime-in anytime."

"Something's really wrong Mr. Murphy," Elder says. "What if we did turn back and the world we knew no longer existed?" He sees the look on my face. "We overheard you talking with the lady doctor sir, right after the meeting. Is it true what she said? That space and time are intertwined? That if we leave this exact position, return to Pearl Harbor and conduct the reset there, we might never get back to our original place in time? That's the reason we haven't moved?"

"It's theoretical. She said it was possible. If we return to Pearl Harbor and things were *different*, trying the reset there would be *off*…forever."

"That's crazy. How Murphy?! Why?"

"Dammit Herndon how would he know?" Chief interjects. "*They* don't even know. But it makes sense to me. This entire boat moved over two thousand klicks during the experiment. I know how to read a goddamn sextant."

"What happens if we go back to Pearl Harbor, repeat the experiment and…" Goldman doesn't finish his sentence.

"Whatever we do Murph we need to do it soon. Rosie's right. I've had to break up two fistfights and a couple dozen quarrels," Chief says running a greasy hand through his beard. "Men who've sailed together for two solid years. The crew's coming apart at the seams."

"Well one thing's for damn sure, I want to go back to the world I came from. I want to see Sally and the kids again, hold them," Stewart says. I see tears forming in his eyes, the first time since I've known him. "What do we got to lose?"

"More than you can probably imagine."

A scratchy record starts over the boat's PA, *Midnight, the Stars and You.*

"Jukes? Playing records?"

"I gave him permission. Under the circumstances, I thought it might relax the crew. Everyone…dismissed."

The control room is quiet, Szotsman asleep by the manifold, Judesay staring into space, the ash of the cigarette between his fingers hanging limp.

"Stay sharp Lynn." He nods, extinguishing his smoke and resumes his observation of the compass. It spins aimlessly, no longer subjected to the authority of a northern magnetic point.

Jukes starts a Bing Crosby record turning, *Ghost of a Chance,* and the boat is filled with the soft drone of the singer's voice. Is the singer pining for a lost love, or is *he* the ghost? I remember my conversation with Lucy concerning the afterlife and my mind suddenly becomes filled with thoughts about her.

What is it that takes me in the direction of her room, the song and its message or some other silent calling? When I tap on the bulkhead near the door, I hear a muffled cry and enter. It's utterly surreal. Fitzgerald has her down on the bunk beneath him ripping at her clothing. I grab his shoulders pulling him off. He slams me backward against the bulkhead with all his weight and follows with an elbow to the solar plexus robbing me of air.

She cries out but he strikes her, forcing her down onto the bunk. I grab him by the collar and rip the shirt off his back, sending him into a rage. He proceeds to pummel me against the bulkhead pounding his fists into my ribs then tripping me onto the floor, upsetting the desk and toppling her reading lamp, the bulb smashing across the deck plate.

Incredibly, he withdraws a switchblade, engaging the blade and lunges at me on the floor. I catch his wrist but he's out of control, putting all his weight into trying to bury the knife into my neck.

We're face-to-face on the floor. I'm straining to keep the knife off me, inches from my neck, but tiring rapidly when a hand reaches in between us and with a great inner strength, raises the knife–and Fitzgerald–to his feet. I watch, frozen, as Porteru clenches Fitzgerald's wrist, bringing the knife up between them. They're literally nose-to-nose and the hatred the men share for each other ignites the space between them like fire. Fitzgerald struggles to free himself, but Coffee has the sailor in a kind of *death grip.*

They struggle fiercely, Fitz trying desperately to get free while Porteru seems to tighten his grip, like a Boa squeezing its prey, using its quarry's movements against him.

A strange *dance of death* ensues in the tiny cramped compartment. When Fitz shoves his free hand up into Coffee's face the Cajun bites into it like a wild animal drawing blood. Porteru, with unrelenting determination, begins to turn the blade in Fitz's hand.

"Coffee don't do it," I say from the floor. What is it I see in those eyes? Controlled rage, a lifetime of it.

"There ain't no choice Mr. Murphy. He won't stop until he hurts her. I'm gonna end this right here and now." He stares into Fitzgerald, terror in the gunner's eyes as he tries to talk his way out of it, actually whimpering, a pathetic, animal-like sound as he watches the blade turning upon him.

"C'mon Port. What are you doing man? I was just joking around. C'mon buddy, let it go. Let it go!"

"I'm ending this right now. Once and for all." He turns the blade into the seaman's chest and leans into it. Fitzgerald screams as Porteru presses the blade home, piercing the ribcage and running the knife deep into his chest up to the hilt. Fitz's eyes bulge with shock, grotesque, blood issuing through his teeth. He drops to his knees, falling atop me. I stare into the man's eyes as he dies; a horrid grimace.

"The crew is coming unglued Murph. Hell, this incident with Fitz is just plain crazy."

"Fitzgerald tried to rape Dr. Charlesworth. It was on his mind from the start."

Stewart exhales loudly. "I know." He shakes off the thought. "How is she?"

"Cooper is with her. Fortunately, she wasn't injured, badly. Where is Fitzgerald's body?"

"We committed him to the deep. Just now. I didn't think you'd mind my addressing the occasion, under the circumstances." I nod. "We weighted the body Murph, heavily, so it would sink. Way things are up top, we were afraid he'd just float there next to the sub." He shakes off the thought.

"How's Coffee?"

"Quiet. He's not going to give us any trouble. He's incarcerated in the after-hold, as per regulations. He's completely at peace about what happened. Said he'd do it exactly the same way again. You saw everything?"

"Fitzgerald was trying to rape her. He came at me with the knife Stewie, for keeps. Porteru saved my life."

"That's not going to change what happens next. Coffee will be up on manslaughter charges, at the very least."

"I know." I breathe deeply, feeling an inner weariness.

"He's asking if we can reassign him his duties until we return…*if* we return." Our situation reasserts itself. I mustn't lose focus on the dire situation we're in. The entire vessel, over seventy human beings, depending on the decisions I make. Cooper joins us looking tired and disheveled. He rechecks the bandage on my shoulder that's begun to bleed again and pokes and prods my ribs.

"How're you feeling Lieutenant?"

"Don't fuss over me Cooper. You've enough on your hands." I winch when he jabs his forefinger into my ribcage.

"He re-cracked your rib. I may still have some painkillers in my kit."

"It's all right Cooper, leave it for now. Is there something you need?"

"Dr. Charlesworth wants to speak with you sir, in private. She's waiting in her room."

I knock and enter the compartment, surprised to find it empty. They've reset her desk. Papers are scattered atop it, notes scribbled on scrap paper, mostly mathematical equations and formulae. Written inside her open notebook is a lengthy series of equations followed by a rather cryptic observation.

'The fields are exerting effects on each other in unanticipated ways, the primary field creating odd pulses, fluctuations of an unknown origin. The new force being created is mysterious but reveals itself when affecting material bodies that lie within the field. Drs Hoffmann and Brauer are baffled.

'What is this strange undefined 'something' within the vortex? And why such strange behavior? Maxwell proved electromagnetic fields travel at the velocity of light, that light photons possess electromagnetic fields. Hence, what difference in regards to time itself? What difference really, space, time and light?'

The curtain opens and she enters, closing it taut. I look at her, her brilliant mind behind her beautiful face; a cut on the left cheek. "Snooping Commander Murphy?"

"What's all this?" I ask pointing to the formulae.

"*This?*" she says thumbing through the clutter of equations and notes. "A waste of...*time.*" She whispers the last word, as if it carried a particular meaning. A bruise has formed and her lip is cracked and bleeding. She sits on the bunk and gently embraces me, pulling my neck close; her body shudders.

"Are you all right?" She nods without looking up from my shoulder. "I shouldn't have let this happen. I failed you. I'm sorry." She raises her sad eyes to mine. Timeless.

"There's nothing for you to apologize about," she sighs, and we quietly embrace, serenely together, alone.

Porteru is in the after-torpedo room. "How are you Coffee?"

"Wasting time Mr. Murphy, sitting here doing nothing. It just don't seem right…a man sitting doing nothing when the Lord give him two good hands and a head on his shoulders…don't seem right."

"I came to see how you were doing."

"One of the men give me this here book to fill time." It's a dog-eared copy of *Mysterious Island* by Jules Verne. The title of the book forces my mind back to *Lost Island*; Wendy Babineaux's dead eyes gazing at the moon, Gil Burlsley's tears falling across the sands of a tiny, far-away island, barely larger than a county park. I throw the thing aside as if it were poison. He shifts his gaze between the book and me, lowering his voice.

"I pretend Mr. Murphy, but I can't read a book like that. I recognize a few words here, there, but…I never went to school. I was oldest, had to cook and clean house so my brothers and sisters could go to school. I cheated my papers into the service." He toes the grating beneath his shoes. "I'd be better inside the galley cooking for the crew Commander Murphy. Dickie's a baker, and McAnulty don't know nothing about feeding grown men essential nutrition. He makes things taste better than just out of a can or cardboard box, but a person's body needs real food, not just sugar and flour…and with Santino dead and gone…well…I just think-"

"Why Coffee? Why did you kill that man?"

He takes a long time to answer, contemplating something deeply before returning his dark eyes to mine, lowering his voice; nearly a whisper.

"I reckon I didn't kill no *man* Mr. Murphy. There weren't nothing left in Fitzgerald resembling the word. Nothing but an awful thing…a thing living on stone-cold hate."

"I asked you a question Coffee, I want an answer. Did you do it out of spite? Anger? I realize you saved my life, and probably Lucy's, but…why did you kill him?" His eyes take on a strange unworldly intensity, as if seeing something at a great distance.

"A *man* got a heart and a soul inside him, gifts given him from *the Graces*; the part that knows the difference between right and wrong. Thing what makes him a man, a human being, is *the voice*, a quiet invisible thing. Almost can't hear it, if a soul's not paying close attention. Soft, like a bird on the wing. *You* know the sound, always know'd it I reckon."

"Yes. I think I do."

"I know you know it."

"But why Porteru? Why kill him? Why not just knock him out?"

"Babineaux knocked him down, now he's dead. Burlsley struck the man down, while back. You never heard about that Mr. Murphy. He struck Fitzgerald down for the shameful thing he said to Miss Lucy. Now he dead too. The *thing* inside'll kill anyone gets in the way." We hang our heads a moment, remembering our fallen comrades.

"But…you killed a man Charles."

"Don't you see? Fitzgerald weren't a *man* no more Mr. Murphy. That hateful thing eating his inside weren't going to rest until he *kilt* Doctor Lucy, sooner or later, sure as the sun rise up. No doubt in my mind. I seen it over and over my whole life, those hateful things that get inside a person. They's forever on the hunt for anything good in this world, anything filled with beauty and light." He quiets, his voice thinning to a mere whisper. "When the duppy inside a man gets so full of hate, so full of disdain for his brother, the soul, the spirit inside the man, up and leaves, leaves nothing but a dead thing walking."

"A *duppy*?"

"The invisible part of a man that makes the body jump up and shout; dance or spit. When the duppy goes bad, he ain't nothing but a dead man walking. There weren't nothing inside Fitzgerald but an eaten out shell. Sure, he look like a man but he's only a *thing* full of dark thoughts. Fitzgerald was dead already, died years ago probably. What I *kilt* was a duppy gone bad…a dead man walking."

I stare into the man, his gaze unflinching.

"I'd do it again, same way as I done. I reckon I'll be doing it over and over, all my days, and those yet to come me…*the glory* forever out of reach. Lifetime after lifetime there *he* is Mr. Murphy, this thing we called *Fitzgerald*. Next time, some other name, other face." I ponder these sobering words, their magnitude. He stares at his hands. "And now my life's done. When we get home, they'll put me in a jailcell. They won't let me cook. If I get out with any years left me; bank won't go a loan. I'll never open my restaurant in New Orleans I dreamt my whole life."

None of the men gathered in the compartment break the silence, each man quiet with his own thoughts.

"Sir, it's better if I get to my duties, feeding the men. Just until we go back to Pearl is fine. Everyone's getting that look comes on with not eating right. I ain't about to hurt nobody Mr. Murphy. Only person on this boat I looked at crosswise was Fitzgerald…and now…he dead. Gone to atone for hisself. Just like I'll do when it's my turn. Stand a'fore the glory. Find out if there's beauty in me, or just a hollow empty shell that never cared for no one, never done nothing for nobody. Just a thing mistook for *a man*."

The crew goes still as I unbind the accouterments incarcerating him. He brushes himself as if shedding dust. I reach my hand to him.

"Thank-you for saving my life." His shake is firm, warmth in his grip. "Charles, when you return to Louisiana, contact Wendall Babineaux's father. He's in Monroe. Tell him about his son, that he died saving our lives." He doesn't speak, doesn't need to, as he heads for the galley. I study the sailors. They quietly disband, exiting the compartment or returning to their stations without a word.

Chapter 14: The Silence

I'm accelerating, a steady rhythmic pulse.

Concentric circles, like expanding bubbles in rapid succession. Each circle, each pulse, increases the sensation that I'm losing form, losing connectivity with my body, becoming lighter, fluid. As the vibrations increase the patterns take on form, becoming waves vibrating through water, like looking into a clear pool, the surface disturbed by a gentle breeze; beams of sunlight in rhythmic intervals.

I awaken from a fitful slumber, rocked to the center of my being. *Everyone to a man is missing from the bunkroom of the submarine.*

Something has happened, something has pulled the men to a different part of the vessel; but why wouldn't they wake me? I hustle into my uniform, enter the control room buttoning my shirt, hardly prepared for what awaits. No one is manning the boat.

Absolute silence.

"Stewart? Chief Bremer?" It's as silent as the grave. "Mr. Duncan?" I head up the ladder into the conning tower. Incredibly, none of the operators are at their stations, the equipment idle. Obviously, something serious has happened and they're all above on deck. I continue topside to the bridge where *reality* takes hold like the icy fingers of a corpse. There's no one on the bridge, the deck as lonely as a prairie at sunset.

Absolute silence.

For miles in every direction the sea stretches–like glass–without a ripple. Not a sound is heard, the boat caught in an eerie unnatural stillness; not a bird or creature, not even a wind or breeze breaks the quietude. Nothing but glass, for miles.

A gnawing sense of wonder drives me on a tour of an empty and lonely boat, not a living person stem to stern. My calls echo through a vacant and hollow boat. I succumb to a horrific realization. I'm a man alone, lost in a sea of time.

I wander the boat like a vagabond meandering the wilds. Not a soul to be found. The chrome wheels of the diving planes are void of their operators, the control room quiet and empty, *the Com* hanging loose as if the men had been spirited away. The sonar and hydrophone stations are without the ears of the technicians. Everything is as still; like stone. I wander aimlessly through the officer's bunkrooms, the only discernable sounds that of my breathing and the soft métier of the Waterbury timepiece on my wrist.

"Hello? Somebody answer me," I shout again, to no one. Only the silence answers with more of itself.

In the crew's mess, coffee is steaming in the decanter, cups of it left sitting on the steel tables but no one drinking from them. Old outdated newspapers and a few of Connie Howard's comic books lie about. I pick one up. Captain Marvel is fighting Doctor Forever. *Dr. Forever.* Perhaps he is me. Perhaps I've become Dr. Forever, to live this way…forever? The thought is unnerving. I pour a cup of coffee and sip the dark liquid. It tastes the same, chicory lacing the liquid; Porteru's personal touch. Nothing has changed, except…where are the men…and Lucy?

Behind the curtain to her cabin, she has a tiny bottle of perfume open; a reprieve from the stifling diesel-laden air.

The small desk in the corner contains her things carefully laid upon it. The ugly antiquated glasses–one of the lenses cracked from the tussle with Fitzgerald–are laid neatly beside her journal. Against my inner voice I open and page through it; mostly mathematical equations, electrical and engineering specs and variances. Then, upon one of the pages written in her scrawling cursive:

'I'm deeply concerned about resonance. Dr. Hoffmann assures me it's of no consequence but the tension and stress on the field is alarming. I've confided with Dr. Brauer but he's so preoccupied with Phoenix that I'm left in a quandary about it. Hawkins has been supportive, but Lawton continues to fuel the assumption I'm a fool to worry and I'm forced to move on. I pray it's nothing, yet I'm deeply concerned about possible effects upon the men. Commander Bradshaw is foolishly insisting we push forward with the actual experiment, and with the men onboard. Dr. Hoffmann is agreeing because of the delays.'

On a previous page I chance upon this entry, dated much earlier:

'Why do I feel this way when I'm near him, like a schoolgirl with a crush? I possess the strongest desire to take him in my arms, despite everyone. He belongs to another, yet why these constant thoughts of us together? As if at some point in time, somewhere, we have been together, have always been together. The very moment we met I've held this thought.'

Another entry dated later:

'Unlikely as this is we were together, very much together, alone, and on a submarine full of other people! Once he was with me, the fear of dying vanished outright. I actually believe I hoped for it. That we might die in this way. Wake up together in some other world.'

And then dated yesterday:

'As much as I wish it, I doubt we will share that moment again. How can it be so? If we somehow return, he resumes his life and career, his beautiful wife. I'll go back to my room at the University. Back to my test tubes and electrodes. Good lord, I've become Frankenstein in a woman's body. A woman's body...what a magical confusing thing. I felt my inner being when we were together, as if we were truly one person. Am I losing my mind over this? I've so many responsibilities yet all I think about is being alone with him. Long for it. The two of us alone, without the demands of the world, its endless problems, endless needs and concerns.

How can I continue to live this way, as if this is who I really am? What's important in a person's life? Work? Career? What about this unfathomable thing they term Love? What is it? What is its source, its secrets? My god, my life has become a plethora of secrets. Secret numbers, secret equations, secret weapons, secret meetings, secret persons, secret secrets. I want to be free of it. Two people who love each other, shouldn't they be together?'

The rest is an unfathomable series of numbers, characters of some unknowable language, the various procedures of the experiment so deeply mired in physics and quantitative analysis it might as well be Greek. Inside the ledger is a letter, the return address, Cambridge University, England. Again, despite the objections of my mind, I open it.

'Lucinda,

'Thank you for your correspondence but I do wish you wouldn't worry over trifles like my health. You've an enormous task at hand. I would suggest you adhere to its schedule in full, not waste valuable time contriving rambling missives to me or others.

'Honestly Lucinda I don't understand your getting mired in something like this. What on earth is going through your head? Why would you want to go to war, in of all things, a submarine? Are you daft? These are the contrivances that murdered your father. If you could poke your nose from your work for one minute's time, you'll see quite plainly war has embraced the planet on all sides. Haven't you realized the realities of war? For what reasons would you desire to get yourself involved in such a dreadful pursuit? I wonder if you've lost your sensibilities entirely.

'As far as University goes, I'll admit Princeton is certainly an exceptional school of learning, but the institution is filling with Germans, the people currently bombing our cities! Use your head. We have all they have nicely here at Cambridge. You could certainly excel here if you would simply put your mind to it, pursue an academic career and put these fanciful ideas behind you. I knew this would happen when you became involved with that charlatan Hoffmann. I say it with the best of intentions, but I dislike the man's theoretical approach to science. Science is factual, not fantastical! The man's theories border on the insane.

'Dear, really, you should favor an empirical course of study and pursue a career within the university, not go parading about the globe like some dilettante. Lucinda, think a moment, do you honestly believe for one second that you've been assigned to this project based solely upon your abilities? Your intellect? You're an expendable commodity dear. A person they can write off. I'm sorry but these are my feelings on the subject. I wish you would reconsider before you become drawn further into such a morass of idiotic tom-foolery.

'There, you have it. From the mouth of the 'old bird' herself and so I can clear my conscience and the decision is entirely yours. How I do wish your father were still alive. I'm certain he would look upon the whole affair rather despairingly wouldn't you agree? Put yourself firmly in your father's shoes and take a good look at the way you're carrying on. I doubt my previous point would be up for debate.

'Lucinda, if you choose to continue with these people, you must put yourself into it in full. It will take every bit of your intelligence and fortitude. If you take this path, you mustn't fail. Should you do so your advancement in science is forfeit. Don't expect me to catch you should you fall. Their response will be as wolves in the fold. You'll be ripped and torn asunder, everything you've built, strived for all these years will be torn away forever. There will be no second chance.

'Let me be frank, your gender serves you not in the least. These people frown upon persons born with a different set of reproductive organs than they, and this puts you at odds with their sense of entitlement. I doubt I need emphasize it. You'll be second-guessed and undermined at every occasion so be strong and fearless and precise! and put all you have into it or for heaven's sake get out now! and leave these people's problems where they belong, with themselves.
'You have all my faith,
'Mum'

Returning the letter to its envelope, I take up her glasses, stare into the vacant frames *seeing* her eyes, her tranquil gaze, and my mind remembers the very first time I saw them at the briefing, deep empathic eyes shining through the smoke, the banter of the people. Where has she gone?

I'm filled with emotion and have to leave the compartment. Why? To wander an empty submarine? How long can I maintain this solitude until I crack?

"Now hear this, now hear this, first officer abandoned on submarine. Requesting immediate instructions, over." The boat's PA system reverberates the vessel's solemn length. Again, only the silence responds. "Attention all crew. There will be sunbathing on deck for the entire week and swimming will be allowed indefinitely. No more five-minute showers once a week, all crew can bath daily, and gambling will be allowed in the mess. Tonight's movie will star Clark Gable and Greta Garbo. Beer and pretzels will be served...horse-shoes on deck..."

How long can I keep going, pretending this is anything normal? *Not long,* is the answer I hear in my head. '*Try to radio Pearl Harbor again,*' the voice repeats, more desperate this time. Why? I already know it's futile. How many times can I speak the same words, the boat's call number and coordinates, over and over, send these utterances out into thin air? There's simply no one out there to hear it. This is solitude, absolute solitude; no voices, laughing or derisive words. No joy or pain anymore, just *time*...apparently an endless amount of it.

I wander through *the Ritz*, the men's personal items strewn across their bunks; pens, knives, books; cigarettes and letters stowed in their lockers. Stinky boots and sweat-stained t-shirts are scattered everywhere; letters from home, wives and girlfriends, carefully hidden. There's an open notebook on Jukes' bunk with a letter written upon it, dated the previous night.

'*Dear Rennie,*

'*Been awhile since I wrote. Things are going good in the subs. I'm eating good but still can't put on weight. Hard to believe I weighed 180 when I worked the mill. I'm lucky if I'm packin a buck fifty. I'm so damn thin Ren cuz the thing thats inside a guy that puts on belly fat was clean burnt outta me from hunger driftin.*

'*Dad said your thinking of driftin. Don't. When I went driftin I was so damn hungry I started eating leather off old shoes. Once got shot in the ass with a loada rock salt for stealing a chicken. The salt was coming out of my butt for near on a month and the chicken got away anyway.*

'*I get you feel the draw little brother. The country is huge, nearly endless. You can hike for days and be in the same state. I've seen mountains, redwoods, desert, cornfields all in the same state. I been to nearly all of em one time or another before the war but living under railroad tressles aint no picnic. Sleeping in culverts or breakin into old barns to keep the rain off gets old after awhile. You do meet some good people but a lot of bad comes with it. I've sat in circles listening to the greatest music you could imagine, never to be recorded or shared with no one else. Its sad and beautiful all at the same time, and the big starry sky goes on forever and ever.*

'*I'm sayin this for your own good. Get your ass into school and get good grades. I'd be lyin to tell you there werent times so beautiful I felt like dyin. I seen the Rockies at dawn all pink and gold you woulda thought heaven ascended to earth. But hoppin rail cars can get a guys head bust in. The vigilantes walk the railyards at night just looking for trouble. Mean men learnt mean ways. Stay out of it. Get into school, dont look back.*

'When I get back I want to settle down this time. I'm planning on being whats called a disc jockey. These are the guys who turn wax on the radio programs. Pays good and the jobs fun. I'm learnin all about radio and radio equipment in the Navy and figure on getting my Navy pension. I'm figuring on going back out there Ren and record some of that music before it disappears forever.

'I like the guys I'm in the subs with. The captains a real war hero. Were sinking more ships than any other boat except this time were on some sort of secret mission. I cant write about it. To hell if I know whats going on anyway. Were under strict radio silence so mostly I just read and turn records for the crew when the XO lets me. We got us a crackerjack XO, I told you about him, guy from California, the guy who got me off the hook for drinking awhile back, when the Navy was fixing to throw me out on my rear for being a dumbass.

'I got one helluva record collection going little brother youd be impressed. I got a 78 of the Scranton Sirens but dont tell dad. I'm taking that bastard back to Scranton in my duffel and giving him it for Christmas. No one here will miss it as much as he will love it.

'I've been off the juice for near on six months now Ren. I aint going back. Stay away from that rotgut. Dads right, a one way street down a mighty lonesome road.

'Well, thats all for now I guess. I'm back on duty in ten minutes. We got ourselves into a scrape and things are a little wacked. Tell you all about it when I see you. Tell Ronnie I love her and tell mom too. Love you little brother.

'Roscoe'

The letter makes me curious and I investigate his record collection surprised to find *Polka Dots and Moonbeams* by Frank Sinatra and Tommy Dorsey on the platter. I turn the disk and pipe it through the PA. The tune's slow meandering beat wanders the empty passages and compartments of the submarine. The Manta Ray seems to *glow* a little more. Is it the music or does her batteries put more juice into the lighting time to time? It was a noticeable effect–mentioned often–when we were far enough from the battle zone to pump music softly through her insides. There were always various theories, but I think *she* liked the music.

The Ritz is excruciatingly vacant and lonely. I flip a few pillows and wonder about the men. Howard's bunk is plastered with comic books, *Action Comics, Detective Comics, Whiz Comics, Captain Midnight*. I laugh thinking about the ribbing he took from the rest of the boat. Looking at their vibrant covers I somehow know the comics will become rarities in the future and worth a small fortune.

Chief's bunk is packed mostly with technical manuals and a couple classic books; *Moby Dick* and *Treasure Island*. Smith's bunk is laced with magazines, *Civil War History;* McClatchy's, *Boxing Life*.

Parmalee's locker is stacked with books, *Electronic Theory; The Electron and You; Electrician's Handbook*. I spy his journal, wonder if perhaps it might shed some light on the mystery. It contains only a handwritten short story.

'The Island, by Anson Wilson Parmalee 1943
'On an island lost deep within the womb of the ocean lives the tattooed woman I existed with during my convalescence. She was the teacher of the children on the island and a healer, a person who knew about magic.

'This remarkable woman was tattooed like an animal, a bush animal, the species I recall inhabiting the tall African grasses. The tattooing was different bands of coloring winding the length of her body from above the ankles to her breasts. Lustrous gold and onyx bands winding vertically about her immaculate skin. Her hair was long and black, her ocular features deep and opiate.

'Only once I saw her naked body. She had taken me into her hut one evening and undressed herself. The room was a thatched hut and illuminated by torch. The motion of her painted body coupled with the monotone words she chanted sent spirals of wondrous anxiety from my feet through the top of my head, invigorating the entirety of my senses with a strange feeling of health. When she finished her chant, I asked about the tattooing, a startling occurrence in what had been up to that point an uneventful repose. "It is illegal for a woman to be tattooed this way," she told me. "Only the initiates know, and now you."

'"This is why you clothe yourself in the long sarong while your children run naked in the sun?"

'"Those in authority would not permit it." I had no understanding of who or what was the authority on the island, only that some vague government or social order existed allowing me to heal after becoming cast-away at sea, my boat lost with all hands, my friends and shipmates all long dead.

'"Why are you painted as you are?" She slowly dressed as she answered my question, a series of mystical interpretations about the earth, her words producing a vertigo behind my eyes and deep within my head.

'"I am a healer. This is my calling."

'She spoke of the people as the eyes, ears, and nose of the earth, that the feet were the earth's most fabulous creation and the reason why no one on the island was permitted to wear shoes.

'"Come," she said taking my hand like a child and we walked the beach. The moon was visible in the night being in its waxing stage and the stars shone like broken glass. Waves cut white daggers into the shore. The ocean was black, no horizon, seabirds called from the darkness.

'"On nights like these, the island speaks about the moon falling from the sky into the sea. This happened many years ago. Only the elders recall these memories. They speak of the moon traveling down into the ocean's darkest regions until its light dimmed and disappeared. I have seen these lights in the sea many times."

'She suddenly addressed the topic of her tattooing by commenting on the sand-like qualities of her skin. "Touch me." Her skin was a plush light-brown and immaculate, without epidermal flaws, the island community marked by some exotic strain of Lupus. "The tattoos are omenistic, the sanctuary of my body, taboo unto disease."

'The entire coast was like a vast luminous ghost, writhing and calling in soft aquatic voices. I'm lulled by the cries of the seabirds into thoughts of quitting the idea of returning to the land of my youth, sheltering within this gentle harbor. Living life as a man lives, atuned to the earth and its desires.

'I said goodnight to the tattooed prophet and retired to my single room hut to watch the roaming of small translucent scorpions from the safety of my hammock. Lying on my back, I watch the moon through the window, imagine it falling into the ocean. I think about the night, its song. Then I'm dreaming about the ocean seeping into the very bowels of the earth.'

That's it, the tale either finished or left unfinished. I set the book down and mix the powdered milk for my cornflakes. Distractions aside; I'm in very serious trouble. The stores on the boat are capable of sustaining me for several more weeks, couple months, perhaps longer if I start rationing. Then what? A dull inexorable panic begins clawing its way through the veneer of my thinking. Relax, think this thing out I remind myself. Think.

I could attempt fishing…but the stillness outside the sub has me wondering whether this sea contains any life at all, being still water? There had been no indication of any life whatsoever, except the crew. Now, even they're gone. Not even birds can be seen in the sky. Even if I manage to find fish, I'll need fresh water. The only way to make potable drinking water is to turn the engines that run the condensers that create it. What happens when the diesel fuel runs out and the generators supplying electricity quit? Panic consumes me. Stop. Think. One thing at a time.

I could gather rainwater by stretching tarps across the deck but there hasn't been a hint of clouds or weather of any kind since the experiment. Is something like that possible? A world without clouds or rain? The indications say yes. There hasn't even been a wind. How can an ocean lie as still as ice? Unperturbed? The answer is evident. There's no movement within this world to create it. No wind or wave currents, no weather; no rain. Is it possible this world is completely unmoving? That would explain what is happening. Nothing to cause these disturbances we take for granted on earth. Is this even earth? This world, this dimension, is somehow locked in a death-grip. There are two principal elements at work here; silence and stillness.

As I eat my cornflakes, staring at Batman on one of Howard's comics, I know I've only two choices; start the boat and return to Pearl Harbor, a nearly impossible endeavor with one man, or conduct the invisibility reset myself.

Option one, the experiment, is a complete mystery, has purposely been kept so, due the secret nature of the project. It had been decided at Pearl Harbor to exclude the officers and enlisted men from any inclusion into the operational aspects of the process, not only to protect the integrity of the experiment itself, but also the crew. Should the submarine fall into enemy hands, it was essential none of the crewmen know anything about the technology and become subjected to interrogation or torture. It was the only way to guarantee their personal safety. Additionally, the science team had been issued cyanide capsules, to be used–or not–at their own discretion. As a result, the experiment's processes were nearly as *invisible* as the experiment's objective. Cyanide capsules…a third option; a very bleak third option.

One thing in my favor was Lucy would share aspects of it with me from time to time. She had explained the layout of the control stations. Station one, the console that controlled the primary field, was set up in the control room with its power and signal relays sequestered in the pump room below the floor. The second station, that controlled the secondary field, had been wired into the only available space–the junior officer's cabin–the retrofit crew actually cutting holes through the bulkheads with torches to allow passage for the cables and circuitry. The two stations were separated by the bulkhead between the control room and the officer's wardrooms. To make the equipment function properly, I would need to be two men. I laugh out loud; the irony of the thought. I *was* two men, in one body. It would be more fortuitous if it were the other way around.

When I look over the *cheat-sheet* Lucy kept with the primary console, it's so technically involved that it might as well be written in Greek. Again, I laugh at the irony. The console actually is in Greek! The control buttons designated Alpha, Beta, Gamma and two levers, one bearing the Theta symbol the other Epsilon. What to do? Turn the machines on, set to full and pray? What happens then? Something worse than my current situation, I surmise.

I drop the manual and sigh, I don't understand the science, the technology or process. The result could be disastrous, quite possibly horrific. I laugh again. For me to run the reset would be like putting a hamster in charge of an aircraft carrier.

Option two suddenly becomes more attractive. Somehow navigate the Manta Ray back to shore, with one man. Ridiculous. How? How can one man work a Gato-class submarine? The answer is unavoidable. He can't. It would be impossible for me to operate this craft without additional personnel. I reason, it would require a bare minimum of six persons at the very least. One man on the bridge, the second– a helmsman–in the conning tower or the helm station in the control room to steer the rudders, a third and fourth person on the radar and sonar stations in the conning tower–necessary to navigate properly–and a fifth and sixth man in the engine and maneuvering rooms to engage and operate the boat's propulsion system; and that just to float, no diving with these few men. Six men, five too many. An unacceptable conclusion. Think.

Okay…drop to four men by removing the radar and sonar operators. It would be traveling completely blind; however, the equipment is nonfunctional anyway. Under the circumstances, that brings me down to four men. Three too many…can't be done. Think.

I could start the motor, engage the drive and pray there are no glitches, effectively removing the need for the motor machinist in the engine room. Possible. Down to three. The electrician in the maneuvering room could then be eliminated by engaging the levers to the diesel drive; as long as I only use the one diesel engine and none of the electric motors, this plan of action could potentially work. I feel my heart pumping, the blood starting to flow.

That leaves two essential positions left to *man*; the navigator on the bridge and the helmsman inside the boat. I hit a rock. Two men. One too many. How? How to navigate from above yet steer the craft from below? Impossible.

I spread the navigational maps and rulers across the table in the mess, lick the graphite on the pencil and begin to plot three courses; one to Midway, one to Hawaii and one toward the American west coast. Incredibly, I realize I could actually *lose* the helmsman.

If I plot a direct course back to Pearl–praying nothing unexpected crops up–I could secure the helm with lanyards and vector in. But how could I navigate into port? The answer is unavoidable. It would be impossible. The helmsman's stations inside the conning tower and control room are *blind*, the operator getting his directions relayed from the bridge or the sonar and radar technicians. No, it has to be two men…unless…I crash the boat. Run her aground and swim to shore, sacrificing the vessel. Under these conditions, a viable alternative. One man could actually do it. I feel the blood pumping again.

My excitement, however, is short-lived. The boat doesn't even possess something as rudimentary as a functioning compass; all of the navigational equipment subjected to some overwhelming force, eliminating even the northern magnetic polarity. Fuck.

Hawaii will prove extremely difficult to locate; Midway nearly impossible. If I'm off the bridge for more than even an hour, it could cost me sighting the island from the distance and making landfall. What if I miss the islands altogether? A highly likely scenario.

Since I'm incapable of navigating by compass or radar, I would be forced to navigate by sextant. My math would need to be impeccable. There would be little room for miscalculations. Even the slightest imperfection in reading the stars could result in the variance of one, possibly up to ten miles. I drop my pencil, refill my coffee and stare.

Who am I kidding? She'll *wander* anyway. The Manta Ray had been nicknamed *the wanderer* by her crew, the *play* inherent in her rudders and connective apparatus a constant subject of discussion on and off the boat. There had never been an explanation as to *why*. The engineers and inspectors at Pearl Harbor–and Mare Island–couldn't really account for the boat's proclivity to wander off course and nothing they ever did–tightening bushings, gaskets, even new shafts– alleviated the *problem*. Canfield, however, loved it. Several times the boat's *wandering* resulted in the spotting of a smoke trail on a far distant horizon, or closing us to an enemy convoy just enough to show on her radar, adding to the mystique that the Manta Ray was somehow endowed with a natural hunter's instinct. *The Queen of Battle*. Her boys–and the leadership at Pearl–loved it.

Reveries aside, there would be no way to keep her on a steady consistent course without constantly taking readings or making readjustments at the helm. How could I do it without sleeping? I would need to wake myself every half-hour. It would make sense to just eliminate vectoring to Midway or Hawaii and set course due east, ground the submarine somewhere along the California coastline.

However, this *solution* could be fatally flawed by one simple undeniable fact, Canfield bypassing Midway on the voyage out and failing to top-off our fuel reserves. Damn.

Grabbing one of Howard's comic books, I run a series of calculations. I calculate the total gallons against our boat's rate of consumption and subtract the mileage traveled and seek the sum, the required fuel for the return transit. Superman is looking at my figures discouragingly. The numbers are bleak. Right on the line.

Another undeniable fact is my certainty that the experiment physically moved the boat over a thousand nautical miles further west. As insane as the concept is, I'm forced to incorporate the figures into my calculations.

When I check the boat's actual fuel levels, my gut drops. Due to the storm and Canfield's insistence of running hard on the surface to make the rendezvous with the O'Malley, the boat's fuel reserves are far below a tenable amount to make the West Coast. I reinvest in my figures running a series of computations before I drop the pencil–and my head. It's hopeless. Even if I run only one engine at low power, I'll be lucky to make Hawaii on fumes. What would happen if I miss it? A very likely scenario running solo and without a compass or radar. The answer is unavoidable. If I miss locating Hawaii, I'll run out of fuel on route to America and drift aimlessly until I die of starvation and thirst.

I come to the conclusion the only viable option would be Midway Island. A tiny coral atoll barely two and a half square miles in the middle of hundreds of thousands of miles of empty ocean. Landing at Midway Atoll, under these conditions, would be like hitting a one-inch bullseye from a thousand yards. Regardless, it's the only viable solution; Hawaii the back-up, should I fail to locate the atoll.

I begin planning the voyage when an unsettling thought hits me. What if no one is even on the island? Any food or fuel? How long could I exist on that pile of sand before I starve or go insane? What about the mainland? Am I to assume this new world of which I'm now a member, harbors the same reserves, the same luxuries, or even another living human being? I come to a very probable conclusion. I'm pretty much fucked no matter what I do.

If I ever needed a drink it was now. However, when I reenter Canfield's cabin the bottle in his desk is empty and the locker where he keeps his *stores* is locked tight, the bolt activated by a combination lock.

I search his desk but come up empty; not even the *Captain's Eyes-Only* file is there for my amusement, only the photo of Rue in her white nurse's uniform. I consider shooting the lock off with my .45, but what if the round accidently pierces the hull? A slow inexorable decent into oblivion. I'm fucked; not even a drink.

At the point panic is beginning to consume my reason, I hear a quiet sound; the sound of a woman whispering. Strangely familiar, nearly more a breath, perhaps a murmur, for the briefest moment, I believe the boat herself is whispering to me, revealing her secret, that she is in fact alive, a living breathing entity; a machine inexplicably endowed with conscious thought. Wandering her insides, I realize the faint sounds are singing, as if the boat were quietly humming a melody to herself.

Exploring the mystery, I discover the music–Lee Wiley singing an era tune by Cole Porter–is emanating from the pump room beneath the control room; the music intermixing with the soft muttering of voices.

When I lift the floor plate that seals the compartment, I'm surprised to discover three sailors making adjustments to the electronic equipment added for the experiment. My shock escalates when I recognize one of the sailors; an older man, known to me. They pause in their labors, gazing at me with smiling faces. The old man then says the words that rattle my world, like shaking a dreamer from sleep.

"Hello my boy. We've been expecting you." I'm stunned, for here stands dressed in grimy blue fatigues, an acquaintance from the future, a man I know well from that time and place.

"I know you. I know who you are. Your name is…" For whatever reason, I cannot pull his name from my memory. "I can't remember, but I know you."

He gestures for me to join them. I take the ladder down into the pump room, actually squeezing his shoulder, more to prove he's material than illusory. His beard is gray, possessing a brownish hue; his dark eyes are intent, penetrating. "How are you holding up?" he asks. I barely control the flood of emotion the question ignites within my mind.

"I don't know…not good I think." Moisture clouds my vision. "I believe I'm rather making a mess of things." He hands his tool to one of the other men who assumes his place and continues the work they're engaged in. "Tell me I'm not imagining this," I ask, expecting *the dream* to melt and I awaken once more, alone.

"You're not imagining this."

"Have I gone insane? I'm actually locked up in some asylum, dreaming all this." His smile dissipates. He takes my shoulder, inadvertently rubbing oil on it and gives it a good shake.

"My, my…look at you. Splendid in your officer's uniform." He exchanges a pleasant glance with the other men unknown to me but vaguely familiar. "A lieutenant commander no less," he says glancing at the others. They share a friendly chuckle.

"What's going on? Why am I here? This is some sort of hallucination." The men grin, finding humor in my comment.

"If you prefer, however, time would be better served if you realize *who* in fact you are."

"*Who* I am?"

"Yes."

"Who am I?"

He takes up an old rag and wipes the oil from his hands, studying me intently, head to toe. "You've become quite obsessed with your role as Michael Murphy I must say." I sense what he's alluding to. "Think. Remember who you are, your life. Do you remember? Is it coming back?" As if turning on a switch a portion of my life floods my psyche; modern things, a modern life.

"I live in the twenty-first century, not 1943." He returns his attention to the men, speaking to them in a tongue I don't understand before returning his attention. His eyes seem to shine, some kind of inner radiance.

"That's a start."

"Who am I? Tell me my name?"

He shakes his head. "I'm sorry old friend. I can't do that for you, even if I wanted to."

"Why?"

"There are reasons, substantial reasons, why certain information, particularly of this sort, shouldn't be bantered about carelessly under circumstances such as these."

"What circumstances?"

"Again, I can't answer that particular question." I study the men. They look like average sailors, wearing standard blue fatigues.

"What are you doing? What are you working on?"

"The boat."

"For what reason?"

"Although your scientists are gifted, you'll never get back home this way."

"What do you mean?"

"Exactly what I've said. Not merely the boat, you as well my friend." He studies my blank expression. "Since your returning here was, in part, our doing, we felt responsible in getting you home. Repairing the anomaly."

"I don't understand."

"Think. What is the last thing you remember? Close your eyes and concentrate." I do as he instructs. Immediately I'm assailed by a series of memories, of a different modern era, modern things, science and technology, physics. "Well?" he asks in response to my look.

"I must be dead. That's what this is, isn't it? I've died and gone to this place. In my mind I think it a submarine. In truth it's some kind of...*interim*." His expression goes grim and he exchanges a rather dour look with the other men, the smiles disappearing from their countenances. He touches the shoulder of the man nearest him.

"Oeen, Oaris, carry on a moment." The men redirect their attention to the equipment while he extracts an ornate meerschaum pipe from his pocket, tamps the bowl, and lights it, exhaling a volume of smoke into the compartment, his expression, sublime. "Ahhh, I was hoping for an opportunity to do that. Take a seat my boy." He points at the vinyl-topped gearboxes the motor machinists use to store their tools, and sits, stretching his leg.

"A fine old craft," he mutters, gesturing at the boat. "How extraordinary. Men actually went to war in these rudimentary machines. Amazing. The fire of the *human will* never ceases to amaze me. War brings out some of the very finest qualities in mankind…yet, alas, also the extremely worst of his tendencies."

"What's going on? What am I doing here in this place?"

"Are you certain you don't remember? You have no recollection in the least?"

"No." He pulls on his beard and smokes, contemplating something deeply.

"As difficult as this is to comprehend at the moment, you're saving this vessel, and in so doing, perhaps the world to an extent, as we know it. All this based entirely on the integrity of *your* character. We're basing our calculations that you'll be true to your nature, a more original, primordial *self.*"

"Are you being flippant?"

"What happened was not, how do we say…*in the cards.* The result, what is referred in the parlance as an *anomaly, a rogue causality.* This experience wasn't supposed to happen, not in your lifetime, as you know it. Inasmuch, it was necessary for us to…adjust the situ. The urgency, the seriousness of the moment, demanded it. It became expedient to send you, for lack of a better way to say it, backward in time, to revisit a previous life."

"For what purpose?"

"A very simple question to an extremely complex and allusive problem. *A voyage,* in this instance, as Michael Murphy, the first officer of this vessel, a vessel that was real and existed, but completely veiled in secrecy for over seventy-five years."

"How was it done?" The men share a laugh. "What's so funny?"

"They know you, so your candor doesn't go unappreciated."

"How do they know me?" I ask and the men laugh again.

"How far down this *rabbit hole* are you prepared to go at this time?"

"How could I have been sent back in time? It's too fantastic." He quietly puffs on the bowl, his eyes shining brightly.

"*Time* is fluid, in actuality lengthens and contracts, slows down or speeds up. But of course, you know this already. The concept of linear time is convenient but hardly complete."

"Part of me somehow understands what you're saying but…no, it's just too fantastic. How could a man who lives in the twenty-first century return to the past? The past is gone, finished and gone. This is some kind of illusion. I believe I'm still in the mess hall dreaming." He raps on the hull with his pipe, expelling some ash.

"You believe yourself to be asleep? You believe this to be a dream?"

"It doesn't feel like I'm dreaming."

"You're not dreaming my friend, well, any more than we do living our normal everyday lives I suppose."

"Meaning?"

"You're aware that you're conscious, that's why you know this is neither dreaming nor illusion. You know you are here now, not only as Michael Murphy, the body and memories you reside in, yet also your true *current state*. Your awareness is here and present; both men."

"This is too incredible. A man can't travel back in time."

"Perhaps I shouldn't have used that phrase, *backward in time*. Perhaps the better phrase is you've been placed into an alternate reality. Does that suit you?"

"You're talking semantics. Science fiction. This is some kind of lucid dreaming."

"Do you agree that *you* and Michael Murphy are both here now fully conscious before me?"

"Well, yes but-" he quiets me with a gesture of his hand.

"Consciousness *is* time and space. Reality isn't a thing in and of itself. It is a process of mind, therefore–technically speaking–has its source, its basis, in nothingness."

"What do you mean by *nothingness*?"

"Non-material manifestation. Recall the teaching of the Buddha, or the Christ for that matter. Nothing exists save mind; *consciousness*. What you *think,* is reality. The great teachers instructed that all is *Maya*, illusion. We are steeped deep within Maya, deep within *the veil*."

"The *veil*?"

"To free oneself of the fetters of Maya is the mission of he who seeks enlightenment. The process of this attainment is the process of subjective non-thought." He studies the confusion on my face. "Let me appeal to your rational side. Quantum Mechanics insists upon an observer, otherwise the particle structure of the universe falls apart; has no body, no reality. Nothing has position until it's observed. Without consciousness, *reality,* as you think you know it, doesn't exist. Or exists in a kind of latent state. Think of it like the recording of a symphony, the musicians long dead, yet they *come to life* when the song is played. Each nuance, each trill, reflecting the individual that created it, brought back to life by the recording, each musician's veritable life, since the music reflects these facts, but where is the man himself?"

"Yes, but..."

"The laws of Quantum Mechanics state implicitly that nothing exists without an observer. What you see doesn't come into existence, without the act of your perceiving it. Consciousness creates the matrix upon which it builds, vibration after vibration, octave after octave, through the material vibrational states–sound and the visual spectrums–to vibrational levels incomprehensible to the senses of man. Thus, different animals experience reality differently. You and I for instance, despite what we think or believe to be substantially objective is in truth reconfirmed through the art of language, *the spoken word*."

"Yes. I know this somehow."

"As you already *know*, reality, is a process that involves consciousness. It's not *seen* outside ourselves at all, but within the brain. Light enters the eyes, is processed by the retinas and formulated within the brain. And–this is imperative–the brain *sees* what it *thinks*." He waits for some sort of response.

"Yes, that's undeniable."

"These treasured particles so essential in propping up our feeble explanation of our universe simply are not out there, or in here either," he says tapping his breast.

"But what you're discussing is like…a dream world."

"What difference really, reality as you think you know it or the dream state? Both occupy the brain as its point of reference. Both exist solely within the confines of the mind. The *universal mind* is infinite in nature, the temporal mind, locked within causality. Maya."

"What about *dreaming*? I had a horrible dream recently. An enormous mushroom cloud."

"Dreaming proves my point. Your mind perceives a world as real as this one, where one moves about, sometimes exhibiting volition, sometimes as if adrift."

"Yes."

"What difference in the actual experience itself except the depth and intensity of that experience? What my mentor referred to as the *focal perception*. What I would term *the varied degrees of awareness*." I mull this over while he smokes, allotting me the time to consider his words.

"What about death? Am I actually dead? Is that what this is? Have I been killed and this is some sort of purgatory?"

"There is no *death*, as you term it, just the passing-on of mind-consciousness through form. The terms *past* and *future* are just that, terms, utterances without substance. They simply, in actuality, do not exist. They are empty concepts, void of meaning. There exists only the moment, and the moment my friend…is eternal."

"The moment…is eternal…"

"It contains all things and yet is nothingness." He pats my shoulder, smiling. "Now, if you don't object, I need to return to our work, and you need to return to your slumbers. Tomorrow, your people will begin the precarious operation of returning to your collective *now*. We must be ready, or a disaster of the highest magnitude will take place."

"What will happen?" His face changes, becoming unreadable.

"The unknown."

When he turns, I take his arm. "There's something I need to tell you."

"Indeed."

"I…I've fallen in love with Lucy Charlesworth." He shares a glance with his fellows gazing up from their labors, an unspoken acknowledgement passing between them.

"We're more than aware of what has transpired between you."

"But what will happen when I return to my former life? I don't think I can bear it. I can't bear returning without her. As difficult as this is…I'd prefer not to return. I'll stay here, in this time and place, to be with her."

Against my will, my eyes well with a rush of emotion and the men grow silent, a warmth emanating from their faces.

"You'll be seeing her again, very soon."

I instantly understand his meaning. "My god, how could I not have realized it? All this time…we are together, in my future life."

"You've known it all along…well, your heart wasn't fooled shall we say. While your mind became obsessed, preoccupied reliving this life as Michael Murphy, your heart could penetrate the veil. It's not merely a convenient phrase but in fact true. *Love*, spirit, permeates all boundaries."

"Spirit…"

"The spirit within *man* is undeniable. Through this mechanism, the power we term *love,* permeates all known boundaries. Nothing is hidden."

"What will happen now?"

"Although your time together was cut short, it was a deeply profound experience for the both of you."

"What do you mean by *this life, cut short?*"

"My dear, dear friend. Soon, you will be forced to make a decision, the greatest decision any man can be asked to make…and that decision, will make all the difference in the world." With those words, he touches the center of my forehead and like a diver plunging into deep water, I fall headlong into an all-encompassing sleep.

Chapter 15: The Reset

*M*usic wafts through the air, *The Mood That I'm In*.

Carroll Gibbon's sweet melody paints the moment with *light*, Lucy's face floating above mine, a smile in her eyes.

"Why, hello." She touches my cheek and warmth floods my body. "It's nice to see your eyes awake again."

"Wha–what's going on?"

Cooper is suddenly at her shoulder. "You passed out here in the pump room. Torsch found you." Sam's rusty-bearded face pokes up from behind.

"Ahoy Commander Murphy." He tips his cap. Sam always wore his hat onboard the sub, most of his rusty hair growing from his chin.

"What's happened?"

"We got a spike in the system sir. I was checking the flow from the auxiliary batteries feeding their induction panel and here you were, stretched out like you'd been in a bar fight."

Stewart maneuvers Torsch aside. "Sorry to interrupt your nap Snow White but what the hell are you doing in the pump room?" I've no answer that I can convey to him. "Never mind, we got worse problems right now. We got a near mutiny on our hands. Somebody needs to make a decision before things get out of hand." I hear the drone of voices coming from the control room above.

"Help me up."

The tension in the control room is electrified. Scientists, officers and sailors all speaking at the same time.

"Everyone just cool down," I shout and the compartment quiets. "What have you decided Dr. Hoffmann?" Hoffmann looks at Brauer who looks at Charlesworth who looks at me.

"We're a divided camp Mr. Murphy," the old man says succinctly. "Some of us want to return to Hawaii. Others want to attempt the reset. Judging from the extraordinary state of affairs we're in no condition to continue with the mission. In truth, the scientists and other officers have no vote. This is a military vessel, a military operation. You are the authority here now Commander. The decision, in lieu of being unable to contact Pearl Harbor, rests entirely with you. Shall we continue with the mission, return to Pearl Harbor...or conduct the reset?" *My decision.* I scan the control room crammed with the senior members of the science and naval teams. Lawton doesn't trust the technology, has been pushing for us to return to Pearl, the junior science team as well and nearly every sailor under my command. The last pair of eyes I look upon are Lucy's. What is it I see in that gentle gaze? *Hope.*

"What do you think Doctor, are we ready?" I ask and her initial surprise quickly diminishes, replaced by a deep knowing look, a look I've known before.

"Yes Mr. Murphy, I believe we're ready." I look at my crew, boys in men's clothing, their anxious countenances filled with expectation.

"Let's do it, the reset. Let's go."

Hoffmann raises his shoulders, nodding. "Bring your men down from the bridge Commander, and please clear the forward and rear torpedo rooms. We can commence countdown in fifteen minutes on your order."

I take up the Com that connects the control room with the bridge and key the button. "Mr. Duncan, clear the bridge."

I press the toggle on the boat's PA and my voice pierces the hubbub within the boat. "All hands, this is the first officer. We're *go* for reset. We'll commence countdown in fifteen minutes. All hands clear the forward and after torpedo compartments. All essential personnel to their stations."

Stompin' at the Savoy, by Benny Goodman, is playing over the PA. A stark contrast to the nervous tension permeating the boat. "Remember Brauer, when we reach the frequency horizon and initiate the field, be sure to time-out precisely as per the math."

"Yes, yes Hoffmann, I'm ready. You and Charlesworth worry about the primary field, I'll synchronize the counter-field. Are your men in position Mr. Murphy?"

"We're ready Professor. The bridge, fore, and stern compartments are clear. The electricians are at their stations, firemen standing-by. Essential positions, manned and ready."

"Well, it's a *go* then gentlemen, let us pray this works," Hoffmann says reaching out his hand. "Commander Murphy, perhaps a somewhat unscientific word but, Godspeed." I shake each of their hands. When I reach for Lucy's she embraces me tightly, unable to release her hold. A smile forms on everyone's face. Hoffmann gently taps her shoulder. "Let's get to it Charlesworth," he says softly. When she retracts, her eyes are wet. "Hawkins, initiate countdown."

Jukes is quietly turning *Mood Indigo* as the countdown proceeds and our cramped and condensed world inside the boat, stands on edge. The last seconds are counted and they engage the levers that send the voltage streaming to the coils.

A loud whirring sound forces many to cover their ears, static electricity from the ionized air dances across the instrument panels. A strange bluish mist permeates the compartment. Sparks leap across the bulkheads and hull.

Lucy suddenly turns. "Dr. Hoffmann…something's wrong. The field…it isn't attenuating." Hoffmann is instantly at her station, the gauges jumping wildly.

"Charlesworth, your conditioning feed from the auxiliary batteries is inactive."

"Good lord, how could I have missed it?"

Parmalee pushes his way inside the circle forming around her station. "It's not her fault. The in-line breaker must have blown. It probably arced."

"We'll never reach *the horizon* now. Brauer, terminate the procedure."

"But Dr. Hoffman," Parmalee interrupts, "it'll take hours to get the batteries back up to operative levels, not without moving the boat."

"Hoffmann, it's critical this ship doesn't move, not one millimeter," Brauer barks. "Even the slightest variance to this exact location could throw off the mathematics."

"I'll reset the breaker," Parmalee says, instantly heading for the bow.

"No! Mr. Parmalee come back," Hoffmann shouts, but he's already ducking through the watertight door leading toward the forward torpedo room.

"What's wrong Dr. Hoffmann?" I ask.

"If he throws that switch with this amount of current passing, it will most certainly kill him."

"Kill him? Are you sure?"

"Of course. The young man knows it. He's sacrificing his life for ours. On a gamble." I hesitate only a fraction of an instant, just long enough to look into her eyes, before I'm racing for the bow. She's calling my name, her voice, receding into the past.

I catch up to Parmalee at the forward torpedo room.

He twists the wheel, swinging back the watertight door, revealing an acidic miasma of smoke and mist and begins to cough uncontrollably. We swim through the fog, finding the electrical panel attached to the coil. When he reaches to reset the breaker, I wrench his arm away and take the handle in my fist.

"No Lieutenant. Don't do it. If you throw that switch…let me do it." He tries to regain the lever, but I push him off. "Commander Murphy, I don't have a wife, or anyone waiting for me."

"Of course you don't. Because you're just a kid Anson. You haven't had a chance to meet a woman or fall in love."

"What does that have to do with anything?"

"When you meet the future Mrs. Parmalee, you'll know." I hesitate a moment–*my decision*–I pull the breaker just as he tries to take my arm from it. There's a solid white flash, then blackness.

Chapter 16: Yesterday, tomorrow

*B*irds cut across the sky; sparrows and finches.

They must have moved me up on deck. Even so, how can there be wrens and sparrows in the middle of the Pacific? When I clear my eyes, I see more of them cutting across white cumulus clouds stacked like cotton balls atop an effervescent blue sky. There are also swallows, definitely swallows, I'm familiar with their erratic flight patterns, the way they dip and weave for insects. Swallows? Now that's odd. I then hear the laughter of children. Painfully, I turn my head and see the tops of trees.

It's excruciating but I manage to sit up. What greets my eyes is a modern world inundated with modern things, new cars, people talking on smartphones, sitting on park benches with laptop computers. Jet airplanes scar the vibrant blue sky. I instantly know it's the future. I've been here before, seen it, felt it, and returned; an old city park, surrounded by new buildings sporting loud and colorful advertising.

The streets skirting the green are bustling with modern automobiles, the sidewalks filled with pedestrians wearing bright and colorful clothing, moving through a cacophony of noise and loud music. Young people in bright fashionable attire are poking at electronic tablets; a man operating a leaf blower drowns out a kid playing an electric guitar for handouts. I'm back.

Almost. Parmalee is prostrate on the grass beside me, his stained blue fatigues unchanged.

As I check his pulse to see if he's alive, he comes-to, looking very bewildered. "My guess is, this complicates things," I say, perhaps to no one.

"What happened Lieutenant?" he moans rubbing his head, shaking off the cobwebs.

"I'm not sure."

"Hey, wait a minute…wait just a doggone minute…" He manages to wobble into something of an upright position. "What in heck? Where are we Lieutenant?"

"I'm not sure. The question might be *when* are we." He's in awe, literally spinning in circles. A newspaper dispenser loiters nearby requiring a dollar in coins. "You got any change on you Anson? A dollar?" I say pointing at the price.

"A buck? For a newspaper?"

"San Francisco Chronicle. We're somewhere in the Bay Area. In fact, I think this is Vallejo." Parmalee fishes his pockets for loose change, watching a kid flipping tricks on a skateboard.

"Look Lieutenant, a tiny surfboard with wheels on it." We manage the fee and yank a copy from the bin. "Oh man. Mr. Murphy, look. Look at the date on the newspaper. Is this some kind of joke?" He shuffles through the paper while I take in the surround.

"This *is* Vallejo. I'm sure of it. I remember this park. It's changed, but I recognize it."

"Holy moly, you're right. I remember throwing coins into that old fountain when it was still working, when we were kids. We would come up for the summers to stay with my grandparents at the house in Berkeley. Grandma said that fountain would grant your wishes." We dumbly stare at each other, wordless. "I remember wishing someday I would travel the world. Mr. Murphy…what the heck's going on?"

"This sounds insane, but I think we've gone forward in time."

I can't tell if he's laughing or crying. "How?"

"I don't know…I'm not sure." Parmalee shakes out the paper and continues to read.

"Holy cow. Read this. It says here United States and Japan are allies. Some kind of conference in San Francisco. A Japanese car company putting in their headquarters down the peninsula. That's crazy." I study the world around us. "Look here Lieutenant, an advertisement for a telephone but without a cord. Is this a joke? How could that work? Without a cord to carry signal or electricity?" I watch a young woman talking on just such a device.

"Parmalee…"

"Wow. Look here Lieutenant. *'Fly to Europe on a jet airplane.'* It doesn't have props. How can it fly without propellers?" I look up into the blue sky and point at a series of jet contrails. "Four and a half hours…to fly to Europe? Lieutenant, what's going on? This has to be some kind of delusion, or practical joke…or something." He stares at the world. I see the wonder in his eyes, and the growing panic. "Mr. Murphy…I feel weird…"

"Let's think this thing out Anson. What do you remember before we woke up here?"

"Well, I remember being on the Manta Ray, the forward compartment. Remember? You were about to pull the breaker. I tried to stop you. It should have killed you, that much juice. We threw the breaker then…" He freezes mid-sentence, his hand in the air as if gripping an invisible lever; staring ahead in a sudden trance.

"What's the matter? Parmalee, what are you doing?"

A weird look forms on his face. "I feel strange Lieutenant."

"What's wrong?" He just stares, eerily unmoving. "Parmalee, answer me. What's wrong?" It's like he's become frozen. He's completely rigid, his eyes unblinking. My pulse is starting to race. "Parmalee, answer me…what's wrong." Nothing. A hotdog stand sits at the corner opposite us. "Hey, how about a dog Anson? Maybe we should eat something, ground ourselves. Okay?" He doesn't even move.

The man behind the pushcart looks me over, loud discordant music playing on the radio near his cash register numbing my senses. "Well? What'll it be bro?"

"Two dogs please."

"Which kind?"

I'm unsure of the vendor's question. "Hot dogs."

"Yeah, yeah but which? The Corndog? Krautdog? Chili-hot, the Bulldog? Which one?"

"Just…hot dogs, mustard and ketchup." The guy gives me a look and hands me two plain hot dogs. I hand him a quarter. "Keep the change."

"What are you a comedian?" he asks.

"Sorry?"

"There a camera hidden around here?" he asks gazing about. "Real funny. Five bucks *Gomer.*"

"Five dollars? For a couple ten cent hot dogs?" The vendor points at the hand-painted sign taped across his cart, *'Hotdogs $2.50.'* I'm shocked. "The same price as a steak?"

His expression goes flat. "You just step off the boat man?" The remark locks my attention.

"*The boat?* The Manta Ray you mean? You know about it, where she's berthed?"

"C'mon bro, give me a break. I'm just trying to make a living. Five bucks or I'm calling the cops." I pull a five out of my wallet and pay him. The man snaps the bill.

"Hey, a silver certificate, and in mint condition. 1943," he declares but I'm already crossing the street. Parmalee is on the bench, he hasn't moved an inch, his arm still extended in mid-air.

"You better enjoy this dog Anson, it cost two and a half bucks." Something is definitely wrong. "Hey. You all right? Parmalee answer me, are you all right?" In slow motion he turns, *tries to tell me something*, then vanishes before my eyes! I drop the hotdogs, feeling the space where he's been sitting. Not a thing remains to indicate he was ever there.

The world inside the park doesn't change. No one seems to have noticed that a man has just disappeared into thin air. How could they have noticed? Everyone is absorbed with their devices, moving about with their heads bowed, staring at their hands. I'm invisible to them, a background element like the trees or shrubs. I stand amidst this collective deference, alone.

The world around me begins to spin. I struggle to collect my sensibilities; control the fear mounting within me, rechecking the space Parmalee just occupied. There's no touch sensation or other. He's simply vanished. Life goes on, unaware of what's taken place.

Like a slap in the face, I realize I can't remember my name, the man I was living in this time period. Why? Why hasn't my memory returned if this is the present? Wait, wasn't Michael Murphy from Vallejo? I'm from a different place, New York or New Jersey. I recall my dreams, the encounter in the pump room when, for a brief moment, I remembered the man I truly am. Then why Vallejo? Could it have something to do with Parmalee? His unexpected appearance in this place? Why did he vanish while I remain? A sudden and profound confusion shrouds my thoughts.

It becomes extant, sitting on the bench in this time and place, that I need to remember who I am; the invisible man that woke up in the submarine. No matter how hard I try, I cannot recall my other self. There's nothing left, only a man from the past, awash in the future, sitting on a park bench like a vagabond from another world. Only an hour ago a man surrounded by friends and colleagues, privileges and responsibilities; all given way to a vast empty chasm growing inside a hollow invisible person.

A slow inexorable panic begins to consume me. I push my brain to remember but there's nothing, nothing but Michael Murphy, former first officer of a doomed ship, a United States fleet-boat that lost its way; got caught up in the backwash and eddies of a distant time and disappeared from the earth, from the memory of man.

Perhaps this isn't real? Perhaps this is some sort of elaborate hoax, designed for some weird ulterior purpose. Perhaps I'm being secretly watched from some remote place. I scan the park, the people, their faces turned toward the ground. No one seems to even notice me sitting there in an old outdated uniform. It's truly like being invisible. Perhaps I am. An invisible man.

I study the old antiquated fountain, now derelict and crumbling, remember standing before it with Hildy in the moonlight. Music was in the air, and a nervous excitement. Europe was at war, America, uncertain. It was prom night. I told her I had enlisted in the Navy; tears in the moonlight.

Without thought, I pull the picture from my breast pocket. Hildy in the flower-print dress, the words '*come home*' written across the bottom of the photograph. "Hildy. I need to find Hildy," I say aloud as if Parmalee were still there; only the air meandering in off the bay. Life goes on; just another casual day in a park in *sunny* California.

———

A taxi idles under a stand of eucalyptus trees across the lawn. "Excuse me. This is Vallejo right? Vallejo California?"

He stares at me placidly. "It was at seven this morning."

"Do you know where 1818 Latimer Street is by chance? Near the corner of Kinney Lane?" The cabbie pulls a smartphone from his pocket and punches in the address.

"That's less than a mile dude. Can't you walk it?" I've no response to this odd request. He tosses his magazine aside and points his thumb toward the backseat. "Hop in."

The address is a vacant lot, but the lay of the land is all too familiar, the gentle slope of the yard cascading toward Latimer Street, reminiscent of an earlier time, the street quieter, life slower. Memory swallows me, absorbing my consciousness like watching an old *Movietone* newsreel.

The Stewart's rusty '32 Ford sits at the curb, his brand-new state-of-the-art Navy *field* radio on full volume. The neighborhood kids gather, enraptured by the sound coming from the automobile, the air filled with music, *Wasting My Love on You* by Annette Hanshaw. The music wafts down the length of Latimer, attracting the children like the Pied-Piper, the singer's melodic voice permeating the moment. Stewart shows the boys his officer's pin, his *dolphins,* each boy committing to volunteer for underwater service when they come-of-age. An argument erupts when the neighborhood girls insist upon enlisting also. Gloria Adder leads their cause, her five-foot-nine stature dominating the consistory of adolescent boys.

Hildy, Sally and Ellis pose for a photograph. Stewie always wore loud clothes; striped jacket and black-and-white wingtips. Sally has their youngest child Ellie in her arms. I photograph them standing before the lot where the house will be built.

It was slow going because of the war, the worst possible time to build a new home. The wood had run out and Drexler was biding his time framing what he could, digging holes where things would eventually go.

The Canfields pull up in Ollie's '39 Studebaker. Rue looks like a million bucks, her hair dyed auburn, her lips scarlet red. She holds Ellie up by the armpits and the child cries for her mother. Everyone is laughing and enjoying the afternoon sunshine when Canfield sides up to me, his hands in his slacks, loafers on his feet. *'Pack your bag Mike. We're heading for Tahiti, Stewart too. You're back onboard the Manta Ray with me. Your orders will be coming in this afternoon. Jim Hudgins won out this time Murph. He'll skipper our flotilla's new boat. Next time will be your turn.'* Everything freezes, like a photograph.

"Hey dude, you want to keep the motor running?" the cabbie asks, cocking his head.

"Yes, thank-you." I pace the sidewalk along Latimer Street, shocked when I realize the enormous elm shading the lot from the south was a mere baby when I planted it the last time I was here, in 1943. It's now a full-grown tree shading an empty corner lot. An elderly neighbor is watering his lawn next door. "Excuse me, do you live here?"

"Yes…"

"Is that lot 1818 Latimer Street?"

"Well, yes, I do believe that is the address of record."

"Where's the house? The house that used to be here. The house I was building back in 1943." The old man adjusts the glasses on his nose and takes a long look at me, head to toe.

"Well now, I do remember when I was a boy, there was a widow who had started building a home there, but it was never finished. A structure was started but they tore it down."

"Tore it down? Why?"

"The walls had been framed in, but the house was never completed. Everyone was so poor back then." He smiles, returning to that time. "That was long ago. We used to play in it, swing from the rafters, play hide-and-seek. It became a neighborhood playground really. A wonderful place for us kids, right next door. I had almost forgotten about that."

"Who owns the lot now?"

"No doubt the family still owns it. If you're thinking of purchasing, don't bother. That old woman always intended to rebuild. I remember now, her husband died long ago, in the second world war, *lost at sea*. They had to move."

"*They?* She…remarried?"

"No, her and the baby…and that craggy old woman from San Francisco. I had completely forgotten about her too."

"*Baby*? What baby?"

"Queer old woman. Mean-spirited. She would chase us out of the house whenever they visited, and they tore it down anyway. All her shouting and ranting and chasing us about was just a colossal waste of time."

"What *baby*?" I ask, arresting his arm.

"Say, are you some kind of relative?" he queries me, eyeing my clothes suspiciously. "No one's asked about them for a very long time. A very long time."

The car horn blares. "Dude! You want a ride back downtown or what? I can't just sit here."

"Thank-you," I say to the man with the hose and climb back into the cab. "Take me to 78 Lafayette Street."

The cab pulls in front of the 1930s era stucco. I instantly recognize the house, its decline surprising me. As I approach the home, I see the name *Canfield* rusting on the mailbox. When I knock on the door, I hear an old man growl from around the corner.

———

"Who's there? State your business." I round the hedge where a bent old man with a shock of pure white hair is holding a pair of shears, drinking from a can of beer. "If you're soliciting I ain't buying. Read the sign on the door." He gives me a thorough looking over. "Where in blazes you get that uniform kid? Hell, I haven't seen a uniform like that in sixty years…or is it seventy? Sonofabitch," he mutters and spits. It's him, an old man. I stand stuttering like an altar-boy meeting the Pope.

"Captain. Captain Canfield?"

"Yeah. I was a captain, submarine captain. *The silent service*, the big war. We were the guys that gave Tojo the blackeye while the Army and the rest of the Navy was sitting around on their asses. I sank more Jap ships in '42 than any other boat in the goddamn fleet yet the lousy sonsofbitches had the nerve to throw me out."

"Skipper, it's me."

He stares at me deadpan. "You want me to dance a jig for you? Kick up my heels and holler halleluiah? How about I blow the national anthem outta my rear-end?"

"Skipper, it's me…Mike Murphy. Your first officer, from the Manta Ray." The old man squints.

"What'd you say? Speak up, I must be hard of hearing." I close the distance that separates us.

"It's me Captain, Mike Murphy."

He drops his can of beer. "Who?"

"Brother, do I got a lot to report sir."

He grabs my shirt. "Who? Murphy? How in the name of God?" He goes into a state of shock. "Murphy! My god it's you," he shouts. "What happened? Where did you go boy? Where did you go?" the old man is barely in control of his emotions. "They said you disappeared. That kid came back, the electrician, but not you. Where in God's name Murphy?"

He begins to shake uncontrollably, dropping to the ground, the cabbie running over. "Dude! That old dude's having a fucking heart attack man!"

"Someone. Is there a doctor?" I call out. "Anyone?!"

"Chill, I'm on it, I'm on it," the cabbie says dialing 911 on his smartphone. "Fuck!"

Canfield stares up at me, clutching my shirt. "Where Murph? Where did you go boy? Tell me."

"Easy Captain, try not to talk."

"Tell me where? Where did you go? I have to know."

"Nowhere Skipper…just…here…right here…" He stares at me, a strange look forming on his face, his pupils dilating wildly. "Skipper?"

"Seventy years Murph. Seventy years. All that time. Where? Where…" He looks through me. His eyes go blank.

"Skipper? Captain!"

He's dead.

An old woman bursts from the house, shattering her teacup on the stoop; Rue, now an old gray-haired woman.

"Ollie? Oliver! Oh my god, Oliver!" she screams above him, a flood of neighbors suddenly converging from every direction. As they congregate, I'm pushed aside, relegated to the wings until I'm like a shadow loitering where it doesn't belong. I begin walking, then run. I just run, not even aware of the direction; a block, then another, then a dozen, now nothing more than a running man, lost in time.

Chapter *17*: Intersections in Time

*N*ight finds me standing before her aunt Ruth's Victorian.

The structure has seen better days, perhaps it just needs of a fresh coat of paint. It seems to contemplate me from the shadows. Cold wisps of foggy dew nip at my collar, pushing me forward. I ascend the stairs, yellow under the dull glow of a weak porchlight. I can hear the sound of voices from inside the home; laughter.

At the door I pause to read the name, *H. Murphy*, and hesitate. She's on the other side of this door. When I go to press the bell, I pause, my finger a mere inch from the button. How old would she be now? Well into her nineties, if she's even alive. If she is still alive, she would most certainly be decrepit, probably bedridden. Perhaps it would be better to just leave, leave her be. Afterall, what if she has a reaction like Canfield? A heart-attack. I shouldn't even be here, this time and place; the idea of it, nearly insane. Perhaps it's better that I remain *lost at sea*. I hesitate again. Just leave…but to where? I push the button. There's the sound of an inner doorbell, the feeling of intense anxiety, then the commotion of someone answering.

I'm unprepared for this.

The door opens…and it's *her*. I'm stunned to the center of my being. Standing before me is Hildy, exactly as she looked in 1943. No different except her clothing and hairstyle, her blue dungarees oddly ripped and shredded, bright garish colors on her shirt. She just stares at me, as if I were a stranger.

"Hildy?"

"Yes?"

"Hildy."

"Yes…" Silence. Her eyes narrow, studying me intently. "Do you want something?"

"My god…Hildy, it's you. You're still the same. How? How can you be the same?" She stares at me, wondering. "You haven't aged. How? It's like a miracle." She gazes at me curiously before turning and calling over her shoulder.

"Grandma, I'm not sure, I think it's maybe for you?" An elderly woman with a cane, joins the girl at the door. She peers at me through the mist that wraps tendrils about our frames.

"May I help you, young man?" I'm unable to speak. She steps out further, her tired eyes fixed on me, studying my uniform. It's her, there's no mistaking it, despite the years. "I'm sorry, do we know you?"

"Hildy…it's me…Mike."

"*Mike?*" she whispers, and I see it, the shock of recognition forming in her tired eyes. "*Mike,*" she echoes barely above a whisper and the moment freezes as if we were locked in ice.

"It's me Hildy." She's incredulous; staring as if she were seeing a ghost. Perhaps she is. A lovely middle-aged woman joins them in the doorway, wiping her hands on a dishtowel. Her dark eyes scrutinize me and the uniform I wear.

"Mom? What is it? Who's here?" She *has* my face. Our eyes meet, a *knowing* emerging in her face. "Mom?"

"No one Mary. It's a mistake. He's at the wrong address." Hildy pushes her daughter and granddaughter inside, retreating behind the door, never taking her eyes from me the entire time. She stares through the crack of the door.

"Hildy…"

"How dare you come here like this…after all these years? Go away. Don't come back here. Ever. If you do, I'll have you arrested." The door shuts. I hear a deadbolt lock in place and the porch light goes out. Silence. I turn my collar against the sting of the breeze, the smell of the ocean saturating the cold air. As I gaze at the night awaiting my return, I chance one last wayward look over my shoulder–the closed door and darkened lamp–then set off into the mist.

"Excuse me, kind sir, can you spare a buck?" I take note of his phraseology, the words *'kind sir'* catching my attention. I give the man a dollar and keep scrolling the computer bolted to the table. The hour is late, the coffee shop closing soon. "You're most generous. Say, another buck and I can get a drink." I'm certain he means alcohol. Although I really can't afford it, I reluctantly slide him another dollar and keep working. I glance over at him. He seems to be contemplating his newly won booty. Incredibly, he actually takes a chair at my table and reaches to the ceiling, snapping his fingers. "Garcon, coffee, sil vous plait."

The waitress saunters over, giving him a dour look. "*Garcon?* Seriously? What do you want Merlin?" she says flexing her tattooed arm in his face as she takes up my spent pastry dish.

"Café American. If you're not too busy *Madam*." She blows a bubble snapping her gum.

"You got money to pay for it?" He extends the two bills I've given him. She snatches them from his grasp. "And this includes my tip this time cheapskate," she says heading for the barista. "*American* for our resident comedian," she shouts loud enough for all to hear.

"Insolent tart," he grumbles. I do my best to ignore him, bent upon the information scrolling the computer screen. I can see him looking at me. "You're not from around here."

"No. Well, yes and no."

"I'll take that in the negative."

"Thank-you," I say, hardly masking my irritation; returning to the computer.

"Two dollars. A novel gesture by the way. Or would that be a *noble* gesture?" I continue to work until I realize he's staring down my neck. "You have a name sir? A nom-de-plume?" I placidly gaze at him. Obviously, he's insisting on some kind of interaction.

"Michael Murphy." He shakes his head.

"Sorry to disagree but you're no more a *Murphy* than I'm a *Smith*…or would that be *Smythe?*" I return to my work on the database while he mulls over my ancestry. "In all fairness you could be a bastard son *Mr. Murphy.* God knows it happens, even in the most religious of families. No, not *Murphy*…your real name sir?"

"My real name?" I ask and laugh softly. "Funny you should ask that, it's what I'm searching for."

"Now we're getting somewhere," he says below his breath. His eyes are dark and penetrating; intelligent and aware, not the vacant gaze of a hobo. A strange feeling emerges in my chest.

"Excuse me but I've quite a lot work to do."

He turns to the crowd in Daniel's Coffee Shop. "He doesn't remember his name. Anyone? Come, come, you've a man here out of place, without a name, without a history." No one seems to care or even take notice.

"Do you mind? I'd rather not-"

"Look at them, hunched over their devices, motionless, wordless. You'd think the *Inquisition* had started again."

The waitress brings his coffee. "Try'n keep it down to a dull roar Merlin?" she says and leaves him to sip the brew.

"Ah…is there a finer drink than the elixir of a properly roasted coffee bean? Methinks not."

"Excuse me but I've quite a bit of work to get done before they close."

"You're homeless?"

"Homeless?" I echo, surprised by the question until I realize the irony of it. "Funny. I suppose so. Yes, I'm homeless, for the moment." His eyebrow elongates.

"A self-confessed homeless man with the wrong name, frantically searching the data files at Daniel's Coffee House before they close for the evening. Hmm," he muses and sips.

"If you don't mind, I'd rather be alone."

"That's more than evident my friend," he says, and I note the irony in his statement. I am alone. I lean back in my chair and study him. He looks like a transient, except his eyes, and his mind; sharp not vacant. Funny, he does remind me of the Merlin in the storybooks of my youth.

"Your name is Merlin?" He's incredulous. "I heard the waitress call you that."

"I wouldn't put faith in what waitresses say my young friend. They'll paint glorious, grandiose pictures of the absurd." He closes the distance between us, lowering his voice. "You know, to pad the tip." I laugh softly. He's beginning to pique my curiosity.

"So, you have a name?" I inquire.

"Completely irrelevant. What's of import here is *you* my fine fellow. Not from around here. Nameless, homeless, yet unbroken."

Unbroken. I shake my head and return to the computer, eyeing the clock on the wall; ten minutes to closing. He becomes lost in his private thoughts.

At the computer, I waste precious time trying to concentrate on the names and addresses scrolling the screen. The waitress walks past, turning the sign in the window.

"Sorry mister but we're closed." The irascible woman actually pulls the cord out of the wall. The screen goes black. I'm left watching other patrons exit the shop.

"Do you have a flop for the night...*kind sir*?"

"Perhaps."

"I'll take that as another negative. Follow me." He dumps his coffee into a takeout cup and urges me on. "Come, come, this way. Unless you prefer a drainage culvert?" I'm amazed by the man's sagacity. I decide to stroll with him for a bit, part company down the block.

We exit the shop into the electrified San Franciscan night. People of all nationalities, in wild colorful clothes, are flocking the nightclubs scattered the length of Haight Street.

"Sorry for the put-on. It's really more for fun and amusement than anything else."

"Put-on?"

"Being on the bum. It's a bit underhanded I'll admit, but a perfect guise."

"What are you talking about? *Guise?*"

"Of course. We all wear a guise. I, you...everyone wears a guise of some sort. It can't be avoided, it's basic human nature. You for instance, the stranger, the outsider...very much the outsider," he says. "You've travelled a great distance, a great deal of *time* to be here...adrift."

"Adrift?"

"Indeed. You're adrift...am I correct?"

"I suppose you could say that. How do you guess it?"

"No *guess*. It's evident in your mannerisms, your state of affairs. You're something of an *anomaly* I should think. There's a bit of the *rogue* about you."

"Why? What makes me different than, say, the guy over there on the street corner?" I point at the derelict panning coins with a paper cup.

"Him? I'll show you." He immediately crosses Haight Street. I catch up to him just as he's addressing the man. "Tell me kind sir, do you know my friend perchance?" he inquires, and the man shakes his cup at us.

"Spare change, any spare change?" My companion extracts a ten-dollar bill from his vest pocket and holds it up, the man's attention instantly locking on the bill. "Please, something to eat."

"Ten dollars my good man for an answer. Can you tell my friend where he might *find* himself? He's lost track of himself apparently. Any good advice?"

"Please, just for a meal, just a meal, please," the man says, actually salivating. He sees nothing but the money, slowly extracting it from my friend's grasp.

"Take care old fellow."

"Bless you. Bless you," he repeats like a mantra, relinquishing his place atop the plastic milk crate. "Bless you," he says once more as he shuffles down the sidewalk. After he's left, I gaze at my odd companion with a genuine sense of curiosity.

"What is that supposed to prove?"

"Watch," he says pointing at our disheveled interloper as he meanders through the press of nighttime revelers. He eventually makes his way to *Rocket Liquors* and disappears into the warmth of the store's neon glow. "There you have it."

"Have what?"

"The answer to your question. Why I know you're not one of the broken."

"One of the broken?" He takes my shoulder and we begin to stroll through the throng of musicians and jugglers.

"The homeless are naked, wearing nothing save the mask of poverty. The material world, its demands and expectations are too painful. Thus, the face they present the world is the *obsession for money*, the acquisition of it. The broken."

"The homeless you mean?"

"I mean the broken. The rich person can be exactly the same as the destitute person, become a slave to an insatiable *obsession for the material*. As odd as it seems, there's no difference between the two really. They sacrifice the sacredness of life, the sacredness of relationships, for this obsession which in turn devours them whole. Like all things in life, it's cyclical, runs full circle. This is the mask they choose to wear, always. You on the other hand...very different."

"What about you? If this is *a guise* you choose, as opposed to being forced into poverty, why?"

"Because it's a good guise."

"Poverty?"

"Invisibility," he says, and I'm rocked to my toes, stopping dead in the middle of the sidewalk.

"Invisibility? You said...*invisibility."*

"I did."

"Why? Why did you use that word?"

He again takes my shoulder and we walk. "Exactly like the rich man hiding behind his gates, in his tower sequestered in his isolation, the homeless man is an invisible person, slowly becomes so. The average person doesn't want to see the man without a home because within every man resides his own fear of failure. Thus, he chooses not to see the man living on the street, begging for his life."

"Go on."

"As hours turn to days, weeks to months, months turn into years, the man becomes an invisible being, slowly becoming nonexistent, eventually leaving this world…an invisible person." He stops abruptly, gazing into me. "Why? What did you think I meant by my choice of words?" His dark eyes are piercing. It occurs to me he knows implicitly why this particular word caught my attention. We continue to wander. "It's not easy being an invisible man…is it?"

"How would I know?"

"Right…how? Hello. Here we are."

He points to a worn series of wooden stairs crammed tightly between a nightclub and a clothing store, leading up to the second story. I cautiously follow him into the darkness. Just when I think it's a really bad idea, what I'm doing, he unlocks the door and an incredible sight greets my eyes.

The apartment is elaborately furnished, antiques and artwork gracing nearly every available space. An old antique radio in the corner plays an old thirties tune, *Begin the Beguine*, by Artie Shaw.

"Have a seat my boy. Coffee? Or do you prefer tea? Sorry, I never keep *spirits* on the premises."

"Coffee is fine." I gaze at the radio. "Do you always play such old music?"

"Not I…*it* does," he says pointing at the aged device. "The cursed thing stopped moving forward in…1943," he says oddly. "Perfectly fine with me. I find that era of music relaxing." As he prepares our drinks, I take-in the splendor of his home. There are more statues of gods and goddesses than I've seen in a private abode. Some–the Asian edifices–seem to resemble demons or monsters, perhaps mystical creatures. Books, many large hardbound editions, are stacked everywhere and a miniature Steinway grand piano sits quietly in the corner.

A large black cat, sleek and elegant, enters through a window overlooking the rooftop. The creature pauses, studying me intently before entering the kitchen.

"What brings you in so early? Not indulging *the goddess of the hunt* tonight?" he questions the animal. "This is Topaz, my roommate," he says *introducing* us and the cat seems to scrutinize me before becoming intent upon what he's doing. "Go track down a rodent if you're hungry," he says and the cat responds loudly, crying for its supper. "Impertinent feline." He places a saucer of milk on the floor, the animal immediately setting to work devouring the plate's contents. When he joins me in the parlor, I'm looking over architectural drawings spread across two tables.

"These are incredible," I say nodding at the drawings. He hands me the coffee; cream and honey, exactly as I prefer it.

"Indeed. Are you an architect?"

"No, I'm afraid not."

"Well, I'll give you the ten-cent tour, that way if you're ever grilled by the architectural snobbery of the world you'll be prepared. This column you see here in this layout is of the Doric order. It's easy to distinguish because the drums have no base," he says and chuckles, apparently quite pleased about the remark.

"What's so funny?"

"It's a pun, a play on words...the drums have no base...*bass* drums...never mind. Ah, this marvelous colonnaded structure here is of the Ionic order, note the capitals and volutes. That's as *Ionic* as it gets my friend. And here, this drawing nicely displays the Corinthian order. Notice the change in the volute? The addition of the rosette and acanthus leaf motifs give the order its unique attributes."

"What's this?" I ask, pointing at the first drawing, what looks like a gargoyle sitting atop the very edge of the roof.

"What was referred to as an *acroterion*…exclusively within the Doric. It was omitted in the Ionic and Corinthian orders." One of the ancient sheets contains a finely drawn plan for a domed structure. I suspect the paper is papyrus.

"A temple?"

"Indeed. Do you recognize it?" he asks. I admit no such knowledge. "Why, it's the temple of Aphaia Aegina my dear boy. A Doric temple of the very highest order."

"It's very old, the drawing," I mutter, stroking the paper.

"Verily. I would dare say ancient." His eyes seem to pulsate as he looks over the crisp and yellowed paper. The drawings seem to be handmade replicas of original graphite and charcoal works; smudges evident upon the paper.

"Why don't you tell me who you are?" I ask.

"Why don't *you* tell *me*?"

"Because we've never met before."

"Then my name is irrelevant. What's of import is you remember yours."

"I told you my name already."

"That's right…*Michael Murphy* was it?"

"Yes, that's correct."

"I see. And why is Michael J. Murphy running amok in this century?"

"I beg your pardon?"

"Shouldn't the Michael J. Murphy we all know, remain in his particular century?"

"I don't think I understand what you're getting at."

"Of course you do. One can't be two people forever my friend. That's a very unhealthy state of affairs." Silence.

"I think I better be leaving. Thanks for the coffee."

"Leaving? I was hoping to have a productive evening. However, if you've pressing matters elsewhere, I'll see you out." At the door I pause. "Something else?" he inquires.

"You're a very strange man."

"My experience likewise. It's been a pleasure…*Mr. Murphy*. Good luck on your enterprise." I slowly descend the stairs. When I get to the bottom, I look back at his silhouette within the dim light of the doorway. "Stop by anytime. The door is always open. By the way, you've a friend that seeks reacquainting."

"A friend?"

"Indeed. A very important friend. I suggest you look her up, as soon as possible."

"Her?"

"That would be the proper gender." He closes the door, and all goes black.

I'm suddenly being nudged awake; it's the tattooed waitress at Daniel's Coffee House. "Hey man, go find a bridge or whatever, we're closed." I've fallen asleep, the dream I felt so real only that, a dream. She takes my cup and pulls the plug on the computer. The gray screen shows my face, the growth of beard.

The barista pulls the string, dropping the blinds and the waitress switches off the light. The cashier is closing out the till, the dishwasher banging dishes in the sink. An old Patsy Cline tune plays on the CD player; *Crazy*. How appropriate, I think to myself, taking up my pack, pulling my collar up around my ears and plunging into the fog rolling in from the Pacific like a freight train.

Out of curiosity, I decide to revisit the old man. When I get to Haight Street, I can't find the stairs between the store and nightclub. Perhaps I'm at the wrong address, but a part of me wonders if the place has vanished from the face of the earth, or more likely, never existed.

Chapter 18: Princeton

A courtyard at the university in Princeton; nearly vacant.

An old bench becomes my home-away-from-home. The reason I took this particular bench on my arrival was because of a book, Heinlein's *Stranger in a Strange Land*. Why it was left behind I've no idea, but the irony of the title had me curious. I end up sitting there waiting for its owner, reading the damn thing nearly cover to cover, until I see her.

How beautiful and alive she seems despite the years. As she walks toward me, I'm so utterly shocked I can't speak, forced to watch her stroll past as if I were invisible. Perhaps I am; the old man's words reverberating in my head. It was true. I was slowly, inexorably, becoming an invisible person.

Watching her interact with the students, I can't help laughing out loud, the way they flock about her as they move from one building to another. Exactly like the fellas on the boat. It all came back, the way they would follow her around like a pack of kids, arguing over whose turn it was to do *this* chore or *that* favor. It wasn't their natures. It was her effect upon them; she brought these qualities out in them. The simple fact was she cared about them, not only the jobs they were tasked with, but *them* as people, people with their own lives, hopes and dreams, joys and sorrows. When they walk out of the laboratory that evening, I realize I'm running out of time. What will happen? Will I get a *door* slammed in my face again? Should that happen, what then?

Two students accompany her. I'm yet to see her alone, someone always there. Now…or never.

She's still an attractive woman; an inner radiance that certain women possess and hold. I pull my cap down and *bump* into her. "Excuse me but aren't you from *Jersey*?"

She studies me. "Yes. I live here, in Princeton." The same knowing eyes; unchanged.

"No kidding. Maybe we're neighbors. That anywhere near Paterson?" She drops her books and papers, then faints.

There are moments in time that become precious. More precious than our very lives really, they are the moments that build our lives, form our personalities, contour the shape of our souls. When she reawakens and takes the palm of my hand, the look in her verdant gaze is like looking into the brilliance of the sun.

"Michael? Is it you? Are you actually here?"

"Hello Lucy. Everything all right?" Her eyes open like rain. We embrace, the students exchanging wondering looks.

"Professor Charlesworth are you okay?" the sandy-haired girl asks, looking at me suspiciously while her partner dusts off Lucy's books.

"Yes, yes Erin, quite." She extracts a snow-white handkerchief from her pocket and dabs her eyes. "I'm quite all right. Forgive me girls. I would like to introduce a very special friend. He's travelled quite a long time to be with us again. This is Lieutenant Commander Michael Murphy, commander of the Manta Ray, a United States submarine. Have you heard of it?" They shake their heads. "I doubt that you have. It's no longer in the history books. Commander Murphy was awarded the Medal of Honor, for bravery...posthumously," she says, her eyes tearing anew. She covers her mouth with her fingers. The girls study me, the raven-haired girl inquisitive, her companion the opposite.

"Michael, this is Mika Thompkins and Erin McMurtry, future physicists." I extend my hand, the blonde girl declining my grasp. "Michael…how is it you're here?" I've no answer to this direct and meaningful question.

"*Posthumously?*" Mika inquires, cocking her head. Lucy fishes through her purse, withdrawing a small stack of photographs from her pocketbook, extracting an old black-and-white photo; a picture of us on the bridge of the Manta Ray, wind in our hair, our faces smiling into the sun.

"Wow, Professor Charlesworth, sexy," Mika says examining the photograph. "You're so young." She studies me, head to toe. "You don't seem to have aged Mr. Murphy."

"I always wondered Michael," Lucy whispers. "What had happened to you? If someday you might return." A thin line of tears cut her cheek. "As if I could feel you, near me." She becomes emotional and the girls converge closer.

"Should I call campus security Dr. Charlesworth?" the sandy-haired girl asks, her expression changing from suspicion to contempt.

"For goodness sake no Erin. Michael is one of my very dearest friends." Emotion emerges within her opulent gaze. "It's just been a very long, long, long time." She covers her eyes with her hand.

"Do you need anything Professor Charlesworth?" Mika asks quietly. "Maybe you two would like to be alone?"

"I'm quite all right girls, forgive me. Yes Mika. We'll see you tomorrow. Bright and early."

Mika yanks the other girl's arm, gesturing with her eyes. They slowly amble off into the evening, shooting several curious looks in our direction until they turn the corner of the building and are gone. Her eyes shine as they search mine.

"If they only knew…those two."

"Knew what?"

"How far you've come…how long. Mika's more intelligent, more intuitive. I'm certain she suspects something is afoot. I'm sure we'll have a lengthy conversation about it tomorrow. My god, what do I tell her?" She brushes tears from her eyes, taking up my hand. "I knew it Michael, wondered if you would come back someday. Perhaps I've wished for it. Look at you, the same handsome young man…exactly as I remember you." Her eyes instantly cloak in a patina of tears. "And here I am…a rickety old woman."

"You're lovely Lucy, as always."

"You're saying that, *solely for my benefit Commander*," she says, remembering her words from seventy years ago. "Welcome home Michael…my god…welcome home." As she studies my expression, the brightness in her face clouds.

"But I'm not *home*, am I? Not yet." She covers her mouth with her hand. "Lucy…Michael Murphy doesn't belong here, in this century. Mike Murphy lived in 1943. He's not supposed to be here…is he?" The look in her eyes fractures.

"No," she whispers softer than a spring rain.

"Who am I? Tell me who I am."

She shakes her head. "I can't."

"Why?"

"Because if I do…I'm afraid of what will happen." I take her shoulders, so thin and frail.

"Lucy, look at me. I'm the same man you knew a century ago."

"Please Michael."

"You're speaking to a man who has existed in your memories for seventy years. I don't belong here, in this place, in this time. Not this way."

"Michael, the machine we built in 1943 still exists, a smaller version than the one on the submarine."

"What do you mean?"

"Yes. It's in the basement of this very building. You went there…to save the boat."

The moment hovers; stars permeating the night above.

"Everyone got back all right? Parmalee? Binkershon's torpedo crew?"

"Yes dear, they did, everyone…everyone…except you." A deep sorrow emanates from the center of her being and we somberly embrace under the sodium lights.

Moths circle our heads in chaotic elliptical orbits, lost within the lamplight, as if trying to seek-out something unattainable. I realize my state of affairs is not altogether different than theirs. "I should have returned, but not this way, not as this man. What happened?"

"My god, you're the same as on the Manta Ray."

"*Parmalee.* The moment I sent the current, he grabbed my arm. It must be the reason I came back as Mike Murphy."

"Yes, I recall it. He came back, but you didn't. You got lost dear…*in between things.*" She cries, quietly, painfully.

"That's what they meant. That I would be true to my nature. They knew I would be the one to throw that switch. It could have happened differently but didn't."

"*They?*"

"That was the trigger, throwing that switch. But they failed to consider Parmalee, his nature…trying to stop me."

"Michael, whatever are you talking about?"

"The submarine survived, but we failed…"

"No Michael, succeeded, gloriously. For goodness sake you're here. You've returned…from 1943! We proved it, together. Time is an ocean, a vast ocean, like the sea, circling back onto itself, forever. Do you understand what this means? We've transcended time. You're living proof of it. This will revolutionize modern science; you and I."

"We did it. We succeeded." Her eyes are exactly the same, untouched by the advent of *time*. Deep verdant pools of wonderment. "Succeeded…almost."

Her eyes search mine. "Michael…your face is changing."

I'm complete. I know who I am now, everything about my life, what's happened and why. A deep inner *knowing* saturates the entirety of my being, like a drowning man letting go, no longer fighting to survive, but letting go to live. I can't help smiling as all the troubling thoughts crowding my mind fade like waking from a dream. Also fading is my youth, rapidly. My strong young sailor's hands that hold her are withering before my eyes.

"Dear god," she whispers. "You're growing old."

The strength in my legs falter, I can no longer stand, falling to the ground. She's bending over me, repeating my name, the object of my search, for seventy years.

Colleagues and students converge, people shout for an ambulance. She's trying to tell me something but there are no words, only her eyes. I can no longer hold her hand.

"Don't leave me, not again," she says, so near her breath caresses my cheek. "Please…don't go."

The sky opens up within the darkness of her pupils. I see, deep within the black, the night above, the thin crescent moon, like a golden jewel, smiling from the firmament, the sky filling with hundreds, thousands, millions of stars, ever expanding into infinity.

Epilogue

*W*e had surfaced in broad daylight.

A rare event in enemy patrolled water; the threat of a surface attack ever-present. There was nothing else we could do, the repairs to the starboard propeller shaft requiring divers in the water and as much light as feasibly possible.

"Twenty, maybe thirty minutes tops Mr. Murphy," Rawlston said before donning his mask and disappearing beneath the water with Howard, the entire *machine-crew* clamoring about the tail-end of the boat.

Taking Lucy's hand, I lead her to the bow where Sorel has lowered the starboard diving plane for us. I lift her down atop the bow-plane jutting out over the water just above the waves, the sea lapping at the Manta Ray's metal fin. It's a beautiful sunny day and despite the gentle breeze that lifts the tendrils of her hair, the ocean rests quietly.

"Look Michael, the ocean looks like it could stretch on forever." Her words convey a truth. The deep cerulean waters of the Pacific are sedate for miles in all directions. She removes her shoes and sticks her legs into the water, her face tranquil, euphoric. "The water's amazingly warm. How wonderful. I'm in heaven." Something occupies her mind. I question what she's thinking about. "Michael, do you remember when you asked me about time travel? For some reason you had been stewing about it the entire day; whether a person could travel in time."

"Yes, I remember. What about it?"

"Let's prove it, together."

"Prove it?"

"Never forget this moment. The ocean so blue it breaks your heart." Her fingers tighten around mine, her eyes moist. "When you're alone or hurting, come back here, to this special place, this moment. I'll be here, waiting for you."

She takes my arm, her head against my shoulder, our feet in the gentle Pacific, the sun painting her hair golden-brown, the ocean wide, flat, and yes, so blue it's heartbreaking; thin wisps of white–the crests of waves–kissing the wind.

"Look!" she points. "What on earth are those?"

"Flying fish."

"Don't tease me. Fish don't fly."

"Those can. They're throughout the Pacific." I watch her study the fish as they take to the breeze, soaring and diving in long slender arcs.

"I wish I could fly," she sighs. "I wish I could just, take wing and fly away," she says speaking to my eyes. "Would you come? Would you come with me?"

"Yes." Timeless.

"Lieutenant Murphy?" Sorel, above us on the deck. "Repairs are finished sir. We're ready to get underway." He extends his hand and helps her up onto the deck. When we make the bridge, Cooper is there with his Argus camera.

"Beautiful day," he says, a rare smile on his young face. "Hey, let me take your picture together." He snaps the photo. "I'll mail you both a copy when we get back."

Black gives the impression of emptiness, lends itself to timelessness. There is no *time* in black for it lacks form, definition; no distinct features or qualities except a feeling of vastness, or its opposite.
Fini.

———

~.~

The author would like to thank the men and women of the United States Navy and armed services for their sacrifices and dedication to peace. To the WWII submariners and their families, a branch of service that suffered a 32% mortality rate between 1941-45. To the 52 US submarines lost during the conflict. Blessed are the brave as they live forever in the hearts of the thankful.

~.~

Sincerest thanks to the USS Silversides (SS-236) and the USS Silversides Submarine Museum in Muskegon, Michigan for allowing my research to continued unabated from 2011 through the present. Special thanks to Executive Director Peggy Maniates; former Executive Director Frank Marczak; the board-members and honorable Neil Mullaly; WWII submariners Don Morrell and Roger Whitman, et al. To the USS Cobia (Manitowac, WI) and USS Pampanito (Mare Island-San Francisco, CA) and Pearl Harbor Memorial Museum (Honolulu, HI) for additional reference and materials. Big thank-you to Don Mangione for the excellent book design, Nicolai Tesla for the science, and to Hayao Miyazaki for teaching me how to *write with my heart*. And last–but hardly least–my family. Without your love it would have all been quite impossible.

This book is dedicated to my father Miles Nyberg, and all men and women, boys and girls, who look to the horizon and think, wonder and dream.

~.~

___

~.~

INVISIBLE published 2020
By M. E. Nyberg. All rights reserved.

~.~

ISBN 13: 978-0-9970986-6-2
eISBN 13: 978-0-9970986-7-9

Registered with U.S. Library of Congress
Copyright # TXu 2-147-103
Writers Guild of America West Reg# 2035484

~.~

Other books by M E Nyberg

...

The Profound Art of Omens
The Man Who Would Be Coyote
The Wicker Woman
Invisible

~.~

www.menyberg.com

~.~

———